The
SPIRIT
of
CANADA

The
SPIRIT
of
CANADA

BARBARA HEHNER, EDITOR

MALCOLM LESTER BOOKS

In memory of my grandfather Edgar Mabbutt, who, on April 9, 1917, fought at Vimy Ridge

To my daughter, Amanda, born April 9, 1989, her mother's birthday

And to my husband, Eric, whose love and encouragement make all things seem possible

Compilation copyright © 1999 by Barbara Hehner

Illustrations copyright © 1999 by the individual artists

CANADIAN CATALOGUING IN PUBLICATION DATA

Main entry under title:

The spirit of Canada

Includes bibliographical references and index.
ISBN 1–894121–14–7

1. Canada—Literary collections. 2. Canadian literature (English).* I. Hehner, Barbara

PS8237.C35S64 1999   C810.8'03271   C99–930398–8
PR9194.52.C3S64 1999

We acknowledge the support of the Canada Council for the Arts for our publishing program.

Malcolm Lester Books
25 Isabella Street, Toronto, Ontario M4Y 1M7

Printed and bound in Canada
99 00 01   5 4 3 2 1

Contents

Barbara Hehner
Introduction

THE SPIRIT OF CANADA TELLS CANADA'S STORY as many different people have felt it in their hearts and expressed it in stories, songs, poems, and journal entries. Each selection conveys how it felt to be alive at a particular time and place in Canadian history, experiencing moments of joy, wonderment, fear, dejection, or triumph.

Sometimes these moments are described by the people who experienced them. Writing home from New France, Jean de Brébeuf gives blunt advice to would-be missionaries. Susanna Moodie reveals the desperation she felt when her pioneer cabin caught fire in the dead of winter. Shizuye Takashima recalls her childhood in a prison camp for Japanese Canadians during the Second World War. At other times, modern writers bring to life the events and emotions of the past. Margaret Atwood, long fascinated by Susanna Moodie, re-imagines the cabin fire in a haunting poem. Willie Dunn writes a sorrowful song about the nineteenth-century Native leader Crowfoot. Joan Clark enters the mind of a bewildered Viking boy who is captured by the Beothuks, and then the minds of his equally puzzled captors.

I've arranged the pieces chronologically, for the most part, with time out for ghost stories, tall tales, and humour. Although there are some famous Canadians in these pages, and some important events, they are not in the form we encounter them in history books. A folk song called "Brave Wolfe" tells of the battle on the Plains of Abraham, which led to the British conquest of New France. Canada's first prime minister, Sir John A. Macdonald, is a supporting character in a story about how his wife rode west on the cowcatcher of a train. *The Spirit of Canada* also balances famous pieces and little-known ones. "The Cremation

of Sam McGee" is here, and so are "In Flanders Fields," Gordon Lightfoot's "Canadian Railroad Trilogy," and even our national anthem, in both official languages. But there are also pieces that will be new to most people, such as Kiakshuk's scary but funny "Giant Bear" and Nancy Prasad's empathetic "You Have Two Voices."

I have written an introduction for each subsection of the book, as well as for each selection. These introductions give the pieces historical context, explaining, for example, the circumstances in which they were written, or the cultural background from which they spring, or unusual words they contain. Although I began this book thinking that I knew Canada's history fairly well, I now grasp much more than I ever expected to about such topics as logging in nineteenth-century Ontario and traditional seal hunting in Nunavut.

As I gathered material for *The Spirit of Canada* over several years, I often felt that I was revisiting my younger self. As a child, I lived in the Canadian North, at a time when the old ways for Native peoples were fast vanishing. When I collected pieces about the Inuit, or the fur trade, or huskies, or biting arctic cold, I thought of those times. We were in the North because my father was stationed there with the army. During the Second World War, my mother had been in the army, too. Both my grandfathers served in the renowned Black Watch Regiment in the First World War. As a child, I felt very much in the shadow of Canada's military history. Remembrance Day was truly a day of remembering, since thousands of veterans of two world wars were still in our midst with their vivid personal recollections.

While I was doing research at the Textbook Archive in the Ontario Institute for Studies in

Education, I saw again the readers I had used in grade school, and I was struck by how many war stories they contained. Several selections in this anthology come from those old readers, including Mona Gould's poignant poem "This Was My Brother." I looked for pieces that did not glorify war, but that would still remind young readers of what Canadians did in those times, and how much they sacrificed.

During the 1960s, like many other teenagers of the time, I was a folksinger, singing and strumming my guitar in coffeehouses. That is when I first learned and sang "Un Canadien errant," and "Nova Scotia Song," both of which appear in the book. A few years later, on the first day of my very first publishing job, I was given a history textbook to copy edit. Over the years, I worked on many more books about Canadian history, and eventually I began to think about a book that would tell Canada's story entirely through songs, stories, and poems.

Assembling the pieces for *The Spirit of Canada* has been a challenge—but also one of the most inspiring experiences of my life. It's a point of pride for me that the contributors to the anthology come from every province and territory in Canada. I have tried to include as wide a range of voices as possible—Inuit, Cree, and Métis; French, English, Scottish, and Irish; Mennonites from Russia and Jews from Poland; Ukrainians and Italians; Chinese, Japanese, South Asians, and Trinidadians—but I was always aware that they would have to represent hundreds of other groups who together make up Canada.

As I was growing up, the phrase used for our multicultural nation was "the Canadian mosaic"—a Canada in which every ethnic group contributed its own little piece to the larger design while still keeping its unique identity. But the mosaic image was always unsatisfying. We know, and story after story in *The Spirit of Canada* makes clear, that immigrants are and must be changed by the experience of coming to Canada. We also know that immigrants change the Canada they find.

Today, when I meet my daughter, Amanda, at her public school in downtown Toronto, I see the world's children tumbling out of its doors. Indeed, the Canadian experiment is more like a kaleidoscope—each little piece of glass keeps its shape and colour, but together they constantly shift and overlap to form something new. At times, some of the pieces are hidden in the larger design, but just a slight shift in viewpoint and they leap out again, plain to see. And the beauty and symmetry of a kaleidoscopic image is, of course, fragile.

At times in Canada's history, certain of its peoples were treated in a way we can recall only with feelings of shame and regret. Some of these injustices—and not only those in the distant past—are remembered in these pages. But the overall spirit of the book is one of celebration. Canada is, once again, at the start of a new century. It has never been a certainty that Canada would stretch unbroken from sea to sea, and it is not now. Still, Amanda's generation shows me an astounding experiment in multiculturalism that, by and large, has worked. They are the hopeful spirit—and the future—of Canada.

A NOTE ON TERMINOLOGY
This is an anthology that includes many ethnic groups and touches on a number of sensitive issues in our history. In my introductions, I have tried to use terminology that shows respect for the people involved. For example, whenever possible, Native Canadian groups are called by their individual, preferred names: Mi'kmaq, Siksika, and so on. When an encompassing term is appropriate, the plural "Native peoples" emphasizes the variety of cultures and languages among first nations. However, the anthologized pieces themselves may use other terms, such as "Blackfoot" and "Indian," and I have not altered these. Similarly, while I use "black" to refer to Canadians of African descent, a nineteenth-century song uses the term "coloured," which was then considered proper usage. Finally, where authors have asked to be described as, for example, Ojibwa rather than Anishinabe, I have respected their wishes.

PART ONE

When the World Was New

Illustrated by

George Littlechild

When the World Was New

All Canadians are descendants of people who came from somewhere else. This is true even of Canada's Native peoples, although they have been here much longer than any other Canadians. There was a time, thousands of years ago, when so much water was locked up in glaciers that sea levels were lower than they are today. Siberia and Alaska were joined by a broad plain, and hunters following herds of deer, bison, and other animals could journey into the New World on dry land. When the glaciers melted and water channels opened up, Asians may have continued to migrate in boats made of hollowed logs or animal hides. These new arrivals spread out across the continent and formed many different nations, each with its own language and customs. They were Canada's first people, and their traditional stories speak of a time when all creation was fresh and new.

C. J. Taylor
How Two-Feather Was Saved from Loneliness

This is a traditional Abenaki story. The name "Abenaki" means "people living at the sunrise"—that is, in the east. The Abenaki lived in what is now Southern Quebec and New England. Most of them moved with the seasons, surviving by hunting and fishing. Some communities, however, began to grow corn for food. Since they did not have ploughs, they would burn a piece of ground to prepare it for planting. This legend explains the origins of fire and corn, and also describes how it became possible for the Abenaki people to live in settled villages.

LONG AGO THE EARTH WAS A COLD AND lonely place. No one knew how to make fire. There were very few people and they wandered far in search of food.

Two-Feather was lonely and hungry. All winter long he had met no one. All he had to eat was the bark he cut off the trees and the roots he dug out from under the snow.

He was glad when at last spring came. The sun grew warmer and the ice melted from the lakes and rivers. As he knelt to drink from a rushing stream, he caught sight of his face in the water and he felt lonely again: "How I wish," he thought, "I could see another face."

To forget his loneliness, Two-Feather lay down to sleep on the soft moss. He was awakened by a voice calling his name. He was afraid to open his eyes and find it was only a dream. But the voice came again and the rustle of leaves told him someone was near.

He opened his eyes and was frightened to find a strange figure above him. His fear passed as he saw a woman, lovely as spring, with long soft hair. He held out his arms to her, but she moved away.

He tried again and again to touch her, but always she stayed just beyond his reach. All day he followed her.

At nightfall they came to a lake. He could not get close to her so he made a drum and, in the moonlight, sang of his love.

"Please," he begged. "I am so lonely and you are so lovely. Stay with me and I will love you and look after you forever."

"I have come to look after you, Two-Feather," she said softly. "If you do what I say, you will never be lonely again."

"What would you have me do?" he asked.

"Follow me," she said, and turned away.

He followed her over mountains, through forests, across streams, always afraid she would get away from him. If he tried to catch up with her, she hurried on ahead. But when he grew tired or hungry and slowed down to rest or eat, she waited for him. After many days, they came to a vast meadow.

At last she stopped and rose up into the air, hovering over him like a bird.

"Two-Feather," she said, "gather some dry grass into a little pile, then take two sticks and rub them together."

Soon sparks flew. The little pile of grass caught fire. Then the tall grass and soon the whole meadow was ablaze. Two-Feather had never seen fire before and he was frightened. Would it spread forever and destroy the earth?

But the soft voice reassured him. "It will be all right, Two-Feather," she said.

When all the grass in the meadow had burned and the fire died down, she spoke again.

"Now, take hold of my hair and pull me over the burned ground."

"I cannot do that," Two-Feather protested. "I cannot hurt you, for I love you."

"If you love me, Two-Feather, you must trust me and do as I say," she said gently.

Two-Feather did as she asked. He pulled her back and forth over the burned meadow. Her hair in his hand was softer than anything he had ever felt before. She seemed to grow lighter and lighter as he pulled.

When he finished and turned, she was no longer there. But where he had pulled her, green shoots appeared. It was the first corn ever grown.

As the corn grew tall and ripened, people found their way to it. Now they no longer had to wander in search of food. They built houses and a village.

Two-Feather married and had children. He was no longer lonely but he never forgot the Corn Goddess. Each summer as he held the first ears of corn, he felt in his hands again the softness of her hair.

Joseph Bruchac
Manabozho and the Maple Trees

This story comes from the Anishinabe (sometimes called Ojibwa), an Algonquian-speaking people
from the area around the Great Lakes. Manabozho (whose name means "old man" and is sometimes also
written as "Nanabozho" or "Nanabush") is a traditional trickster hero. In some stories, like this one, he has a serious
purpose: to keep his people from becoming lazy and ungrateful. In other stories, he plays pranks on people.
Gitchee Manitou is the great spirit, the creative force in the universe, according to the
traditional beliefs of many Algonquian peoples.

A LONG TIME AGO, WHEN THE WORLD was new, Gitchee Manitou made things so that life was very easy for the people. There was plenty of game and the weather was always good and the maple trees were filled with thick sweet syrup. Whenever anyone wanted to get maple syrup from the trees, all they had to do was break off a twig and collect it as it dripped out.

One day, Manabozho went walking around. "I think I'll go see how my friends the Anishinabe are doing," he said. So he went to a village of Indian people. But there was no one around. So

Manabozho looked for the people. They were not fishing in the streams or the lake. They were not working in the fields hoeing their crops. They were not gathering berries. Finally he found them. They were in the grove of maple trees near the village. They were all just lying on their backs with their mouths open, letting the maple syrup drip into their mouths.

"This will not do," Manabozho said. "My people are all going to be fat and lazy if they keep on living this way."

So Manabozho went down to the river. He took with him a big basket he had made of birch bark. With this basket he brought back many buckets of water. He went to the top of the maple trees and poured the water in so that it thinned out the syrup. Now thick maple syrup no longer dripped out of the broken twigs. Now what came out was thin and watery and just barely sweet to the taste.

"This is how it will be from now on," Manabozho said. "No longer will syrup drip from the maple trees. Now there will be only this watery sap. When people want to make maple syrup they will have to gather many buckets full of the sap in a birch bark basket like mine. They will have to gather wood and make fires so they can heat stones to drop into the baskets. They will have to boil the water with the heated stones for a long time to make even a little maple syrup. Then my people will no longer grow fat and lazy. Then they will appreciate this maple syrup Gitchee Manitou made available to them. Not only that, this sap will drip only from the trees at a certain time of the year. Then it will not keep people from hunting and fishing and gathering and hoeing in the fields. This is how it is going to be," Manabozho said.

And that is how it is to this day.

Frances Fraser
How the Thunder Made Horses

Although horses first evolved in North America some forty million years ago, paleontologists believe that they later became extinct here. In the sixteenth century, they were brought back by the Spanish and gradually moved northward, passing from one group of Native people to another. By the mid-eighteenth century, they had arrived in what is now Southern Alberta, home of the Siksika (Blackfoot) people. Horses quickly transformed their lives and became their most precious possessions. The animals could haul their belongings and their buffalo-hide homes from place to place. Mounted on horses, hunters could pursue and kill buffalo. This traditional Siksika story of how horses were given to them by the god of thunder shows how much they valued the strength and beauty of the animals.

ONE FINE DAY, WHEN THE MOON OF Frogs was rising, Ka-tsi-tís-kuma, the Thunder, had nothing to do. And he was very bored. He sat up there in the Sky Country, looking about for some way of amusing himself.

Down on the earth he saw a lake, shining in the sunlight. He leaned away over, and reached down to get a big handful of mud out of the middle of it. Then he sat by his fire, making little figures, and baking them in the ashes. When they were well baked, he took them out, and sat idly turning them over and over in his hands.

One caught his eye.

"Aie!" said the Thunder, delighted. "Here is something good!" Something useful! Maybe pretty, too! I must make this one better, and make more like it!" He threw some more sticks on the fire and reached down into the lake again.

All day long the Thunder worked hard, making horses. He made big ones, and little ones, mares, and stallions. When he had gotten them all modelled and baked, he lined them up evenly, and looked at them again.

"Sometimes it is cold," he said. "They

must have fur, or hair, to keep them warm." But how to get it, and put it on?

Ka-tsi-tís-kuma looked down to earth again, and his eyes brightened. There were a great many animals down there with the kind of hair he wanted. So he took the hair from the white dogs, from the gophers, from the moose, and the deer, and even the little grey mice, and all these colours of horses he made. Sometimes he had bits of two colours left, and with these he made pintos. Some of the hair fell into the soot by the fire, and that made the black horses.

Ka-tsi-tís-kuma was very happy. He lined up all the horses he had made, and the lightning went flickering down the row, touching each one in turn, and the little horses came alive, and began to cavort around. Ka-tsi-tís-kuma sat, smoking his pipe, and watching them. He was very proud of what he had done.

Suddenly, he noticed that his beautiful horses weren't running and jumping any more. They were limping, slowly, and painfully. He had forgotten to make hooves for them! They had to have hooves to protect the tender parts of their feet, but what to make them of?

Ka-tsi-tís-kuma sighed, and set to work to find something that could be made to serve as hooves. First, he tried making hooves out of buckskins, like moccasins.

These were not bad, but then he thought, "No. These animals will have to travel over rough and stony ground. Moccasins would wear out."

Then he tried making the hooves out of rock. But the poor little horses limped worse than ever. He tried a lot of other things, but nothing worked. So, up in the Sky Country, Ka-tsi-tís-kuma sat with his chin on his hand, looking gloomily down to the earth.

Down on the lakeshore, queer little creatures were crawling in the mud. The Thunder reached down and snatched a handful of them. And the hooves of his horses were made from the shells of the turtle. (That, say the Old Ones, is why there are no turtles around this part of the country, now. The Thunder used every one of them for the hooves of his horses.)

Then the Thunder dropped the horses one by one down to earth for the Indians to use. And he watches them, even to this day. For if you are cruel to your horses, and run them hard, till they sweat, in a thunderstorm you are likely to lose them. Ka-tsi-tís-kuma will send lightning to strike them, and take them back to the Sky Country. Ka-tsi-tís-kuma does not like his gifts to be abused.

"E-ma-ne-ya! True!" say the Old Ones.

Joan Skogan
Scannah and the Beautiful Woman

The traditional lands of the Tsimshian lie along the Nass and Skeena rivers and the northern coast of British Columbia, near present-day Prince Rupert. The Tsimshian relied on and respected the ocean and its inhabitants, especially the salmon that fed them. They built large sea-going canoes, and also put their wood-carving skills to work on totem poles and other ceremonial objects, such as the cedar box described in this story. This traditional Tsimshian story of how a man rescued his wife from a sinister undersea kingdom of sea otters was first published by the Metlakatla Band Council.

LONG AGO, AT THE HEAD OF A BAY NEAR the present village of Metlakatla, the Tsimshian people's finest hunter walked on the beach with his wife. This woman had beauty as well as a shining spirit, and her husband loved her well. The two of them stood arm in arm in the sun, looking at the bright ocean, when they saw a white sea otter drifting in on the tide.

Calling out in delight at such a rare find, the woman ran to the water's edge and waded into the waves. As the hunter watched, she and the white otter disappeared beneath the sea. Her husband swam far out, looking for her, and waited on the shore until near dark before he admitted to himself that she was truly gone. He returned to the village, hoping to find the truth about his great loss from Ska-geh, the One-Who-Sees-Visions.

Ska-geh crouched, silent, in a shadowed corner of the longhouse as the hunter told his tale. He looked long into the fire, and after a time he said, "The woman was taken by Scannah, the sea otter people. She is far away in their underwater home, wife to their chief. No human can rescue her."

"I shall not rest until I have tried," the hunter declared. "You must help me."

So Ska-geh instructed the sorrowing husband, "You must take two companions, the martin and the swallow, to help you on your journey. You will search the seas until you find two heads of kelp tied together. These mark the road under the ocean to the home of the Scannah people. I cannot tell what will happen to you there, but I can give you a small power that may strengthen you." The old man fastened a deerskin bag around the hunter's neck, saying, "The dried leaves within will make whole that which is broken." The hunter bade farewell to all in the longhouse. Ska-geh returned to his fire.

Softly and clearly the hunter called, "Brothers, I am ready," and the martin and the swallow flew to his side. The canoe moved quickly through Metlakatla Pass to the open sea with the martin flying ahead and the swallow above. Many days the three of them travelled, seeing nothing but wind-tossed foam and sea birds, until they were near despair. At last, the martin returned to the canoe, saying, "Far ahead yet, I see two kelp bulbs tied together." The three travellers went towards this place.

The hunter tied the canoe to one of the kelp heads, and he and the two birds talked together. "All we can do," said the martin, "is to separate. I will guard the canoe while you continue your journey to the home of the Scannah. The swallow will fly home and tell our people what has happened." To this, they all agreed, and they parted in sadness with small hope of seeing each other again. The brave hunter put his hands on the kelp heads and took his first step onto the undersea road.

The way before him led to the green gloom of the undersea world. The sunlight was far above the hunter now. He knew not when he would reach the end of the road, or what he might find there.

In the world above, day had turned into night, but the hunter walked on, travelling forever downwards until he heard fearful noises ahead. A flock of geese jostled one another and muttered angrily. Their searching beaks terrified him, and he waited until he could pass among them unnoticed.

The hunter ran. He could only continue his journey now, or be lost forever in this shadowed world. Once again he stopped, his own breathing loud in his ears, when he heard sounds farther along the path. Three men he thought to be slaves were taking turns chopping at an old hemlock tree. Their stone axe was clumsy and dull, and the work went slowly. As he watched, the head flew off the axe, and the slaves tried in vain to mend it. They moaned, "How shall we finish this work? The master will be angry and his rage is fierce."

From the deerskin bag Ska-geh had hung around his neck, the hunter took some of the dried leaves. He stepped forward to sprinkle the leaves over the axe, and the head came together with the handle as strong as before. The slaves stared at him in awe. When they saw that he was human, the first slave said, "How do you come to be in this world?"

"I have come from the land above to find my wife. The Scannah took her from

the shadows while the slaves took up a large cedar box and filled it with water. Even the cooking boxes here were beautifully carved with the sea otter crest. The slaves brought the box to the coals. The hunter moved a little closer to the silent woman. Suddenly, the carved box tipped and clouds of smoke and steam rose around the woman. The hunter leaped forward and clasped her in his arms. "Come, my wife!" he cried.

The two of them ran, hand in hand, as the Scannah roused themselves to give chase.

They fled along the undersea road, past the quarrelsome geese, ever upwards, closer and closer to the top. The sounds of pursuit faded behind them until at last they placed their hands together on the two heads of kelp that marked the beginning of the sea road.

Their canoe was safe, still tied to the kelp, but the faithful martin lay in the bottom of the boat, faint and near death from thirst. "Oh, my brother," murmured the hunter. Gently he placed some of Ska-geh's dried leaves on the martin's body. The bird stirred to life. The hunter and his beautiful wife wept a little in thankfulness that they all lived in the sunlight once more.

They travelled home to find the swallow safe with Ska-geh, and told their adventures to all the people of the longhouse. The hunter and his wife passed the rest of their days in peace and comfort at Metlakatla.

our home to be wife for their chief."

The slaves looked at one another. The first slave spoke again, "The sea otter chief is our master, and though we fear him greatly, we will help you as you have helped us. First, you must beware of the geese. They, too, were once the Scannah chief's wives, until he tired of them. He has changed them into blind creatures to act as his messengers. Now, here is the plan."

The hunter drew close to the slaves and listened.

"The woman who was your wife in the world above will be standing beside the cooking fire," said the slave. "We will fetch water for her and spill it onto the fire." The hunter agreed that the resulting confusion would give him his only chance to rescue his wife. He and the slaves set out for the Scannah chief's dwelling place.

Soon enough they came to the fire. The hunter saw the figure of a woman standing nearby. Her cloak was wrapped about her body as if to shield herself, and her face was hidden, but he knew this was his wife. Saying nothing, he withdrew into

PART TWO

The New Found Land

Illustrated by

Alan Daniel

Explorers and Adventurers

As far as we know, the first Europeans came to the shores of North America about one thousand years ago. They were called the Norse, or Vikings, and were seafarers from Scandinavia. They settled first in Iceland, later in Greenland, and finally made their way to Labrador and Newfoundland. Some five hundred years passed before there are records of Europeans arriving again. It has long been believed that John Cabot, sponsored by the king of England, reached Newfoundland in 1497 and 1498. He found the Grand Banks teeming with codfish, but did not find what he was really looking for: a route to the spices and silks of Asia. Nevertheless, from that time onward, fishing fleets from England, France, Portugal, and Spain crossed the ocean every summer to fill their nets with fish on the Grand Banks. Meanwhile, English explorers such as Martin Frobisher and Henry Hudson began the long quest for a northern water route (the Northwest Passage) over North America to the Far East. And in 1534, Jacques Cartier planted the French flag on the Gaspé Peninsula and claimed it for the king of France. The territories being explored and claimed by these Europeans were, of course, already occupied by Native peoples. Coastal people, and later those farther inland, had to decide how they would respond to these baffling, and often arrogant, new arrivals.

Joan Clark
Thrand and Abidith

At first, the Norse people who came to Newfoundland simply harvested timber and vines and returned to Greenland, but eventually they settled on the coast. Unfortunately, the Norse colonists mistrusted and fought with the Beothuks, the Native people they encountered there. Because of this feuding, and also because of the harsh climate, they eventually gave up their North American settlements. Joan Clark's novel *The Dream Carvers* tells of a young Greenlander named Thrand who is captured by Beothuks—he calls them *skraelings*—and gradually learns to accept their ways. In this excerpt from the early pages, Thrand finds his captors hard to understand, while a young Beothuk girl named Abidith, whose brother was killed by a countryman of Thrand's, finds him equally strange.

THEY HAVE PLACED ME OUTSIDE THEIR tents where they can keep an eye on me. I notice they took care to stake me in a grassy area empty of anything except myself. There is nothing close by that I can use to cut the bindings that tie my wrists to the stake. The bindings are strips of caribou skin. My feet have been left unbound, which means I can move my legs as I please. My captors have cleverly placed a crosspiece at the top of the pole to prevent me from lifting the ties off the stake. At night they take me into one of their tents—there are three altogether— and tie me in a sleeping place, feet towards the fire. In the morning they bring me out here to the stake. For seven days it's been like this. All this time I've been watching my captors, waiting for a chance to escape. And I've been remembering Greenland.

My name is Thrand. I was born fourteen years ago in Gardar, in Greenland. My father and I came to Leifsbudir for wood, which is scarce at home. We Greenlanders regard the name of our island as something of a joke since, except for the pastures along the fjords, it is less green than blue and white. There are no trees in Greenland, only rock and grass, water and ice. Alders and osiers grow in the hollows; dwarf birch and juniper survive here and there, but these hardly count as trees since they can't be made into houses or ships. Occasionally enough driftwood comes ashore to make a small rowboat or a bench, perhaps a chest. But wood has to be fetched from forested lands in order to build houses with posts and beams and furnish them with tables and sleeping platforms. At home in Gardar my family lives in a stone hut and sleeps on alder branches and furs spread on the floor.

The year I was born, 1001, Leif Eriksson crossed the western sea looking for the forested lands and found this country. He built some houses on the edge of the sea about a two-day journey by boat from where I am now, and named them Leifsbudir. That is where my father and I, along with seventy-odd Greenlanders and Icelanders, have been this past year. Mainly we have been harvesting and dressing timber to take back to Greenland. At last my mother will have a fine house in Gardar built with posts and beams. It will have sleeping benches, chests and whatever furniture she wants us to make.

As soon as I find my chance, I intend to take one of my captors' boats—I see two from where I am sitting—and use it to escape to Leifsbudir. If I run into trouble with the boat, I'll go ashore and return on foot. I'm quick on my feet and would make good time along the shore. My escape will have to be soon. My father and the others can't delay their departure much longer without running into ice in Greenland. Late Summer is the only time ships can move in and out of the Eastern Settlement before the fjords become choked with ice.

My captors use boats made of birch bark. In my view this is short-sighted. Why make a boat from bark when wood is plentiful and sturdier by far? If I could speak to these skraelings, I would tell them how Norsemen build ships. Of course, I can't talk to my captors since they speak a language unknown to me.

Before coming to Leifsbudir, I had never seen a skraeling. In Northsetur, far to the north of Gardar where we Greenlanders trap white bears, hunters have seen the occasional skraeling dressed in sealskin and paddling a skin boat. The skraelings on this side of the sea appear to be different from the Greenland skraelings. For one thing, they are as tall and well built as Norsemen; for another, they are completely red. They rub their skin and clothing with what appears to be red earth mixed with grease. Their tents are covered with this red powder as are their tools and utensils, as well as the bone ornaments they wear around their necks. Even the boat that brought me here is red. This makes me think I have entered another world. It's true that the sky and sea are blue, the trees and grass green, the rocks and stones grey, but these skraelings seem to inhabit a world of redness where everything they make or use is red. It's as if they imagine themselves living within a red world of their own that's side by side or within the larger world that I know.

As a boy in Greenland I was told skraelings were wretches who lived on the outermost reaches of the world. They weren't people but wild savages who lurked in unknown places. The first skraeling I saw was the thief we killed in Leifsbudir. When I saw him lying near the woods, I

was surprised to see how much he resembled me. Now that I've seen many more of them, I know these skraelings eat and sleep and work the way people do. There are men and women, old and young, children and babies just as there are among folk in Greenland. The main difference between skraelings and myself is their redness, at least on the outside.

Other than feeding me and moving me between tent and stake, the skraelings ignore me completely. It's as if by not being red, I don't exist. I am outside their world of redness. Except for one. That's the old woman who brings me my food twice daily, usually a roasted fish speared on a wooden stick. She pats my hair and says something that sounds like "Wobee." Over and over, she says this word, "Wobee." I eat the fish because I want to be strong enough to escape. I don't understand why people would feed some-

one they intend to kill. Do they intend to set me free and then run me down?

The tent where I sleep at night is occupied by the old woman and an old man I take to be her husband. I notice both of them have creased faces, wrinkled necks and move slowly as if from the joint-ill, which is how I know they are the oldest people here. The other two tents are occupied by younger men and women and their children, all of them dark-eyed. The hair beneath the red covering seems to be black. It's difficult to know the colour of their skin beneath the red. All of them go about barefoot as well as bare-armed and bare-legged. The women wear some sort of skin tunic, the men a skin hanging from a belt. I myself am wearing skin breeches, a shirt and deer-skin shoes. I can see for myself that my hair is light brown and my skin white and sunburnt. I can't, of course, see my eyes but I know that like most Greenlanders', they are more or less blue.

[Thrand makes an unsuccessful escape attempt, and finds himself back in the care of the old woman, whose name is Imamasduit.]

In the morning Imamasduit brings me a roasted fish but I refuse to eat. If I can't escape, what's the point of being strong? In any case, I've no appetite for food. The old woman takes my face in her hands and lifts it to hers. "Wobee," she says and shakes her head. Her forehead wrinkles in the way my father's does when he's confused or distressed. Imamasduit doesn't seem angry at me for trying to escape. If anything she's more gentle and patient with me than she was before. "Wobee," she says over and over then leaves me alone. I put my head between my knees and stare at the ground.

I don't know how long the girl has been sitting there. I didn't hear her approach. But I know when I look up and see her that she's been there for some time. Once again, I am convinced that my captors live in a different world from mine. There's an invisible wall between us, which is why they can move about without my hearing them.

One of the silly games my brother Magnus likes to play with anyone patient enough to sit with him is Stare Me Out. In this game, two people cast a spell on each other by locking their gaze until the loser breaks the spell by looking away. This is the kind of game the girl seems to be playing with me now. Though she isn't giggling the way Magnus does, I refuse to

play. I can't avoid stealing glances at her all the same. She's sitting hands clasped around her bended knees. She's wearing a tunic trimmed with what looks like pieces of bone and has a bone ornament around her neck. Like the others, she's covered with red earth, which gives her a sharp, bitter smell. I can see that beneath the covering she is pleasingly shaped.

Is this creature human? Grandmother says he is. It's true that except for his white skin and blue eyes, the one she calls Wobee looks human, which is to say he has two arms, two legs and a head with two eyes. But some spirits are said to shape themselves into humans and Wobee could be that kind of spirit. Grandmother insists Wobee is human. She says creatures with white skin can be human. Wobee was one of several white men who were recently hunting bear in the woods to the North of us. She reminds me, as if I needed reminding, that there were many more white men in the place of the ice seals where my brother, Awadasut, was killed. Grandmother says that if Wobee had been a spirit, our hunters wouldn't have been able to capture him and bring him here to replace Awadasut.

Wobee can never replace my brother. Nobody can. I despise Wobee for killing my brother. I wouldn't be sitting here with him if it weren't for Grandmother's urging. This morning she insisted we talk about Wobee.

"Unless one of us can enter his mind, Wobee won't survive," Grandmother said.

I didn't say that I didn't care if Wobee

survived. To speak so would dishonour Grandmother's words. I told her I was deeply offended that our captive had chosen to hide himself near my brother's grave mound across the water on the island of birches.

"Wobee didn't know that the island was a burial ground. How can he be blamed for hiding there?"

I chose not to answer this. I want to blame Wobee for everything—for the water I spilled early this morning, the finger I pricked with an awl yesterday, the ache I have behind my eyes today.

"Being unkind to Wobee won't bring Awadasut back," Grandmother said.

"Wobee was also born of the Creator," she went on, her voice soft as lapping waves. "He's not an evil person, and has more years ahead of him than behind. We must help him become one of us."

"Why must he become one of us?" I said. I did not know until later that I was shouting. "Why can't we send him away to live on his own? That is what he wants, or he wouldn't have tried to escape. Why not give him what he wants?"

"Because we need him to do the things Awadasut did," Grandmother said. "We must persuade him of this and teach him our ways. That is why you must learn his thoughts. You have been given special powers to do this." Then she added slyly, "Wobee may welcome a young woman inside his head."

So here I am, sitting close enough to Wobee so that Grandmother can see I am obeying her wishes, yet not so close that I can smell his whiteness, which is the odour of rancid fat. How pale he is, like a newly dug root. Because of his whiteness

it's hard for me to believe he's alive. If I pricked his finger with an awl, would it bleed?

The girl isn't playing a staring game with me as I thought. Each time I've stolen a glance her way, she's made no attempt to lock eyes with me. It's true her face is turned in my direction, but it seems she's looking through rather than at me, and there's an angry, hostile expression on her face. Why is she staring at me like that? is she trying to put an evil spell on me? In Greenland there are folk who are said to have the evil eye. They have the power to change others' luck by staring at them. That's why we never look an evil spell caster in the eye. As long as we can avoid looking at the evil eye, we can withstand the spell.

After a time, Imamasduit comes out of the tent and stands between us. She looks at the girl and pats my head.

"Wobee," she says.

"Wobee," the girl repeats, her voice hard and clipped.

Imamasduit looks at me and pats the girl.

"Abidith," she says.

I hesitate. The girl's name doesn't sound difficult to say. Perhaps I should try.

"Abidith," I repeat and look at the girl. It's the first word I've spoken since my capture. It sounds strange coming from my mouth.

The girl doesn't smile but Imamasduit does, showing her worn teeth.

I say Abidith's name once more aloud, then over and over, liking the sound of it in my ears.

Elma Schemenauer
Hunting for Unicorns

Seafaring on wind-driven ships in the fifteenth and sixteenth centuries was risky and uncertain.
Expeditions were also expensive undertakings—only kings or wealthy nobles could afford to sponsor them.
But the possibility of discovering riches, along with the age-old desire to see new wonders, brought
many European explorers to North America. Elma Schemenauer's story reminds us of one
quest for fabulous treasure that is almost forgotten today—the search for unicorns.

DURING THE MIDDLE AGES, STORIES OF unicorns took a very firm hold on the imagination of most people in Europe.

The head and body of the unicorn were like those of a slender white stag or horse. It had the swift cloven hoofs of a stag. Its tail was like that of a lion. Its cry was like the sound of bells, and it lived for a thousand years!

"The unicorn can cleanse a polluted spring or stream," people said. "All the noble animal needs to do is make the sign of the cross in the water with its horn.

The miraculous horn of the unicorn can also cure a fever. It can prevent the plague, and it can kill poisonous spiders."

Clearly, the unicorn was an amazing creature. The most important part of its anatomy seemed to be its fantastic horn, which was said to sprout from the middle of the animal's noble forehead.

Because the fabulous animal was supposed to be able to cure illness, it became the special symbol of doctors and chemists.

In those days, some Europeans had the

unfortunate habit of poisoning people they didn't like. Kings and queens and other wealthy individuals were particularly in danger of being poisoned. Consequently, such persons were most anxious to protect themselves by buying pieces or even tiny shavings of the wonder-working horn. Soon the bony "treasure of the unicorn's brow" was worth its weight in gold.

However, as everybody knows, the unicorn is a shy and elusive creature. It is extremely difficult to catch. As a matter of fact, nobody has ever even seen a unicorn—except in pictures. So how could anyone possibly hope to obtain the horn of the animal?

Well, the crafty merchants of the day had an idea. From the ice-choked waters of the far north came exactly the "product" they were seeking. It was the horn of a little-known Arctic creature called the *narwhal*.

The narwhal, a type of whale, is a blunt-bodied ocean mammal about the length of an average-sized living room. It has a spotted greyish brown back and white belly. By far the most outstanding feature of its anatomy is its dramatic single tusk.

This sword-like projection, which appears only in the male narwhal, juts straight out through the animal's upper lip. The tusk is two to three metres long, and *it spirals just like the horn of the legendary unicorn*!

People living in the far north knew about the narwhal from the earliest times. In Iceland, they called it *Nähvalhr*, or Death-whale, because it was supposed to appear to sailors before a shipwreck.

The European trade in narwhal horns probably began about 1000 A.D. By that time, Vikings from Iceland and Norway had established colonies on the bleak and rocky shores of southwestern Greenland. From this vantage point, square-sailed Viking *knorrs* (cargo ships) sliced their way northward into the grey waters of Baffin Basin—one of the richest narwhal areas in the world.

Needless to say, the blond-bearded sea-rovers quickly sold every narwhal tusk that they managed to bring back from their bold ventures into the far north. However, only a handful of shrewd European merchants were permitted to deal with the Norse traders. All trading was done in an atmosphere of great secrecy and mystery. Only a very few people in Europe knew the true source of the magnificent "unicorn horns" that the merchants offered for sale. As a result, supplies were always limited and the price remained high.

For centuries, European and British merchants carried on the valuable trade in narwhal horns. For centuries, most people continued to believe in the legends of the fabulous unicorn.

Strong belief in the unicorn might have gone on for several more centuries—if it hadn't been for a man called Martin Frobisher. Frobisher, an Englishman, was one of the earliest explorers of Canada's North. It was he who finally exposed the age-old secret of the horn of the unicorn.

One bright August day in 1577, during Frobisher's second voyage to the North, some members of his crew found a large dead fish floating in the water close to the Baffin Island shoreline. The creature had a long spiralling tusk projecting through its upper lip. The excited sailors immediately concluded that they had discovered a "unicorn of the sea." Here is how one of them described the event:

On this West shoare we found a dead fish floating, whiche had in his nose a horn streight & torquet (twisted), of lengthe two yards lacking two ynches, being broken in the top, where we might perceiue it hollowe, into which some of our Saylers putting Spiders, they presently dyed…we supposed it to be the Sea Unicorne.

High Admiral Frobisher was most interested in the amazing discovery. He ordered his men to cut the dead narwhal's tusk from its blimp-like body. He took this tusk home with him as a special present for Queen Elizabeth I, who had sent him on his voyage.

The Queen was overjoyed at receiving such a rare and valuable gift. She referred to it as a jewel and placed it in her wardrobe.

In later years, several of Frobisher's men published books about their experiences in the Arctic. In their accounts they included the story of the large single-tusked fish that they had found on that bright August day off the coast of Baffin Island.

People in both Britain and Europe read the accounts with great interest. Some thoughtful individuals began to "put two and two together." Nobody had ever actually seen the stag-like land unicorn, but dozens of Frobisher's crewmen had seen the narwhal. The tusk that the explorers had brought home with them looked exactly like what Europeans had always regarded as the horn of a unicorn. Perhaps, just perhaps, the mystical white unicorn wasn't a real animal after all.

Of course, treasured beliefs die hard. Besides, merchants dealing in narwhal tusks did their best to maintain the air of magic and mystery that had always surrounded their product.

In the long run, however, it was a losing battle. Knowledge of the Canadian North increased rapidly with the voyages of explorers such as Henry Hudson, William Baffin, and the French fur-traders Radisson and Groseilliers. As narwhal tusks became more and more common, interest dwindled and the price dropped. By the late 1600s, hardly anyone was buying unicorn horns any more. The "fad" had finally run its course.

Barbara Hehner
The Village That Stretched from Sea to Sea

CANADA OWES ITS NAME TO TWO YOUNG men named Taignoagny and Domagaya. They were the sons of Donnacona, chief of the land around the village of Stadacona on the St. Lawrence River. In August 1536, the two were nearing the end of a long journey. The previous year, the explorer Jacques Cartier had taken them all the way to his birthplace of France. Now he was bringing them home again. As the ship neared Anticosti Island, the young men excitedly pointed out the route that would take the ship to Kanata—"Kanata" was the Huron-Iroquois word for "village"—meaning their own home of Stadacona. From then on, Cartier used the word "Canada" to refer not only to Stadacona (where Quebec City would one day stand) but also to the land around it. One hundred years later, the name was being used for all of New France, and as explorers and fur traders pushed west, the name Canada spread with them. The first official use of Canada came in 1791, when the provinces of Upper Canada and Lower Canada were established. In 1867, Canada became a country with four provinces; these were gradually followed by six more. Today, Stadacona's village stretches more than five thousand kilometres, from the Pacific Ocean to Newfoundland in the Atlantic Ocean.

Geordie Georgekish, William Kapsu, John Mukash, and Jane Pachano
Chikabash and the Strangers

We have many written records from Europeans that describe their first meetings with Native peoples, but the Native reaction to the Europeans was not written down for a long time. The first North Americans to see white people lived on the eastern coast of Canada. One Mi'kmaq traditional story tells of a young woman who had a strange dream. She saw a small island floating towards land. As it came close to shore, she saw that there were many trees sticking up from it, and that there were bears climbing these trees. A man dressed all in white left the island and came ashore. The young woman told her dream to the wisest elders of her people, but they could not understand what it meant. A few days later, an island covered in trees, with bears climbing in the branches, really did float towards shore. As it came closer, the Mi'kmaq people saw that the island was actually a large boat, and that the bears were men climbing its masts. Some of these strangers got into a small boat and came ashore, and among them was a man dressed all in white, just as the girl had dreamed. Word of the strange new arrivals spread inland, so many Native people heard about the Europeans long before they saw them. This story about Chickabash and his sister, which comes from Cree storytellers, is similar in many ways to the Mi'kmaq tale.

LONG, LONG AGO, THERE WAS A YOUNG Cree boy named Chikabash who lived with his older sister. The two of them travelled all over the place, never staying in any one place for long.

Now there was one thing that Chikabash loved doing best of all and that was to hunt squirrels. He and his sister travelled all over just so he could go hunting for squirrels.

One day while Chikabash was out hunting near a bay, he saw a huge canoe way off in the distance. It looked as if it had a big tree growing out of its middle. The huge canoe came closer and closer to shore.

Chikabash was very curious and he decided to have a look at it. He walked to the shoreline and waited.

When the canoe was very near, he saw

men with pale faces and light-coloured hair and eyes. They were wearing strange clothing he had never seen before and speaking a strange language he had never heard before. They stared at him and he stared back.

They waved to him and he waved back. They beckoned to him to come on board. When he had climbed aboard, they kept touching his clothing and poking at him. They finally set some food down for him and although he had never seen such food before, he decided to eat it so they wouldn't be offended.

He knew his sister would be interested in this new food, so he saved some to take back to her.

"Nimsa, nimsa," he called as soon as he was within shouting distance of their camp. "I have some food for you."

"Where did you get this?" she asked when he laid out the unfamiliar food in front of her.

"From some strange-looking men who came in a huge canoe with a tall tree growing out of the middle. They have pale faces, light-coloured hair and eyes. They wear clothes which are not made out of hides and they speak a language which I cannot understand. They invited me to climb into their canoe and then they fed me. They kept touching my clothing and poking at me," Chikabash recounted.

"And you went on board?" his sister asked, horrified. "Weren't you scared that they would kill you? I have heard that a race of people like the ones you have described would someday come to this land, and we would have a lot of problems after that."

"Where did you hear this?" Chikabash asked.

"From our mother and father, and they got it from their grandparents," she replied.

"These people are very friendly," he said.

"Well, we don't want to be unfriendly," his sister said. "Take some meat to them as a token of our friendship."

Chikabash did as his sister had told him and he took one squirrel thigh to the pale-faced men in the huge canoe. Now, the squirrels in this land were so huge that when Chikabash climbed aboard the strangers' canoe and put the squirrel thigh down, the canoe listed to one side and almost capsized.

New France

Although Jacques Cartier first sailed up the St. Lawrence and claimed the land for the French king in 1534, almost seventy-five years passed before the French arrived to stay. Samuel de Champlain founded Quebec in 1608, and under his leadership New France was explored and mapped and the fur trade grew. Missionaries started the first hospitals and schools. Ville Marie (as Montreal was originally called by the French) was founded in 1642. However, the French had allied themselves with the Hurons and other Native groups who were the fur-trade rivals and traditional enemies of the Iroquois. As a result, the Iroquois considered the French to be their enemies as well, and they frequently attacked the newcomers' small, struggling settlements. For a time, it looked as if the colony of New France might fail. But beginning in the 1660s, King Louis XIV gave the colony new hope in the form of three able and energetic leaders: Intendant Jean Talon, Governor Louis de Buade de Frontenac, and Bishop François de Laval. He also granted tracts of land called *seigneuries* to army officers who wanted to settle in New France, and encouraged other settlers to take up farming in the New World. The golden age of New France had begun, and for almost one hundred years the colony prospered.

Jean de Brébeuf
Try Not to Be Troublesome

Jean de Brébeuf was a Jesuit priest who journeyed to New France and lived as a missionary among the Huron people from 1626 to 1649. Like many of the Jesuit missionaries, Brébeuf came from a noble family in France, and could have spent his life in comfort. However, he was willing to suffer any hardship to bring his Christian religion—which to him was the only true religion—to Native peoples. While he wanted them to accept Christianity, Brébeuf also made an effort to understand the way the Hurons saw the world. In 1637, he wrote down some practical advice for other Jesuits who were planning to become missionaries in New France. His ideas were recorded in *The Jesuit Relations*, a record of missionary work that was sent home to the Jesuit order's headquarters in France.

THE FATHERS WHOM GOD SHALL CALL TO the holy Mission of the Hurons should exercise careful foresight about all the hardships, annoyances and perils that must be encountered in making this journey. In this way, they will be prepared for all emergencies that may arise.

You must provide yourself with a tinder box or with a burning mirror, to furnish the Indians with fire in the daytime to light their pipes, and in the evening when they encamp. These little services win their hearts.

You should try to eat their sagamité [boiled cornmeal] in the way they prepare it. It is well to take everything they offer, although you may not be able to eat it all. When one becomes used to it, it does not seem like too much.

You must try to eat at daybreak unless you can take your meal with you in the canoe; for the day is very long. The Indians eat only at sunrise and sunset when they are on their journeys.

You must be careful never to make them wait for you in embarking. You must tuck up your gowns so that they will not get wet, and so that you will not carry either water or sand into the canoe. Keep your feet and legs bare. Be careful not to annoy anyone in the canoe with your hat [the missionaries' hats had wide brims]; it would be better to wear your nightcap.

You must conduct yourself so as not to be at all troublesome to even one of these people. Don't ask too many questions. Silence is good equipment at such a time.

Do not undertake anything unless you want to continue it; for example, do not start paddling unless you intend to continue paddling.

Finally, understand that the Indians will keep the same opinion of you in their own country that they formed of you while on the journey. If they decide you are an annoying and troublesome person, you will have a hard time changing their minds later. Show them a cheerful face, and thus prove that you are able to endure the fatigues of the voyage in good spirits.

All the fine qualities that would make you loved and respected in France are worthless here. If you could carry the load of a horse on your back, they would recognize you as a great man; otherwise not.

Jean de Brébeuf
The Huron Carol

Jean de Brébeuf learned the Huron language, and in that language he is thought to have written the words to "Jesous Ahatonhia." (The haunting melody is from a traditional French carol.) "Jesous Ahatonhia" tells the story of the birth of Christ, but uses words and settings that would be familiar to the Huron people. It was first sung in the settlements of Huronia (the area between Lake Simcoe and Georgian Bay) around 1642. In 1649, the Iroquois, who were enemies of the Hurons, invaded Huronia and destroyed their settlements. Brébeuf and Gabriel Lalemant, another missionary working among the Hurons, were captured by the Iroquois and killed. A few Hurons fled to Lorette, near Quebec City, and one hundred years later their descendants were still singing "Jesous Ahatonhia." A Jesuit priest, Father de Villeneuve, heard the carol and wrote it down. It was later translated into French as "Jésus est né," and in 1926 J. E. Middleton wrote its English words and called it "The Huron Carol."

1.

'TWAS IN THE MOON OF WINTER TIME
When all the birds had fled,
That mighty Gitchi Manitou
Sent angel choirs instead;
Before their light the stars grew dim
And wand'ring hunters heard the hymn:

Chorus:
"Jesus your King is born,
Jesus is born: *In excelsis gloria!*"

2.

Within a lodge of broken bark
The tender Babe was found,
A ragged robe of rabbit skin
Enwrapped His beauty 'round;
And as the hunter braves drew nigh
The angel song rang loud and high:
"Jesus your King is born,
Jesus is born: *In excelsis gloria!*"

Chorus

3.

The earliest moon of winter time
Is not so round and fair
As was the ring of glory on
The helpless Infant there.
The chiefs from far before Him knelt
With gifts of fox and beaver pelt.
"Jesus your King is born,
Jesus is born: *In excelsis gloria!*"

Chorus

4.

O children of the forest free,
O sons of Manitou,
The Holy Child of earth and heaven
Is born today for you.
Come kneel before the radiant Boy
Who brings you beauty, peace, and joy.
"Jesus your King is born,
Jesus is born: *In excelsis gloria!*"

FIRST STANZA IN FRENCH
Chrétiens, prenez courage,
Jésus Sauveur est né!
Du malin les ouvrages à jamais sont ruinés
Quand il chante merveille, à ces trou-
    blants appas
Ne prêtez plus l'oreille:
"Jésus est né: In excelsis gloria!"

FIRST STANZA IN HURON
Estennialon de tsonoue, Jesous ahatonhia.
Onna-ouaté oua d'oki n'ou ouanda skoua
    en tak,
En nonchien skouatchi hotak, n'on
    ouandi Ionra chata,
Jesous ahatonhia, Jesous ahatonhia, Jesous
    ahatonhia.

Suzanne Martel
The King's Daughter

Far more men than women came to New France in its early days. Jean Talon, who
became the first intendant (chief administrator) of New France in 1665, realized that the colony
could not survive unless people married and raised families in the new land. To achieve this, he asked
France to send hundreds of healthy young women to New France. These young women were known as *filles du roi*
(daughters of the king). Each was given a trousseau (the items needed to set up housekeeping) and a small dowry (a
sum of money). In this excerpt from Suzanne Martel's novel *The King's Daughter* (translated from the French by
David Homel and Margaret Rose), a young orphan named Jeanne Chatel has almost completed her voyage to
New France. The nun who is escorting her was a real person. Marguerite Bourgeoys first came to Ville
Marie in 1653 and was one of its most important leaders, establishing schools and a teaching order of
nuns. In 1982, she was the first Canadian woman to be declared a Roman Catholic saint.

ONE DAY, THE LOOKOUT SIGHTED LAND at last. The travellers were a little disappointed to spot only a thin dark line on the horizon. Soon the ship sailed past the high rocky cliffs of Newfoundland. Then the coast of Nova Scotia paraded before their eyes.

The St. Lawrence narrowed, but still appeared gigantic compared to the watercourses of France. Sometimes they rounded a green island set like an emerald in the steel-grey ribbon of the river. The wind brought them the invigorating scent of the pines that bordered the shores and came down right to the banks.

One morning as the passengers gathered on deck were admiring the rocks jutting over the Saguenay River, Sister Bourgeoys took Jeanne to the narrow cabin she shared with five of the novices. With a laugh, the seasoned traveller told her companions that the dark little cubby-hole represented a luxury for her. Indeed, she had already made the crossing on deck, sleeping in the open on the ropes, in the days when she had been too poor to afford a bed on board.

"Jeanne," said Sister Bourgeoys, "I've prepared this bag for you. It will help you help others. I can see in you a great need for devotion; that will be your greatest asset in your new life."

She handed Jeanne a heavy, square leather sack, fitted with a strap so it could be carried over the shoulder.

"I've filled this bag with medicines and curative herbs. I collected ample supplies before I left France," the nun went on.

Setting the sack on the narrow bench that served as a bed, she opened it and showed her charge an assortment of smaller sacks, glass bottles and flasks, all carefully labelled. A small book full of notes came along with it.

"Here you will find the description of every remedy, the illnesses they're used for, doses and the effects to expect. I know you are diligent enough to study it and benefit from it. And you must not neglect the knowledge of the many wise people you will meet.

"Always be on the alert for new curative plants. New France has many that the Indians or settlers will show you. Sometimes those simple people possess the secrets of some very efficient cures."

Marguerite Bourgeoys closed the sack and added a little slyly, "And neither should you forget the very positive moral effect of a harmless potion when the true nature of the illness escapes you. I have often cured dizziness with sugared warm water. And mothers sleep better when they have a medicine to give their children at regular intervals. It reassures them and doubles their courage."

Jeanne listened attentively, her grey eyes intently watching her benefactress' wrinkled face. She considered herself a soldier being entrusted with a mission.

"You will not have put your confidence in me in vain, Sister," the orphan passionately declared. "I've already learned much during this crossing, and before we set foot in Québec, I will know this notebook by heart."

Jeanne's zeal confirmed the founder's opinion; after all, the old nun was a good judge of women of action. She had discovered one of that breed in this difficult student in whom Mother de Chablais couldn't find one good quality.

Jeanne carried the heavy sack to her cabin, took out the notebook and emptied the medicines onto the straw mattress. She plunged into the study of this new science, and every free moment found her murmuring,

"Marseilles vinegar for the plague.
Melissa cordial for migraine.
Poppy for bronchitis.
Hawthorn for the heart.
Paregoric for relief of pain."

If it was up to Jeanne Chatel, the colony would be bursting with perpetual health and would soon contain only alert hundred-year-olds and bouncing babies.

Québec, August, 1672

On a beautiful evening in the month of August, the sailing ship passed Île d'Orléans and approached the fortified city of Québec, perched on the heights of its gigantic cliff.

The royal flag was flapping in the wind above the log fortifications of Château Saint-Louis, which towered over the rock. Jeanne looked up proudly at that symbol of the courage and tenacity of her compatriots.

Several wooden houses nestled in the shadow of Cap Diamant. Canoes and small boats of all types were beached on

the shore. In the distance, a steep road scaled the cliff, leading to the upper part of the town.

If the departure from Le Havre had seemed picturesque to Jeanne, the arrival in Québec left her speechless. Besides the Governor's delegation presenting arms with a flourish of trumpets, she saw a crowd of citizens on the wharf attracted by this much anticipated event: the arrival of a ship. The *coureurs de bois* with their strange fringed shirts and their fur caps never parted with their guns. To her the Indians seemed peaceful, even somewhat dazed, and she couldn't figure out why people spoke of them with such terror. At the time she did not know those Indians had been trans-

formed by living with the whites; they had nothing in common with their brothers, the fierce kings of the forest.

The passengers, gathered on deck with their trunks and suitcases, silently studied the grand scenery spread before them. The less courageous felt overwhelmed by that immense rock, that gigantic river, those endless forests they had been sailing by for days. How distant were the peaceful contours and gentle colours of the French countryside!

Leaning against the rail between Jeanne and her lieutenant, Marie looked around with frightened eyes.

"Everything seems so big, so threatening," she shivered.

"No, it's all magnificent," contradicted Jeanne enthusiastically. "The air smells of pine. You can see that the country is brand new."

With a great uproar of shouting and noise, the gangplank finally linked the ship with solid ground.

Monsieur de Frontenac, the Governor who had just taken office, came forward, hat in hand. Sister Bourgeoys was the first to cross the narrow wooden plank. The Quebeckers cheered her, knowing that each of her numerous voyages contributed to the colony's well-being.

At a signal from the captain, the king's daughters, led by Jeanne, set foot on the soil of New France. Many of them were disappointed that the rolling and pitching sensation of the ship didn't disappear, but persisted for several hours.

From a distance, the awed Quebeckers inspected these girls daring enough to land in a wild country with no other protection than that offered by a potential husband. The married men looked at what they had missed, and the bachelors took inventory of the possibilities.

The girls, embarrassed by all those covetous glances, blushed and lowered their eyes. Only Jeanne, filled with wonder and fascination, looked at everything around her and answered the murmured words of welcome with an open smile.

Traditional
Mon Canot

Native peoples who were allies of the French brought furs to trade at Quebec, Trois-Rivières, and Montreal. But any young Frenchmen who were willing to leave the settlements and journey by canoe could bring back beaver pelts themselves, earning high profits. Many of these young men came to prefer the freedom of life in the woodlands and adopted the ways of the Native peoples who lived there. They were known as *coureurs de bois* (runners of the woods). They sang songs like "Mon canot" (My canoe) to the rhythm of their canoe paddles. Marius Barbeau, a scholar of French-Canadian music and folklore, found that about 90 per cent of French-Canadian songs had their roots in music from France. This song, however, is believed to have originated in Canada.

As - sis sur mon ca - not d'é - cor - ce, As - sis à la
frai - che du temps; Oui, je bra - ve tous les ra - pi -
des, Je ne crains pas___ les bouil - lons blancs!___
4)...Et là, je l'ver - se sur la pla - ge C'est ma ca - ba -
ne pour la nuit. Et là, je l'ver - se sur la pla -
ge C'est ma ca - ba - ne pour la nuit.___

1.

Assis sur mon canot d'écorce,
Assis à la fraiche du temps;
Oui, je brave tous les rapides,
Je ne crains pas les bouillons blancs!

2.

Je prends mon canot, je le lance
A travers des rapid's, des bouillons blancs,
Et là, à grands sauts, il avance.
Je ne crains mêm' pas l'océan.

3.

Mon canot est fait d'écorce fine
Que l'on pleume sur les bouleaux blancs.
Les côt's ell's sont fait's de racine
Et les avirons de bois blancs.

4.

Et quand ça vient sur le portage,
Je prends mon canot sur mon dos;
Et là, je l'verse sur la plage
C'est ma cabane pour la nuit.

5.

J'ai traversé les flancs des côtes,
Aussi le grand fleuve St-Laurent.
J'ai connu les tribes sauvages
Et leurs langages différents.

6.

Un labourer aim' sa charrue,
Un chasseur, son fusil et son chien,
Un musicien aim' sa musique.
Moi, mon canot, c'est tout mon bien.

1.

Seated in my bark canoe,
Seated in the coolness of the day;
Yes, I brave all the rapids,
I do not fear the white foam!

2.

I take my canoe and I launch it
Across the rapids, the white foam,
And then by great leaps it advances.
I am not afraid even of the ocean.

3.

My canoe is made of fine bark
That they strip from the white birches.
The sides are made of root
And the paddles of white wood.

4.

And when we reach the portage
I take my canoe on my back;
And there I turn it over on the shore,
It is my home for the night.

5.

I have travelled along the coasts,
Also the great St. Lawrence River.
I have known the Indian tribes
And their different languages.

6.

A farmer loves his plough,
A hunter his dog and gun,
A musician loves his music.
As for me, my canoe is all my wealth.

The Great Northwest

How could you get around it? How could you get through it? For hundreds of years, European explorers saw Canada's geography as a frustrating problem that had to be solved. To get easier access to the spices, silks, and jewels of the Far East, they needed to find a northern sea route to the Pacific: the Northwest Passage. The English explorers Martin Frobisher and John Davis journeyed as far as what is now Baffin Island in the late sixteenth century, but they found the way west blocked with pack ice. In later centuries, explorers found their way into Hudson Bay but could go no farther by ship. In fact, it was not until the years 1940 to 1942 that the *St. Roch,* a Royal Canadian Mounted Police vessel skippered by Sgt. Henry Larsen, threaded its way through the Northwest Passage from west to east. In 1944, again in the *St. Roch,* Larsen finally completed the journey from east to west that had thwarted so many earlier explorers.

Meanwhile, land-based explorers, looking for routes to expand the fur trade, searched for rivers that would lead to the Pacific Coast. Guided by Native people, Samuel Hearne, David Thompson, and Simon Fraser all explored and mapped the rivers of the west. But it was Alexander Mackenzie, in July 1793, who first reached the Pacific.

Samuel Hearne
A Coppermine Feast

In 1769, the Hudson's Bay Company sent Samuel Hearne to search for a water route to the Pacific Ocean from their post, Prince of Wales's Fort, on Hudson Bay. Hearne's first two attempts ended quickly in failure. Then he found a skilful Chipewyan guide, Matonabbee, and followed his instructions for organizing his third expedition. For instance, Matonabbee insisted that strong and resourceful Native women should be part of the group. They left Hudson Bay in December 1770, travelling west and then north to the Coppermine River, which they followed to the Arctic Ocean. Hearne did not reach the Pacific on his eighteen-month journey, but he was the first European to see and write about the landscape and people of the Barren Lands. In this excerpt from his book, *A Journey from Prince of Wales's Fort in Hudson's Bay to the Northern Ocean*, you can see Hearne's willingness to adapt to Native ways.

WE WALKED FIFTEEN MILES, IN expectation of finally reaching the Coppermine River that day. But when we had reached the top of a long chain of hills through which the river was said to run, we found it to be no more than a branch which emptied into the main stream about forty miles from its influx into the sea.

Seeing some woods to the westward, we directed our course towards them. The Indians now destroyed several fine bucks and we enjoyed the luxury of cooking them over abundant fires, for these were the first woods we had seen since shortly after leaving Clowey Lake.

As such favourable opportunities for indulging the appetite happen but seldom, we did not neglect any art, in dressing our food, which the most refined skill of Indian cookery has been able to invent. These consist chiefly of boiling, broiling and roasting, but also of a dish called *beeatee*, which is most delicious. It is made with the blood, a good quantity of fat (shredded small), some of the tenderest flesh, and the heart and the lungs torn into small shivers. All of this is put in the deer's stomach and roasted by being suspended before the fire. When it is sufficiently done it will emit steam, which is as much as to say, "Come and eat me now!"

This preparation is somewhat related to the most remarkable dish known to both the Northern and Southern Indians, which is made of blood mixed with the half-digested food found in the deer's stomach, and which is then boiled to the consistency of pease-porridge. Some fat and scraps of tender flesh are also boiled with it. To render this dish more palatable, they have a method of mixing the blood with the stomach contents in the paunch itself, and then hanging it up in the heat and smoke of the fire for several days. This puts the whole mass into a state of fermentation, and gives it such an agreeably acid taste that, were it not for prejudice, it might be eaten by those who have the nicest palates.

It is true that some people with delicate stomachs would not be persuaded to partake of this dish if they saw it being prepared. Most of the fat is first chewed by the men and boys in order to break the globules, so that it will all boil out and mingle with the broth. To do justice, however, to their cleanliness in this particular, I must observe that neither old people with bad teeth, nor young children, have any hand in preparing this dish.

At first, I must admit that I was rather shy of partaking of this mess; but when I was sufficiently convinced of the truth of the above statement, I no longer made any scruple, but always thought it exceedingly good.

Ainslie Manson
The Long Journey of "Our Dog"

Alexander Mackenzie was a Scottish-born fur trader who became a partner in the North West
Company in 1784. Like Samuel Hearne before him, he wanted to find a water route to the Pacific Ocean.
On his first expedition in 1789, he travelled along the river known to the Native people of the region as Deh Cho.
Today it is usually called the Mackenzie River. To Mackenzie's great disappointment, the river emptied into the
Arctic Ocean, not the Pacific. In 1793, he tried again. It is this journey that Ainslie Manson describes in her book
A Dog Came, Too, from which this excerpt is taken. Mackenzie travelled with nine men and a big brown dog in
a single canoe. Following the advice of the Native Carrier people, the expedition left the treacherous
Fraser River for the final part of the journey and travelled overland to the Pacific Ocean. On July 22,
1793, at the mouth of the Dean Channel, Mackenzie took some fish grease and red dye
and wrote on a rock: "Alex Mackenzie / from Canada / by land / 22^d July 1793."

LONG, LONG AGO, TWO NATIVE GUIDES, an explorer, and seven voyageurs set off to find a route across Canada to the Pacific Ocean.

A big brown dog travelled with them.

He was not a pet. He was a working dog. All his life he had slept under the stars, not under a kitchen table.

He had never had his dinner served to him in a dog dish. He had never worn a collar or had a family to call his own.

The big brown dog didn't even have a name.

"Send Our Dog after him," the guides would say when they shot down a great white swan for food.

"Our Dog will swim and fetch it," six voyageurs would say when the seventh voyageur dropped his paddle into a swift-flowing river.

"Our Dog will keep watch," the explorer would say when there were bears or wolves near the campsite.

The explorer, the voyageurs, and the guides grew more and more fond of Our Dog as they travelled towards the Pacific Ocean.

Each night, under the stars, Our Dog would lie down by the explorer's side.

Our Dog was a guard dog at night, and so he slept very lightly. He was aware of every sound in the deep, dark forest.

Once he saw a wolf prowling a little too close to the sleeping men. He barked to warn them.

Once he discovered a hungry bear trying to take their food. He chased it away.

Another time he growled to warn the explorer when a stranger crept by the campsite on his hands and knees.

It was a long, long way to the Pacific Ocean. Our Dog grew very tired. His paws were cut by sharp, jagged rocks.

He was bitten by mosquitoes, wasps, blackflies, and fleas.

Sometimes there was little to eat, and there were no scraps for Our Dog. Tired and hungry, he would have to go hunting late at night for his meal.

The explorer, the voyageurs, and the native guides knew Our Dog was tired. They were tired, too. Often they had to carry their canoe and their boxes and bundles up one side of a mountain and down the other to avoid a dangerous rapid. They had little time or strength to sit by a warm fire removing burrs and twigs from Our Dog's tangled fur. They had little time or strength to look after their own comforts.

Then they came to a river that was worse than all the others. Our Dog could tell the explorer was worried. Time and time again they had to stop to repair the canoe. Eventually it was more patch than bark. It had become a patchwork canoe!

The men decided to leave that impossi-ble river and travel overland to the ocean. New native guides they met in the mountains showed them a route that natives had travelled for hundreds of years.

After many days they reached a cool, beautiful valley. Our Dog noticed a different smell in the air. It was the smell of salt water. The sea could not be far away.

Before the last lap of their journey the men rested and were treated kindly at a friendly native village. They ate well and they slept well.

Our Dog knew his friends were safe in the village. He did not lie down at the explorer's side. He limped wearily off into the forest and found a deep, dark cave. He curled up and fell sound asleep.

Our Dog slept too well. The next morning the men were ready and eager to go on to the Pacific Ocean.

The explorer whistled. For the first time ever, Our Dog did not come. He did not hear the whistle in his deep, dark cave.

The voyageurs called and called. Still Our Dog did not come.

The guides searched the nearby forest, but they didn't find him. In his deep, dark cave Our Dog was sleeping more soundly than he had ever slept in his whole life.

The men were sad and worried, but they had to go on. Joined by more guides from the friendly village and equipped with more canoes, they set off down the river on the last lap of their journey. Our Dog slept on.

When he finally awoke the next day, he trotted down the hill to the friendly village. Our Dog's friends were nowhere to be found.

He tried to follow their scent, but he could not follow it past the water's edge. He laid his head down upon his matted paws and stared at the river. He felt lost and lonely. He whimpered and whined.

When darkness came, he howled mournfully. Eventually the villagers could stand the noise no longer. They chased him away.

Again Our Dog laid his head down upon his matted paws. Again he whimpered and whined and howled. He was so sad and lonely that he stopped eating. He wandered up and down the river. He grew weaker and weaker.

Our Dog knew the explorer usually followed rivers. So he, too, followed the river to the Pacific Ocean.

Where the river met the ocean, high mountains rose up into the clouds on either side of a long inlet. Our Dog caught the scent of his friends. They had camped here. But they had moved on. Now they were far down the inlet, well out of sight...and scent.

The explorer, the voyageurs, and the guides had problems, too. Rain, fog, and high winds made travel dangerous.

One afternoon, when unfriendly natives surrounded their canoes, the men were

forced to land on a small rocky point. The
explorer, the voyageurs, and the guides
spent a sleepless night. Our Dog was not
with them to warn of further danger.

In the morning the men were alarmed
to see that more and more unfriendly
natives were landing on their rocky point.
The voyageurs quickly packed up the
canoes. But before they departed, the
explorer painted a message on a rock. In
years to come he hoped people would see
his message and know he had truly
reached the Pacific Ocean.

When Our Dog saw the explorer, the
voyageurs, and the guides, who had
returned up the river, he barked joyously.

Our Dog wagged his tail enthusiastically, but he was almost too weak and
tired to stand up. The explorer knelt
beside him, patted him gently, and whispered in his ear.

The voyageurs lifted Our Dog
carefully and carried him to a canoe. Our
Dog travelled as a passenger for the very
first time.

With food and loving care, Our Dog
recovered quickly. Soon he was well again
and ready for the homeward journey all
the way back across the vast country.

Stan Rogers
Northwest Passage

The story of John Franklin is one of the most famous tales of Arctic exploration. In 1844, Franklin set out from England on his third expedition to find the Northwest Passage. Franklin died while his ship was trapped in Arctic ice, and all of the crew perished on a desperate overland journey to seek aid. Another British explorer, John Rae, later pieced together their tragic tale from Inuit accounts. The mentally befuddled crew, probably poisoned by lead from their canned food tins, had lugged tons of useless goods across the Arctic ice until they collapsed. Stan Rogers's song, whose words are printed here, recalls the tragic Franklin expedition and also the names of other explorers of the Northwest. "Kelso" is actually Henry Kelsey, a young Hudson Bay fur trader who was the first European to see the Canadian plains. He created a remarkable account of his journey, written in verse.

AH, FOR JUST ONE TIME, I WOULD TAKE THE NORTHWEST PASSAGE
To find the hand of Franklin reaching for the Beaufort Sea
Tracing one warm line through a land so wide and savage
And make a Northwest Passage to the sea

Westward from the Davis Strait, 'tis there 'twas said to lie
The sea-route to the Orient for which so many died
Seeking gold and glory, leaving weathered broken bones
And a long-forgotten lonely cairn of stones

Three centuries thereafter, I take passage overland
In the footsteps of brave Kelso, where his "sea of flowers" began
Watching cities rise before me, then behind me sink again
This tardiest explorer, driving hard across the plain

And through the night, behind the wheel, the mileage clicking West
I think upon Mackenzie, David Thompson and the rest
Who cracked the mountain ramparts, and did show a path for me
To race the roaring Fraser to the sea

How then am I so different from the first men through this way?
Like them I left a settled life, I threw it all away
To seek a Northwest Passage at the call of many men
To find there but the road back home again

PART THREE

Creating a Country

Illustrated by

Bill Slavin

Don Kilby

Turbulent Times

England and France were rivals in Europe and had been at war many times over the centuries. In the seventeenth century, their rivalry spread to their colonies in North America. The British and French clashed in Acadia (now the Maritime provinces), where there were rich fishing grounds. In New France, French settlers struggled with British colonists from the south for control of the fur trade. Finally, in the 1750s, full-scale war came to North America, with Britain determined to seize all of New France. The people of New France fought hard for the land where they had been settled for 150 years, but their troops were badly outnumbered. The colony surrendered to Britain in the spring of 1760.

In 1775, Britain's thirteen American colonies went to war against the Mother Country to win their independence. Some forty thousand colonists who were still faithful to Britain, known as Loyalists, moved north to the Maritimes, to Quebec, and to the territories that would become Upper Canada (later Ontario).

Even after the United States won its independence, there were tensions between the new country and Britain. In 1812, the Americans decided to try to take over Britain's remaining North American colonies by invading them. As well as British troops, Native warriors (some led by the brilliant Tecumseh) and ordinary citizens of the Maritimes, Lower Canada (later Quebec), and Upper Canada fought successfully to keep the Americans from seizing their homeland. The war ended with a treaty between Britain and the United States in 1814. The Americans considered that they had won a victory, because Britain finally treated them as a free and separate country. But Canadians believe they won this war—even though Canada did not yet exist as a country.

Mary Alice Downie and George Rawlyk
Leaving Acadia

The first French colonists arrived in Acadia—the Maritime region of Canada—in 1604,
even before Quebec was founded. Over the years, as more settlers arrived, the people of Acadia built
dikes to hold back the sea and farmed the rich marshlands they created. But it was Acadia's misfortune that
both England and France wanted to claim the territory. Over the next 150 years, control of Acadia passed back
and forth between the two countries more than half a dozen times. For the most part, the Acadians managed to
continue their traditional way of life and avoid taking sides—until 1755. In that year, the British began to round up
members of the Acadian population. Some were deported to British colonies farther south (many of these
made their way to the French colony of Louisiana, where they were called Cajuns) or were returned to
France. A few were able to escape to Quebec. Some of the exiled Acadians made their way slowly back
to their homeland and eventually rebuilt their shattered lives. In *A Proper Acadian,* from which this
excerpt is taken, Timothy, a boy from Boston, has come to live with relatives in Acadia. When
they learn that they are to be deported, Timothy must make a hard choice…

IT WAS OCTOBER AND STILL THE TRANS-
ports did not come.

"Soon," Timothy thought, "Ebenezer
will be here. Then we will all be safe." He
packed his few belongings in order to be
ready to leave at once.

The mists were swirling in from the bay
on the morning that William brought a
message. Timothy met him at the door as
he was on his way in with a few sticks of
wood for the fire.

"We're anchored in the bay by the new
dike," William said. "You're to come at
once." He plunged back into the mist like
a sturdy phantom.

"He's here!" Timothy found his aunt
and cousin sitting gazing into the tiny fire
in the giant fireplace where once huge
logs had burned. "We'll soon be safe.
Come quickly."

Martin looked at him calmly, but said
nothing. Aunt Madeleine embraced him.

"Goodbye, dear Timothy. We will stay."

Timothy could not believe it. "You *must* come. No one knows what will become of us here."

Martin shook his head.

"But we'd be happy together," Timothy pleaded. "We'd forget all this." He was frightened by what he saw around him and he wanted to flee to safety. But he found it almost impossible to move. How could he leave his Acadian family to an uncertain fate? Finally, Timothy hoisted his pack on his shoulder and, followed by the faithful Nip, he walked along the overgrown pathway. Through the wet mists he went, avoiding the pathetic heaps of belongings that had been piled outside by the distraught women. The scarlet and gold leaves of fall, rusted and mildewed by the rain, lay in dank heaps.

He trudged on past the Mass House. The lawn was overgrown and no flowers bloomed now on the tall white crosses. Only their blackened skeletons remained. He passed a drunken soldier, who looked at him curiously but said nothing.

It took a long time to reach the little hidden bay where *The Reliant* was anchored. He looked around in the fog. The figure of Ebenezer detached itself from a concealing tree.

"Good lad. What kept you?"

"Many things." Timothy sighed and dropped his pack to the ground. "Give my love to Father and Priscilla," he said unsteadily.

"What are you talking about?" Ebenezer bent down to pick up the pack. Nip laid back her ears and growled. Timothy reached out to calm her. "I'm staying here," he whispered. "I can't go back to Boston. Tell Father and he'll understand." He told Ebenezer about all that had happened.

Ebenezer looked at him in silence for a moment. "Well, lad," he said slowly, "You face a grim future, but I'm not going to try to dissuade you. You're old enough to make up your own mind. God go with you and grant that we meet again in happier times." He embraced the boy, smiled sadly, and was gone.

Timothy started back towards home. On the way he found a wild plum tree.

"This will please Aunt Madeleine." He pulled the frost-bitten plums from the tree. Wizened and sour though they might be, they would be a welcome treat in these hungry times.

The fog was lifting and masses of clouds were battling each other for mastery of the sky. Long streaks of gleaming light were flung from the warring cloud battalions. Their colour changed from snowy white to icy green.

"Such strange colours," Timothy thought. These reflections suddenly gave place to others—blood red, bright orange—against the jet black of the forest.

No, these were not strange reflections in the sky! As Timothy came over the crest of the hill, he saw columns of black smoke rising from the village. Minas was ablaze. There were four ships out in the bay.

"The transports have come!" he cried aloud. Timothy began to run. He ran as he had never run before, but it seemed to take forever.

He stopped, gasping for breath, with a stitch in his side, at the outskirts of the village. Smoke filled the air. There were

soldiers everywhere. He could hardly move without bumping into someone or something: carts of furniture, boys staggering under the weight of trunks with dogs barking at their heels.

Some houses were in ashes, others were in flames, burning like torches. Worst of all was the noise. The old women who used to sit gossiping by the well were making a horrible wailing sound. They beat the walls with their hands and tore at their black shawls and dresses.

Timothy ran to his house and went inside but there was no one there. On his way out he met two soldiers. They had flaring torches and were about to set fire to the building.

"Stop, wait. Don't burn this house," he cried. They looked up quickly when they heard the English words but relaxed when they saw it was only a young Acadian.

"We got our orders, lad, and even if we don't like 'em, we got to do it all the same. Some of the Acadians have slipped away to the woods. We can't have 'em sneaking back and setting up here again."

Nearby a burning house collapsed and sent thousands of sparks flying. Several landed on Nip, who cried in pain.

Timothy ran towards the wharf, to find Aunt Madeleine and Martin. But it was even more confusing there. The beach was piled with boxes, baskets, and bundles. Crowds of weeping women and children were being pushed towards the longboats by soldiers.

Timothy hurried from group to group, Nip yelping at his heels. "Have you seen Aunt Madeleine? Has anyone seen Martin?"

He could hear no answer except the crackling of flames and the tragic cries of women and children.

"Here, what are you doing standing about?" The sharp point of a musket poked his back. "Into the longboat with you." Timothy turned around and saw a soldier pushing him towards the water. Just then he saw Aunt Madeleine. She was struggling to help Martin lift a box of their belongings into a longboat. Timothy broke away and ran to them.

"Wait for me," he cried. "Aunt Madeleine, Martin, wait for me!" They stared bleakly as if they didn't recognize him. Aunt Madeleine's face was pale, Martin's was smeared with soot and blood from a gash in his forehead.

Nip's frantic barks broke their trance.

"Timothy," Aunt Madeleine faltered. "I hoped you were safely off with Ebenezer." She sat down suddenly on the box and began to weep. The damp mists swirled in off the bay and mingled with the smoke.

"I decided to stay," he said, comforting her. "Don't cry, Aunt Madeleine. We'll be together."

"Idiot," said Martin, coughing from the acrid smoke. "Now you'll be a homeless wanderer, too." But he smiled and added, "God bless you anyway."

Timothy looked steadily at his family.

"One and all," he said. They helped Aunt Madeleine into the longboat and heaved the box in after her.

"Hurry up there, you!" shouted a soldier. Nip bared her teeth and growled. "All right, all right, good girl." The soldier retreated a few paces. "The dog can't go," he snarled.

Nip stood whining on the shore. Timothy leaned down to stroke her soft head. "You always hated water," he told her gently. "You'll be better off here. Home, Nip!" he shouted and she ran off into the fog and smoke. Timothy and Martin climbed aboard.

In the growing darkness they were all herded into the transports. In the end, most of their goods were abandoned on the shore. They were crowded to near suffocation, packed together like cattle on the slippery decks. They sat, shivering in the cold, silently watching the bright orange flames all up and down the coast.

"We need a song, Timothy," Martin said. "It will comfort everybody."

Quietly at first, Timothy began to sing the song that had swept through the villages during the time of their trials. "Gather and join us, or give us a grave." He sang again. "We will return to the land of our ancestors, our beloved land. We Acadians will return."

Proud and clear his voice rang over the water, as darkness descended on that last night in Acadia.

The small dog lay panting in the shade of a drooping willow. The hollow shell of the ruined house she guarded was hidden by a healing web of wild roses. Only the outline of the bench by the deserted well could be seen through the mass of green leaves and riotous blossoms.

The dog pricked up her ears at an unaccustomed sound in the silence, which was usually broken only by the hum of a wild bee or the cry of an animal. With short urgent barks she ran down the hill to see who was invading her kingdom.

In the bay was an old boat with a ragged sail. Half-savage after three years alone, the small dog hid behind a bush and watched, growling softly.

The boat drifted closer. The dog ran to the shore, jumped into the water and paddled out. She scratched impatiently on the side of the boat until Timothy hauled her in. She shook herself, spraying him with water, then began to lick their faces.

"Nip!" Timothy hugged the small wet dog.

They had spent two years in South Carolina as indentured servants after the deportation, then months working their way up the Atlantic coast in their home-made boat, creeping ashore by night to sleep and to find food. But Timothy, Martin and Aunt Madeleine together with hundreds of other exiled Acadians, like the wild geese they knew so well, had returned to their northern home.

Richard Nardin
The Piper's Refrain

"The Piper's Refrain" commemorates a battle at the south end of Lake Champlain between the French, aided by their Native allies, and the British in July 1758. It took place near a fort that the French called Carillon (chimes) because of the sound of nearby rapids. The French, under the command of Louis-Joseph de Montcalm, had built an abatis (a barricade of piled-up trees and brush) in which they trapped the Scottish soldiers of the Black Watch Regiment, who were serving in the British army. The Scots were all killed. Although the French won this battle, Carillon was taken by the British the following year and renamed Fort Ticonderoga. This song also makes reference to a ghost story that became popular after the battle. Back in Scotland, young Duncan Campbell had been told by the ghost of his murdered cousin that they would meet at a place called Ticonderoga. When Duncan later hears this name, he knows his death is imminent.

I'll tell it to you as they told it to me In the glow of the camp-fi-re burn-ing By the banks of the wa-ter we've sport-ed and played But they once felt the fu-ry of bat-tle.

Chorus

And up to the Cham-plain came the High-land Bri-gade The pipes and the drum-mers played "Scot-land the Brave" But when they sailed home, the pi-per's re-frain Was "Oh, how cru-el the vol-ley."

2. And for one Duncan Campbell it came in a dream
That he'd meet his fate where he never had been
Where the blue waters roll and the stickerbush tear
Travel well, Duncan, I'll wait on you there.

3. For the French and Indians have challenged our king
To a soldier like Duncan, no need to explain
It's many the time I've travelled the waves
To find my place in the fire.

Chorus

4. From Fort William Henry the boats pushed away
For the north of Lake George in the morning
To the place the Frenchmen call Carillon
To the Indians, Ticonderoga.

5. And the word struck Duncan like a thunderbolt there
And everyone knew of the warning
So give us a tune to remember me by
For tomorrow I'll not be returning.

Chorus

6. In the gunpowder's flash, the Highlanders died
Never again to sit by the Clyde
In the wilderness green, in the sun and the rain
It's here they're forever remaining.

Chorus

7. And I've told it to you as they told it to me
Of one Duncan Campbell and the Highland Brigade
But when the campfires crackle in the summertime's wane
Through the mist on the water comes the piper's refrain.

Traditional
Brave Wolfe

In 1759, British forces under the command of Brig.-Gen. James Wolfe sailed up the St. Lawrence River
to capture the city of Quebec. But the French commander, the Marquis de Montcalm, held the British at bay
for weeks, even though Quebec was battered by British cannonballs and mortar bombs. Finally, before dawn on
September 13, Wolfe ordered his troops to climb the steep cliffs a few kilometres upriver from Quebec. Taken by
surprise, Montcalm quickly marshalled his troops for battle, but the British overpowered them. Within a few
months, all of New France would fall to the British. Versions of "Brave Wolfe" first appeared very shortly after the
battle. Some of the details in the song are correct: Wolfe became engaged just before coming to Canada; both
leaders were mortally wounded; and Wolfe died knowing that he had gained a victory. However, it is not
true that the two generals spoke before the battle, and Wolfe was not on a horse when he was shot.

Come, all you old men— all, Let— this de - light you,—— Come,

all you young men— all, Let— nought af - fright you.—— Nor—

let your— cou - rage— fail When— comes the tri - al,——— Nor

do not be dis - mayed At the first de - ni - al.———

1.

COME, ALL YOU OLD MEN ALL,
Let this delight you,
Come, all you young men all,
Let nought affright you.
Nor let your courage fail
When comes the trial,
Nor do not be dismayed
At the first denial.

2.

I went to see my love.
Thinking to woo her;
I sat down by her side,
Not to undo her;
But when I looked on her
My tongue did quiver;
I could not speak my mind
While I was with her.

3.

"Love, here's a diamond ring,
Long time I've kept it
All for your sake alone,
If you'll accept it.
When you this token view,
Think on the giver;
Madame, remember me,
Or I'm undone forever."

4.

Then forth went this brave youth
And crossed the ocean,
To free America
Of her division.
He landed at Quebec
With all his party,
A city to attack
Both brave and hearty.

5.

Brave Wolfe drew up his men
In a line so pretty,
On the Plains of Abraham
Before the city.
The French came marching down
Arrayed to meet them,
In double numbers 'round
Resolved to beat them.

6.

Montcalm and this brave youth
Together walkèd;
Between two armies they
Like brothers talkèd,
Till each one took his post
And did retire.
'Twas then these numerous hosts
Commenced their fire.

7.

The drums did loudly beat,
With colours flying,
The purple gore did stream,
And men lay dying.
When shot from off his horse
Fell that brave hero.
Long may we lament his loss
That day in sorrow.

8.

Brave Wolfe lay on the ground
Where the guns did rattle,
And to his aide he said,
"How goes the battle?"
"Quebec is all our own,
They can't prevent it."
He said without a groan,
"I die contented."

Stan Rogers
MacDonnell on the Heights

The Battle of Queenston Heights was fought on October 13, 1812. Some six hundred American troops crossed the Niagara River from Lewiston, New York. They planned to capture the village of Queenston, at the foot of the steep Niagara Escarpment, and then take control of the heights. Gen. Isaac Brock, commander of the British forces in Upper Canada, was at Fort George, eleven kilometres (seven miles) away. When he heard cannon fire, he jumped on his horse and rode to Queenston. By the time he arrived, some of the Americans had reached the heights and were firing down on the troops below. As Brock led the attack up the hill, he was shot in the chest and killed. Brock's aide, Lt. Col. John Macdonell (the way he spelled his name) led a second charge. He, too, was killed. But after a day of fierce fighting, the Americans were eventually defeated. General Brock was greatly mourned in Upper Canada, and a statue was erected in his honour on Queenston Heights. Stan Rogers, who was struck by how unfair it is that history honours some brave men and forgets others, wrote a song about Macdonell. These are the words.

TOO THIN THE LINE THAT CHARGED THE HEIGHTS
And scrambled in the clay.
Too thin the Eastern Township Scot
Who showed them all the way,
And perhaps had you not fallen,
You might be what Brock became
But not one in ten thousand knows your name.

> To say the name, MacDonnell,
> It would bring no bugle call
> But the Redcoats stayed beside you
> When they saw the General fall
> 'Twas MacDonnell raised the banner then
> And set the Heights aflame,
> But not one in ten thousand knows your name.

You brought the field all standing with your courage and your luck
But unknown to most, you're lying there beside old General Brock.
So you know what it is to scale the Heights and fall just short of fame
And have not one in ten thousand know your name

    At Queenston now, the General on his tower stands alone
    And there's lichen on "MacDonnell" carved upon that weathered stone
    In a corner of the monument to glory you could claim,
    But not one in ten thousand knows your name.

        You brought the field all standing with your courage and your luck
        But unknown to most, you're lying there beside old General Brock
        So you know what it is to scale the Heights and fall just short of fame
        And have not one in ten thousand know your name.

Rebels

In the years after the War of 1812, many people in both Upper and Lower Canada were discontented with the way they were being governed. In Lower Canada, power was held by a British governor and a small group of wealthy advisers known to their opponents as the Château Clique. In the elected assembly, which spoke for the French-Canadian majority, Louis-Joseph Papineau and his Patriote Party pushed for reforms, but the governor was not obliged to consider them. In the fall of 1837, and again in 1838, armed rebellion broke out. Patriotes defeated British troops at St-Denis before being outnumbered and crushed at St-Eustache. Some of those who were not able to flee into exile were hanged or sent to prison colonies in Australia.

In Upper Canada, too, power was in the hands of a small number of wealthy citizens, Tories known as the Family Compact. Many of them owned large tracts of land that they left undeveloped as they waited for prices to rise. But the farmers of Upper Canada wanted the land developed so their communities could grow, schools for their children could be built, and roads could be constructed. In the 1820s, William Lyon Mackenzie scolded and mocked the Tories in his newspaper, the *Colonial Advocate.* When he was eventually elected to the assembly, he pushed for reform. Frustrated with the slow pace of change, however, Mackenzie began to speak of armed rebellion.

James Reaney
The Boy with an R in His Hand

James Reaney's novel *The Boy with an R in his Hand* is about a high-spirited orphan named Alec who comes to live with his Tory aunt and uncle in York (as Toronto was formerly called). Alec is soon hired as an apprentice in William Lyon Mackenzie's printing shop. After witnessing several injustices, Alec comes to agree with his employer that the small group of people who govern Upper Canada are holding too much power. In this excerpt, Alec finds out just how far some of them will go to silence Mackenzie, one of their most outspoken critics.

ALEC HAMMERED AT THE MACKENZIE house door. It seemed ages before Mr. Mackenzie's old mother came down to answer. Both she and Mr. Mackenzie's oldest boy, James, an apprentice to the printing trade like Alec, wondered what Alec was so excited about on such a calm Sunday evening. Old Mrs. Mackenzie had a cup of tea in her hand.

"The Tory boys are coming to wreck the shop. We've got to try to stop them. Rebecca says she can't get Mr. Allan to stir. James, you go over and tell him. I'm too small. Surely he won't stand by and watch a man's house get broken into."

While James, who really had the red hair that was represented in his father by a red wig, flew over to Mr. Allan's house, Alec tried to push some of the heavy tables up against the front door. James

came back with the same news Rebecca had. Magistrate Allan could not be bothered, although he now emerged from his house to watch whatever needed watching. Needless to say, Mr. Allan was of the Government party.

"They're singing," said James. They could hear quite a few voices singing something like

Since he prints tripe,
We'll smash his type.
All for King and Country.

"They've each one got a big stick," said James.

About twelve young men and youths headed by Mr. Jarvis came up from beneath the bank onto Palace Street, marching in single file. They came straight towards the door of the printing office, and James hurried both Alec and his grandmother out of the place for fear they would be hurt.

The rioters acted as if there were nothing more legal or worthy to do on a Sunday evening than to smash up the press and type of a newspaper that had dared to criticize their fathers and poke fun; had dared to say that Grandfather, instead of being a noble lord, had been a humble cobbler in the army. Underneath the lampblack some of the attackers had daubed on their faces, Alec easily recognized Cousin Allan, John Lyons, who was the Lieutenant-Governor's private secretary, quite a few law students from Uncle John's office and the offices of other prominent officials, and Raymond Baby and his brother Charles.

Their leader pushed open the door, the rioters filed into the shop, and soon the sounds of smashing and throwing drifted out.

Alec looked over at Magistrate Allan, who was grinning and laughing with the rioters.

"What a shame this is!" cried James to Mr. Jarvis. "What a shame to wreck a man's livelihood."

"You say a word," blustered out Jarvis, his face reddening under the lampblack, "and I'll knock you down."

With hammer and sticks, the Tory boys soon finished pounding the type that was set up. Then they pied it by sweeping it onto the floor. Six of them heaved at the press until they had toppled it over. It went over with a tremendous big crash, heard up and down the street. Some passers-by stopped to watch, and one of them, a carpenter, would have helped if he had not seen Mr. Allan standing by. What could he, one man, do against a dozen men? Why should he move when the law itself did not move? Even Charley French, when he came running up, and he was more reckless than most, decided watching was best.

The quoins and leads were smashed and bent. The composing stone was pushed over and cracked. The picture cuts were mutilated with nails—and last of all each one of the rioters seized a tray of type and came outside with it. Some chose to dump their tray in Mr. Mackenzie's garden. Others raced down to the wharf and threw the cases into the lake.

"Well done, boys!" cheered Mr. Allan as they filed off again, leaving the door of the printing-shop open behind them. Alec could hear a familiar voice laughing under the bank. While James comforted his grandmother, who was weeping and very disturbed, Alec watched the Tory boys leave their cudgels at his uncle's office and then disperse, laughing and joking, in great high spirits.

He went down to the lake to wash off the lampblack that Cousin Allan had smeared on his cheeks as a parting gesture. In the water he saw something gleaming. It was a great capital letter R that had fallen out of the cases thrown into the lake by the rioters.

He picked it up and turned about. The swallows were flitting back and forth from their nests under the wharf. He caught sight of his uncle sneaking down the beach, hugging the shadows of the bank and thinking, no doubt, that no one saw him. Alec put the capital letter R in his pocket.

William Lyon Mackenzie
Mackenzie's Call to Rebellion

William Lyon Mackenzie was first elected to the assembly of Upper Canada in 1828. As a fiery opponent of the Family Compact, he was expelled from the assembly several times, but his rural constituents always voted him in again. In 1837, Mackenzie began to plan an armed revolt, and he travelled through the towns of Upper Canada seeking support. Less than a month before the Rebellion in Upper Canada broke out, he printed and distributed a handbill that included the stirring words reprinted here. Unlike the Rebellion in Lower Canada, however, Mackenzie's uprising ended with its first fight. On December 5, 1837, he and a small group of supporters marched down Yonge Street towards the city of York. They were met by soldiers, a few shots were fired, the rebels scattered, and Mackenzie eventually fled to the United States. Although the Rebellions of 1837 did not succeed, Britain was forced to take a hard look at how its Canadian colonies were governed. Within ten years, the elected assemblies were given much more power.

CANADIANS! DO YOU LOVE FREEDOM? I know you do. Buckle on your armour and put down the villains who oppress and enslave our country; you must put down those governments which trample on the law. The bounty you must pay for freedom (blessed word) is to give the strength of your arms to put down the tyranny of Toronto. One short hour will deliver our country, and freedom in religion, peace, equal laws and an improved country will be the prize. Up then, brave Canadians! Get ready your rifles and make short work of it. Now's the day and the hour!

M. A. Gérin-Lajoie
Un Canadien errant

Antoine Gérin-Lajoie grew up in rural Quebec. He was only fourteen years old when the Rebellion in Lower Canada took place in 1837, and its tragic events made a deep impression on him. After the rebellion was put down, many of the men who had taken part, including the leader, Louis-Joseph Papineau, had to travel to the United States or Europe to escape arrest and punishment. Five years later, Gérin-Lajoie wrote a song about the exiles, using a traditional French folk tune. In the song, an unhappy exile wanders beside a river that flows towards Canada, and he asks the waters to carry a message to his friends back home. The song spread quickly through French Canada, and remained popular there for more than one hundred years. The English words were written by folk-music scholar Edith Fowke.

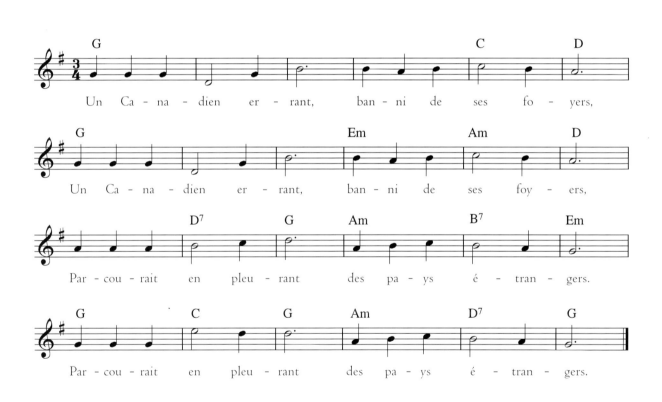

Un Ca - na - dien er - rant, ban - ni de ses fo - yers,

Un Ca - na - dien er - rant, ban - ni de ses foy - ers,

Par - cou - rait en pleu - rant des pa - ys é - tran - gers.

Par - cou - rait en pleu - rant des pa - ys é - tran - gers.

1.

Un Canadien errant, banni de ses foyers,
Parcourait en pleurant des pays étrangers.

2.

Un jour, triste et pensif, assis au bord des flots,
Au courant fugitif il adressa ces mots:

3.

"Si tu vois mon pays, mon pays malheureux,
Va, dis à mes amis que je me souviens d'eux.

4.

"O jours si pleins d'appas vous êtes disparus,
Et ma patrie, hélas! Je ne la verrai plus!

5.

"Non, mais en expirant, O mon cher Canada!
Mon regard languissant vers toi se portera…"

1.

Once a Canadian lad, exiled from hearth and home,
Wandered, alone and sad, through alien lands unknown.
Down by a rushing stream, thoughtful and sad one day,
He watched the water pass and to it he did say:

2.

"If you should reach my land, my most unhappy land,
Please speak to all my friends so they will understand.
Tell them how much I wish that I could be once more
In my beloved land that I will see no more.

3.

"My own beloved land I'll not forget till death,
And I will speak of her with my last dying breath.
My own beloved land I'll not forget till death
And I will speak of her with my last dying breath."

Freedom-Seekers

There were black slaves in New France from its earliest days. By 1760, the year of the British conquest, there were about eleven hundred of them, mostly working as house servants or in the dockyards. There were slaveholders in the Maritimes, too, and as settlers moved into Upper Canada, they also had the right to own slaves. By the end of the century, though, there was a growing belief in Britain and its colonies that slavery was morally wrong. In 1793, Lt.-Gov. John Graves Simcoe passed a law declaring that any slave coming into Upper Canada would be made free on the spot. The Maritimes and Lower Canada soon followed with their own anti-slavery legal decisions. Although most areas of the northern United States also passed anti-slavery laws, the economy of the American South was built on slave labour. Even in the northern states, it was against the law for anyone to help a fleeing slave. After the strict Fugitive Slave Law was passed by the Americans in 1850, slave catchers could even seize blacks in the northern states and take them back to slavery in the South. Escaping slaves realized that they had to go farther to find freedom—all the way to Canada.

Traditional
Follow the Drinkin' Gourd

It took immense courage for black slaves to escape from the American South. They had to make
their plans in secret and travel alone or in small groups. All knew that if they were recaptured, they would
be severely punished. Most slaves had been denied an education, and few could read, so written instructions or maps
were useless to them. Songs such as "Follow the Drinkin' Gourd" were one way for directions to be given and
remembered. The Drinking Gourd is another name for the group of stars known as the Big Dipper. The stars in the
bowl of the Big Dipper make a line that points to the North Star. In North America, following the North
Star will take you almost straight north. Other words in the song carry messages as well—how to find
a safe route along a riverbank, for example, following charcoal marks left on dead trees
by a man named Peg Leg Joe, who guided many slaves to freedom.

When the sun goes back and the first quail calls, ____ Fol - low the drink - in' gourd, For the Ole Man's wait - in' for to car - ry you to free - dom, Fol - low the drink - in' gourd. Fol - low the drink - in' gourd, Fol - low the drink - in' gourd, For the Ole Man is a -wait - in' for to car - ry you to free - dom, Fol - low the drink - in' gourd. ____

1. WHEN THE SUN GOES BACK AND THE FIRST QUAIL CALLS,
Follow the drinkin' gourd,
For the Ole Man's waitin' for to carry you to freedom,
Follow the drinkin' gourd.

Chorus:
Follow the drinkin' gourd,
Follow the drinkin' gourd,
For the Ole Man is awaitin' for to carry you to freedom,
Follow the drinkin' gourd.

2. Oh, the riverbank makes a mighty fine road,
Dead trees to show you the way,
The left foot, pegfoot, travellin' on,
Follow the drinkin' gourd.

Chorus

3. The river ends in between two hills,
Follow the drinkin' gourd,
There's another river on the other side,
Follow the drinkin' gourd.

Chorus

4. I thought I heard the angels say,
Follow the drinkin' gourd,
The stars in the heavens gonna show you the way,
Follow the drinkin' gourd.

Traditional
The Underground Railroad

The Underground Railroad was not a railroad at all—it was a secret network of people who were willing to help escaping slaves get to Canada. The "conductors" met escaping slaves ("passengers") and gave them directions or sometimes guided them to safety. One of the most famous conductors was Harriet Tubman, an escaped slave who had settled near St. Catharines, Ontario. She made at least nineteen dangerous journeys back into the American South to help others to freedom, but she was never captured and she never lost a passenger. Many white people who were against slavery were involved in the Underground Railroad, too. Some of them were "station masters," sympathizers who offered hiding places in their homes, as well as food and warm clothing. This song, probably by a white abolitionist (a person who wanted slavery ended), was first printed in a black newspaper, *The Voice of the Fugitive*, published in Sandwich, Ontario, in 1851. It is sung to the tune of "O Susannah."

I'm on my way to Ca-na-da, that cold and drea-ry land, The dire ef-fects of sla-ver-y I can no lon-ger stand. My-soul is mixed with-in me so, to think that I'm a slave, I'm now re-solved to strike the blow, For Free-dom or the grave. Oh Right-eous Fa-ther, wilt thou not pi-ty me, And aid me on to Ca-na-da, where co-loured men are free?

1.

I'M ON MY WAY TO CANADA, THAT COLD AND DREARY LAND,
The dire effects of slavery I can no longer stand.
My soul is mixed within me so, to think that I'm a slave,
I'm now resolved to strike the blow,
For Freedom or the grave.

Chorus:
Oh Righteous Father, wilt Thou not pity me,
And aid me on to Canada, where coloured men are free?

2.

I heard old Queen Victoria say if we would all forsake
Our native land of slavery and come across the lake,
That she was standing on the shore, with arms extended wide,
To give us all a peaceful home, beyond the rolling tide.

Chorus:
Farewell old master, this is enough for me,
I'm going straight to Canada where coloured men are free.

3.

I've served my master all my days without a dime's reward,
And now I'm forced to run away to flee the lot abhorred.
The hounds are baying on my track, the master's just behind,
Resolved that he will bring me back before I cross the line.

Chorus:
And so, old master, don't come after me,
I'm going straight to Canada where coloured men are free.

Barbara Greenwood
A Visit from the Slave Catcher

Even in Canada, escaped slaves were not entirely safe. American slave catchers, bounty hunters seeking rewards from southern American slave owners, sometimes crossed the border into Canada and kidnapped blacks. In this excerpt from "A Parcel for Joanna," by Barbara Greenwood, a young girl named Melanie has escaped slavery and made her way safely to St. Catharines, Ontario. Melanie is being sheltered by Joanna Reid's family until her mother, from whom she was separated during the journey north, can come to claim her. One day, while Joanna's parents are away from the house, a threatening stranger arrives at the door.

HUMMING HAPPILY, JOANNA CLATTERED mugs and muffin tins onto the kitchen table and was reaching for the kettle when a movement outside caught her eye. A slim shape flitted furtively past the window. Then suddenly it was back, and a face peered in at her. Joanna felt her heart lurch into her mouth as the face grinned and disappeared. Who was it? In the distorting bubbled glass she had caught only an impression....

It doesn't matter who. I mustn't open the door to anyone while we're alone. As a precaution she flew towards the inside bolt—but she was too late. The handle turned and

the door swung inward. The stranger she had seen in the shop that morning stepped politely into the kitchen.

"Yes?" she asked breathlessly, standing close to the doorway so that he would have to stop or push her aside. "What do you want?"

"Afternoon, missy." A thin-lipped smile stretched his stubbly cheeks. "Got some real good news for your little guest."

"Melanie?" Joanna exclaimed, and then could have bitten her tongue. Did she imagine it or were his eyes glinting in triumph?

"The very one." He smiled broadly,

showing yellow teeth. "Got a message from her ma," he said, raising his voice and craning his neck to see around Joanna, who stood firm. "She's safe here in Canada and she wants her little girl to come right away so they can take the steamer to Toronto."

Joanna frowned. "Why didn't you tell my father that this morning?"

He raised his eyebrows and shrugged. "Didn't know the little lady existed this morning. Just met my good friend Abram Fuller on the road. Soon's I heard what he was about, I said, 'Don't you worry. I'll be right in that neighbourhood. Seein' as how y're a busy man, I'll pass on the joyful news and bring the little girl out meself.'" He grinned at her again. "Now you just fetch your little friend and we'll be on our way."

Joanna felt confused. Should she believe him? Everything about him made her wary. "Never judge a parcel by its wrappings," her mother always said. But it wasn't just his dirty hands and scruffy appearance that bothered her.

"Hurry up now! I ain't got all day."

The sharp demand rattled her so that she half-turned to the bedroom to call Melanie. Instantly he stopped acting friendly and pushed past her into the room. Panic-stricken, she retreated further.

"You're mistaken," she gasped. "There's no one else here."

The stranger's face flushed with rage. "You fetch me that girl," he hissed. "Now!"

Terrified, Joanna turned to run, but he reached out and caught her wrist. She twisted wildly and bit the hand that held her.

"Thunderation!" He spat venomously

and let go just as a living tornado swept out of the bedroom. Head down, Melanie charged full-tilt into the stranger and knocked him off balance. He staggered backwards, tripped on the doorstep, and fell sprawling on the porch. Joanna jumped for the door, slammed it shut, and shot all the bolts.

Weak with relief the girls stared at each other.

"The slave catcher?"

Melanie nodded.

"How did you know?"

Melanie shrugged. "Had a feelin'. I just know 'bout folks like that. Anyway, what call has Mr. Fuller got to send him here? He knows your daddy's bringin' him barrels today. And if my mama was in Queenston, she'd never send the likes of that one to come and fetch me."

Joanna sat down limply but Melanie still stood, frowning, in the middle of the room. "What's he at now?" she asked, listening tensely to the silence.

Joanna tiptoed to the window. To her horror, the slave catcher was standing in the yard, hands on hips, staring thoughtfully at the roof, then along the side of the house.

"He's not going away," she said, half-turning to Melanie. But when she looked back, he had vanished. Where had he gone? Anxiously she imagined him prowling around the house, looking, looking. There was no way in at the back. The lean-to that ran across the back of house and shop had only one very small window. There was another window along the side of the shop. Surely he wouldn't dare try the front door. Anyway it was locked—wasn't it? She raced into the parlour, Melanie at her heels.

Yes, the door, which opened directly into the front parlour, was locked. As an added precaution, Joanna shot the bolts, then checked the door that led from the back parlour out to the lean-to.

As she latched it firmly, she said, "Perhaps we should make a run for it. Mother's just down the street. The neighbours might hear us if we screamed." And then again, they mightn't, she thought, remembering how far apart houses were here on the outskirts of St. Catharines.

Just then Melanie clutched at her and pointed. A shadow was passing in front of the window. The front door handle rattled briefly, then the shadow passed in front of the next window.

"He's circling the house!" Joanna whispered. "Listen, Melanie, as soon as he's around the back, we'll make a run for it."

"How'll you know when he's around the back? What if he's crouched out there ready to pounce on us?"

The girls looked at each other in despair.

"Surely Mama can't be much longer!"

"Better if we just wait right here. Long as he's outside, we're safe inside."

"Sh!" Joanna said. "What was that?"

From somewhere had come the tinkle of breaking glass. The girls stood rigid, straining to hear. Their own heartbeats seemed to echo through the silent house. A sudden thud made them start convulsively. Then a door hinge creaked.

"He must have broken into the shop," Joanna gasped, as she guessed where the sounds came from. Then a loud crash and a sharp oath exploding into the silence told her the stranger had stumbled over something in the dark lean-to. Now only the flimsy back parlour door with its hook-and-eye latch barred the slave catcher's way.

"We've *got* to run for it!" Joanna gasped, but Melanie was already tugging frantically at the lower bolt of the front door.

Joanna flew at the upper one, willing her mind to concentrate, to blot out the sounds of the blows that were shattering the back parlour door. With a sudden lurch the bolt yielded. Now the key. Just as the teeth of the big key tripped the tumblers of the lock, the back door splintered open.

"Run, run!" Joanna screamed, pushing Melanie out in front of her. As they sped down the front steps, Joanna felt a hand on her shoulder, twisted from under it, and darted after Melanie. They turned down the road. Joanna spurted ahead, leading the way towards neighbours, towards Mother. Suddenly Melanie stumbled in a wagon rut and fell.

Joanna heard a triumphant "Gotcha!" and whirled around as the slave catcher dragged Melanie roughly to her feet. Fear turned to fury. With a shriek of rage she threw herself at the man, pummelling him with her fists.

"Let go. Let go. Let go!" Then suddenly he was plucked away and the girls were left clutching each other.

As her wild heartbeats calmed, Joanna raised her head and looked around. At the side of the road was her father's wagon and team. In the centre of an excited knot of neighbours, firmly grasping the slave catcher, was her father. The crowd fell silent. Mr. Reid, clutching his captive by the lapels of his coat, and deliberately shaking him for emphasis, was almost whispering in repressed rage.

"Listen, my friend…in this town we don't take kindly…to anyone terrorizing…our children. Neither…do we like vermin…who traffic…in the slave trade. If you value your hide…you won't

show your face…on this side of the river…again!"

Then there was a flurry among the watchers, and two mothers swooped down on two daughters to hug, and scold, and cry.

"Mama!" Melanie cried. "Look, Joanna. Here's my mama safe at last."

It was almost Christmastime when the parcel arrived. Joanna undid the string and opened one end. A piece of cream-coloured linen slithered out. It was a small sampler.

Around the edges, Melanie had worked a garland of the crimson hedgeroses she would have seen all up and down the Niagara Peninsula on her autumn ride to Toronto. Across the top, in emerald green cross-stitch, it said:

JOANNA

Along the bottom in matching green:

MELANIE

1852

In the centre, in bold black, she had embroidered:

I was a stranger
And ye took me in.
Matt. 25:35

Joanna looked at the accompanying letter, her eyes almost too blurred by tears to read it.

"My dearest friend," it began.…

Settlers

The first population boom in Upper Canada came in the opening decade of the nineteenth century. Lt.-Gov. John Graves Simcoe advertised in American newspapers that free land was available for anyone who would move north. More than fifty thousand "late loyalists" took him up on his offer—until the War of 1812 broke out. The next batch of immigrants—many of them desperately poor—came from England, Scotland, and Ireland in the years between 1815 and 1850. Some settled in the Maritimes and Lower Canada, but the greatest number—several hundred thousand—travelled on to Upper Canada. Some of the English settlers—including Susanna Moodie's husband (p. 82)—were "half-pay officers" from the British army, which had finally ended its long war with France. They had once lived a comfortable life in England, and many had never done hard physical work until they reached the so-called backwoods of Ontario. Their first homes were hand-built log cabins with thatched roofs and dirt floors. Before they could plant their first crops, they had to clear the land of trees. They also made their own clothing from sheep's wool that they spun and wove. In fact, almost everything they had—furniture, soap, candles—was the work of their own hands. Neighbours would get together for barn-raisings and quilting bees, which were also a prized opportunity to socialize with other people.

Catharine Parr Traill
Canadian Crusoes

Catharine Parr Traill immigrated to Upper Canada with her husband when she was thirty. She
had already published several books in England, and she kept on writing in her new home, despite her
challenging pioneer life and the birth of nine children. Her novel for young people, *Canadian Crusoes*, published in
1852, contains a great deal of practical information about how to survive in the wilderness. Scottish-Canadians
Catharine, twelve, and her fourteen-year-old brother, Hector, along with their French-Canadian friend
Louis, who is also fourteen, become lost in the wilderness. But as self-reliant pioneers, they are able to
live off the land for several years until they are reunited with their families. In this excerpt, we
see them building a snug house, finding food, and even creating clothes and utensils.

"CATHARINE," SAID LOUIS, ONE DAY, "THE huckleberries are now very plentiful, and I think it would be a wise thing to gather a good store of them, and dry them for the winter. See, ma chère, wherever we turn our eyes, or place our feet, they are to be found; the hill sides are purple with them. We may, for aught we know, be obliged to pass the rest of our lives here; it will be well to prepare for the winter when no berries are to be found."

"It will be well, mon ami, but we must not dry them in the sun; for let me tell you, Mr. Louis, that they will be quite tasteless—mere dry husks."

"Why so, ma belle?"

"I do not know the reason, but I only know the fact, for when our mothers dried the currants and raspberries in the sun, such was the case, but when they dried them on the oven floor, or on the hearth, they were quite nice."

"Well, Cath, I think I know of a flat thin stone that will make a good hearth-stone, and we can get sheets of birch bark and sew into flat bags, to keep the dried fruit in."

They now turned all their attention to drying huckleberries. Catharine and Louis (who fancied nothing could be contrived without his help) attended to the preparing and making of the bags of birch bark; but Hector was soon tired of girl's work, as he termed it, and, after gathering some berries, would wander away over the hills in search of game, and to explore the neighbouring hills and valleys, and sometimes it was sunset before he made his appearance. Hector had made an excellent strong bow, like the Indian bow, out of a tough piece of hickory wood, which he found in one of his rambles, and he made arrows with wood that he seasoned in the smoke, sharpening the heads with great care with his knife, and hardening them by exposure to strong heat, at a certain distance from the fire. The entrails of the woodchucks, stretched, and scraped and dried, and rendered pliable by rubbing and drawing through the hands, answered for a bow-string; but afterwards, when they got the sinews and hide of the deer, they used them, properly dressed for the purpose.

Hector also made a cross-bow, which he used with great effect, being a true and steady marksman. Louis and he would often amuse themselves with shooting at a mark, which they would chip on the bark of a tree; even Catharine was a tolerable archeress with the long-bow, and the hut was now seldom without game of one kind or other. Hector seldom returned from his rambles without partridges, quails, or young pigeons, which are plentiful at this season of the year; many of the old ones that pass over in their migratory flight in the spring stay to breed, or return thither for the acorns and berries that are to be found in great abundance. Squirrels, too, are very plentiful at this season. Deer, at the time our young Crusoes were living on the Rice Lake Plains, were plentiful, and, of course, so were those beasts that prey upon them—wolves, bears, and wolverines,

besides the Canadian lynx, or catamount, as it is here commonly called, a species of wild-cat or panther. These wild animals are now no longer to be seen; it is a rare thing to hear of bears or wolves, and the wolverine and lynx are known only as matters of history in this part of the country; these animals disappear as civilization advances, while some others increase and follow man, especially many species of birds, which seem to pick up the crumbs that fall from the rich man's board, and multiply about his dwelling; some adopt new habits and modes of building and feeding, according to the alteration and improvement in their circumstances.

While our young people seldom wanted for meat, they felt the privation of the bread to which they had been accustomed very sensibly. One day, while Hector and Louis were busily engaged with their assistant, Wolfe, in unearthing a woodchuck that had taken refuge in his burrow, on one of the gravelly hills above the lake, Catharine amused herself by looking for flowers; she had filled her lap with ripe May-apples, but finding them cumbersome in climbing the steep wooded hills, she deposited them at the foot of a tree near the boys, and pursued her search; and it was not long before she perceived some pretty grassy-looking plants, with heads of bright lilac flowers, and on plucking one pulled up the root also. The root was about the size and shape of a large crocus, and, on biting it, she found it far from disagreeable, sweet, and slightly astringent; it seemed to be a favourite root with the woodchucks, for she noticed that it grew about their burrows on dry gravelly soil, and many of the stems were bitten, and the roots eaten, a warrant in full of wholesomeness. Therefore, carrying home a parcel of the largest of the roots, she roasted them in the embers, and they proved almost as good as chestnuts. Hector and Louis ate heartily of the roots, and commended Catharine for the discovery.

The boys were now busy from morning till night chopping down trees for house-logs. It was a work of time and labour, as the axe was blunt, and the oaks hard to cut; but they laboured on without grumbling, and Catharine watched the fall of each tree with lively joy. They were no longer dull; there was something to look forward to from day to day—they were going to commence housekeeping in good earnest and they would be warm and well lodged before the bitter frosts of winter could come to chill their blood. It was a joyful day when the log walls of the little shanty were put up, and the door hewed out. Windows they had none, so they did not cut out the spaces for them;* they could do very well without, as hundreds of Irish and Highland emigrants have done before and since.

A pile of stones rudely cemented together with wet clay and ashes against the logs, and a hole cut in the roof, formed the chimney and hearth in this primitive dwelling. The chinks were filled with wedge-shaped pieces of wood, and plastered with clay: the trees, being chiefly oaks and pines, afforded no moss. This

deficiency rather surprised the boys, for in the thick forest and close cedar swamps, moss grows in abundance on the north side of the trees, especially on the cedar, maple, beech, bass, and iron-wood; but there were few of these, excepting a chance one or two in the little basin in front of the house. The roof was next put on, which consisted of split cedars; and when the little dwelling was thus far habitable, they were all very happy. While the boys had been putting on the roof, Catharine had collected the stones for the chimney, and cleared the earthen floor of the chips and rubbish with a broom of cedar boughs, bound together with a leathern thong. She had swept it all clean, carefully removing all unsightly objects, and strewing it over with fresh cedar sprigs, which gave out a pleasant odour, and formed smooth and not unseemly carpet for their little dwelling. How cheerful was the first fire blazing up on their own hearth! It was so pleasant to sit by its gladdening light, and chat away of all they had done and all that they meant to do. Here was to be a set of split cedar shelves, to hold their provisions and baskets; there a set of stout pegs were to be inserted between the logs for hanging up strings of dried meat, bags of birch bark, or the skins of the animals they were to shoot or trap. A table was to be fixed on posts in the centre of the floor. Louis was to carve wooden platters and dishes, and some stools were to be made with hewn blocks of wood, till something better could be devised. Their bedsteads were rough poles of iron-wood, supported by posts driven into the ground, and partly upheld by the projection of the logs at the angles of the

---

* Many a shanty is put up in Canada without windows, and only an open space for a door, with a rude plank set up to close it in at night.

wall. Nothing could be more simple. The framework was of split cedar; and a safe bed was made by pine boughs being first laid upon the frame, and then thickly covered with dried grass, moss, and withered leaves. Such were the lowly but healthy couches on which these children of the forest slept.

———————

One day Hector, who had been out from dawn till moonrise, returned with the welcome news that he had shot a young deer, and required the assistance of his cousin to bring it up the steep bank—(it was just at the entrance of the great ravine)—below the precipitous cliff near the lake; he had left old Wolfe to guard it in the meantime. They had now plenty of fresh broiled meat, and this store was very acceptable, as they were obliged to be very careful of the dried meat that they had.

This time Catharine adopted a new plan. Instead of cutting the meat in strips, and drying it (or jerking it, as the lumberers term it), she roasted it before the fire, and hung it up, wrapping it in thin sheets of birch bark. The juices, instead of being dried up, were preserved, and the meat was more palatable. Catharine found great store of wild plums in a beautiful valley, not far from the shanty; these she dried for the winter store, eating sparingly of them in their fresh state; she also found plenty of wild black currants, and highbush cranberries, on the banks of a charming creek of bright water that flowed between a range of high pine hills, and finally emptied itself into the lake. There were great quantities of watercresses in this pretty brook; they grew in bright round cushion-like tufts at the bottom of the water, and were tender and wholesome.

As the cool weather and frosty nights drew on, the want of warm clothes and bed-covering became more sensibly felt: those they had were beginning to wear out. Catharine had managed to wash her clothes at the lake several times, and thus preserved them clean and wholesome; but she was often sorely puzzled how the want of her dress was to be supplied as time wore on, and many were the consultations she held with the boys on the important subject. With the aid of a needle she might be able to manufacture the skins of the small animals into some sort of jacket, and the doe-skin and deer-skin could be made into garments for the boys. Louis was always suppling and rubbing the skins to make them soft. They had taken off the hair by sprinkling it with wood ashes, and rolling it up with the hairy side inwards. Out of one of these skins he made excellent moccasins, piercing the holes with a sharpened bone bodkin, and passing the sinews of the deer through, as he had seen his father do, by fixing a stout fish-bone to the deer-sinew thread; thus he had an excellent substitute for a needle, and with the aid of the old file he sharpened the point of the rusty nail, so that he was enabled, with a little trouble, to drill a hole in a bone needle, for his cousin Catharine's use. After several attempts, he succeeded in making some of tolerable fineness, hardening them by exposure to a slow steady degree of heat, till she was able to work with them, and even mend her clothes with tolerable expertness. By degrees, Catharine contrived to cover the whole outer surface

of her homespun woollen frock with squirrel and mink, musk-rat and wood-chuck skins. A curious piece of fur patch-work of many hues and textures it presented to the eye—a coat of many colours, it is true; but it kept the wearer warm, and Catharine was not a little proud of her ingenuity and industry: every new patch that was added was a source of fresh satisfaction, and the moccasins, which Louis fitted so nicely to her feet, were great comforts.

Whenever game of any kind was killed, it was carefully skinned and the fur stretched upon bent sticks, being first turned, so as to present the inner part to the drying action of the air. The young hunters were most expert in this work, having been accustomed for many years to assist their fathers in preparing the furs which they disposed of to the fur traders, who visited them from time to time, and gave them various articles in exchange for their peltries; such as powder and shot, and cutlery of different kinds, as knives, scissors, needles, and pins, with gay calicoes and cotton handkerchiefs for the women.

As the evenings lengthened, the boys employed themselves with carving wooden platters: knives and forks and spoons they fashioned out of the larger bones of the deer, which they often found bleaching in the sun and wind, where they had been left by their enemies the wolves; baskets too they made, and birch dishes, which they could now finish so well that they held water, or any liquid.

Susanna Moodie
Caught Between Fire and Ice

Susanna Moodie—like her sister, Catharine Parr Traill—was an English immigrant who had to make a new life for herself in Upper Canada. Unlike Traill's cheerfully written *Backwoods of Canada*, Moodie's book *Roughing It in the Bush* often emphasizes the hardship and dangers of pioneering life and how out of place she felt in her rough surroundings. But she could be strong and resourceful when she had to be. In this excerpt, she describes how she coped with a fire that broke out in her house while her husband was away. Her daughter Katie, who was only about six years old, pitched in bravely, too.

THE HOUSE WAS BUILT OF CEDAR LOGS; in all probability it would be consumed before any help could arrive. There was a brisk breeze blowing up from the frozen lake, and the thermometer stood at eighteen degrees below zero. We were placed between the two extremes of heat and cold, and there was as much danger to be apprehended from the one as the other. In the bewilderment of the moment, the direful extent of the calamity never struck me: we wanted but this to put the finishing stroke to our misfortunes, to be thrown, naked, houseless, and penniless, upon the world. "*What shall I save first?*" was the thought just then uppermost in my mind. Bedding and clothing appeared the most essentially necessary and without another moment's pause, I set to work with a right good will to drag all that I could from my burning home.

While little Agnes, Dunbar, and baby Donald filled the air with their cries, Katie, as if fully conscious of the importance of exertion, assisted me in carrying out sheets and blankets, and dragging trunks and boxes some way up the hill, to be out of the way of the burning brands when the roof should fall in.

How many anxious looks I gave to the head of the clearing as the fire increased, and large pieces of burning pine began to fall through the boarded ceiling, about the lower rooms where we were at work. The children I had kept under a large dresser in the kitchen, but it now appeared absolutely necessary to remove them to a place of safety. To expose the young, tender things to the direful cold was almost as bad as leaving them to the mercy of the fire. At last I hit upon a plan to keep them from freezing. I emptied all the clothes out of a large, deep chest of drawers, and dragged the empty drawers up the hill; these I lined with blankets, and placed a child in each drawer, covering it well over with the bedding, giving to little Agnes the charge of the baby to hold between her knees, and keep well covered until help should arrive. Ah, how long it seemed coming!

I found that I should not be able to take many more trips for goods. As I passed out of the parlour for the last time, Katie looked up at her father's flute, which was suspended upon two brackets, and said,

"Oh, dear Mamma! do save papa's flute; he will be so sorry to lose it."

God bless the dear child for the thought! The flute was saved; and, as I succeeded in dragging out a heavy chest of clothes, and looked up once more despairingly to the road, I saw a man running at full speed. It was my husband. Help was at hand, and my heart uttered a deep thanksgiving as another and another figure came upon the scene.

I had not felt the intense cold, although without cap, or bonnet, or shawl; with my hands bare and exposed to the bitter, biting air. The intense excitement, the anxiety to save all I could, had so totally diverted my thoughts from myself, that I had felt nothing of the danger to which I had been exposed; but now that help was near, my knees trembled under me, I felt giddy and faint, and dark shadows seemed dancing before my eyes.

The moment my husband and brother-in-law entered the house, the latter exclaimed,

"Moodie, the house is gone; save what you can of your winter stores and furniture."

Moodie thought differently. Prompt and energetic in danger, and possessing admirable presence of mind and coolness when others yield to agitation and despair, he sprang upon the burning loft and called for water. Alas, there was none!

"Snow, snow; hand me up pailfuls of snow!"

Oh! it was bitter work filling those pails with frozen snow; but Mr. T—— and I worked at it as fast as we were able.

The violence of the fire was greatly checked by covering the boards of the loft with this snow. More help had now arrived. Young B—— and S—— had brought the ladder down with them from the barn, and were already cutting away the burning roof, and flinging the flaming brands into the deep snow.

"Mrs. Moodie, have you any pickled meat?"

"We have just killed one of our cows, and salted it for winter stores."

"Well, then, fling the beef into the snow, and let us have the brine."

This was an admirable plan. Wherever the brine wetted the shingles, the fire turned from it, and concentrated into one spot.

But I had not time to watch the brave workers on the roof. I was fast yielding to the effects of overexcitement and fatigue, when my brother's team dashed down the clearing, bringing my excellent old friend, Miss B——, and the servant-girl.

My brother sprang out, carried me back into the house, and wrapped me up in one of the large blankets scattered about. In a few minutes I was seated with the dear children in the sleigh, and on the way to a place of warmth and safety.

Margaret Atwood
The Two Fires

In 1970, Margaret Atwood published *The Journals of Susanna Moodie*, a book of poems inspired by
Moodie's account of pioneering in Upper Canada. Atwood wrote that Moodie fascinated her because she
seemed "divided down the middle" in her feelings about Canada. Did she want to be here or back home in England?
Did she love the land or fear it? "The Two Fires" is a poem about how hard it is for Moodie, in her isolated pioneer
home, to feel secure anywhere, inside or out. As a summer fire rages outside, she tells herself that her home
is a haven. But later, in winter, a fire in her house (Moodie describes it herself in the previous
selection) forces her to shelter her family outside in the snow.

ONE, THE SUMMER FIRE
outside: the trees melting, returning
to their first red elements
on all sides, cutting me off
from escape or the saving
lake

I sat in the house, raised up
between that shapeless raging
and my sleeping children
a charm: concentrate on
form, geometry, the human
architecture of the house, square
closed doors, proved roofbeams,
the logic of windows

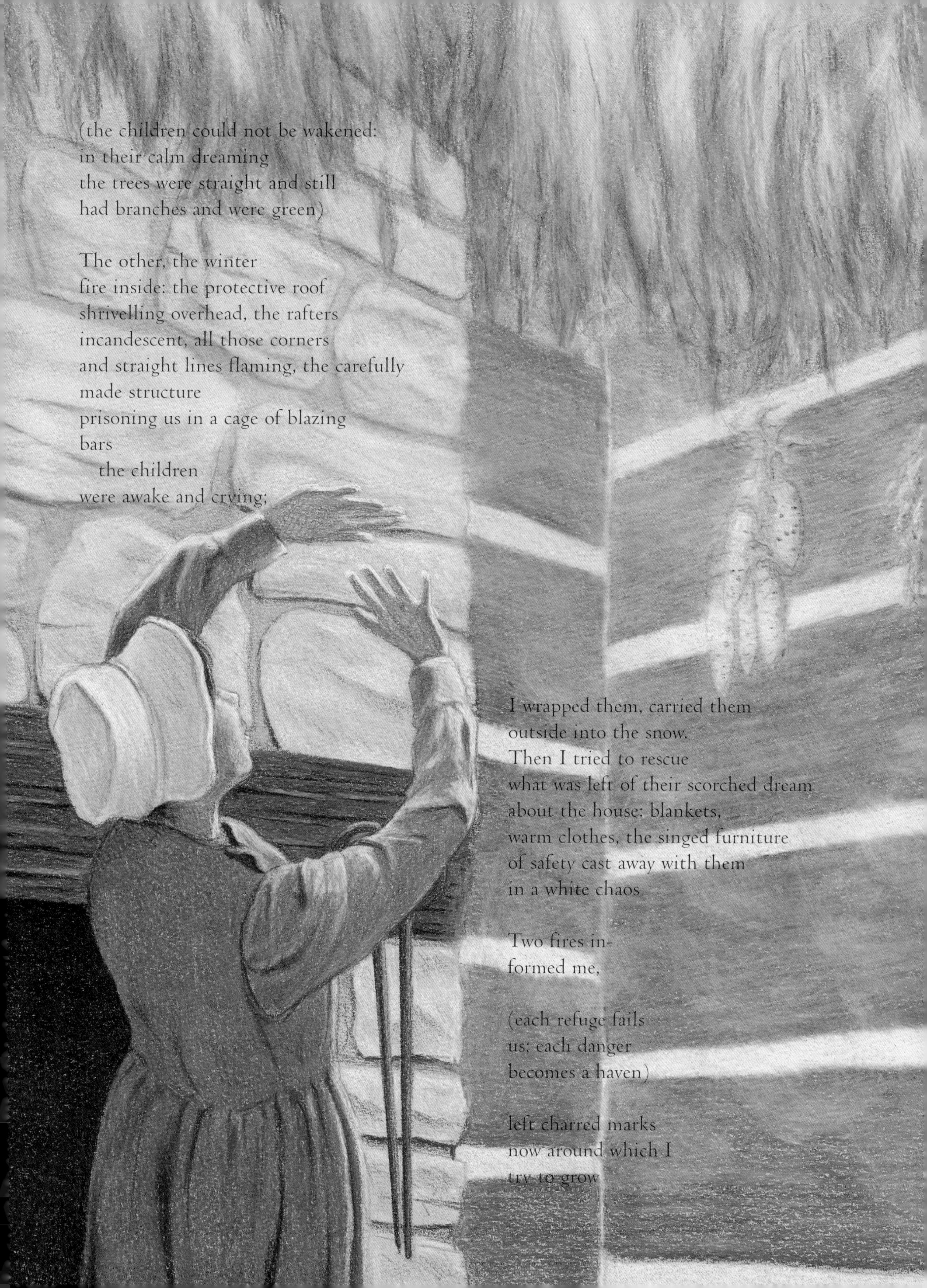

(the children could not be wakened:
in their calm dreaming
the trees were straight and still
had branches and were green)

The other, the winter
fire inside: the protective roof
shrivelling overhead, the rafters
incandescent, all those corners
and straight lines flaming, the carefully
made structure
prisoning us in a cage of blazing
bars
   the children
were awake and crying;

I wrapped them, carried them
outside into the snow.
Then I tried to rescue
what was left of their scorched dream
about the house: blankets,
warm clothes, the singed furniture
of safety cast away with them
in a white chaos

Two fires in-
formed me,

(each refuge fails
us; each danger
becomes a haven)

left charred marks
now around which I
try to grow

Loggers

Forests have long played an important role in Canada's economy. In the early nineteenth century, Britain needed timber for its navy. In Atlantic Canada, tall trees were cut down to provide masts for ships. As the forests were used up, lumbering moved into Quebec and Ontario. By the end of the nineteenth century, nearly all the white pine, prized for ship-building, had been cleared from this part of Canada.

In British Columbia, home of gigantic Douglas fir and Sitka spruce, the forest industry did not develop until the 1850s. When the railway link to the rest of Canada was being constructed in the 1880s, huge amounts of wood were needed for railway ties, bridges, and train stations. Later, with the line completed, B.C. began to ship lumber to Eastern Canada. Today, the forest industry—logging, wood processing, and pulp and paper manufacturing—employs more than forty thousand Canadians. But bitter struggles are being waged in several regions between loggers and environmentalists. Environmental groups often include Native peoples who see themselves as guardians of their traditional homelands.

Tom C. Connors
Big Joe Mufferaw

Unlike other tall-tale heroes such as Paul Bunyan (p. 162) and Johnny Chinook (p. 164), Joe Mufferaw actually existed. His real name was Joseph Montferrand, and he was born in Montreal in 1802 and died in 1864. Joe was about 185 cm (6 foot 2)—unusually tall for a nineteenth-century man—and exceptionally strong. When he became a logger in the Ottawa Valley, word quickly spread that Joe could do twice as much work in a day as any other man. One of the most famous stories about Joe—which just might be true—is that one evening, after drinking in a tavern, he discovered he didn't have enough money to pay the bill. The tavern keeper told him not to worry about it, so to thank him, Joe said he was going to leave his calling card. He leaped in the air and aimed a kick at the ceiling, leaving a clear bootmark stamped there. From then on, business boomed in the tavern, with people coming from far and wide to gaze up in wonder at Joe's footprint.

RECITATION 1
AND THEY SAY BIG JOE HAD AN OLD PET FROG,
bigger than a horse and he barked like a dog.
And the only thing quicker than a train upon a track
was Big Joe ridin' on the bull-frog's back.

RECITATION 2
And they say Big Joe used
    to get real wet
From cuttin' down timber
    and workin' up a sweat,
And everyone'll tell ya 'round
    Carleton Place,
The Mississippi dripped off of
    Big Joe's face.

Refrain
Heave hi, heave hi ho!
The best man in Ottawa was Mufferaw Joe,
Mufferaw Joe!

RECITATION 3
And they say Big Joe put out a forest fire
Halfway between Renfrew and old Arnprior.
He was fifty miles away down around Smiths Falls,
But he drowned out the fire with five spit balls.

Refrain

RECITATION 4
Well, he jumped in the Calabogie Lake
    real fast,
And he swam both ways to catch a
    cross-eyed bass;
But he threw it on the ground and said,
    "I can't eat that,"
So he covered it over with Mount St. Pat.

Bill Freeman
The Log Jam

In the novel *Shantymen of Cache Lake*, John Bains, age fourteen, and his thirteen-year-old sister, Meg, must take work in a lumber camp after their father dies. The story is set in the 1870s, at Cache Lake in the Algonquin Highlands (where Algonquin Park is today) and in the Ottawa Valley. In those days, the area around Cache Lake was covered in white pine trees, some as much as sixty metres (two hundred feet) tall and two metres (six feet) in diameter. Lumbermen, called shantymen (from the French word *chantier*, which refers to the huts they lived in), travelled to lumber camps in October or November and spent the winter there, felling trees and "squaring" them (trimming them into straight-sided logs). In this excerpt from the book, spring has come and Meg and John participate in the most dangerous part of the lumbermen's work: driving the logs downriver to Ottawa. Their peavy poles are long poles with an iron point and a hinged hook, while pike poles are three-metre (ten-foot) poles with no moving parts. Pointers are small boats in which the lumbermen follow the log drive.

THE DRIVE REPRESENTED MANY THINGS to the shantymen: it was the start of a new round of activities, it was the end of the isolation of camp life, it meant, with each turn of the river, that they were getting closer to their homes; and for many, the log drive was the final and ultimate test of their courage and skill as shantymen. That night John and Meg felt a part of all of those things.

After a fitful sleep on the half-frozen ground, the men were up before the dawn, ate a hurried breakfast, climbed into their pointers and followed the logs downstream. At every bend of the river some of the logs had washed ashore, and a crew would have to get out and, using their peavy poles, roll the logs back into the river again. By midday the pointers were stretched the whole ten miles from below the log chute to the point where the river emptied into Lake of Two Rivers. The cook and one of the older shantymen, who had taken the job of cook's help, were first with most of the supplies, and they hurriedly set up camp at the mouth of the river and began preparing the evening meal. A small log jam had formed in some shallow water near a group of islands, and it took an hour's work for a half a dozen men to free them, but by nightfall the river had been cleared and all of the men had made it to the camp.

A different technique had to be used to get the logs across the lake. If they waited for the current to drift the logs to the other side, it would take months to complete the drive. The shantymen broke into two teams. One hurriedly made a huge log boom large enough to enclose all of the timbers that had been cut. The other crew built a square raft out of timbers, and on it they set up the large capstan they had been carrying. They paddled the raft out into the middle of the lake and firmly anchored it in shallow water near an island. Then they took a long rope leading back from the capstan to tie securely around the boom. The capstan was a large spool-shaped cylinder that revolved when the men turned it by pushing on the long poles that projected out of the centre. The men walked around and around and slowly wound the rope around the capstan, gradually pulling the huge log boom towards the raft. The men took turns at the exhausting, monotonous work, ten at a time turning the capstan, and slowly they winched the boom up to the raft and then moved the raft ahead, anchored it, and began winching again. Finally, two days after they had started, they had winched the logs to the end of Lake of Two Rivers.

The next few days were so exhausting that Meg and John wondered if signing on for the log drive had been wise. When they got to the end of the lake they broke up the boom and drove the logs down to Whitefish Lake. Then it was back to the capstan raft for what seemed to be days and days of winching the enormous boom. Finally at the end of Galeairy Lake they released their logs into the powerful waters of the Madawaska.

It was not surprising that the log run was considered the most dangerous part of the shantyman's life. Anyone who fell into those surging waters could be dragged under by the current. The heavy woollen clothing of a shantyman would soak with water, and his big boots would make him sink like a stone. It would take good luck and superhuman strength to come out alive, and it was not surprising that there were a number of shantymen who never returned home after the annual log run.

Both John and Meg stuck to their jobs with grim determination. No one would say that they were not good workers. From sunup to sundown they were in pointers sweeping the river for timber that had gone ashore. At rapids and waterfalls log chutes had been built and log booms had been strung across the river to catch the timber. As soon as all of their logs had been trapped the chute would be opened and the shantymen would begin guiding the logs into it with their long pike poles. It was dangerous work. The men would often leave their pointers and run across the squared timbers to free a log, knowing full well that if they fell into the water they could be swept under the boom and into the waterfall before they could get a handhold.

The final test came in the fourth week

of the drive. A few of the experienced men knew that they were coming to a treacherous part where the river narrowed and was pitted with small islands and rocks. John and Meg went with them ahead of the logs, and they positioned themselves on the rocks and river bank with their long pike poles to help steer the logs through the narrows. About a quarter of the logs had passed through when suddenly one lodged sideways, jamming up against two rocks across the flow of the river. Within moments other logs hurtling along behind got caught and a twisted pile of timbers grew as each log added to the numbers.

"Jam! Jam!" the men shouted up and down the bank, and as the news spread every man ran to the spot as fast as he could. The most dangerous of all possible things had happened.

John stood beside the others, holding on to his pike pole and listening to the men anxiously debating what to do. He studied the jam in every detail. The key log, which the others were all wedged into, could be seen quite clearly. If a man could get into the water, he thought, and lift one end of the timber up and over the rock, it would slip away downstream and the whole jam should tumble free. The sooner it was done, the less the risk, because there would be fewer timbers in the jam. John did not hesitate a moment.

was hooked in exactly the right place, then he heaved upwards, pushing with every ounce of strength that he had in his sinewy body. Slowly, ever so slowly at first, the squared timber lifted upwards, until gradually the end came out of the water a trifle, hesitated, and then began to slip across the top of the rock that it had been wedged into.

Suddenly, John felt the timber give away. He glanced back. The jam was moving towards him, logs tumbling down on top of him as the bottom slipped out. He dropped the peavy pole and started the dash for shore. Suddenly, the rope around his waist came taunt as the men frantically dragged his body wildly through the water towards the shore. John was hit by a log, then another, but finally, miraculously, he felt himself being dragged over hard ground. He looked back; the jam had broken with a deafening roar as the logs suddenly surged downstream.

The men surrounded John, exuberantly congratulating him. Breaking a jam was the most dangerous job that a shantyman was ever called on to do, and few men had the strength or nerve to do it. Over and over again the men shook his hand and slapped him on the back, telling him what a great shantyman he had become. It was only Jacques and Cameron who disapproved. Over the season's work they had come to feel responsible for the two children of their dead friend, and although they marvelled at John's daring they scolded him that night after supper, and told him in no uncertain terms that he was not to take such risks again.

He explained to the others how he thought the jam could be freed, then bound a rope around his waist, took a peavy pole, and waded into the cold, swift-flowing water.

Meg was there and was about to protest, but even by then there was little she could do except stand with the others and slowly play out the rope that was around her brother's waist. The current was up to his thighs, surging so strongly that he had to lean against his peavy pole to hold his balance, but he waded on until finally he was by the rock and the key timber. The jam was huge, a tangled mass of logs towering over his head. He leaned into the water to make sure his peavy pole

Traditional
Way Up the Ucletaw

Lumbering in British Columbia at the end of the nineteenth century was dangerous work. Loggers from Vancouver first had to journey up the treacherous Yuc'ta (Ucletaw) Rapids, between Quadra Island and Sonora Island, to reach the trees known as pitchbacks. These were Douglas firs that stood more than sixty metres (two hundred feet) high and were more than two metres (six feet) in diameter. The bark on the lower part of these trees was so hardened by pitch (tree sap) that the loggers could not cut through it. Instead, they hammered boards into the tree above the pitch layer, and stood on these shaky platforms to chop the tree down with hand axes. In the song, the loggers' misery is made greater by a greenhorn (inexperienced) cook who serves them runny, undercooked hotcakes.

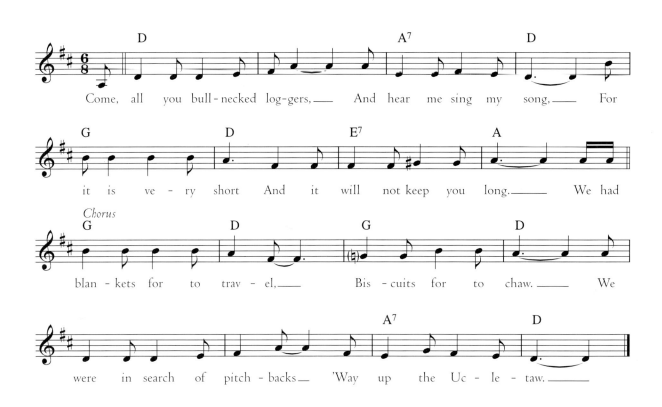

Come, all you bull - necked log-gers,___ And hear me sing my song,___ For

it is ve - ry short And it will not keep you long.___ We had

Chorus

blan - kets for to trav - el,___ Bis - cuits for to chaw. ___ We

were in search of pitch - backs___ 'Way up the Uc - le - taw. ___

1.
COME, ALL YOU BULL-NECKED LOGGERS,
And hear me sing my song,
For it is very short
And it will not keep you long.

Chorus:
We had blankets for to travel,
Biscuits for to chaw.
We were in search of pitchbacks
'Way up the Ucletaw.

2.
We're leaving Vancouver
With sorrow, grief and woe,
Heading up the country
A hundred miles or so.

Chorus

3.
We hired fourteen loggers,
And we hired a man to saw.
We had a greenhorn cook,
And he run the hotcakes raw.

Chorus

The True North

Where does Canada's North begin? For many Canadians, especially those who live in a narrow band of cities and towns along the American border, the North begins in the more rugged areas of their own provinces. Sometimes the North is defined more narrowly as the Yukon, the Northwest Territories, and the new territory of Nunavut. For thousands of years, these areas have been the homelands of the Yukon First Nations, the Dene, and the Inuit. European explorers often saw the Canadian North, which has some of the most extreme climatic conditions on earth, as a test of their strength and courage. Some learned from its Native inhabitants how to survive there; others set out on their own, fiercely pitting themselves against harsh weather and terrain until they gave up or died. Even in the nineteenth century, contact between the Native peoples of the Far North and visitors from the outside was rare. Then, with the discovery of gold in 1896, more than one hundred thousand fortune-seekers flooded into the Yukon. In the years that followed, other resources, such as oil and natural gas, attracted more non-Native people to the North, and by the middle of the twentieth century most Native people had given up their traditional nomadic life and moved into settled communities.

Pauline Johnson
The Train Dogs

Pauline Johnson was the child of a Mohawk father and a non-Native mother. Around
the turn of the twentieth century, she became famous in North America and England for her
dramatic readings of her own poems. While visiting Edmonton one year in the early spring, she saw
a train of yelping husky dogs pulling a sled loaded with skins down the street. The dogs were exhausted,
their ribs showing, and the Native driver was worn out too. However, the driver was pleased to have completed his
run from the North before the last of the frost was gone. Inspired by this incident, Johnson wrote "The
Train Dogs." The Inuit have used *qimmiit* (huskies) to pull *qamutiit* (sleds) in the North for more than
a thousand years. The strong, thick-coated dogs are ideally suited to a vigorous outdoor life. In recent
years, snowmobiles have begun to do much of their work. However, breeders have made sure that
the dogs do not disappear from the Canadian North. They are still used to transport
tourists, and for challenging long-distance sled races.

OUT OF THE NIGHT AND THE NORTH;
   Savage of breed and of bone,
Shaggy and swift comes the yelping band,
Freighters of fur from the voiceless land
   That sleeps in the Arctic zone.

Laden with skins from the north,
   Beaver and bear and racoon,
Marten and mink from the polar belts,
Otter and ermine and sable pelts—
   The spoils of the hunter's moon.

Out of the night and the north,
   Sinewy, fearless and fleet,
Urging the pack through the pathless
    snow,
The Indian driver, calling low,
   Follows with moccasined feet.

Ships of the night and the north,
   Freighters on prairies and plains,
Carrying cargoes from field and flood
They scent the trail through their wild
    red blood,
   The wolfish blood in their veins.

Robert W. Service
The Cremation of Sam McGee

On August 17, 1896, three men found gold in Bonanza Creek, a tributary of the Klondike River.
As word of their find spread throughout North America and beyond, one hundred thousand people
headed for the North in hopes of striking it rich. Most would be bitterly disappointed. Although Robert
Service became famous by writing about "sourdoughs"—the Klondike prospectors—he was never one of them. He
arrived in the Yukon in 1905, when the rush was over, and worked as a bank clerk. "Moiling" for gold
means hard physical work, while "mushing" means travelling by dogsled. Lake Laberge (not
Lebarge) is a Yukon River lake, and its "marge" is its shoreline.

There are strange things done in the
  midnight sun
By the men who moil for gold;
The Arctic trails have their secret tales
That would make your blood run cold;
The Northern Lights have seen queer sights,
But the queerest they ever did see
Was that night on the marge of Lake Lebarge
I cremated Sam McGee.

Now Sam McGee was from Tennessee,
where the cotton blooms and blows
Why he left his home in the South to
  roam
'round the Pole, God only knows.
He was always cold but the land of gold
seemed to hold him like a spell;
Though he'd often say in his homely way
that he'd sooner live in Hell.

On a Christmas Day we were mushing our
    way
over the Dawson trail.
Talk of your cold! through the parka's
    fold
it stabbed like a driven nail.
If our eyes we'd close, then the lashes
    froze
till sometimes we couldn't see,
It wasn't much fun, but the only one
to whimper was Sam McGee.

And that very night, as we lay packed
    tight
in our robes beneath the snow,
And the dogs were fed, and the stars o'er-
    head
were dancing heel and toe,
He turned to me, and "Cap", says he,
"I'll cash in this trip, I guess;
And if I do, I'm asking that you
won't refuse my last request."

Well, he seemed so low that I couldn't say
    no;
then he says with a sort of moan,
"It's the cursed cold, and it's got right
    hold
till I'm chilled clean through to the bone
Yet 'taint being dead—it's my awful dread
of the icy grave that pains;
So I want you to swear that, foul or fair,
you'll cremate my last remains."

A pal's last need is a thing to heed,
so I swore I would not fail;
And we started on at the streak of dawn
but God! he looked ghastly pale.
He crouched on the sleigh, and he raved
    all day
of his home in Tennessee;
And before nightfall a corpse was all
that was left of Sam McGee.

There wasn't a breath in that land of
    death,
and I hurried, horror-driven
With a corpse half hid that I couldn't get
    rid,
because of a promise given;
It was lashed to the sleigh, and it seemed
    to say,
"You may tax your brawn and brains,
But you promised true, and it's up to you
to cremate these last remains."

Now a promise made is a debt unpaid,
and the trail has its own stern code,
In the days to come, though my lips were
    dumb
in my heart how I cursed that load!
In the long, long night, by the lone fire-
    light,
while the huskies, round in a ring,
Howled out their woes to the homeless
    snows—
Oh God, how I loathed the thing!

And every day that quiet clay
seemed to heavy and heavier grow;
And on I went, though the dogs were
    spent
and the grub was getting low.
The trail was bad, and I felt half mad,
but I swore I would not give in;
And I'd often sing to the hateful thing,
and it hearkened with a grin.

Till I came to the marge of Lake Lebarge,
and a derelict there lay;
It was jammed in the ice, but I saw in a
    trice
it was called the Alice May,
And I looked at it, and I thought a bit,
and I looked at my frozen chum;
Then "Here", said I, with a sudden cry, "is
    my cre-ma-tor-eum"!

Some planks I tore from the cabin floor
and I lit the boiler fire;
Some coal I found that was lying around,
and I heaped the fuel higher;
The flames just soared, and the furnace
    roared
such a blaze you seldom see,
And I burrowed a hole in the glowing
    coal,
and I stuffed in Sam McGee.

Then I made a hike, for I didn't like
to hear him sizzle so;
And the heavens scowled, and the huskies
    howled,
and the wind began to blow,
It was icy cold, but the hot sweat rolled
down my cheeks, and I don't know why;
And the greasy smoke in an inky cloak
went streaking down the sky.

I do not know how long in the snow
I wrestled with grisly fear;
But the stars came out and they danced
    about
ere again I ventured near;
I was sick with dread, but I bravely said,
"I'll just take a peep inside.
I guess he's cooked, and it's time I
    looked."
Then the door I opened wide.

And there sat Sam, looking cool and calm,
in the heart of the furnace roar;
And he wore a smile you could see a mile,
and he said, "Please close that door.
It's fine in here, but I greatly fear
you'll let in the cold and storm—
Since I left Plumtree, down in Tennessee,
it's the first time I've been warm."

There are strange things done in the midnight
    sun
By the men who moil for gold;
The Arctic trails have their secret tales
That would make your blood run cold;
The Northern Lights have seen queer sights,
But the queerest they ever did see
Was that night on the marge of Lake Lebarge
I cremated Sam McGee.

Alootook Ipellie
I Shall Wait and Wait

Alootook Ipellie is an Inuk writer and artist who was born on the north shore of Frobisher Bay in 1951. His poem describes a winter seal hunt as it would have been carried out in his grandfather's day. The hunter would search the ice for a seal's breathing hole, and then wait beside it until the seal came up for air. Seals have many breathing holes and can stay underwater for long periods. It might be hours, or even days, before a seal appeared at the place the hunter had chosen. The hunter had to wait patiently, but still be ready at any moment to lunge with his harpoon. Seals provided the Inuit not only with food, but also with warm sealskin clothing and oil for heat and light. The Inuit did not hunt for sport—only for their own survival.

AS I STAND ALONE ON THE MIDDLE OF THE ICE,
the sky above gets darker by the minute.
The seal has not yet come.
It must be somewhere out there where I cannot see it.
It must be playing in the water below the ice,
or searching for food as I am doing now.
He has his life too, as I do.

I came here to bring food to my family,
so it is most important I stay and wait.
Wait till the seal comes up to the hole below me,
A hole that is filled with salted water.
Food is waiting there.

My children are waiting for me too.
Waiting to be fed from the seal that has not come.

The long wait is worth every single length of time.
I shall wait until the seal arrives to breathe for life.
Then I shall push my spear down into the hole
as hard as I can and let the blood appear.
Then I shall pull the seal out, smiling with the wonderful
feeling that food is on its way to my family;
to my wife, to my children.

They are still waiting for the moment
when fresh meat will touch their tongues
and visit their tummies,
when they can enjoy the taste of the seal
that hasn't made an appearance yet through the hole below.

I shall wait and wait until it comes.

Voices of Sadness

The nineteenth century was the period when Canada was pieced together, a time of immigration, growth, and optimism. But for Native Canadians, the century holds many bitter memories. Almost everywhere that colonists of European origin settled, Native peoples were pushed aside. Although the Canadian government did not wage war on Native peoples as the American government did, their lives and livelihoods were often taken away from them by unfair treaties and broken promises that left them hungry, sick, and impoverished. At the same time, they were excluded from decisions that affected their future: wars were declared; peace treaties were signed; land that belonged to them was bought and sold as if it were uninhabited; an international boundary was drawn and divided the territories of some groups in half. Native peoples were not given a voice in any of these matters. Even today, many Native bands are involved in legal struggles to have their rights and land claims recognized.

Stella Whelan
The Ballad of Mary March

The Beothuk people lived in Newfoundland when the first Europeans arrived there. Because they painted their bodies with a mixture of oil and red ochre, the Europeans called them Red Indians. The Beothuks roamed from place to place with the seasons, hunting caribou inland in the fall, then moving to the coast for the summer to catch seals and fish. When Europeans settled along the coast, they kept the Beothuks away from their traditional summer camps. Some even hunted the Beothuks down and killed them, and by the early 1800s very few Beothuks remained. In 1819, a Beothuk woman named Demasduwit was taken prisoner. Her husband was killed coming to her aid, and her baby, left behind, died soon after. The white settlers decided to keep Demasduwit, whom they called Mary March, in their community for a time. They planned to teach her English and then return her to her people, but she died of tuberculosis before she could go home. Stella Whelan's poem imagines Mary March's bitter feelings about her captivity. Shawnandithit, the last of the Beothuks, died in 1829.

THEY WILL TELL YOU IF YOU ASK THEM, THEY WILL TELL YOU I AM DEAD.
They will tell you I am lying in my cold and narrow bed.
They will tell you I am sleeping with my husband by my side,
But I wake and walk and wander and I tell you that they lied.

Many centuries ago my fathers settled here to make
Their homes about the margin of this dark and shining lake,
Where the silver-footed river from the mountains running free,
Linked us close to one another on a roadway to the sea.

The wild game of the forest gave us food and clothes to wear
There were marten, fox and otter, beaver, sable, wolf and bear;
We smoked and dried the carcasses and fashioned from the skins
All the garments that we needed—cassocks, hose and moccasins.

When I look back I wonder if the prophet could describe
The doom and devastation that were waiting for our tribe,
For the white man fell upon us like an awesome avalanche
With the grim determination to destroy us, root and branch.

Every red man was the target for some white man's deadly gun,
They relentlessly pursued us, and they shot us, one by one;
They drove us from the river and from the camp fire site,
They drove us from the hunting grounds, they stalked us day and night.

Oh my lost and stricken loved ones! I would turn away my head
From a memory that fills me with a sickness born of dread,
For the child that was abandoned and left alone to die;
For his father bruised and broken underneath that bitter sky.

They say they came in friendship but they shot him with a gun,
They stabbed him in the back and they were seven to his one;
They say they came in friendship but the child that was my own
In that dark wilderness of ice was left to die alone.

The white men took me prisoner but they could not keep me long,
For the ties that bound me to my own were rooted deep and strong.
And there is neither room nor door nor lock that can be found
To stay the captive spirit in its journey homeward bound.

And when I could no longer see or hear or feel or care
They took the empty shell of me and brought it back to where
Beneath the sullen sky upon another winter day
The tides of death came in and swept all that I loved away.

Now the wigwam is deserted and the winter winds blow through.
And nearby lies the wreckage of the little birch canoe,
But the silent trees remember and the glossy pond and lake
Still watch along the shore line in the morning when they wake;
For the vanished Indian hunter, bow and arrow in his hand,
And there is blood upon the rock and tears upon the sand.

Shinguacouse
A Letter from Shinguacouse

Shinguacouse was an Ojibwa leader who fought alongside General Brock in the War of 1812. Later, in the 1830s, he asked the lieutenant-governor of Upper Canada to establish a settlement for his people near Sault Ste. Marie. In 1850, the government negotiated treaties with several Native leaders who lived north of Lake Superior and Lake Huron, including Shinguacouse. The Native groups were given immediate cash payments and small continuing allowances, a guarantee of fishing and hunting rights, and twenty-one reserves to live on. In return, they were to "cede, grant and convey to her Majesty" some 129, 500 km² (50,000 square miles) of land, including potentially rich mining properties. After holding out for several days, Shinguacouse reluctantly agreed. This letter, written by Shinguacouse to a government official in 1849, expresses the anguish and sense of betrayal that many Native people were feeling as their land was taken away from them.

WHEN YOUR WHITE CHILDREN FIRST came into this country, they did not come shouting the war cry and seeking to wrest this land from us. They told us they came as friends to smoke the pipe of peace; they sought our friendship, we became brothers. Their enemies were ours, at the time we were strong and powerful, while they were few and weak. But did we oppress them or wrong them? No! And they did not attempt to do what is now done, nor did they tell us that at some future day you would.

Father,
Time wore on and you have become a great people, whilst we have melted away like snow beneath an April sun; our strength is wasted, our countless warriors dead, our forests laid low, you have hunted us from every place as with a wand, you have swept away all our pleasant land, and like some giant foe you tell us "willing or unwilling, you must now go from amid these rocks and wastes, I want them now! I want them to make rich my white children, whilst you may shrink away to holes

and caves like starving dogs to die." Yes, Father, your white children have opened our very graves to tell the dead even they shall have no resting place.

Father,

Was it for this we first received you with the hand of friendship, and gave you the room whereon to spread your blanket? Was it for this that we voluntarily became the children of our Great Mother the Queen? Was it for this we served England's sovereign so well and truly, that the blood of the red skin has moistened the dust of his own hunting grounds, to serve those sovereigns in their quarrels, and not in quarrels of his own?

Father,

We begin to fear that those sweet words had not their birth in the heart, but that they lived only upon the tongue; they are like those beautiful trees under whose shadow it is pleasant for a time to repose and hope, but we cannot forever indulge in their graceful shade—they produce no fruit.

Father,

We are men like you, we have the limbs of men, we have the hearts of men, and we feel and know that all this country is ours; even the weakest and most cowardly animals of the forest when hunted to extremity, though they feel destruction sure, will turn upon the hunter.

Father,

Drive us not to the madness of despair. We are told that you have laws which guard and protect the property of your white children, but you have made none to protect the rights of your red children. Perhaps you expected that the red skin could protect himself from the rapacity of his pale-faced bad brother.

Willie Dunn
The Ballad of Crowfoot

Willie Dunn (Roha'tiio) made a film in 1968 called *The Ballad of Crowfoot*, and this was the haunting theme song. Crowfoot (Isapo-Muxika) was a chief of the Siksika (Blackfoot) people. When he was born, in 1821, there were about nineteen thousand Siksika on the Western plains, and about fifty million bison. By the time Crowfoot died in 1890, the bison herds had been wiped out by white hunters, and the Siksika, devastated by disease and starvation, numbered only about six hundred. Crowfoot did his best. In his youth he was a brave warrior, and he later negotiated a treaty with the Canadian government that kept his people out of the Northwest Rebellion (p. 119). These verses not only tell Crowfoot's often tragic story, but also describe the deplorable conditions for Native Canadians in Dunn's own time.

COMES THE SPRING, AND ITS WARM THAW,
Around your neck, the eagle claw.
Upon your head, the buffalo horn
To-day a great new chief is born.
So raise him fast towards the sun,
A heart now beats, a life's begun.
It's eighteen hundred twenty-one,
Today a Blackfoot soul is born.

Chorus:
Crowfoot, Crowfoot, why the tears?
You've been a brave man, for many years.
Why the sadness? Why the sorrow?
Maybe there'll be a better tomorrow.

The years have gone, the years have past.
Your heart has set, your soul is cast,
You stand before the Council Fire,
You have the mind and the desire,
Of notions wise you speak so well
And in brave deeds you do excel
And it's eighteen hundred fifty-three.
And you stand the chief of Confederacy.

Chorus

You are the leader, you are the chief.
You stand against both the liar and thief,
They trade braves' whiskey and steal your
    land,
And they're coming in swift like the
    wind-blown sand.
They shoot the buffalo and kill the game.

And send their preachers in to shame.
And it's eighteen hundred sixty-four,
And you think of peace and you think of
    war.

Chorus

See the settlers in more numbers
He takes whatever he encounters,
You've seen the Sioux all battered, beaten.
They're all in rags, they haven't eaten.
The Nez Percé are much the same
It seems like such a heartless game.
And it's eighteen hundred seventy-six.
And the enemy's full of those death-
    dealing tricks.

Chorus

Today the treaty stands on the table.
Will you sign it, are you able,
It offers food and protection too.
Do you really think they'll hold it true?
It offers a reserve, now isn't that grand.
And in return, you cede all your land.
And it's eighteen hundred seventy-seven.
And you know the scales are so uneven.

Chorus

Well, the buffalo are slaughtered, there's
    nothing to eat,
The government's late again, with the
    meat
And your people are riddled with the
    white man's disease,

And in the summer you're sick, and in the
    winter you freeze,
And sometimes you wonder why you
    signed that day,
But they broke the treaties themselves
    anyway,
And it's eighteen hundred eighty-nine,
And your death star explodes and then it
    falls.

Chorus

The years have gone, the years have flown,
A nation since has swiftly grown,
But for the native, it's all the same,
There's still the hardship, there's still the
    pain,
There's still the hardship, there's still the
    strife,
It's bitterness shines like a whetted knife,
There's still the hypocrisy, and still the
    hate,
Was that in the treaties, was that our fate?
We're all unhappy pawns in the govern-
    ment's game,
And it's always the native who gets the
    blame,
It's a problem which money can never
    lessen,
And it's nineteen hundred seventy-one.

Chorus

Maybe one day you'll find honesty,
Instead of the usual treachery,
Perhaps one day the truth may prevail,
And the warmth of love which it does
    entail.

Chorus

PART FOUR

The New Nation

Illustrated by

Janet Wilson

Paul Mombourquette

Confederation

 On July 1, 1867, the Dominion of Canada was born. It had only four provinces: Ontario, Quebec, New Brunswick, and Nova Scotia. The push towards Confederation had started in earnest in 1864. In that year, John A. Macdonald, George-Étienne Cartier, and George Brown, government leaders in the United Province of Canada (which was made up of Ontario and Quebec), asked if they could come to Charlottetown, Prince Edward Island, to discuss a union of Britain's North American colonies. The Maritime provinces agreed. In September 1864, fifteen official delegates from Prince Edward Island, Nova Scotia, and New Brunswick met with eight delegates from the Province of Canada. These men are known as the Fathers of Confederation. Everyone agreed to meet again in Quebec City in October to try to draft a constitution (the basic set of rules by which the new country would be governed). They decided that much of the new country's constitution would be based on Britain's. However, instead of having just one central government, Canada would be a federal union. This meant that each province would have its own government and would control some of its own affairs, such as education. At the time the Canadian leaders were meeting, the United States, also a federal union, was being torn apart by a civil war. Macdonald believed that the American constitution gave too many powers to the states, and that this had led to the conflict. So the Fathers of Confederation reached a consensus that the central (federal) government of Canada should be stronger and have more powers than any of the provinces.

Donald Creighton
The First of July, 1867

Even after the meetings in Charlottetown and Quebec, it was not certain that Canada would actually become a nation. Each of the delegates had to return to his home province and get approval there. (And because the provinces were British colonies, they also had to get Britain's permission.) Ontario and Quebec supported Confederation. But in the Maritimes, many people were opposed. There were hard-fought provincial elections in Nova Scotia and New Brunswick before pro-Confederation leaders won the day. In Prince Edward Island, however, Confederation was rejected. (The island joined in 1873.) Fortunately, it turned out that the British Parliament was very happy to approve Canada's plan, and passed the British North America Act with very little debate. Eventually, the name "Canada" was chosen for the new union, and on July 1, 1867, Canada became a nation.

MOST OF THE POPULATION OF CANADA had gone on holiday. The parades were over; the proclamation had been read; everything official—civil or military—was finished. And the people had picked up, left their houses, and gone off to sports, games, and picnics. At Three Rivers, a large crowd of spectators watched the Union Club and the Canadian Club play "une partie de cricket." There were games in the cricket grounds at Kingston, while the band of the Royal Canadian Rifles played faithfully on during the long after-noon, and out on the waters of the bay the competing sailboats moved gracefully along the course round Garden Island and back. The citizens of Barrie turned out to Kempenfelt Bay to watch the sailing and sculling races, and to amuse themselves at the comic efforts of successive competitors to "walk the greasy pole," which extended thirty feet beyond the railway wharf, with a small flag fluttering at its end. At Dunnville, down in the Niagara Peninsula, a new race-course had just been laid out. People came from all around "to witness the birthday of the course as well as that of the nation," and while "the Dunnville and Wellandport brass bands discoursed sweet music to the multitude," the spectators watched the exciting harness race between Black Bess and Jenny Lind.

In dozens of small villages, where there were no bands or race-courses, and where there could be no water sports, the farmers and their wives and children thronged out early in the afternoon to the local fair grounds or picnic place. Sometimes this common occupied a piece of high ground just outside the village, where a great grove of maple trees gave a pleasant shelter from the heat, and sometimes it lay a mile or two away—a broad, flat stretch of meadowland, through which a shallow river ran. The wagons and buggies stood together in a row; the unharnessed horses were tethered in the shade of a group of tall elm trees; and out in the sunshine the young people and the children played their games and ran off their sports. For an hour or two the small boys who were later to drive the Canadian Pacific Railway across their country and who were to found the first homesteads in the remote prairies, jumped across bars and ran races. The long shadows were creeping rapidly across the turf when they all sat down to a substantial supper at the trestle tables underneath the trees. Afterwards they gossiped and chattered idly in the still calm evening. Then it grew slowly darker, and the children became sleepy; and they drove home over the dusty summer roads.

By nine o'clock, the public buildings and many large houses were illuminated all across Canada. And in Toronto the Queen's Park and the grounds of the private houses surrounding it were transformed by hundreds of Chinese lanterns hung through the trees. When the true darkness had at last fallen, the firework displays began; and simultaneously throughout the four provinces, the night was assaulted by minute explosions of coloured light, as the roman candles popped away, and the rockets raced up into the sky. In the cities and large towns, the spectacle always concluded with elaborate set pieces. The Montrealers arranged an intricate design with emblems representing the three uniting provinces—a beaver for Canada, a mayflower for Nova Scotia, and a pine for New Brunswick. At Toronto the words "God Save the Queen" were surrounded by a twined wreath of roses, thistles, shamrocks, and *fleur-de-lys*; and at Hamilton, while the last set pieces were blazing, four huge bonfires were kindled on the crest of the mountain. In Ottawa, Parliament Hill was crowded once again with people who had come to watch the last spectacle of the day. The Parliament buildings were illuminated. They stood out boldly against the sky; and far behind them, hidden in darkness, were the ridges of the Laurentians, stretching away, mile after mile, towards the north-west.

Traditional
Anti-Confederation Song

When the Charlottetown Conference was held in 1864, Newfoundland was not invited to attend.
The delegates knew that most people there liked their British colony just as it was. Newfoundland exported
salt fish to Europe and the West Indies, and imported food and manufactured goods from the United States.
Newfoundlanders had little to do with people in the Canadas, and even distrusted them, as this song shows very
clearly. In fact, Newfoundland stayed out of Confederation for more than eighty years. In 1949, the island
finally became Canada's tenth province, and its premier, Joey Smallwood, could rightly refer to
himself as "the only living Father of Confederation" for the rest of his long life.

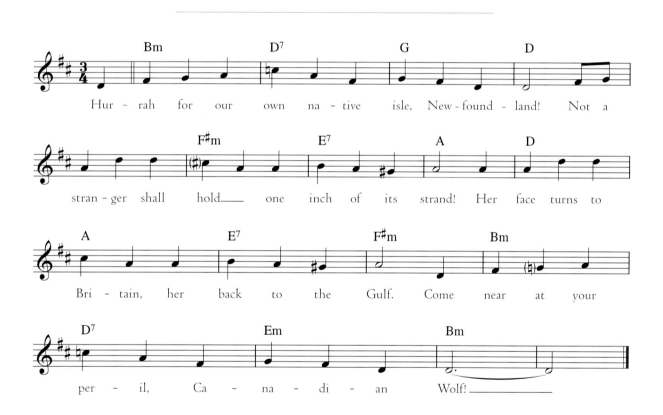

Hur – rah for our own na – tive isle, New-found-land! Not a

stran – ger shall hold___ one inch of its strand! Her face turns to

Bri – tain, her back to the Gulf. Come near at your

per – il, Ca – na – di – an Wolf!_____

1.

HURRAH FOR OUR OWN NATIVE ISLE, NEWFOUNDLAND!
Not a stranger shall hold one inch of its strand!
Her face turns to Britain, her back to the Gulf.
Come near at your peril, Canadian Wolf!

2.

Ye brave Newfoundlanders who plough the salt sea
With hearts like the eagle so bold and so free,
The time is at hand when you'll all have to say
If Confederation will carry the day.

3.

Cheap tea and molasses they say they will give,
All taxes take off that the poor man may live;
Cheap nails and cheap lumber our coffins to make,
And homespun to mend our old clothes when they break.

4.

If they take off the taxes how then will they meet
The heavy expense of the country's up-keep?
Just give them the chance to get us in the scrape
And they'll chain us as slaves with pen, ink, and red tape.

5.

Would you barter the right that your fathers have won,
Your freedom transmitted from father to son?
For a few thousand dollars of Canadian gold
Don't let it be said that your birthright was sold.

Kim Morrissey
Address to the Jury

Louis Riel is one of Canadian history's most fascinating figures. As a leader of the Northwest Rebellion of 1885, an uprising of Native and Métis (people descended from both Native Canadians and Europeans) in what is now Saskatchewan, he was denounced by many people as a threat to the country. But to the rebels, who'd been pushed out of their homeland by new settlers and felt that they were fighting for survival, he was a hero. The rebels were soon overwhelmed by the government's troops, however, and Riel was arrested and put on trial. This "found poem," which uses some of the actual words of Riel's long, rambling address to the jury, touches on issues that are still with us today: the tensions between French and English, Native and non-Native, Western Canada and the government in the East.

Your Honours

Gentlemen of the Jury:
I cannot speak
English well, but am trying
because most here
speak English

When I came to the North West
I found the Indians suffering
I found the half-breeds
eating the rotten pork
of the Hudson's Bay Company
and the whites
deprived

And so:
We have made petitions I
have made petitions
We have taken time; we have tried
And I have done my duty.

My words are
worth something.

Louis Riel
Song of Louis Riel

In 1870, the Canadian government purchased the Hudson's Bay Company's vast fur-trading lands in the northwest. Suddenly, Canada was six times as big as it had been in 1867. However, the Métis people who lived in the Red River settlement (in the valley of the Red River, in what is now Manitoba) had not been consulted. Under the leadership of Louis Riel, they demanded that the Canadian government make Red River a province with its own legislature. The government agreed, but trouble broke out between the French-speaking Métis and some English-speaking settlers. After Riel had one of the English settlers executed, the government sent troops to take control of the settlement, and Riel had to flee to the United States to escape arrest. He eventually returned to Canada and, after the Northwest Rebellion of 1885, was tried and sentenced to death by hanging, an event that caused great discord in the new nation of Canada. (In fact, it wasn't until 1998 that members of Parliament of all parties supported a bill that would overturn Riel's conviction and recognize him as one of the Fathers of Confederation—almost 130 years after Manitoba became a province in 1870.) Riel, or one of his supporters, wrote this song at the time of his imprisonment. The English translation is by Barbara Cass-Beggs.

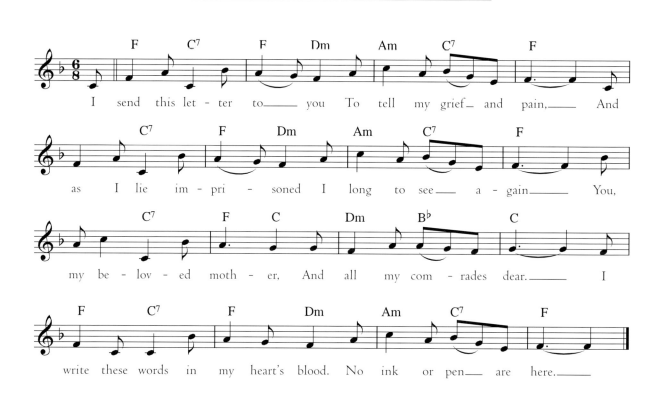

1.

I SEND THIS LETTER TO YOU
To tell my grief and pain,
And as I lie imprisoned
I long to see again
You, my beloved mother,
And all my comrades dear.
I write these words in my heart's blood.
No ink or pen are here.

2.

My friends in arms and children.
Please weep and pray for me;
I fought to keep our country
So that we might be free.
When you receive this letter,
Please weep for me and pray
That I may die with bravery
Upon that fearful day.

1.

C'est au champ de bataille,
J'ai fait crier mes douleurs,
Où tout 'cun doute se passe
Ça fait frémir les coeurs.
Or je r'çois-t-une lettre
De ma chère maman.
J'avais ni plum' ni encre.
Pour pouvoir lui écrire.

2.

Or je pris mon canif,
Je le trempai dans mon sang,
Pour écrir'-t-une lettre
A ma chère maman.
Quand ell' r'çevra cett' lettre
Toute écrit' de sang,
Ses yeux baignant de larmes,
Son coeur s'allant mourant.

3.

S'y jette à genoux par terre
En appelant ses enfants:
Priez pour votr' p'tit frère
Qui est au régiment.
Mourir, c'est pour mourir,
Chacun meurt à son tour;
J'aim' mieux mourir en brave,
Faut tous mourir un jour.

Railway Builders

Canada's first public railway line—the Champlain and Saint Lawrence Railroad in Lower Canada—opened in 1836. By the time of Confederation, New Brunswick, Quebec, and Southern Ontario were well connected by railways. In 1871, Prime Minister John A. Macdonald offered British Columbia a railway link to the rest of Canada if it would join Confederation. B.C. agreed, and became a province on July 20, 1871. The Canadian government promised to start construction from the Pacific towards the Rocky Mountains and from a point east of the Rocky Mountains towards the Pacific. Sir Sandford Fleming was appointed engineer-in-chief of the enormous project, which the government assured Canadians would be completed by 1881. And so one of the great epic achievements in Canadian history began.

Gordon Lightfoot
Canadian Railroad Trilogy

By 1880, the Canadian government had managed to build only a few short stretches of the transcontinental railway. In 1881, a group of wealthy investors formed the Canadian Pacific Railway Company and, in return for large cash payments and millions of acres of western land, promised to complete the line. They hired a strong-willed American, William Cornelius Van Horne, to push the railway through. Dynamiting through the hard rock of the Canadian Shield, the railway workers inched west. In one summer, they laid 900 kilometres (more than 550 miles) of track. Gordon Lightfoot's song commemorates both the beauty of the vast land that was transformed by the railway and the dangerous work of the "navvies" (workers) who built it.

THERE WAS A TIME IN THIS FAIR LAND WHEN THE RAILROAD DID NOT RUN,
When the wild majestic mountains stood alone against the sun.
Long before the white man, and long before the wheel
When the green dark forest was too silent to be real.

But time has no beginnings and hist'ry has no bounds,
As to this verdant country they came from all around.
They sailed upon the waterways and they walked the forests tall
Built the mines, mills and factories for the good of us all.

And when the young man's fancy was turning in the spring
The railroad men grew restless for to hear the hammers ring.
Their minds were overflowing with the visions of their day
And many a fortune won and lost and many a debt to pay.

For they looked in the future and what did they see
They saw an iron road running from the sea to the sea.
Bringin' the goods to a young growin' land
All up from the seaports and into their hands

Bring in the workers and bring up the rails
We gotta lay down the tracks and tear up the trails.
Open her heart let the lifeblood flow
Gotta get on our way 'cause we're movin' too slow.

Get on our way 'cause we're movin' too slow.
Behind the blue Rockies the sun is declinin'
The stars they come stealin' at the close of the day.
Across the wide prairie our loved ones lie sleepin'
Beyond the dark forest in a place far away.
We are the navvies who work upon the railway
Swingin' our hammers in the bright blazin' sun.
Livin' on stew and drinkin' bad whiskey
Layin' down track 'til the long days are done.
Yeah, bendin' our backs 'til the railroad is done.

Now the song of the future has been sung,
All the battles have been won,
On the mountain tops we stand,
All the world at our command,
We have opened up the soil
With our teardrops and our toil.

Paul Yee
Spirits of the Railway

In the early 1880s, some six thousand Chinese labourers were brought to Canada to build the railway that would link British Columbia to the rest of the country. They were paid a dollar a day—wages that were much lower than those of white labourers, but that were still more than ten times what they could earn in China. From the labourers' meagre earnings, foremen deducted money for the boat trip to Canada, their clothes, their room and board, and even the shovel they needed for their backbreaking work—preparing the level bed on which the railway ties were laid. Many men were injured by rock slides, but the most dangerous work, as described in this story by Paul Yee, was blasting tunnels through the mountains. Many Chinese labourers were killed when fuses went off before they could run to safety.

ONE SUMMER MANY, MANY YEARS AGO, heavy floodwaters suddenly swept through south China again. Farmer Chu and his family fled to high ground and wept as the rising river drowned their rice crops, their chickens, and their water buffalo.

With their food and farm gone, Farmer Chu went to town to look for work. But a thousand other starving peasants were already there. So when he heard there was work across the ocean in the New World, he borrowed some money, bought a ticket, and off he sailed.

Long months passed as his family waited to hear from him. Farmer Chu's wife fell ill from worry and weariness. From her hard board bed she called out her husband's name over and over, until at last her eldest son borrowed money to cross the Pacific in search of his father.

For two months, young Chu listened to waves batter the groaning planks of the ship as it crossed the ocean. For two months, he dreaded that he might drown at any minute. For two months, he thought of nothing but his father and his family.

Finally he arrived in a busy port city.

He asked everywhere for his father, but no one in Chinatown had heard the name. There were thousands of Chinese flung throughout the New World, he was told. Goldminers scrabbled along icy rivers, farmers ploughed the long low valleys, and labourers travelled through towns and forests, from job to job. Who could find one single man in this enormous wilderness?

Young Chu was soon penniless. But he was young and strong, and he feared neither danger nor hard labour. He joined a work gang of thirty Chinese, and a steamer ferried them up a river canyon to build the railway.

When the morning mist lifted, Chu's mouth fell open. On both sides of the rushing river, grey mountains rose like walls to block the sky. The rock face dropped into ragged cliffs that only eagles could ascend and jutted out from cracks where scrawny trees clung. Never before had he seen such towering ranges of dark raw rock.

The crew pitched their tents and began to work. They hacked at hills with hand-scoops and shovels to level a pathway for the train. Their hammers and chisels chipped boulders into gravel and fill. Their dynamite and drills thrust tunnels deep into the mountain. At night, the crew would sit around the campfire chewing tobacco, playing cards, and talking.

From one camp to another, the men trekked up the rail line, their food and tools dangling from sturdy shoulder poles. When they met other workers, Chu would run ahead and shout his father's name and ask for news. But the workers just shook their heads grimly.

"Search no more, young man!" one grizzled old worker said. "Don't you know that too many have died here? My own brother was buried alive in a mudslide."

"My uncle was killed in a dynamite blast," muttered another. "No one warned him about the fuse."

The angry memories rose and swirled like smoke among the workers.

"The white boss treats us like mules and dogs!"

"They need a railway to tie this nation together, but they can't afford to pay decent wages."

"What kind of country is this?"

Chu listened, but still he felt certain that his father was alive.

Then winter came and halted all work. Snows buried everything under a heavy blanket of white. The white boss went to town to live in a warm hotel, but Chu and the workers stayed in camp. The men tied potato sacks around their feet and huddled by the fire, while ice storms howled like wolves through the mountains. Chu thought the winter would never end.

When spring finally arrived, the survivors struggled outside and shook the chill from their bones. They dug graves for two workers who had succumbed to sickness. They watched the river surge alive from the melting snow. Work resumed, and Chu began to search again for his father.

Late one afternoon, the gang reached a mountain with a half-finished tunnel. As usual, Chu ran up to shout his father's name, but before he could say a word, other workers came running out of the tunnel.

"It's haunted!" they cried. "Watch out!

There are ghosts inside!"

"Dark figures slide soundlessly through the rocks!" one man whispered. "We hear heavy footsteps approaching but never arriving. We hear sighs and groans coming from corners where no man stands."

Chu's friends dropped their packs and refused to set up camp. But the white boss rode up on his horse and shook his fist at the men. "No work, no pay!" he shouted. "Now get to work!"

Then he galloped off. The workers squatted on the rocks and looked helplessly at one another. They needed the money badly for food and supplies.

Chu stood up. "What is there to fear?" he cried. "The ghosts have no reason to harm us. There is no reason to be afraid. We have hurt no one."

"Do you want to die?" a man called out.

"I will spend the night inside the tunnel," Chu declared as the men muttered unbelievingly. "Tomorrow we can work."

Chu took his bedroll, a lamp, and food and marched into the mountain. He heard the crunch of his boots and water dripping. He knelt to light his lamp. Rocks lay in loose piles everywhere, and the shadowy walls closed in on him.

At the end of the tunnel he sat down and ate his food. He closed his eyes and wondered where his father was. He pictured his mother weeping in her bed and heard her voice calling his father's name. He lay down, pulled his blankets close, and eventually he fell asleep.

Chu awoke gasping for breath. Something heavy was pressing down on his chest. He tried to raise his arms but could not. He clenched his fists and summoned all his strength, but still he was

paralyzed. His eyes strained into the darkness, but saw nothing.

Suddenly the pressure eased and Chu groped for the lamp. As the chamber sprang into light, he cried, "What do you want? Who are you?"

Silence greeted him, and then a murmur sounded from behind. Chu spun around and saw a figure in the shadows. He slowly raised the lamp. The flickering light travelled up blood-stained trousers and a mud-encrusted jacket. Then Chu saw his father's face.

"Papa!" he whispered, lunging forward.

"No! Do not come closer!" The figure stopped him. "I am not of your world. Do not embrace me."

Tears rose in Chu's eyes. "So, it's true," he choked. "You...you have left us...."

His father's voice quavered with rage. "I am gone, but I am not done yet. My son, an accident here killed many men. A fuse exploded before the workers could run. A ton of rock dropped on us and crushed us flat. They buried the whites in a churchyard, but our bodies were thrown into the river, where the current swept us away. We have no final resting place."

Chu fell upon his knees. "What shall I do?"

His father's words filled the tunnel. "Take chopsticks; they shall be our bones. Take straw matting; that can be our flesh. Wrap them together and tie them tightly. Take the bundles to the mountain top high above the nests of eagles, and cover us with soil. Pour tea over our beds. Then we shall sleep in peace."

When Chu looked up, his father had vanished. He stumbled out of the tunnel and blurted the story to his friends.

Immediately they prepared the bundles and sent him off with ropes and a shovel to the foot of the cliff, and Chu began to climb.

When he swung himself over the top of the cliff, he was so high up that he thought he could see the distant ocean. He dug the graves deeper than any wild animal could dig, and laid the bundles gently in the earth.

Then Chu brought his fists together above his head and bowed three times. He knelt and touched his forehead to the soil three times. In a loud clear voice he declared, "Three times I bow, three things I vow. Your pain shall stop now, your sleep shall soothe you now, and I will never forget you. Farewell."

Then, hanging on to the rope looped around a tree, Chu slid slowly down the cliff. When he reached the bottom, he looked back and saw that the rope had turned into a giant snake that was sliding smoothly up the rock face.

"Good." He smiled to himself. "It will guard the graves well." Then he returned to the camp, where he and his fellow workers lit their lamps and headed into the tunnel. And spirits never again disturbed them, nor the long trains that came later.

Elma Schemenauer
The Lady and the Cowcatcher

On November 7, 1885, in a small ceremony at Craigellachie, B.C., Donald A. Smith, president
of the Canadian Pacific Railway, drove in the last spike. The first transcontinental passenger train left
Montreal on a Monday evening, June 28, 1886, and arrived at Port Moody, B.C., at noon on Sunday, July 4—a
journey that just a few years before had taken weeks or months. Finally, Prime Minister John A. Macdonald's dream
of seeing the country linked by rail had become reality. He was too busy with his duties to be on that first train,
but he and his wife made the journey just a few days later. After her adventurous ride, Lady Agnes Macdonald
wrote an article about it for a British magazine. Inspired by her example, many passengers on the
early transcontinental trains made part of the journey on the cowcatcher.

THE MACDONALDS SETTLED THEMSELVES into the railway car that had been especially prepared for them. It was called the *Jamaica*, in honour of Lady Agnes, who had lived in the West Indies as a child. Everything possible had been done to make the coach comfortable and attractive. Its walls and ceiling were finished with richly carved panels of polished wood. Thick, soft velvet cushions covered the seats. The windows had even been fitted with special fine-meshed screens to keep out dust and insects.

The doors clanged shut. A shudder ran through the length of the train. There was a sudden jolt. Then slowly, ever so slowly, the locomotive began to pull out of the station. The Macdonalds watched the lights of Ottawa glide past their window. Little by little the train gathered speed. Soon it was rumbling along through the dark countryside to the west of the city. The engine whistle gave a deep full-throated roar that echoed and re-echoed and then slowly died along the track behind the speeding train.

Lady Agnes's eyes sparkled. What an adventure! She glanced across at her husband. There were tired lines across his high forehead and around his eyes. But a satisfied smile played on his lips. Perhaps he didn't feel quite the same excitement as his wife did. At seventy-one, he was much older than she was. However, in his own quiet way, he was enjoying the fruits of his long labours.

For the next two days, the train rattled along through the rock and forest of western Ontario. During the morning of July 13, the landscape started to change. Behind them now were the dark evergreens, the shining rivers and lakes, and the rocky outcroppings of pink granite. Ahead was flat open prairie, blue sky, and seemingly endless sunshine.

It wasn't long before the train rattled into the booming young city of Winnipeg. The Macdonalds stopped there for a few days to visit with friends and to attend several meetings. On July 16 they took their places in the *Jamaica* once again and continued across the prairie. Lady Macdonald remarked that it looked like perfect farming country. There were no trees to root out, no stones to pick—just beautiful rich land stretching on and on right to the horizon. Soon the train reached Regina. The Macdonalds stopped to visit there for a few days. Then they continued their westward journey.

Gleichen, a small village in what is now southern Alberta, was their next major stop. At Gleichen Sir John met with Crowfoot, a leader of the Blackfoot nation. Chief Crowfoot had done a great deal to aid the progress of the CPR by keeping peace between his people and the railway-builders. He and Sir John each made a long speech. Then the two leaders exchanged gifts. When their meeting was over, the locomotive slowly pulled out of

Gleichen and steamed across the gently rounded hills towards Calgary.

Until this time Lady Agnes had watched the changing landscape either through the wide windows of the *Jamaica*, or from a small outdoor platform at the rear of the coach. But as the train approached the mountains, she became more and more restless. She squirmed in her seat and tapped her foot on the floor. The beauty of the foothills was starting to unfold outside the windows, and she felt that she just couldn't see well enough from the coach. When the train stopped in Calgary, she asked an official to take her forward to the cab of the locomotive.

There she seated herself on a bench close to the windows right at the front of the train. She smiled happily. Ah yes, now the view was much better. Ahead of her she could see the narrow steel track stretching on and on and finally disappearing among the hazy blue mountains in the distance. And on either side she could see the soft green and brown and gold of the rolling foothills.

At length the train entered the first mountain range, which had been visible in the distance for some time. Lady Agnes craned her neck, trying to see the top of a rugged snow-capped peak. The next minute she turned to gaze down into a yawning canyon so deep that it seemed bottomless. Then the train rounded a sharp bend and she caught her breath in delight and amazement. There, tumbling straight down a sheer rock wall, was the most magnificent waterfall she had ever seen. But seconds later the plunging cataract was lost from her narrow view. She heaved a deep sigh, twisting restlessly

on her bench. If only she could see better!

When the train stopped near Banff, Alberta, the superintendent politely offered to take Lady Agnes on a tour of the outside of the locomotive. He showed her the large headlight at the front of the cab, and the little flag fluttering below it. Then he pointed out the cowcatcher. This V-shaped iron "beak" extended low over the track. Its purpose was to push aside animals or logs or anything else that lay in the path of the speeding locomotive. In the winter, the superintendent explained, it could be fitted with metal plates and used as a snowplow.

Lady Macdonald was fascinated with the cowcatcher. She noticed the large smooth platform that formed the top of it. In an instant she decided that this metal platform would be the perfect place for her to ride. From there she would be able to see the full magnificence of the mountain scenery. Nothing would obstruct her view. And how exciting it would be to ride out in the open, right at the very front of the train!

"I'm afraid you would find it too windy and dusty and noisy, madam," said the superintendent. "And besides," he added stiffly, "it would be extremely dangerous."

"You can tie me on if you like," suggested Lady Macdonald brightly. "That way, you'd be sure I couldn't fall off."

"But—" protested the superintendent.

"I'll sit right up on that box there," interrupted Lady Agnes.

Soon she was seated on the candle-box, with a felt hat pulled low over her forehead. She tucked a linen carriage-cover around herself to keep off the dust. The train superintendent felt that he simply couldn't allow the prime minister's wife to ride the cowcatcher alone. So he seated himself, somewhat grimly, on the other side of the headlight.

"This is lovely. Quite lovely," Lady Agnes shouted across to him as the train jolted itself into motion once again.

Soon it was roaring down into the deep valley of the Kicking Horse River, near the British Columbia border. The descent was swift. Hot winds whipped past Lady Agnes's face. Gritty dust sifted in through the folds of the carriage cover, turning it grey. But the view was magnificent. And what a thrill it was to hear the loud blaring of the locomotive's whistle echoing off the high canyon walls!

When the train stopped at Palliser, British Columbia, Sir John and some of his friends strolled up to pay Lady Agnes a visit. She acted in a rather "superior" manner. After all, she had shown herself to be much braver and more daring than any of them. She asked the "chief" if he would care to "step up and take a drive."

To the horror of everyone watching, the prime minister nodded his head in agreement. He nimbly leapt up to take the place of the superintendent, who then seated himself on the platform at the Macdonalds' feet. With this trio on its

cowcatcher, the locomotive raced across the flat valley of the Columbia River.

Sir John enjoyed the thrill of riding at the front of the train. He joined his wife there on several occasions later. But he really preferred the comfort of the coach and usually returned to it after a few hours.

As for Lady Agnes, she insisted that she would ride the cowcatcher right through the mountains and down to the sea. And she kept her word. The train edged its way along narrow ledges overlooking sheer dizzying cliffs. It rattled over high creaking bridges. It rumbled through dark tunnels where cold mountain springs gushed down on her. But nothing would persuade her to leave her perch.

At one point the engineer saw the billowing black smoke and the flickering orange light of a forest fire beside the track ahead. He brought the train to a shrieking halt. Then he stepped down from the cab and walked up to where Lady Agnes was sitting. He urged her to go back and sit in the coach until the train had safely passed the fire. But she refused. She simply lowered her head and gathered her long skirts tightly about her as the locomotive rushed past the bank of crackling leaping flames.

At last, on July 24, 1886, the train reached the salt water of the Pacific at Port Moody—the small town at the end of the railway track. Flushed with excitement Lady Agnes climbed down from her perch. She beamed at her husband, and at the crowds that had gathered to meet them.

Seafarers

From the days when the earliest Native peoples lived there, Atlantic Canada has traditionally drawn its livelihood from the sea. Indeed, Europeans were first attracted to the Eastern shores of Canada by the vast schools of codfish off Newfoundland. Some historians refer to the nineteenth century as "the golden age" of this region. Not only did the fishing fleets prosper, but the East Coast also became famous for its shipbuilding—fast and beautiful three- and four-masted ships. Yet most fishermen went to sea not in schooners, but in their own small fishing boats, risking the dangers of wind and storm. This age-old contest of man versus nature is a common theme in many of Atlantic Canada's traditional songs about the sea—sea shanties, songs about whaling and sealing, and ballads about disasters and ghost ships (see "The Spirit Song of George's Bank," p. 172). Folk-song scholars have pointed out that the tunes and rhythms of many of these songs, especially those from Newfoundland, have an Irish flavour.

A. R. Scammell
Squid-jiggin' Ground

"The Squid-jiggin' Ground," one of the best-known Newfoundland songs, was written by
Arthur Scammell when he was just fifteen years old. He grew up in a fishing village called Change Island on
the north coast of Newfoundland, where generations of fishermen had gone out to catch squid in the late summer
and early fall. At that time of year, large schools of squid approached the coast and were caught with "jiggers" (fish
hooks) that were jiggled up and down on the ends of lines. The song describes the fishermen's clothing as "oilskins"
(coats and pants made of cloth treated with oil to make it waterproof) and "Cape-Anns" (rainhats with an
extension on the back to protect the neck). The Squires who is referred to is Sir Richard Squires, a
corrupt former prime minister of Newfoundland. Bobby and Uncle Billy are hit
by the inky liquid that squids squirt in self-defence.

Oh! this is the place where the fish - er - men ga - ther In
oil - skins and boots and Cape - Anns bat - tened down; All
si - zes of fig - ures, with squid lines and jig - gers, They
con - gre - gate here on the squid - jig - gin' ground.

1.

OH! THIS IS THE PLACE WHERE THE FISHERMEN GATHER
In oilskins and boots and Cape-Anns battened down;
All sizes of figures, with squid lines and jiggers,
They congregate here on the squid-jiggin' ground.

2.

Some are workin' their jiggers while others are yarnin',
There's some standin' up and there's more lyin' down;
While all kinds of fun, jokes and tricks are begun,
As they wait for the squid on the squid-jiggin' ground.

3.

There's men of all ages and boys in the bargain,
There's old Billy Cave and there's young Raymond Brown,
There's a red rantin' Tory out here in a dory,
A-runnin' down Squires on the squid-jiggin' ground.

4.

There's men from the harbour; there's men from the tickle
In all kinds of motorboats, green, grey and brown;
Right yonder is Bobby and with him is Nobby,
He's chawin' hard tack on the squid-jiggin' ground.

5.

God bless my sou'wester, there's skipper John Chaffey,
He's the best hand at squid-jiggin' here, I'll be bound,
Hello! what's the row? Why, he's jiggin' one now,
The very first squid on the squid-jiggin' ground.

6.

The man with the whisker is old Jacob Steele,
He's gettin' well up but he's still pretty sound;
While uncle Bob Hawkins wears six pairs of stockin's
Whenever he's out on the squid-jiggin' ground.

7.

Holy smoke! what a scuffle, all hands are excited,
'Tis a wonder to me that there's nobody drowned,
There's a bustle, confusion, a wonderful hustle,
They're all jiggin' squids on the squid-jiggin' ground!

8.

Says Bobby, "The squids are on top of the water,
I just got me jiggers about one fathom down";
But a squid in the boat squirted right down his throat,
And he's swearin' like mad on the squid-jiggin' ground.

9.

There's poor Uncle Billy, his whiskers are spattered
With spots of the squid juice that's flying around;
One poor little boy got it right in the eye,
But they don't give a darn on the squid-jiggin' ground.

10.

Now if ever you feel inclined to go squiddin',
Leave your white shirts and collars behind in the town,
And if you get cranky, without yer silk hanky,
You'd better steer clear of the squid-jiggin' ground.

Traditional
Jack Was Every Inch a Sailor

This humorous song recalls the biblical story of Jonah and the Whale, though the setting has been changed to Newfoundland and Labrador. Bacalhao (pronounced "Buck-a-loo") is a rocky island off the east coast of Newfoundland whose Portuguese name means "codfish." Indian Harbour, on the Labrador coast, was a cod-fishing centre around the beginning of the twentieth century. Whaling was an important economic activity in nineteenth-century Newfoundland, when whale oil was used for streetlamps and soap, and baleen (whale-bone from the roof of whale's mouth) was used for buggy whips, skirt hoops, umbrellas, and fishing rods. As long as whales were hunted with hand-held harpoons, whaling was a dangerous contest between man and animal, but more powerful weapons such as the harpoon gun turned the whale hunt into a slaughter. Many whale species were all but wiped out by the early twentieth century, although some are now making a comeback. In 1972, the Canadian government ordered the last two Newfoundland whaling operations to shut down. Today, only the Inuit are allowed to hunt whales.

Now, 'twas twen-ty-five or thir-ty hears since Jack first saw the light. He came in-to this world of woe one dark and storm-y night. He was born on board his fa-ther's ship as she was ly-ing to 'Bout twen-ty-five or thir-ty miles south-east of Bac-al-hoo. Jack was ev'-ry inch a sai-lor, Five and twen-ty years a whal-er, Jack was ev'-ry inch a sai-lor, He was born up-on the bright blue sea.

1.

NOW, 'TWAS TWENTY-FIVE OR THIRTY YEARS SINCE JACK FIRST SAW THE LIGHT.
He came into this world of woe one dark and stormy night.
He was born on board his father's ship as she was lying to
'Bout twenty-five or thirty miles southeast of Bacalhoo.

Chorus:
　　Jack was ev'ry inch a sailor,
　　Five and twenty years a whaler,
　　Jack was ev'ry inch a sailor,
　　He was born upon the bright blue sea.

2.
　　When Jack grew up to be a man, he went to Labrador;
　　He fished in Indian Harbour, where his father fished before.
　　On his returning in the fog, he met a heavy gale,
　　And Jack was swept into the sea and swallowed by a whale.

Chorus

3.
　　The whale went straight for Baffin's Bay 'bout ninety knots an hour,
　　And ev'ry time he'd blow a spray he'd send it in a shower.
　　"Oh now," says Jack unto himself, "I must see what he's about";
　　He caught the whale all by the tail and turned him inside out.

Chorus

Traditional
Nova Scotia Song

Helen Creighton was a folklorist who collected more than four thousand traditional folksongs
sung in Nova Scotia in English, French, Gaelic, Mi'kmaq, and German. Perhaps the most famous song in
her collection was "Nova Scotia Song," which she first heard sung about seventy years ago in Petpeswick and
Chezzetcook, near Halifax. In the 1960s, it was the theme song of a popular CBC Television show from Halifax
called "Singalong Jubilee," and it became well known across Canada. It tells a story of leave-taking,
apparently by a young man who is headed for naval service in a war. However, the melody and chorus—
perhaps based on an old sea shanty—are so stirring that the overall effect of the song is not sad.

1.

THE SUN WAS SETTING IN THE WEST,
The birds were singing on ev'ry tree,
All nature seemed inclined for rest,
But still there was no rest for me.

Chorus:
Farewell to Nova Scotia, the sea-bound
  coast!
Let your mountains dark and dreary be,
For when I am far away on the briny
  ocean tossed
Will you ever heave a sigh and a wish for
  me?

2.

I grieve to leave my native land,
I grieve to leave my comrades all,
And my parents whom I hold so dear,
And the bonny, bonny lass that I do
  adore.

Chorus

3.

The drums they do beat and the wars do
  alarm.
The captain calls, we must obey,
So farewell, farewell to Nova Scotia's
  charms,
For it's early in the morning I am far, far
  away.

Chorus

4.

I have three brothers and they are at rest,
Their arms are folded on their breast,
But a poor simple sailor just like me
Must be tossed and driven on the dark
  blue sea.

Chorus

obvious disadvantages of everybody carrying his own coins and safeguarding them from thieves and pickpockets led to an acceptable compromise. Strong cases were built, the money packed into them, and six sturdy young men were assigned to guard them at all times. By the time they reached Canada more and more men asked for some of their money in order to buy whatever they thought they would need to make a fresh start in Manitoba. It was in Collingwood, Ontario, while they waited to transfer from the railway to a Great Lakes steamer that Erdman agreed to redistribute the money.

"Spread some sheets on the floor. Now, you gold carriers, get ready to empty your cases. I'll come around to each pile and count it with you to make sure it's all there." The six did as they were told while the rest of the men filled the hall like a crowd around a boxing ring.

"The count in every pile is correct," Erdman announced presently. "Now I want all of you to come past one by one with your receipts to collect what belongs to you. No pushing or shoving, please."

The distribution had hardly begun, however, when there was an interruption. A Canadian employee of the Immigration Hall opened the unbolted door without knocking, presumably to bring a message or announcement. What his business was was never established. When he saw more gold on the floor than he had ever dreamed of, his eyes protruded, his mouth dropped open, and without saying a word he turned and half ran out the door, closing it firmly behind him.

The crowd reacted with alarm. "I wonder what he wanted?" one man asked.

"I don't know," said another, "but I'd feel an awful lot safer about taking my money if he hadn't seen this."

"It was stupid of us not to lock the door," said Erdman. "However, I think we should go ahead with the distribution. What this means is that every one of us must be very careful, at least until we leave Collingwood. I think it would be better if we all stayed together from now on and none of us went into town any more."

So, the division of the money continued. As each man got what belonged to him, he countersigned the receipt he had brought from Russia and returned it to Erdman. At last it was finished. With a sigh of relief Erdman said, "There, it looks as if it's all come out even. Is everybody satisfied?"

There were general expressions of approval. Peter, stolid though he was, considered himself somewhat of a wit, so he said, "If you have any left over or if anybody has more than they want, I could be talked into taking a little more."

As the first man to leave reached the door he opened it but then quickly closed it again. "Police!" he exclaimed. "There are policemen out there."

An uneasy quiet fell over the crowd. In their almost self-governing villages in Russia they seldom had dealings with the czar's security forces and when they did, the experience was usually not a happy one.

"We haven't done anything wrong, have we?" asked Jacob Friesen. "Is it wrong to have money in Canada, Erdman? Or to get it out and count it?"

"No," answered Erdman, "I'm sure that

Canadians have money and enjoy looking at it and counting it from time to time just as you do. I think the servant acted so strangely because he was surprised to see so much gold in one place."

The crowd became a babble of voices. Most of the comments and questions were addressed to nobody in particular. Some were directed to Erdman because it was generally acknowledged that he had more worldly experience and financial sense than the others.

"Maybe he doesn't realize that it belongs to all of us and that it's all we have. If he thinks it all belongs to one of us, then he would naturally think it was stolen."

"How can we prove it's not stolen? Erdman, you have our receipts. Show the police our receipts to prove that we each own only a little bit."

"If we can convince them that none of us is rich they may feel sorry for us."

"For sure we'll have to bribe them to let us go on. If we don't they'll think of some reason to keep us here for weeks."

"Maybe we should give it back to you, Erdman. It would be easier to hide a few packages than all our separate money bags."

Erdman tried to keep a semblance of order in the anxious crowd. "I'm sure we've broken no law. Stay here for a few minutes. I'll go out and talk to them and find out what they want of us."

So he went out alone to speak to the police. But first he took out a few coins and hid them in his hand where they would be readily available. In Russia there had been similar occasions when he dealt with representatives of the law and he knew they sometimes made an opportunity for him to slip them something discreetly. As luck would have it, one of the guards spoke a little German.

"Good day, honoured sirs." Erdman addressed them as humbly and respectfully as he knew how. "To what do we owe the pleasure of this visit?"

The policeman had never been in a situation remotely resembling this one before, so, if possible, he was even more uncertain about how to handle it than Erdman was. "We wondered if we could be of help to you," he said lamely.

"Thank you, but we wish only to be allowed to proceed in peace to our destination in Manitoba."

"But all that gold," he was emboldened to ask. "What are you doing with all that gold?"

"It belongs to us," Erdman assured him, "obtained by honest work and not through theft or unlawful means. And although it may appear to be a great deal, it is pitifully little when you consider how many owners claim it. For many it will be much less than is needed to establish a working homestead." Erdman was willing to offer a sizeable bribe but he didn't want the Canadians to get any unreasonable expectations so he wanted to make sure they realized that they were dealing with a group of extremely poor immigrants.

"But all that gold!" the guard exclaimed again. "Why did you have it lying on the floor? And without even locking the door."

"We brought it across the ocean in a safe way. Now that everybody needs it for his own uses we were distributing it to the individuals to whom it belongs,"

Erdman explained quite simply and truthfully. "As to the open door, I agree that was careless. But we thought we were among ourselves, among friends."

"Lucky for you, you are among friends." Then, as he turned to indicate the meeting was finished, he added to his companions in English, "Anybody that does things like that sure needs friends."

Erdman returned the handful of coins to his pocket and went back into the hall. Had the signal for a bribe been given so subtly that he had missed it? But he didn't have time to think about that question because he was met by a barrage of demands from the anxious crowd.

"Can we keep our money?"

"Will they let us go?"

"How much blood money did you have to give them?"

"What excuse did he give you for making trouble for us?"

"Quiet, quiet," said Erdman. "I'm still just as much in the dark as you are. He accused us of nothing. He didn't give me a cue for a bribe, or if he did I missed it. He even suggested they were our friends."

"Did you ever hear of a policeman being a friend to anybody?" Peter was trying to be funny again. "To his own wife, maybe."

"What do we do now?" Jacob was more practical. "They know we have it, so it's no use trying to hide it. Would it be possible to put it all back into the cases again and send a few secretly to Manitoba by a different way?"

"What other way is there to Manitoba?" asked Erdman. "Is there anyone among us who can find his way to Manitoba?"

There were no volunteers. Up to now their journey had been through settled

parts of the world. But they all knew they were presently waiting for a ship to take them to the United States because the alternative Canadian route was through a wilderness that presented great difficulties. Certainly they would need a guide. But how could they find a guide and still maintain secrecy? And how could they be sure they could trust the guide? After a considerable pause Erdman continued. "I suggest we carry on as if nothing had happened. Stay in or near the Immigration Buildings. Certainly don't wander into town alone. Sleep on your money bags until we get away from here."

Just as the gathering was breaking up news arrived that the ship was ready for

boarding. In the bustle of rounding up children and belongings and making sure that nobody or nothing was left behind there was little opportunity for discussion of the occurrence in the Immigration Hall. Erdman returned to the subject as he and Jacob stood in the crowd at the rail watching the sailors prepare to cast off. "I'm relieved that we've got this far without any more interference. I'll be even more relieved when we leave this ship at Duluth and get on an American train, because then we'll be beyond the power of the Canadian police."

"And by the time we get back into Canada in Manitoba we'll be hundreds of miles from here, and there the police won't know anything about our gold," Jacob continued the train of thought. "You and I could afford to give up a few coins by way of a bribe. But some of our brethren—a few coins is all some of them have. How will they ever manage to start a farm?"

"Let me remind you that when we decided to leave Russia we agreed that the five villages of our Bergthal Colony would go as a group except for the few who didn't want to come. This meant that nobody would have to stay behind for lack of means. In one way or another those who can do so will pay the expenses of those in need. When we get to the land reserved for us we must make sure that

Mamma, she just nurses the baby. She brings her back when you are well. Have no fear."

My father smiled at me. "She knows. That is not why she cries," he said, so the tears remained a mystery to me.

The train trip took a long, long time of noise and soot-grimed seats and a tunnel through a dark forest. Finally it was time to take our boxes and bags down the steep steps to a little wooden platform. A cold March wind assaulted our faces and the sun on the snow dazzled our eyes. But there was Wasyl Demetruk, our neighbour from the Ukraine, now two years in this country, pounding my father on the back in unrestrained joy, and the two of them talking all at once in an amazing way.

I remember being huddled beside Maria and Lena in the back of a big sleigh with double runners and Wasyl wrapping heavy robes about us. We went past the little station-house with the sign spelling "Whitemouth" and a few more buildings and then suddenly we were in the bush again. I had felt a joy on leaving the train, but the bush, so dark, so close, robbed me of it for a while.

We stayed with the Demetruks for two weeks or more, and that was a happy time. I tumbled in the snow with Metro and John and leaned my forehead against the warm, familiar flank of a cow while I streamed milk into a pail. I fed the geese and took eggs from beneath the protesting hens, and best of all, felt the earth solid and unmoving beneath my feet.

Each day Wasyl and my father went off through the trees and I understood that a home was being prepared for us—a log house with a low loft, like the Demetruks'.

By late March the sun was beginning to show some strength against the snow.

Brown patches of earth were appearing along the south sides of the stable and the house.

My father explained to my mother. "Wasyl tells me that when the break comes, the swamp between our place and this place will flow like a river for a time. We must move now. First, I go to Whitemouth to buy a bed and a stove, then we go to our own place while the ice still holds."

He took from his pocket a little roll of bills and spilled some silver coins on the table and counted all of it twice over. Then he wrote down on a paper what would be needed; besides the bed and stove, a barrel of flour, sugar, tea, oatmeal. We had a small supply of quilts and dishes and the Demetruks gave us straw for our ticking and feathers for our pillows and even meat, still frozen. We had enough.

"Potatoes," Wasyl said as we were leaving. "Plant potatoes first and cabbages. They spring from the earth! Next year when the stumps are out, oats and maybe a little barley. There's wild hay a-plenty, east of the swamp. You'll do all right. You'll do all right."

But it was not all so easy. Still, there was no despair in us until that day of the empty flour barrel. I remember that day, hour by hour, even minute by minute.

Father had gone away. He and Wasyl had planned that in July they would go, the two of them, to Whitemouth and then down the CPR line from farm to farm, haying for cash payment. When we had first come to our homestead Father had a dollar bill, soft with much handling, and some coins, still remaining from his little hoard, but by June this money was entirely gone. Cash from the haying would buy provisions, geese, maybe even a cow. He had been gone two weeks on that particular day.

I awoke to the sound of rain...rain softening the continuous swish of the poplars, rain drumming against the roof and dripping through the poplar shakes that covered it. My mother was already up, putting a pot to catch the drips that came by the stove, and pulling the bed where Maria and Lena still slept away from the wall to escape a dampening from another leak.

I lay awhile, pretending sleep. There had been so much rain, so many days when the grey sky seemed to rest on the treetops, when the earth was slippery beneath my bare feet, the wood smoking in the stove and everything smelling of damp and rot. I was weary of it. I had sense enough to realize, too, that while it rained there would be no haying for Wasyl and my father.

I did not get up until I smelled the porridge cooking. It was thin, watery stuff, without milk or sugar and I was weary of it also, but not so unknowing as my eight-year-old sister Maria who protested loudly.

"I don't want porridge, Mamma. Can't we have bread?"

Mother went and brought out half a loaf from the crock and held it up and said, "This is the last of the bread. If you eat it now you eat porridge for supper. It makes no difference. There is this bread and oatmeal and tea and potatoes. That is all."

"Make more bread, Mamma," said Lena, who was barely five.

"There is no flour in the barrel," said my mother.

I was cross with Maria because she went and took the lid off the flour barrel and peered in, disbelieving.

"It's all scraped out bare," she said in dismay.

"When Papa comes home he will bring flour," I said hastily. "Any day now. Flour and meat and sugar and canned milk, even."

Then my mother looked at me, a long look. Only her eyes and the corners of her mouth spoke, but I read their message well. Unless the sun shone hot and strong for several days, only two things could happen—either Father would come home without flour or he would be gone many, many more days.

By noon the rain stopped and the clouds thinned, so that the sun showed

through, pale and hazy. It was cheering to see even the faint shadows made by the light coming in the little square windows and we went outside to walk around on the wet earth, a welcome release from the heavy air of the house, so long closed against the rain.

I don't know how much later it was that we missed the baby. Anna was almost two now, and could walk well, her short legs being sturdy and straight. She wandered here, she wandered there, always with Maria or Lena or myself to catch her under the arms and propel her back to the doorstep before she went too far. Who was at fault that she evaded us this time? I was, after all, the eldest. Still, minding the baby was surely girls' work. Couldn't Maria have kept better watch? In any case, Anna was suddenly out of sight.

We went down among all the potatoes and cabbages, expecting to find her there in the garden patch. But she was not. We tore along the edge of the entire clearing—it was but an acre after all—peering into the bush for a glimpse of her bright blue dress or pale yellow hair. There was nothing but moving grey-green shadows. So then, with fear pressing hard against our chests, we had to go and tell Mother.

Her eyes flashed with quick alarm, but she kept her voice composed as she spoke to us.

"She cannot be far. Those little legs. She may even have dropped off to sleep, curled up, hidden by bushes. You go that way, Joseph; Maria, Lena, this way. Call her, then listen. She will cry if she's frightened."

So we went again, up and down,

between the stumps, and into the edge of the bush all around, calling, "Anna, Anna" and listening. But the only sound that came back to us was the cruel tapping of a woodpecker against a dead tree.

When Mother called us all to her, her face was grey, as grey as it had been on the ship. We stood, all four, and turned slowly to survey the wall of poplar and thick underbrush that hemmed us, looking for something that might have attracted the baby to that shadowy world. Finally Mother said, "No, I do not think she would go into the bush. It must be that she has gone along the trail towards"—her voice dropped to a whisper—"the swamp."

In a dry year the swamp was not formidable in summer, being an area of bulrushes, coarse reeds, and grasses. But that first summer, the swollen creek had spilled from its deep trench and spread out in a wide circle on both sides to within a few rods of our clearing. The trail that led to town skirted deep holes and jumped from hummock to hummock. In places Father had laid logs across some of the pools, otherwise he would have been completely cut off. So Mother breathed her words with terror, and turned and began to run, looking wildly from side to side, calling, "Anna, Anna, Little One!"

She splashed through ankle-deep water and her dress was soon flapping wetly about her knees. She darted this way and that, pushing the bulrushes aside with her arms, drawing back in alarm when her feet sank deeply in the soft earth. We followed, Maria, Lena, and I, more nimbly perhaps, but less quickly. Maria began to wail and I turned on her in fierce anger.

"Stop it. Stop it. What good to bawl? Listen for the baby."

Finally Mother stumbled and fell full length into mire and water. I thought how small she looked, lying there, but I did not reach out to help her to her feet. Somehow it seemed to me that we must stay apart, that she would not wish her children to share too closely in her anguish.

She got up slowly, first on her elbows, then sitting, but still did not rise to her feet. We all stood back a little. Then she began to speak and never before and not since have I heard her express in words the full emotions of her heart. Although her head was raised and her gaze directed along the ill-defined trail to town, I was not sure whether she spoke to my father somewhere out there, or just to herself.

"It cannot be. We cannot survive it. It rains and rains till nothing remains dry. The roof leaks in a new place every day and there is no straw or hay for thatching. We are so alone, so alone. There is no church, no priest, no school for the children. There is no meat and no flour in the barrel. And now what happens? The baby is lost, lost."

She gave a hoarse cry as though the sound were torn from her throat. Maria began to whimper again and I think I slapped her.

"Come," I said, "we keep looking."

We went back the way we had come, more slowly, I with my heart wild beneath my ribs, Maria sniffing loudly, and little Lena, pale and frightened and not quite understanding why. Mother had not come back to herself and we left her sitting huddled on the wet grass.

We had retraced our steps nearly all the way back to the clearing when I saw the first sign, the prints of tiny bare feet in the mud at the very beginning of the low ground. I began to holler, but I can't remember if it was the baby or Mother I called. There were low, scrubby willows in that place and in a moment, I saw Anna, sitting in a tangle of branches, her blue eyes wide but without tears. I picked her up, and how warm and tight her plump little arms were around my neck.

Then Mother was there and took her from me. She hugged her hard against herself for a moment and then sat down on a high hummock with Anna on her knee, brushing her silky light hair back from her little round face, examining the scratches on her arms and legs, all the time murmuring, "Naughty little Anna to run away," in a tone that denied the reproachful words. Suddenly she stopped and stared hard at the baby's face and then at her chubby little hands.

"Joseph, look at her, look at her," she said excitedly.

I looked. There were red stains on the baby's lips, on her chin and her little fingers and the palms of her hands were deeply stained.

"She's been eating berries," said Mother. "Look at the scratches! Somewhere near are raspberries!" Her eyes had a bright look I had not seen since we left the Demetruks.

"Do you understand, Joseph? We pick these berries and we take them to Whitemouth. The storekeeper buys them. Sophie Demetruk tells me. A dollar, sometimes a whole dollar for a pail. Find the bushes, Joseph. They cannot be far.

Maria, Lena, to the house. Get pails. We all pick, every one of us." She glanced at the sky, where the sun was still a pale ball behind clouds. "There is time. Joseph goes today with a pail, maybe two. He comes home before dark with flour. When your father comes we already have flour in the barrel."

After the exhausting fear of losing the baby I felt weary to my bones, but Mother seemed charged with energy. It did not take us long to find the berry patch. It was on a rise of gravelly ground behind the willows. A fire had gone through there some years before because the dead trunks of big trees were there, almost hidden now in a tangle of Saskatoon, chokecherry and raspberry bushes. Beyond were the tall poplars that screened the place effectively from our house and clearing. Still, we scolded each other for not having discovered it sooner and marvelled again and again that Anna had been the one to lead us to it.

As we picked, Mother kept repeating. "Think of it, flour in the barrel when your father comes!"

Listening to her, I began to view the tiresome five-mile walk into town that was ahead of me as a privilege.

Everything came about in time: first, flour in the barrel, then Father home with cash money, and before fall, a cow and a good thatch for the roof. Then, a lime wash for our mud-chinked walls and even, as the years passed, a church, a priest and a school.

This I know, once we had filled the flour barrel by our own efforts, my mother knew all things could be accomplished.

PART FIVE

Imagination

Illustrated by
Zhong-Yang Huang

Tall Tales

You may think that tall tales take their name from the fact that many of their heroes, like Paul Bunyan and Joe Mufferaw, are gigantic in size and strength. But in fact, the word "tall" in this sense means exaggerated to the point of being unbelievable. Every culture has its own folklore—the songs, legends, and proverbs that are passed on from one generation to the next. Traditional tall tales, so enjoyable to tell and to hear, are part of folklore. Sometimes they begin with a grain of truth, but as they pass from one person to another and another, they grow more and more fanciful. Stories about Ti-Jean date back hundreds of years in French Canada; Paul Bunyan and Johnny Chinook have been around for generations. Tall tales don't have to be old, however—anyone can invent one, as bp Nichol's "Fish Story" shows.

Eva Martin
Ti-Jean Brings Home the Moon

Tales about Ti-Jean (the short form of Petit Jean, which means Little John) were brought to Canada by the early settlers of New France. They were passed from one storyteller to another for many generations, without ever being written down. In the twentieth century, folklorists collected more than a hundred Ti-Jean stories just in Quebec and Ontario, and hundreds more have been collected in France, Louisiana, and the French-speaking Caribbean countries. Ti-Jean lives in a magic fairy-tale world of kings, princesses, and giants. He usually begins the story as a humble peasant; his parents and neighbours may even think him a fool. Yet Ti-Jean has complete confidence in his own powers, and he takes on seemingly impossible tasks that others are afraid to try. Many Ti-Jean stories have never been published— or even told—in English; this one is a modern retelling by Eva Martin.

ONE DAY THE KING CALLED TI-JEAN TO appear before him. "Ti-Jean," he asked, "is it true that you are telling everyone that you can bring back the seven-league boots that the giant keeps chained under his bed?"

"No," said Ti-Jean, "I did not say that, Your Majesty. But if you wish me to do it, I will try. But I will need two things to take with me."

"What will you need?"

"I will need an invisible coat and a file that cuts through one inch of steel with each scrape."

It took the king some time to find those things, but finally he handed them over to Ti-Jean.

Ti-Jean put on the invisible coat, thrust the file in his pocket, and set off through the forest.

The giant lived in the heart of the forest, far beyond the old ruined church where the unicorn had been captured. Ti-Jean travelled and travelled until finally he came to the giant's house. He peeked in the window. The giant and his wife and little girl were having their supper. The little girl was sitting on the floor, but even so, she was so tall that she towered over Ti-Jean. Still wearing the invisible

coat, Ti-Jean crept into the giant's house, found the bedroom and crawled under the bed. There were the seven-league boots anchored to the floor with a three-inch chain.

When supper was finished, the giant had a long smoke and finally they all went to bed. Soon they were snoring loudly. Carefully, Ti-Jean took the file from his pocket, grasped the chain and made one scrape. The sparks flew and the noise was so great that the giant jumped out of bed, saying, "Hey, hey, someone is in this

room. There is someone under that bed, I know there is!"

"Go back to bed, you lout," said his wife. "You were only dreaming."

"I know there is someone under this bed and I am going to get down and see who it is," roared the giant.

The giant's wife gave him such a cuff on the head, saying, "Go to sleep, you old fool," that he finally lay down, and soon they were all snoring again.

Ti-Jean put a boot on each foot. Then he took the file and quickly made two scrapes. The chain lay in pieces. Wearing the seven-league boots, Ti-Jean leapt out the door and was halfway through the forest, travelling seven leagues at each step, leaving the giant roaring in the doorway, shaking his fist.

The king was very pleased to receive the seven-league boots. They would come in handy when he went striding vigorously throughout the countryside. But the coachman was more jealous than ever, because everyone was talking about Ti-Jean's exploits.

One day, the coachman said to the king, "Your Majesty, do you know what that fellow Ti-Jean is saying now? He is telling everyone that he could go back to the giant's house and bring back the moon that the giant keeps there."

"Well," said the king, "if he said that, then he must do it." He called Ti-Jean before him and said, "Ti-Jean, is it true that you are telling people that you are not afraid to go to the giant's house and bring back the moon that he keeps hanging from the ceiling?"

"No," replied Ti-Jean, "I did not say that at all. But if you want me to, I will try to do it. But I will need something to take with me."

"What will you need this time? I hope it will not be too difficult to find."

"This time I will only need a five-pound bag of salt," Ti-Jean replied.

"That's easy," said the king, and he provided the five-pound bag of salt. Ti-Jean put on the invisible coat again and away he went through the forest to the giant's house. When he arrived there, he peeked in the door, and there was the giant bending over an enormous pot, making soup.

Ti-Jean waited until the giant turned away to cut up the vegetables for the soup. Then he crept into the house, climbed up on a stool, and dumped the five-pound bag of salt into the soup. Then he hid behind the door. The giant finished cutting up the vegetables and threw them into the soup and stirred and stirred until the soup was done. Then he and his wife sat at the table and began to drink the soup.

Something was not quite right about the soup. The giant began to hiccup. "Wife, hiccup," he said. "Why did you put so much salt in the soup, hiccup?"

"I didn't put any salt in the soup," said his wife.

"Well, hiccup, there is certainly something wrong with it, hiccup." Then he said to his little girl, "Go out to the well in the yard and bring me a barrel of water so I can quench my thirst and get rid of these hiccups."

"Oh, no," cried the little giant girl. "I can't do that. I am too afraid. It is too dark out there in the yard."

"Then take down the moon from its hook in the ceiling and it will light your way to the well."

The giant's daughter got down the moon from its hook and held it in front of her so it would light a path to the well. Ti-Jean, still wearing the invisible coat, crept out the door and followed her. When she was well across the yard, he grabbed the moon from her and was halfway through the forest before the giant family realized what had happened.

The king was very pleased to receive the moon. He hung it up in a tree where everyone in the countryside could see it. And Ti-Jean was pleased, too.

Dell J. McCormick
Paul Bunyan Digs the St. Lawrence River

About one hundred years ago, lumberjacks in Canada and the United States began to tell
tales about a giant woodsman named Paul Bunyan and his huge blue ox, Babe. Paul could chop down
whole forests in a single day and break the tallest tree in half with his hands. In 1914, the Blue River Lumber
Company of Minnesota started printing and giving away booklets of Paul Bunyan stories to promote their business.
Soon people all over North America, even those far away from the lumber camps, knew about Paul Bunyan.
Although more of the stories are set in the United States, some Canadians who study folklore think the
first Paul Bunyan stories may have come from north of the border. "Bunyan" might come from
"Bon Jean," one of the names for Ti-Jean, a well-known French-Canadian character (see
p. 159). This version of one of Paul's adventures was first published in 1936, and
appeared in Canadian school readers in the 1940s and 1950s.

ONE SUMMER PAUL DECIDED TO LEAVE
the North Woods and go back to Maine
to visit his father and mother. When he
arrived, they talked about old times, and
Paul asked about Billy Pilgrim, the
biggest man in that part of the country.

"What is this Billy Pilgrim doing?"
asked Paul.

"He is digging the St. Lawrence River
between the United States and Canada,"
said Paul's father. "There was nothing to
separate the two countries. People never
knew when they were in the United

States and when they were in Canada."

Paul Bunyan went to see Billy. He
found that Billy Pilgrim and his men had
been digging for three years and had dug
only a very small ditch. Paul laughed
when he saw it.

"My men could dig the St. Lawrence
River in three weeks," said Paul.

This made Billy angry, for he thought
no one could dig a large river in three
weeks.

"I will give you a million dollars if you
can dig the St. Lawrence River in three

weeks!" said Billy Pilgrim.

So Paul sent for Babe the Blue Ox, Ole the Big Swede, Brimstone Bill, and all his woodsmen.

Paul told Ole to make a huge scoop shovel as large as a house. They fastened it to Babe with a long buckskin rope. He hauled many tons of dirt every day and emptied the scoop shovel in Vermont. You can see the large piles of dirt there to this day. They are called the Green Mountains.

Every night Johnnie Inkslinger, who did the arithmetic, would take his large pencil and mark one day off on the wall calendar.

Billy Pilgrim was afraid they would finish digging the river on time. He did not want to pay Paul Bunyan the million dollars, for at heart he was a miser. So he thought of a plan to prevent Paul from finishing the work.

One night Billy called his men together and said, "When everybody has gone to bed we will go out and pour water on the buckskin rope so it will stretch, and Babe the Blue Ox will not be able to pull a single shovelful of dirt!"

The next day, Babe started towards Vermont with the first load of dirt. When he arrived there, he looked around, and the huge scoop shovel was nowhere to be seen. For miles and miles the buckskin rope had stretched through the forests and over the hills.

Babe didn't know what to do. He sat down and tried to think, but everyone knows an ox isn't very bright; so he just sat there. After a while the sun came out and dried the buckskin and it started to shrink to normal size.

Babe planted his large hoofs between two mountains and waited. The buckskin rope kept shrinking and shrinking. Soon the scoop shovel came into view over the hills. Then Babe emptied it and started back after another load.

In exactly three weeks the St. Lawrence River was all finished, but still Billy Pilgrim did not want to pay Paul the money.

"Very well," said Paul, "I will remove the water!" So he led Babe the Blue Ox down to the river, and Babe drank the St. Lawrence River dry.

Billy Pilgrim only chuckled to himself, for he knew that the first rain would fill it again. Soon it began to rain, and the river became as large as ever.

So Paul picked up a large shovel.

"If you do not pay the money you owe me I will fill the river up again," said Paul.

He threw in a shovelful of dirt. He threw in another and another, but still Billy Pilgrim would not pay him the money.

"I will pay you half your money," said Billy.

Paul again picked up his shovel and tossed more dirt into the river.

"I will pay you two-thirds of your money," said Billy.

Paul kept throwing more dirt into the river until he had thrown a thousand shovelfuls.

"Stop! I will pay you all your money!" cried Billy.

So Paul Bunyan was finally paid in full for digging the St. Lawrence River. The thousand shovelfuls of dirt are still there.

They are called the Thousand Islands.

Robert E. Gard
Johnny Chinook

Although Johnny Chinook's outrageous adventures could never really happen, they are inspired by an amazing weather condition—the chinook—that actually exists. The chinook is a warm, dry wind that swoops down the eastern slopes of the Rocky Mountains into southwestern Alberta. Gusting up to 160 kilometres (100 miles) per hour, the chinook can raise the temperature by as much as ten to fifteen degrees in an hour. In the midst of winter, the chinook melts snow and brings the warmth of spring, sometimes just for a few hours and sometimes for many days.

JOHNNY CHINOOK IS A FAMOUS YARN spinner. His best tall tale is the one he tells about the Chinook wind. One day during the big snow, Johnny had to go to Calgary. He harnessed the horse, hitched him to the sleigh, and set out. When he was about halfway to town, he heard a rustling noise. He knew what that was. It was a Chinook stealing up behind him. He whipped up his horse, but the harder he whipped, the harder blew the Chinook wind. The snow melted like magic!

"Boys," said Johnny, "'Twas all I could do to keep the front runners on the snow! The back runners were raising a dust storm."

One of Johnny's best yarns is the one he tells about the hot winter.

"The fall was mighty warm," says Johnny, "just like summer. It cooled off a little in October, though we were mostly working in our shirt sleeves. Middle of December came and no snow. In fact it was warmer than ever. Some of the boys began to plant a few potatoes just to see what would happen. When they started to sprout, a lot of the homesteaders put in wheat and garden stuff.

"The crops came up and by February were doing well. We got rain instead of snow. Indeed the weather was like one long Chinook. Biggest trouble we had was with the mosquitoes. They were as big as sparrows by this time, not having died off in the fall. We carried baseball bats to fight them off. They were too fat to fly much, just buzzed round slowly.

"In the spring the boys decided not to do any spring seeding because the winter-sown stuff was doing so well. By midsummer the potatoes were up to our shoulders and the wheat had stems like small willows. It came mighty hot in August and fearing fire, we cut the grain with bucksaws. The straw made fine drainpipes once it dried out.

"We took up the potatoes in September. That *was* a job. The little ones we could lift, but the big ones we just heaved up with a crowbar and let them lie. Carrots we drew off with a block and tackle. 'Twas lucky we had a good crop that year, though, for the next year there wasn't any summer at all."

Johnny's very best story is the one about the high wind. "One day when we were on the roundup," says Johnny, "a terrific wind started to blow. I knew it was going to be a humdinger, so I picked out the biggest steer I could find and slung him back of my saddle to hold down the horse and keep us from being blown away. The other boys saw what I was doing and they did the same. The wind blew so cold, so hard and so long that we got pneumonia. All the other fellows died and I was left alone.

"The wind blew for days, but the horse and I and the steer stuck together. Barns, houses, chickens, fences, and all kinds of things kept blowing past us. The funniest thing of all was an old fellow sitting in a rocking chair, sailing through the air. As he came near, he yelled for a match to light his pipe. By the time I'd dug one out, he was out of sight. Pretty soon a telephone came blowing by, so I grabbed it and told the operator in the next township that an old fellow in a rocking chair was heading her way and would she see to it that somebody had a light ready for his pipe.

"The storm finally blew itself out, so I dumped off the steer and rounded up the ten thousand head of cattle that had drifted for more than a hundred miles! When I got home to the ranch, I saw a big hat lying on the ground, so I picked it up. Under it was my old friend still in his rocking chair and puffing away at his pipe.

"Ah," I said, "so you got a match."

"Oh, no," said he, "but I got her going just the same. They gave me one of the new-fangled cigarette lighters. It lights my pipe fine, but it isn't so good for picking my teeth."

bp Nichol
A Fish Story

(for Howard Gerhard)

Fish stories are perhaps the most common type of tall tails—the tale-spinners hold their hands far apart and describe their outsized catch or "the one that got away." This comic poem by bp Nichol is a fish story with a difference, however, as he imagines what might happen if the one that got away decided to get even.

WHEN I GO TO THE SEASHORE,
or up north to a lake,
or walk beside the ocean
where the flakey tuna flake,
I often think of fishes,
of how their lives must be,
and I wonder if they ever,
oh ever, think of me.

Once, on Lake Superior
in a rowboat, a friend
lowered in his fishing line
which soon began to bend and
out leapt this big father fish,
the biggest he had caught,
fixed my friend with a fishy stare
then tied his line in knots,
took his hook, snapped it in two,
smashed in his starboard side,
and as my friend swam away
shouted out, "Don't try to hide!
'Cause if I catch you fishing,
from sea to shining sea,
by all the fish in this great lake
I'll make you pay. You'll see!!"

Later, on Athabasca,
fishing with some folks,
schools of fish swam up
cracking filthy, fishy jokes—
"tuna" this & "fillet" that,
"salmon," "red snapper" too—
turned my friend's boat upside down and
what could my good friend do?

They filled his mouth with seaweed,
ears with octopus ink,
plugged his nose with rubber hose,
tickled him till he turned pink,
saying: "Don't fish in the lake
and don't fish in the sea
and don't fish in the ocean,
don't fish where fish might be."

Oh they made it very plain
with that hose in his nose,
with all that ink in his ears,
with the seaweed, his wet clothes.
So plain that now he never
goes out fishing, you see,
because with him it just doesn't
no it doesn't agree.

Ghosts and Spirits

 In traditional ghost stories from the British Isles, the setting is usually a dank, forbidding castle or at least a rambling old house.
Although Canada does have its tales of haunted houses, it seems to
be easier for Canadians to imagine terrors that confront them outside—in
darkness, or wild weather, or unearthly cold.

Ken Stange
Windigo Spirit

The most terrifying creatures people can imagine are the ones that grow out of their own
deepest fears. For the Native peoples of Canada's Eastern Woodlands, the greatest threats were winter cold
and starvation, and what they might drive a desperate person to do. The Windigo ("Windigo" is the Algonquian
word for "cannibal") was a supernatural beast with a heart of ice and a ravenous hunger for human flesh. He might
appear in the form of a wild beast or, as in Ken Stange's poem, take over the body of a human being.

THE WINDIGO IS A SPIRIT OF THE North, THE CREE TOLD US.
The Windigo is a cannibal spirit, the Cree told us.
The Windigo will possess a man
     form ice inside his soul
     cause fur to cover his skin
     create a craving for human flesh
The Cree told us,
Two bitter nights ago.
Two nights ago, we left their dismal camp, to check
Our traplines. It was twenty below zero
Two nights ago, but now it has gotten
Really cold. Windigo, Windigo,
Passing through our thoughts
Like wind at thirty-five below.
Windigo.
The Windigo moves thru the five moons of winter
     shrouded in a blizzard
     blown by high winds over frozen lakes
     or creeps inexorably on
     thru those still days
     when life is locked immutable in minus
     fifty skies, those cloudless, breathless
     days when neither air nor man dare move.
The Windigo crosses a portage
     then a sun-blind lake
     then the soul of any fool
     alone
          out here,
               like us

Now.
Two nights out, out from another man, we are still
Strangers in front of our fire,
        our meek fire melting
        melting just enough
        night air
        to breathe.
A shadow moves.
Windigo.
Two nights ago, the Cree told of a trapper lost,
Near here,
Now surely, host of
The Windigo Spirit.
Cold.
Windigo. Windigo.
Two nights out, the dead trapper enters the ring of our fire
        his own lips and fingers chewed off in hunger
        a gaping chasm of a mouth ringed with frozen
Blood.
Two nights out, I turn to my companion,
        behind his eyes ice forms
        his hands are matted with hair
This night, I rise and scream.
My scream crosses the frozen lake and dies somewhere in the
spruce
        dies somewhere in the spruce.
Windigo. Windigo.
Windigo.

Kiakshuk
The Giant Bear

This poem comes from a Netsilik Inuk writer. The Netsilik live near the Gulf of Boothia, in what is now Nunavut. "The Giant Bear" puts a grimly humorous twist on a theme that is familiar from folktales around the world, including some versions of "Little Red Riding Hood." All is not lost when a monster or fierce animal swallows somebody up. If you cut it open, its victims may tumble out, safe and sound!

THERE ONCE WAS A GIANT BEAR
who followed people for his prey.
He was so big he swallowed them whole:
Then they smothered to death inside him
if they hadn't already died of fright.

Either the bear attacked them on the run,
or if they crawled into a cave
where he could not squeeze his enormous
    body in,
he stabbed them with his whiskers like
    toothpicks,
drawing them out one by one,
and gulped them down.

No one knew what to do
until a wise man went out and let the bear
    swallow him,
sliding right down his throat into the big,
    dark, hot, slimy stomach.
And once inside there, he took his knife
and simply cut him open,
killing him of course.

He carved a door in the bear's belly
and threw out those who had been eaten
    before,
and then he stepped out himself
and went home to get help with the
    butchering.

Everyone lived on bear meat for a long
    time.
That's the way it goes:
Monster one minute, food the next.

Traditional
The Spirit Song of George's Bank

In 1920, Elizabeth Bristol taught school in the small community of Sally's Cove, Newfoundland, and also began collecting folksongs common to the area. She learned this song from a man named Daniel Endicott, who knew hundreds of songs by heart. In March 1866, during a storm at sea, a ship called the *Haskell* accidentally struck and sank another ship. The next year, on George's Bank, a fishing ground south of Newfoundland, some crewmen on the *Haskell*'s "dog watch" (the watch around sundown) claimed to have seen the ghostly seamen described in this song. It was said that the *Haskell* never went to sea again—because no one would sail on her.

You can smile if you've a mind to, but per-haps you'll lend an ear; We've been men and boys to-geth-er well on for fif-ty year, I've sailed up-on the wa-ter in the sum-m'ry pleas-ant days And through the storm-y win-ter when the how-ling wind do rage.

YOU CAN SMILE IF YOU'VE A MIND TO, BUT PERHAPS YOU'LL LEND AN EAR;
We've been men and boys together well on for fifty year,
I've sailed upon the water in the summ'ry pleasant days,
And through the stormy winter when the howling wind do rage.

I've been out in early seasons, most everywhere to pay:
I've been tossed about on George's, I've been fishing in the bay,
I've been out in different vessels from Western Banks to Grand,
I've been in herring vessels that sailed down to Newfoundland.

O, not to brag myself, but I'll say nothing else but this—
I'm not much easier frightened than most of other men,
For I've seen storms, I'll you tell, when things looked rather blue,
But someways I was lucky, and I always did get through.

This night as I am telling you, we were off shore a ways;
I never will forget it, in all my mortal days;
I've been in our grand dog-watch, I felt a shivering dread
Came over me, as if I heard one calling from the dead.

'Twas over our rail they climbed, all silent one by one,
A dozen dripping sailors—just wait till I am done—
Their face shone pale with seaweed, shone ghostly through the night,
And each man took his station as if he had a right.

We moved along together there till land did heave in sight,
And rather than I should say so, the lighthouse shoned his light,
And then those ghostly seamen moved to the rail again
And vanished in a moment before the sun of men.

We sailed right in the harbour, and every mother's son
Will tell you the same story, the same as I have done;
The trip before the other, we was on George's Bank then,
Ran down another old vessel, and sank her and all her men.

I think it was the same pore fellows—may God now rest their souls!—
That our old craft runned over that night on George's Shoals.
So now I've told my story, to you I will confess,
I have believed in spirits from that day unto this.

PART SIX

Canada's Century

Illustrated by

Laura Fernandez and Rick Jacobson

Luc Melanson

O Canada!

When Wilfrid Laurier was campaigning to become prime minister of Canada in 1896, he promised a "sunny ways" approach to politics. He meant that he would end the constant squabbles that threatened to break the country apart. Laurier's Liberal Party easily won the election of 1896 and he remained prime minister until 1911. Laurier made his most famous speech on January 18, 1904. "I thank Providence that I was born in Canada," he said, "but Canada's history is only commencing. As the nineteenth century was that of the United States, so I think the twentieth century shall be filled by Canada. For myself, I cannot see much of it, but when my eyes close I hope it will be on a United Canada cherishing an abundant hope for the future."

Calixa Lavallée and A. B. Routhier
English words by Stanley Weir
O Canada!

"O Canada!" wasn't proclaimed Canada's official national anthem until July 1980. By then, the song had been sung for one hundred years—at least in Quebec. Calixa Lavallée and Adolph-Basile Routhier wrote the patriotic song for a day of French-Canadian celebration in June 1880. The song was unknown in English Canada until the early 1900s, when various English versions began to appear. One began, "O Canada, our heritage, our love, / Thy worth we praise, all other lands above . . ." When Stanley Weir wrote his English words in 1908, however, they quickly became the accepted lyrics. But some Canadians grumbled about the five repetitions of "stand on guard." And what about all the immigrants, for whom Canada was not their "native" land? In 1967, a special government committee recommended changing two "stand on guard" phrases to "from far and wide" and "God keep our land," giving us the English lyrics we sing today. A. B. Routhier's French words have remained unchanged.

1.

O CANADA! TERRE DE NOS AÏEUX,
Ton front est ceint de fleurons glorieux!
Car ton bras sait porter l'épée,
Il sait porter la croix!
Ton histoire est une épopée
Des plus brillants exploits,
Et ta valeur, de foi trempée,
Protégera nos foyers et nos droits,
Protégera nos foyers et nos droits.

2.

Sous l'oeil de Dieu, près du fleuve géant,
Le Canadien grandit en espérant.
Il est né d'une race fière,
Béni fut son berceau:
Le ciel a marqué sa carrière
Dans ce monde nouveau,
Toujours guidé par sa lumière
Il gardera l'honneur de son drapeau,
Il gardera l'honneur de son drapeau.

3.

De son patron, précurseur du vrai Dieu,
Il porte au front l'auréole de feu,
Ennemi de la tyrannie,
Mais plein de loyauté,
Il veut garder dans l'harmonie
Sa fière liberté,
Et par l'effort de son génie,
Sur notre sol asseoir la vérité,
Sur notre sol asseoir la vérité.

1.

O Canada! Our home and native land!
True patriot love in all thy sons com-
    mand!
With glowing hearts we see thee rise
The true north strong and free!
From far and wide, O Canada
We stand on guard for thee.
God keep our land glorious and free!
O Canada we stand on guard for thee.
O Canada we stand on guard for thee.

2.

O Canada! Where pines and maples grow,
Great prairies spread and lordly rivers
    flow,
How dear to us thy broad domain,
From East to Western Sea,
Thou land of hope for all who toil!
Thou True North, strong and free!

3.

O Canada! Beneath thy shining skies
May stalwart sons and gentle maidens
    rise,
To keep thee steadfast through the years
From East to Western Sea,
Our own beloved native land!
Our True North, strong and free!

Alexander Muir
The Maple Leaf Forever

Alexander Muir, who wrote "The Maple Leaf Forever," was born in Scotland in 1830.
He immigrated to Canada and became a schoolteacher in the village of Scarborough (now part of
Toronto). In the fall of 1867, Muir was walking through a park when a maple leaf fell on his coat sleeve and
stuck there. "The maple leaf forever," he said to himself, jokingly. The line lingered in his mind, however, and
eventually he composed a poem about it. At his wife's suggestion, he later set his poem to music so his students
could sing it. The maple leaf was already a widely used symbol of Canada, and the song quickly became
popular. By the early 1900s, "The Maple Leaf Forever" was English Canada's unofficial anthem, and
was sung in classrooms across the land. It reflects a time when Canada was very much part of the
British Empire, with its mention of Scotland's thistle, Ireland's shamrock, and England's rose.
But the song makes no mention of Native Canadians or of non-British immigrants. As
Canada became more and more multicultural, the song fell out of favour.

1.

IN DAYS OF YORE, FROM BRITAIN'S SHORE,
Wolfe, the dauntless hero, came,
And planted firm Britannia's flag on
    Canada's fair domain.
Here may it wave, our boast, our pride,
And joined in love together
The Thistle, Shamrock, Rose entwine
The Maple Leaf forever.

Chorus:
The Maple Leaf, our emblem dear,
The Maple Leaf forever.
God save our Queen, and heaven bless
The Maple Leaf forever.

2.

At Queenston Heights and Lundy's Lane
Our brave fathers, side by side,
For freedom, homes, and loved ones dear
Firmly stood and nobly died;

And those dear rights which they
    maintained
We swear to yield them never!
Our watchword ever more shall be
The Maple Leaf forever!

Chorus

3.

Our fair Dominion now extends
From Cape Race to Nootka Sound;
May peace forever be our lot,
And plenteous store abound:
And many those ties of love be ours
Which discord cannot sever,
And flourish green o'er Freedom's home
The Maple Leaf forever!

Chorus

Mark Shekter and Charles Weir
The New Land

These words were written in 1980 for a musical comedy revue called *Toronto Toronto*. Its
refrain of "O Canada" reminds us of our national anthem, but this song focuses on immigrants. It tells
of impoverished people who came to Canada from Europe around the turn of the century and pioneered on the
Prairies. And it reminds those Canadians "working in a tower of glass" that many of them owe their
prosperity to people who were willing to leave behind everything they knew and start again.

A BOAT ARRIVES IN HALIFAX,
All they own is on their backs—
Heading west on railroad tracks,
O Canada, O Canada.

Changing trains in Montreal,
Standing out in boots and shawls—
A language they don't speak at all,
O Canada, O Canada,
Their home.

Sailing past a sea of trees,
Lakes reflecting brilliant leaves,
A hawk suspended on the breeze—
So free to fly an endless sky.

Prairie grasses ebb and flow,
So much space for them to grow,
With bags of wheat they've brought to
    sow—
The fields that run beneath the sun.

They worked the land as they knew best,
And when they died they took their rest—
Their babies scattered east and west,
O Canada, O Canada.

Working in a tower of glass,
A life flows through me from my past—
A boat touched port in Halifax,
O Canada, O Canada,
My home.

A Vanished Way of Life

"The past is a foreign country. They do things differently there." These are the words of a British writer, L. P. Hartley, but they can easily apply to Canada. All the pieces in this section are about day-to-day life in the first half of the twentieth century—in a Canada that would seem very strange if today's children could visit it. It is a slower-moving place, where houses are heated by coal, and milk and bread are delivered by horse-drawn wagons. As we start a new century, there are still many older Canadians who can remember these earlier ways of doing things, but the Canada they once lived in has disappeared forever.

L. M. Montgomery
Anne Comes to Green Gables

Anne Shirley may be the most famous fictional character Canada has ever produced. The outspoken, warm-hearted orphan girl is known all over the world, and every year thousands of visitors travel to Prince Edward Island to see her home for themselves. Although Anne was not a real person, the setting and way of life described so vividly by L. M. Montgomery *were* real. Montgomery had a more privileged life than Anne's, but she saw farming families just like those in *Anne of Green Gables* when she taught school in rural Prince Edward Island. At that time, families depended on their sons to do the heavier work on the farm as the parents aged. But Marilla and Matthew Cuthbert, who are brother and sister, have no young relatives. To get some help, they decide to take in an orphan boy, which was common practice at the time. As this excerpt from the novel shows, however, Matthew is in for a surprise when he gets to the train station.

MATTHEW CUTHBERT AND THE SORREL mare jogged comfortably over the eight miles to Bright River. It was a pretty road, running along between snug farmsteads, with now and again a bit of balsamy fir wood to drive through or a hollow where wild plums hung out their filmy bloom. The air was sweet with the breath of many apple orchards and the meadows sloped away in the distance to horizon mists of pearl and purple.

When he reached Bright River there was no sign of any train; he thought he was too early, so he tied his horse in the yard of the small Bright River hotel and went over to the station house. The long platform was almost deserted; the only living creature in sight being a girl who was sitting on a pile of shingles at the extreme end.

Matthew encountered the stationmaster locking up the ticket office preparatory to going home for supper, and asked him if the five-thirty train would soon be along.

"The five-thirty train has been in and gone half an hour ago," answered that brisk official. "But there was a passenger dropped off for you—a little girl. She's sitting out there on the shingles. I asked her to go into the ladies' waiting room, but she informed me gravely that she preferred to stay outside. 'There was more scope for imagination,' she said. She's a case, I should say."

"I'm not expecting a girl," said Matthew blankly. "It's a boy I've come for. He should be here. Mrs. Alexander Spencer was to bring him over from Nova Scotia for me."

The stationmaster whistled.

"Guess there's some mistake," he said. "Mrs. Spencer came off the train with that girl and gave her into my charge. Said you and your sister were adopting her from an orphan asylum and that you would be along for her presently. That's all I know about it—and I haven't got any more orphans concealed hereabouts."

"I don't understand," said Matthew helplessly, wishing that Marilla was at hand to cope with the situation.

"Well, you'd better question the girl," said the stationmaster carelessly. "I dare say she'll be able to explain—she's got a tongue of her own, that's certain. Maybe they were out of boys of the brand you wanted."

He walked jauntily away, being hungry, and the unfortunate Matthew was left to do that which was harder for him than bearding a lion in its den—walk up to a girl—a strange girl—an orphan girl—and demand of her why she wasn't a boy.

Matthew groaned in spirit as he turned about and shuffled gently down the platform towards her.

She had been watching him ever since he had passed her and she had her eyes on him now. Matthew was not looking at her and would not have seen what she was really like if he had been, but an ordinary observer would have seen this: A child of about eleven, garbed in a very short, very tight, very ugly dress of yellowish-gray wincey. She wore a faded brown sailor hat and beneath the hat, extending down her back, were two braids of very thick, decidedly red hair. Her face was small, white and thin, also much freckled; her mouth was large and so were her eyes, which looked green in some lights and moods and gray in others.

Matthew was spared the ordeal of speaking first, for as soon as she concluded that he was coming to her she stood up, grasping with one thin brown hand the handle of a shabby, old-fashioned carpet-bag; the other she held out to him.

"I suppose you are Mr. Matthew Cuthbert of Green Gables?" she said in a peculiarly clear, sweet voice. "I'm very glad to see you. I was beginning to be afraid you weren't coming for me and I was imagining all the things that might have happened to prevent you. I had made up my mind that if you didn't come for me to-night I'd go down the track to that big wild cherry-tree at the bend, and climb up into it to stay all night. I wouldn't be a bit afraid, and it would be lovely to sleep in a wild cherry-tree all white with bloom in the moonshine, don't you think? You could imagine you were dwelling in marble halls, couldn't you? And I was quite sure you would come for me in the morning, if you didn't to-night."

Matthew had taken the scrawny little hand awkwardly in his; then and there he decided what to do. He could not tell this child with the glowing eyes that there had been a mistake; he would take her home and let Marilla do that.

[Matthew and the young girl leave the station and start on their way home in Matthew's buggy.]

The girl opened her eyes and looked about her. They were on the crest of a hill. The sun had set some time since, but the landscape was still clear in the mellow afterlight. To the west a dark church spire rose up against a marigold sky. Below was a little valley and beyond a long, gently rising slope with snug farmsteads scattered along it. From one to another the child's eyes darted, eager and wistful. At last they lingered on one away to the left, far back from the road, dimly white with blossoming trees in the twilight of the surrounding woods. Over it, in the stainless southwest sky, a great crystal-white star was shining like a lamp of guidance and promise.

"That's it, isn't it?" she said, pointing.

Matthew slapped the reins on the sorrel's back delightedly.

"Well now, you've guessed it! But I reckon Mrs. Spencer described it so's you could tell."

"No, she didn't—really she didn't. All she said might just as well have been about most of those other places. I hadn't any real idea what it looked like. But just as soon as I saw it I felt it was home. Oh, it seems as if I must be in a dream. Do you know, my arm must be black and blue from the elbow up, for I've pinched myself so many times today. Every little while a horrible sickening feeling would come over me and I'd be so afraid it was all a dream. Then I'd pinch myself to see if it was real—until suddenly I remembered that even supposing it was only a dream I'd better go on dreaming as long as I could; so I stopped pinching. But it is real and we're nearly home."

With a sigh of rapture she relapsed into silence. Matthew stirred uneasily. He felt glad that it would be Marilla and not he who would have to tell this waif of the world that the home she longed for was not to be hers after all. They drove over Lynde's Hollow, where it was already quite dark, but not so dark that Mrs. Rachel could not see them from her window vantage, and up the hill and into the long lane of Green Gables. By the time they arrived at the house Matthew was shrinking from the approaching revelation with an energy he did not understand. It was not of Marilla or himself he was thinking of the trouble this mistake was probably going to make for them, but of the child's disappointment.

The yard was quite dark as they turned into it and the poplar leaves were rustling silkily all round it.

"Listen to the trees talking in their sleep," she whispered, as he lifted her to the ground. "What nice dreams they must have!"

Then, holding tightly to the carpet-bag which contained "all her worldly goods," she followed him into the house.

David Tipe
Picking Coke

More than sixty years had passed when David Tipe wrote this story about the early 1900s in Toronto—but he still remembered his childhood vividly. His neighbourhood was called Cabbagetown because the low-income people who lived there, many of them Irish Canadians, often ate cabbage, which they grew in their front yards. In those days, Toronto burned coal at the Gas House to generate fuel for lighting the city. Poorer people heated their homes with coke, little pieces that were left over after the gases had been extracted from the coal. As Tipe recalls, Cabbagetown's families often depended on their children to collect the coke.

IT USED TO BE THIS WHOLE CITY WAS run by coal. The coal would burn to make gas and what they had left over were little pieces they called coke. The coke wasn't good for much but it did burn and all summer the poor people, children and adults alike, would come to the Gas House and pick the coke.

For them it was the only way to keep warm during the winter. Every house in Cabbagetown burned coke in their fireplace during the winter. Oh how horrible it would be if you had not picked enough of it during the summer! You would have to get up very early in the morning in winter and pick coke before going to school. Some of the boys used to burn holes in other people's bags and steal their supply. When things were really bad, gangs used to fight over coke. Some of the

older children would collect extra coke to sell to the old and sick people who could not pick it themselves. This way they had a little money to buy some treats or to go to the movie show. The show was only ten cents in those days.

When the coke was first piled up in the morning, it would still be hot from the furnace. You had to move very quickly to get that coke in the bag and sometimes the boys managed to get more than the girls. One day a good man dumped all the coke into two piles and said that from now on, one pile would be for the boys and one pile for the girls.

Most of the people who picked coke in those days are old now; but they remember, because it was something they all shared, a kind of community event.

Quentin Reynolds
A Secret for Two

In the first half of the twentieth century, horse-drawn wagons brought bread and milk right to
Canadians' doors. Delivery men (they were almost always men in those days) followed the same route
every day and would remember the regular order—a quart of milk and a pint of cream, for example—for each
customer. People left their empty glass milk bottles on the porch for the delivery man to pick up, often with money
tucked in the top to pay for their orders. Over time, delivery trucks replaced the horse-drawn wagons, and
gradually the service died out. Today there are many more dairy products available than those long-ago
milkmen dreamed of, but you have to go to a store to buy them.

MONTREAL IS A VERY LARGE CITY, BUT,
like all large cities, it has some very small
streets—for instance, Prince Edward
Street, which is only four blocks long,
ending in a cul-de-sac. No one knew
Prince Edward Street as well as did Pierre
Dupin, for Pierre had delivered milk to
the families there for thirty years.

During the past fifteen years the horse
which drew the milk wagon used by Pierre
was a large white horse named Joseph.
When the big white horse first came to the
Provinciale Milk Company he didn't have
a name. They told Pierre that he could use
the white horse henceforth. Pierre stroked
the softness of the horse's neck; he stroked
the sheen of its splendid belly and he
looked into the eyes of the horse.

"This is a kind horse, a gentle and a
faithful horse," Pierre said, "and I can see
a beautiful spirit shining out of the eyes
of the horse. I will name him after good
St. Joseph, who was also kind and gentle
and faithful and a beautiful spirit."

Within a year Joseph knew the milk
route as well as Pierre. Pierre used to
boast that he didn't need reins—he never
touched them. Each morning Pierre
arrived at the stables of the Provinciale
Milk Company at five o'clock. The wagon
would be loaded and Joseph hitched to it.
Pierre would call, "*Bonjour, vieil ami*," as he
climbed into his seat and Joseph would
turn his head and the other drivers would
smile and say that the horse would smile
at Pierre. Then Jacques, the foreman,

would say, "All right, Pierre, go on," and Pierre would call softly to Joseph, "*Avance, mon ami*," and this splendid combination would stalk proudly down the street.

The wagon, without any direction from Pierre, would roll three blocks down St. Catherine Street, then turn right two blocks along Roslyn Avenue, then left, for that was Prince Edward Street. The horse would stop at the first house, allow Pierre perhaps thirty seconds to get down from his seat and put a bottle of milk at the front door and would then go on, skipping two houses and stopping at the third. So down the length of the street. Then Joseph, still without any direction from Pierre, would turn around and come back along the other side. Yes, Joseph was a smart horse.

Pierre would boast at the stable of Joseph's skill. "I never touch the reins. He knows just where to stop. Why, a blind man could handle my route with Joseph pulling the wagon."

So it went on for years—always the same. Pierre and Joseph both grew old together, but gradually, not suddenly. Pierre's huge walrus moustache was pure white now and Joseph didn't lift his knees so high or raise his head as much. Jacques, the foreman of the stable, never noticed that they were both getting old until Pierre appeared one morning carrying a heavy walking stick.

"Hey, Pierre," Jacques laughed. "Maybe you got the gout, hey?"

"*Mais oui, Jacques*," Pierre said a bit uncertainly. "One grows old. One's legs get tired."

"You should teach that horse to carry the milk to the front door for you,"

Jacques told him. "He does everything else."

He knew every one of the forty families he served on Prince Edward Street. The cooks knew that Pierre could neither read nor write, so instead of following the usual custom of leaving a note in an empty bottle if an additional quart of milk was needed they would sing out when they heard the rumble of his wagon wheels over the cobbled street, "Bring an extra quart this morning, Pierre."

"So you have company for dinner tonight," he would call back gaily.

Pierre had a remarkable memory. When he arrived at the stable he'd always remember to tell Jacques, "The Paquins took an extra quart this morning; the Lemoines bought a pint of cream."

Jacques would note these things in a little book he always carried. Most of the drivers had to make out the weekly bills and collect the money, but Jacques, liking Pierre, had always excused him from this task. All Pierre had to do was to arrive at five in the morning, walk to his wagon, which was always in the same spot at the

curb, and deliver his milk. He returned
some two hours later, got down stiffly
from his seat, called a cheery "*Au 'voir*" to
Jacques, and then limped slowly down the
street.

One morning the president of the
Provinciale Milk Company came to
inspect the early morning deliveries.
Jacques pointed Pierre out to him and
said: "Watch how he talks to that horse.
See how the horse listens and how he
turns his head towards Pierre? See the
look in that horse's eyes? You know, I
think those two share a secret. I have
often noticed it. It is as though they both

sometimes chuckle at us as they go off on
their route. Pierre is a good man,
Monsieur President, but he gets old.
Would it be too bold of me to suggest
that he be retired and be given perhaps a
small pension?" he added anxiously.

"But of course," the president laughed.
"I know his record. He has been on this
route now for thirty years and never once
has there been a complaint. Tell him it is
time he rested. His salary will go on just
the same."

But Pierre refused to retire. He was
panic-stricken at the thought of not driving Joseph every day. "We are two old

men," he said to Jacques. "Let us wear out together. When Joseph is ready to retire, then I, too, will quit."

Jacques, who was a kind man, understood. There was something about Pierre and Joseph which made a man smile tenderly. It was as though each drew some hidden strength from the other. When Pierre was sitting in his seat, and when Joseph was hitched to the wagon, neither seemed old. But when they finished their work, Pierre would limp down the street slowly, seemingly very old indeed, and the horse's head would drop and he would walk very wearily to his stall.

Then one morning Jacques had dreadful news for Pierre when he arrived. It was a cold morning and still pitch-dark. The air was like iced wine that morning and the snow which had fallen during the night glistened like a million diamonds piled together.

Jacques said, "Pierre, your horse, Joseph, did not wake up this morning. He was very old, Pierre, he was twenty-five and that is like being seventy-five for a man."

"Yes," Pierre said slowly. "Yes. I am seventy-five. And I cannot see Joseph again."

"Of course you can," Jacques soothed. "He is over in his stall, looking very peaceful. Go over and see him."

Pierre took one step forward, then turned. "No...no...you don't understand, Jacques."

Jacques clapped him on the shoulder. "We'll find another horse just as good as Joseph. Why, in a month you'll teach him to know your route as well as Joseph did. We'll..."

The look in Pierre's eyes stopped him.

For years Pierre had worn a heavy cap, the peak of which came low over his eyes, keeping the bitter morning wind out of them. Now Jacques looked into Pierre's eyes and saw something which startled him. He saw a dead, lifeless look in them. The eyes were mirroring the grief that was in Pierre's heart and his soul. It was as though his heart and soul had died.

"Take today off, Pierre," Jacques said, but already Pierre was hobbling off down the street, and had one been near one would have seen tears streaming down his checks and have heard half-smothered sobs. Pierre walked to the corner and stepped into the street. There was a warning yell from the driver of a huge truck that was coming fast and there was the scream of brakes, but Pierre apparently heard neither.

Five minutes later an ambulance driver said, "He's dead. Was killed instantly."

Jacques and several of the milk-wagon drivers had arrived and they looked down at the still figure.

"I couldn't help it," the driver of the truck protested, "he walked right into my truck. He never saw it, I guess. Why, he walked into it as though he were blind."

The ambulance doctor bent down. "Blind? Of course the man was blind. See those cataracts? This man has been blind for five years." He turned to Jacques, "You say he worked for you? Didn't you know he was blind?"

"No...no..." Jacques said softly. "None of us knew. Only one knew—a friend of his named Joseph.... It was a secret, I think, just between those two."

James Reaney
The Royal Visit

Queen Elizabeth and other members of the royal family now visit Canada fairly often.
But until 1939, no reigning monarch had ever made the journey. On May 17, 1939, King George VI
and Queen Elizabeth (the parents of the present queen) stepped ashore at Quebec City to begin a month-long
tour that included every province. There was a serious reason for their trip: Adolf Hitler, the Nazi dictator who led
Germany, was threatening countries in Europe, and the British government knew that war would likely come
soon. When it did come, Britain wanted to be sure that Canadians would support them in their struggle.
But as James Reaney's poem recalls, most Canadians were not thinking about the threat of war as they
waited for the royal train. They were simply eager to see the king and especially the glamorous,
beautifully dressed queen, even if only for a fleeting moment.

WHEN THE KING AND THE QUEEN CAME
    to Stratford
Everyone felt at once
How heavy the Crown must be.
The Mayor shook hands with their
    Majesties
And everyone presentable was presented
And those who weren't have resented
It, and will
To their dying day.
Everyone had almost a religious
    experience
When the King and Queen came to visit
    us
(I wonder what they felt!)
And hydrants flowed water in the gutters
All day.

People put quarters on the railroad tracks
So as to get squashed by the Royal Train
And some people up the line at
    Shakespeare
Stayed in Shakespeare, just in case—
They did stop too,
While thousands in Stratford
Didn't even see them
Because the Engineer didn't slow down
Enough in time.
And although,
But although we didn't see them in any
    way
(I didn't even catch the glimpse
The teacher who was taller did
Of a gracious pink figure)
I'll remember it to my dying day.

The Wars

There were no wars on Canadian soil in the twentieth century, but Canadian troops fought in many international conflicts, including the Boer War in South Africa (1899–1902) and the Korean War (1950–53). Acting on their own, small groups of Canadians also followed their consciences to join in other struggles. The Mackenzie-Papineau Battalion fought in the Spanish Civil War (1936–39), and hundreds of Canadians fought in the Israeli War of Independence in 1948. But above all, Canadians suffered through two terrible conflicts—the First World War and the Second World War—that engulfed much of the world.

In 1914, Britain declared war on Germany, which had attacked Belgium and France. Canada, as part of the British Empire, was automatically at war as well. At a time when its population was only 8 million, Canada sent 600,000 men and 3,000 women, who served as nurses, to the war. About 60,000 Canadians had been killed by the time victory came in 1918. Only a generation later, in 1939, there was a second global war. On one side were the Axis powers—including Germany, Italy, and later, Japan. On the other were the Allies, which included Britain, the Soviet Union, and, after its naval base at Pearl Harbor was attacked by the Japanese in December 1941, the United States. Eventually, most countries in the world were drawn into the conflict. This time, Canada declared war on Germany (and, later, on Japan) on its own. From 1939 to 1945, about one million Canadians, including 45,000 women (who now filled most military roles, except combat), served in Canada's armed forces, and more than 42,000 service people were killed.

John McCrae
In Flanders Fields

John McCrae was a Canadian doctor who served at a field hospital in Flanders (an area of Belgium) during the terrible battle at Ypres in the spring of 1915. He had seen a great deal of death and suffering, but one death particularly affected him. On May 2, 1915, a friend and former student of his was killed by a shell burst. McCrae performed the funeral ceremony. The next day, seated on the back of a parked ambulance with a view of the military cemetery, he wrote the poem "In Flanders Fields." The small cemetery was full of blood-red wild poppies blowing in the breeze. No one in Flanders had ever seen so many wild poppies until that spring. The ground had been churned up by warfare, and had become just the kind of soil wild poppies need to grow. McCrae's resulting poem was first published in a British magazine called *Punch* in 1917, and soon became the most famous poem of the First World War. Every year on Remembrance Day, November 11, Canadians wear poppies to honour those who died in all wars.

IN FLANDERS FIELDS THE POPPIES BLOW
Between the crosses, row on row,
That mark our place; and in the sky
The larks, still bravely singing, fly
Scarce heard amid the guns below.

We are the Dead. Short days ago
We lived, felt dawn, saw sunset glow,
Loved and were loved, and now we lie,
In Flanders fields.

Take up our quarrel with the foe:
To you from failing hands we throw
The torch; be yours to hold it high.
If ye break faith with us who die
We shall not sleep, though poppies grow
In Flanders fields.

Edgar McInnis
Our Dugout

When the First World War began in August 1914, many Canadians believed that the soldiers
would be home by Christmas. However, it was soon obvious that no quick end would come. In France
and Belgium, soldiers from both sides became bogged down in battles over small patches of ground. The men
began digging ditches called trenches to provide cover from machine-gun fire and artillery. (The term "Woolly
Bears," used in this poem, was a nickname for artillery fire. "Crumping" describes the sound of their explosion.) The
trenches of the First World War were horrible places filled with dirt, mud, rats, and lice, but for soldiers like
Edgar McInnis the dugouts in these trenches were home. McInnis even describes his "bivvy" (short for
"bivouac," an army camp) as a comfy, cosy place. His fellow soldiers, however, would have
recognized that he was only joking, to make the best of a bad situation.

WHEN THE LINES ARE IN A MUDDLE—AS THEY VERY OFTEN ARE—
When the break's a mile away from you, or maybe twice as far,
When you have to sort the trouble out, and fix it on the run,
It's fine to know that you can go, when everything is done,

To a cosy little dugout (and the subject of this ode)
Just a comfy little bivvy on the —— Road,
A sheltered, sandbagged doorway with the flap flung open wide,
And a pal to grin a greeting when you step inside.

When the weather's simply damnable—cold sleet and driving rain—
When the poles snap off like matches and the lines are down again,
And you rip your freezing fingers as you work the stubborn wire,
It's great to get back home again, and dry off by the fire,

In a cheery little dugout (and you know the kind I mean)
With a red-hot stove a-roaring, and a floor that's none too clean,
A pipe that's filled and waiting and a book that will not wait,
And a cup of steaming coffee if you come back late.

It may look a little crowded, and the roof's a trifle low,
But it's water-tight—or nearly—and it wasn't built for show,
And when Woolly Bears are crumping and the shrapnel sprays around,
You feel a whole lot safer if you're underneath the ground,

In a rat-proof, rain-proof dugout (and it's splinter-proof as well)
Where we got the stuff to build it is a thing I mustn't tell,
But we've made it strong and solid, and we're cosy, rain or shine,
In our happy little dugout on the firing line.

John Gillespie Magee
High Flight

"High Flight" is one of the most famous pieces of writing about aviation. Although it was composed in the midst of war, it is not about fighting, but is about the pure joy of flight. The poem was written in September 1941 by a nineteen-year-old Royal Canadian Air Force pilot named John Gillespie Magee. He had received his pilot's wings only in June of that year, and was in Wales for advanced training. After his first flights in a Spitfire fighter plane, he scribbled his exhilarated feelings on the back of a letter. He wrote home to his parents: "It [the poem] started at 30,000 feet, and was finished soon after I landed. I thought it might interest you." Just a few weeks later, Magee was killed in a plane crash. In May 1942, "High Flight" was first published in *Flying* magazine, whose editors rightly predicted that the poem would become a classic.

OH! I HAVE SLIPPED THE SURLY BONDS OF EARTH
And danced the skies on laughter-silvered wings;
Sunward I've climbed, and joined the tumbling mirth
Of sun-split clouds,—and done a hundred things
You have not dreamed of—wheeled and soared and swung
High in the sunlit silence. Hov'ring there,
I've chased the shouting wind along, and flung
My eager craft through footless halls of air....

Up, up the long, delirious, burning blue
I've topped the wind-swept heights with easy grace
Where never lark, or even eagle flew—
And, while with silent, lifting mind I've trod
The high untrespassed sanctity of space,
Put out my hand, and touched the face of God.

Mona Gould
This Was My Brother

For Canadians who sent their loved ones off to war, there were long months of anxious waiting. Mail did not always arrive regularly. When it did, soldiers were not allowed to say where they were or what military actions they were involved in. Families often had no way of knowing whether their fathers, sons, and brothers were on the front lines of the battles they read about in the newspapers. The mail everyone dreaded receiving most of all was a telegram beginning "We regret to inform you . . ." In August 1942, Mona Gould lived through this terrible experience. Her beloved brother was one of nine hundred Canadians killed in a disastrous raid on Dieppe, France, a coastal town strongly held by the Germans.

For Lt. Col. Gordon Howard McTavish,
killed in action at Dieppe, August 19, 1942

THIS WAS MY BROTHER
At Dieppe,
Quietly a hero
Who gave his life
Like a gift,
Withholding nothing.

His youth…his love
His enjoyment of being alive
His future, like a book
With half the pages still uncut—
This was my brother
At Dieppe—
The one who built me a doll house
When I was seven,
Complete to the last small picture frame—
Nothing forgotten.

He was awfully good at fixing things,
At stepping into the breach when he was needed.

That's what he did at Dieppe;
He was needed.
And even Death must have been a little shamed
At his eagerness.

Shizuye Takashima
A Child in Prison Camp

After the Japanese attack on Pearl Harbor in Hawaii, on December 7, 1941, Canadians, like Americans, were afraid of a Japanese invasion on their Pacific coast. Suddenly, twenty-two thousand people of Japanese origin who lived in British Columbia were seen as the enemy, even though many were Canadian citizens. Although no Japanese Canadian was ever accused of any act of spying or sabotage, the government seized their belongings and property. They were shipped to camps far away from the coast and kept there, stripped of all their civil rights, for three years. Shizuye (Shichan) Takashima lived through this experience as a young girl, and described it in her book *A Child in Prison Camp.*

New Denver, British Columbia
September 1942

Our Home at Night

It is night. We light our two candles. There is no electricity. The frail, rationed candles burst into life and the darkness slinks away. The smell of fresh-cut trees burning fills the room. The pine pitch cracks and pops in the fire. I sit, watch my mother. She places the rice pot on the black, heavy stove. The wet, shiny pot begins to sputter.

"Rice tastes better cooked like this," she says, smiles. Her dark eyes look even darker in this semi-light and I feel love for her.

"Why?" I ask.

"Because natural fire is best for cooking. Food tastes pure."

I stare at the now boiling rice and wonder why all people do not use such stoves and fuel.

Yuki brings wood. I help her pile it near the hot stove, for the raw wood is damp. The family who share the kitchen, the stove and the house, begin their dinner. Mrs. Kono appears quietly from her nooklike curtained bedroom, bows to my mother, washes her rice. The wood sink gurgles as the water scooped from the lake plunges quickly down the narrow pipe. Soon her rice too is cooking on the big, black stove. The bare, tiny, candle-lit room is filled with the smell of rice and Japanese food. Mrs. Kono is still young. I notice she watches her rice pot with care as Mother does. "This is very important," Mother has often said.

Mrs. Kono lives with her husband and their small child, a girl of three. Kay-ko is her name. A lovely girl with black, black hair cut in straight bangs, huge round dark eyes that look very merry when she smiles. She always has rosy, rosy cheeks. Now she comes shyly to me, calls me "Big Sister" in Japanese, which sounds nice, for I have never been called this. I smile. She squats and watches as I pile the wood. The white part of the wood looks strange in this dim light.

"Would you like to help?" I ask. Half joking, she nods, begins to hand me the pieces, one by one with her tiny, round hands. Some of the pitch sticks to our hands. I look at the sticky, yellow liquid coming out of the wood. Kay-ko stares at it.

"What is it? It smells funny."

I reply, "It's pitch. Comes from the pine tree. We learnt this in school."

Yuki joins in and adds, "It's the sap of the tree. It's full of the sun's energy. This is why it cracks and pops as it burns."

Kay-ko and I both listen, and we hear the sharp snap of the pitch burning. The fresh smell of the pine reaches us. We both wrinkle our noses. Kay-ko laughs. I dab a bit of soft pitch on her nose; she does the same to me. Soon we forget all about piling the wood and end up laughing and laughing.

The table is set; the white candles create a circle of light on the wood table. I sit by the flame. I notice the far corners of the room are dark. This gives an eerie feeling. Though eyes and mind are getting used to this kind of light. On the other side of the room I can hear the Konos talking quietly. It took us several days to get used to living with them. But the Konos are so quiet, speak very little, except for Kay-ko, who talks a lot. I do not mind. I think it bothers my mother and father more. Older people seem more sensitive to other people's noises. I'm glad I'm still young, for things do not bother me, even as much as they bother Yuki.

Our First Snow

We children continue to go to school. It was not the best, but school is school and I have no choice. Finally, our first sign of winter.

As I pick my way along the brushes, stumps and broken, twisted twigs and grass (a short-cut from the school to our home) I see our first snow. It falls quietly, gently from the low, grey cloud. I stop, put out my hands. The star pattern of the snow looks perfect as it falls on my hand. I wonder how it can be so lovely. I touch it carefully with my other hand. But then, as if I have broken its secret, it melts, leaving a tiny, clear drop of water. I try it again. The same thing happens. I look up. Now it's beginning to snow harder. I hurry home. The tall grass and dead leaves feel wet. I'm excited and happy.

That night Yuki and I stare out of our small window. The snow has stopped. We see the lemony-yellow moon shine so nice

and bright, her silver falling on the white earth. It looks beautiful. The trees outside are heavy with snow. Their dark green spiky branches are hidden. The shimmering winter magic light makes the neighbours' houses look suddenly beautiful. How kind snow is!

"Yuki, is your friend Rose coming?"

Yuki replies, "Yes, she should be here soon. I'm making some hot chocolate, and Mother bought a cake."

I wonder if I can stay up too. I wish I were older. It seems unfair to have to go to bed so early. I finally ask, "Can I stay up for a while? Please. Mom is out. She won't know. And Dad's gone to play cards."

Yuki stares out the window. "There she is. Rose." I peek out. Then I see her walking slowly towards our house. Her tall, thin body is bent forward. The snow is all around her, all white and magic. "Okay, Shichan. You can have hot chocolate and a piece of cake. Maybe we could have it now. It's cold. Then you can go to bed before Mother comes home. All right?"

I feel so happy. I rush to the shelves to bring out the cups. Yuki goes to the door to let Rose in. The cold air comes rushing from the open door. I put out the big pot for the hot chocolate. The big, black stove is hot and warm.

I smile at Rose. She is bundled up like a hunter. "Hi! Yuki's making hot chocolate." Rose nods, too cold to speak. I laugh. We all laugh.

The small candle casts an orange glow on my book. I am reading about Marco Polo again. My mind leaves our house. I hear Yuki and Rose talking quietly, but soon their voices fade away. I feel like a princess being rescued by a brave, dark Tartar. I see the Chinese palace as my hero carries me to his emperor's magnificent summer home, all tile and mosaic, filled with fountains in the lush gardens. I close my eyes, and dream. The Tartar comes to life, hands me splendid jewels to be placed around my hair. He takes my hand and guides me gently into the garden. I am not afraid as I reach for another world.

Christmas at Home

I swing my legs to and fro. Japanese music fills our tiny room. Mrs. Kono has a small record player. From this black leather box, with shining handles which we turn from time to time, glorious music comes. In the hot, burning oven, our Christmas chicken is cooking. It sputters and makes funny noises. The lemon pies Father baked are already on the table. He has been cooking all day. They look so nice, my favourite pies. Only Father can bake such lovely, tasty pies. He must put magic into them.

Father is an excellent cook. Before he became a gardener, he worked as a chef in a big restaurant and in hotels. And now he still cooks on holidays or when we have many guests. I love watching him cook. He never uses a measuring cup, mostly his hands. He's always tasting, making gurgling, funny noises in his throat (for Japanese are allowed to make a lot of noise when they eat, especially when they drink tea or eat soup). Father closes his eyes and tastes it, then he gives me a tiny bit. He and Mother always treat me specially, I guess because I'm the youngest and not as strong as Yuki. She doesn't mind; she knows I love her. I watch my father cook and I listen. The old song sounds full of joy....

Father ties a towel around his head. Mother hands him a bowl. He raises his arm, dances around. He is graceful as he waves his arm and bowl in time with the music. We all laugh. Mr. Kono joins him and sings. It is an old folk song. Mother claps her hands in time with the rhythm. She is looking at my slippers, the ones David sent us for Christmas. She has a little smile. I know her thoughts are with David; this is the first Christmas he is not with us. The music seems to grow louder. Little Kay-ko too joins us. We all sing. Yuki, the Konos, the whole room seems to fade. I see Japan. The snow is gone. I see the happy rice planters with their bright kimonos, their black hair tied with printed towels, the gentle wind, with lovely Mount Fuji, Fuji-san itself, in the distance. The music, our voices, go beyond our house, out into the snow, past the mountains and into space, and this special day is made more magic, and I know I shall remember it forever.

Farley Mowat
The Coming of Mutt

Farley Mowat is one of Canada's most beloved writers, and *The Dog Who Wouldn't Be*, with its unforgettable Mutt, is perhaps his most popular book. The story is based on Mowat's own childhood experiences, when his family moved from Ontario to Saskatoon. In the foreground are his eccentric father, always with a new hare-brained scheme; his exasperated mother; and especially Mutt, the family's energetic, goggles-wearing, skunk-chasing pet. But the dusty landscapes and personal hardships of the Depression are always there in the background. This excerpt from the early pages of the book describes how the author's family came to Saskatchewan, and how a poverty-stricken child brought Mutt to them.

AN OPPRESSIVE DARKNESS SHADOWED the city of Saskatoon on an August day in 1929. By the clock it was hardly noon. By the sun—but the earth had obliterated the sun. Rising in the new deserts of the southwest, and lifting high on autumnal winds, the desecrated soil of the prairies drifted northward; and the sky grew dark.

In our small house on the outskirts of the city my mother switched on the electric lights and continued with the task of preparing luncheon for my father and for me. Father had not yet returned from his office, nor I from school. Mother was alone with the sombre day.

The sound of the doorbell brought her unwillingly from the kitchen into the hall. She opened the front door no more than a few inches, as if expecting the menace of the sky to thrust its way past her into the house.

There was no menace in the appearance of the visitor who waited apologetically on the step. A small boy, perhaps ten years of age, stood shuffling his feet in the grey grit that had been falling soundlessly across the city for a day and a night. He held a wicker basket before him and, as the door opened, he swung the basket forward and spoke in a voice that was husky with the dust and with the expectation of rebuff.

"Missus," he asked in a pale, high tone, "would you want to buy a duck?"

Mother was a bit nonplussed by this odd echo of a catch phrase that had already withered and staled in the mouths of the comedians of the era. Nevertheless, she looked into the basket and to her astonishment beheld three emaciated ducklings, their bills gaping in the heat, and, wedged between them, a nondescript and bedraggled pup.

She was touched, and curious—although she certainly did not want to buy a duck.

"I don't think so," she said kindly. "Why are you selling them?"

The boy took courage and returned her smile.

"I gotta," he said. "The slough out to the farm is dry. We ate the big ducks, but these was too small to eat. I sold some down to the Chinee Grill. You want the rest, lady? They're cheap—only a dime each."

"I'm sorry," Mother replied. "I've no place to keep a duck. But where did you get the little dog?"

The boy shrugged his shoulders. "Oh, *him*," he said without much interest. "He was kind of an accident, you might say. I guess somebody dumped him out of a car right by our gate. I brung him with me in case. But dogs is hard to sell." He brightened up a little as an idea struck him. "Say, lady, you want him? I'll sell him for a nickel—that way you'll *save* a nickel for yourself."

Mother hesitated. Then almost involuntarily her hand went to the basket. The pup was thirsty beyond thirst, and those outstretched fingers must have seemed to him as fountains straight from heaven. He clambered hastily over the ducks and grabbed.

The boy was quick to sense his advantage and to press it home.

"He likes you, lady, see? He's yours for just *four* cents!"

Less than a month had elapsed since my parents and I had come out of the verdant depths of southern Ontario into the arid and dust-shrouded prairies.

It had seemed a foolhardy venture then, for those were the beginnings of the hard times, even in the east; while in the west the hard times—the times of drought and failure—were already old. I do not know what possessed my father to make him exchange the security of his job in Windsor for a most uncertain future as Saskatoon's librarian. It may be that the name itself, Saskatoon, Saskatchewan, attracted him irresistibly. It may have been simply that he was tired of the physical and mental confines of a province grown staid and stolid in its years.

Father spent that winter building a caravan, a trailer-house which was destined to carry us westward. It was a long winter for me. On Saturdays I joined my father under a shed and here we hammered and sawed industriously, and the caravan took shape. It was an unconventional shape, for my father was a sailor at heart and he had had but little experience in the design of land conveyances. Our caravan was, in reality, a houseboat perched precariously on the four thin wheels of an old Model T chassis. Her aspect was bluff and uncompromising. Her sides towered straight

from the frame a full seven feet to a gently cambered deck (which was never referred to as a roof). She was big-boned and buxom, and she dwarfed poor Eardlie—our Model A Ford convertible—as a floating derrick dwarfs the tug which tows it.

Perhaps our caravan was no thing of beauty, but she was at least a thing of comfort. My father was an ingenious builder and he had fitted her cabin with every nautical convenience. There was a compact galley with a primus stove on gimbals, gimballed lamps, great quantities of locker space, stowage for charts, a Seth Thomas chronometer on the forward bulkhead, two luxurious berths for my parents, and a folding pipe-berth for me. Dishes, our many books, and other loose oddments were neatly and securely racked in fitted cupboards so that even in the wildest weather they could not come adrift.

It was as well that my father took such pains to make the interior seaworthy, for, as we headed westward, we discovered that our wheeled vessel was—as sailors say— more than somewhat crank. Slab-sided and immense, she was the prey of every wind that blew. When a breeze took her from the flank she would sway heavily and, as like as not, scuttle ponderously to the wrong side of the road, pushing poor Eardlie with her. A head wind would force

Eardlie into second gear and even then he would have to strain and boil furiously to keep headway on his balky charge. A stern wind was almost as bad, for then the great bulk of the tow would try to override the little car and, failing in this, would push Eardlie forward at speeds which chilled my mother's heart.

All in all it was a memorable journey for an eight-year-old boy. I had my choice of riding in Eardlie's rumble seat, where I became the gunner in a Sopwith Camel; or I could ride in the caravan itself and pilot my self-contained rocket into outer space. I preferred the caravan, for it was a private world and a brave one. My folding bunk-bed was placed high up under the rear window, and here I could lie—carefully strapped into place against the effect of negative gravity (and high winds)—and guide my spaceship through the void to those far planets known as Ohio, Minnesota, Wisconsin, Michigan, and North Dakota.

When we re-entered Canada at the little town of Estevan, I no longer needed to exercise my imagination by conjuring up otherworldly landscapes. The desolation of the southeast corner of Saskatchewan was appalling, and it was terrifyingly real. The dust storms had been at work there for several years and they had left behind them an incipient desert. Here and there the whitening bones of abandoned build-

ings remained to mark the death of hopes; and the wind-burnished wood of engulfed fences protruded from the drifts of subsoil that were overwhelming the works of man.

We were all subdued. Although my father tried hard to reassure us, saying that things would improve as we went north, I can remember no great improvement in that lunar landscape as we passed through endless little hamlets that appeared to be in the last stages of dry rot, and as we traversed the burning expanses of drought-stricken fields.

Mother was openly mutinous by the time we reached Saskatoon and even my father was a little depressed. But I was at an age when tragedy has no permanent reality. I saw only that here was a land foreign to all my imaginings, and one that offered limitless possibilities for totally new kinds of adventures. I was fascinated by the cracked white saucers that were the

dried-up sloughs; by the dusty clusters of poplar trees that, for some reason which still escapes me, were known as bluffs; and by a horizon that was limitless.

The innumerable little gophers roused my speculative interest, as did the bitter alkaline waters of the few remaining wells, the great soaring shapes of the hawks that rose from the fence posts by the roadsides, and the quaver of coyotes in the evening that sent a shiver down my back. Even Saskatoon, when we found it at last sprawled in exhausted despair beside the trickle of the river, was pregnant with adventure.

Father rented a house for us in the northern section of the city. To me it seemed admirable, for it was close to the outskirts of the city—and having been so recently grafted on the face of the plains, Saskatoon had as yet no outer ring of suburbs. You had but to step off the streetcar at the end of the last row of houses, and you were on virgin prairie. The transition in space and time was abrupt and complete and I could make that transition not only on Saturdays, but on any afternoon when school was over.

If there was one drawback to the new life in Saskatoon, it was that we had no dog. The prairies could be only half real to a boy without a dog. I began agitating for one almost as soon as we arrived and I found a willing ally in my father—though his motives were not mine.

For many years he had been exposed to the colourful tales of my great-uncle Frank, who homesteaded in Alberta in 1900. Frank was a hunter born, and most of his stories dealt with the superlative shooting to be had on the western plains. Before we were properly settled in Saskatoon my father determined to test those tales. He bought a fine English shotgun, a shooting coat, cases of ammunition, a copy of the *Saskatchewan Game Laws*, and a handbook on shotgun shooting. There remained only one indispensable item—a hunting dog.

One evening he arrived home from the library with such a beast in tow behind him. Its name was Crown Prince Challenge Indefatigable. It stood about as high as the dining-room table and, as far as Mother and I could judge, consisted mainly of feet and tongue. Father was annoyed at our levity and haughtily informed us that the Crown Prince was an Irish setter, kennel bred and field trained, and a dog to delight the heart of any expert. To my eyes he seemed a singularly useless sort of beast with but one redeeming feature. I greatly admired the way he

drooled. I have never known a dog who could drool as the Crown Prince could. He never stopped, except to flop his way to the kitchen sink and tank up on water. He left a wet and sticky trail wherever he went.

Mother might have overlooked his obvious defects, had it not been for his price. She could not overlook that, for the owner was asking two hundred dollars, and we could no more afford such a sum than we could have afforded a Cadillac. Crown Prince left the next morning, but Father was not discouraged, and it was clear that he would try again.

Mother realized that a dog was now inevitable, and when chance brought the duck boy—as we afterwards referred to him—to our door on that dusty August day, Mother showed her mettle by snatching the initiative right out of my father's hands.

By buying the duck boy's pup, she not only placed herself in a position to forestall the purchase of an expensive dog of my father's choice but she was also able to save six cents in cash. She was never one to despise a bargain.

When I came home from school the bargain was installed in a soap carton in the kitchen. He looked to be a somewhat dubious buy at any price. Small, emaciated, and caked liberally with cow manure, he peered up at me in a nearsighted sort of way. But when I knelt beside him and extended an exploratory hand he roused himself and sank his puppy teeth into my thumb with such satisfactory gusto that my doubts dissolved. I knew that he and I would get along.

William W. Smith
Saskatchewan

This folk song has an interesting history. Originally it was a hymn called "Beulah Land." On the American plains, where song parodies were popular, the words were changed to fit the local situation. So instead of the paradise referred to in the hymn, the song described heat, dust, and starving animals and was renamed "Sweet Dakota Land," "Sweet Nebraska Land," and so on. "Saskatchewan," with words by William W. Smith of Swift Current, is the Canadian version. To the miseries of the American songs, it adds a complaint about the bitter cold. Yet while most of the American songs end with a sigh—"We only stay 'cause we're too poor to move away"—the northern version ends on a hopeful note. The people of Saskatchewan, it seems to say, are tough enough to make it through to better times.

Sas - kat - che -wan, the land of snow Where winds are al - ways
on the blow, Where peo - ple sit with fro - zen toes, And why we stay here
no one knows. Sas - kat - che -wan, Sas - kat - che - wan, There's
no place like Sas - kat - che -wan. We sit and gaze a - cross the plain, And
won - der why it ne - ver rains, And Ga - briel blows his
trum - pet sound; He says: "The rain, she's gone a - round."

1.

SASKATCHEWAN, THE LAND OF SNOW
Where winds are always on the blow,
Where people sit with frozen toes,
And why we stay here no one knows.

Chorus:
Saskatchewan, Saskatchewan,
There's no place like Saskatchewan.
We sit and gaze across the plain,
And wonder why it never rains,
And Gabriel blows his trumpet sound;
He says: "The rain, she's gone around."

2.

Our pigs are dying on their feet
Because they have no feed to eat;
Our horses, though of bronco race,
Starvation stares them in the face.

Chorus

3.

The milk from cows has ceased to flow,
We've had to ship them east, you know;
Our hens are old and lay no eggs,
Our turkeys eat grasshopper legs.

Chorus

4.

But still we love Saskatchewan,
We're proud to say we're native ones,
So count your blessings drop by drop,
Next year we'll have a bumper crop!

Chorus

Bobby Gimby
CA-NA-DA

"CA-NA-DA" was the bilingual theme song of Canada's centennial celebration in 1967. The song was composed by Bobby Gimby, who was known as "the pied piper of Canada." Gimby toured the country wearing a pied piper's costume, tootling on a horn, and trailed by a group of children singing, "It's the hundredth anniversary of Confederation. Everybody sing together!" Thousands of Canadians did—a recording of "CA-NA-DA" was a hit pop single and seventy-five thousand copies of its sheet music were sold.

Pierre Berton
The Centennial Train

One of the most successful projects put together to celebrate Canada's birthday was the Centennial Train. The exhibits inside the train presented a lively history of the country and saluted the contributions of Canada's many ethnic groups. The train began its journey in Victoria, B.C. Dignitaries gathered there to send it on its way, pushing a button that made the train's whistle play "O Canada." The train visited sixty-three cities, but those Canadians beyond its reach were not forgotten. Caravans of tractor trailers, with exhibits similar to those on the train, made their way over 65,000 kilometres (40,000 miles) of Canadian road, journeying as far as Tuktoyaktuk in the Northwest Territories. In all, ten million people visited the Centennial Train or one of the caravans.

AS SOON AS THE SIX WINDOWLESS CARS that contained the confederation exhibits were opened, the crowds began to line up. Mary Isobel Winstone, a forty-five-year-old Victoria widow who decided to visit the train with her ten-year-old daughter, Jenny, learned that the best time to go was between five-thirty and six in the afternoon. And so, at half-past five on January 11, she and Jenny took their places. If this was supposed to be a lull, she wondered, what was it like during peak hours? The rain drizzled down as they arrived, but each had brought an umbrella and the queue seemed to be

moving ahead in fairly frequent spurts. A policeman told them that it would take three hours to reach the entrance, but they didn't believe him.

After half an hour the rain stopped. In another half hour they reached the railway yard office that was doing duty as an emergency first-aid post and unofficial comfort station. A stiff breeze chilled them, and the line seemed to move more and more slowly; but they kept on. At last they reached the end of the train proper. Visitors who had already gone through cheered them as they passed by. "It was worth that long wait," Mrs. Winstone

heard one remark. She felt relieved.

At the two-hour mark, a small child, tired but still game, sighed, "Isn't it lucky the Centennial comes only once in a lifetime?" Mrs. Winstone longed for something hot to drink; a sign announced "free coffee after the train," but the need was now. Mrs. Winstone took heart from the fact that they were inching closer. "We felt we were paying a tribute to Canada by being there," she recalled later, "and that we would somehow be letting her down if we left, so we continued to wait."

At last, after three hours in the queue, they reached the intricately designed entrance to the travelling museum. A ripple of excitement ran down the line. "Is the train going to leave now?" a tiny three-year-old wanted to know.

At 9:09 p.m. they made it inside. The train was an experience on wheels, complete with the sights, sounds, and smells of a country one hundred years in the making. Mary and Jenny Winstone entered Car No. 1, walking the floor of a primeval forest, listening to sounds the archaeologists told them were heard long before the Ice Age. They walked past a huge photograph of a family of eight huddled on an English dock in the 1920s, preparing to leave hearth and home for Canada, then entered a replica of a steerage cabin on an immigrant ship, complete with bunks housing plastic figures of sickly, emaciated passengers in rags. A lantern swayed above them as they heard the cries of children, the coughs of men, and the groan of timbers as the musty smells of crowded humanity assailed their nostrils. They stood on a plank floor and

press, stroked a 1920s coonskin coat, picked up a few grains of Marquis wheat, goggled at Louis Riel's pistol and Sitting Bull's tobacco pouch. And once every hour, some small fortunate child was allowed to press the button that sounded the train's familiar whistle.

After spending an hour among the displays, Mrs. Winstone and her daughter were exhilarated by a sense of Canadian history. To plan and build the train had taken two years and $1.5 million. Mary Winstone considered it time and money well spent.

The purple train caught the imagination of the country. In Calgary, thousands waited four hours in a blizzard to climb aboard. Although the train was designed to handle no more than four thousand visitors a day, the attendance was never less than five thousand. In a single day in Vancouver twice that many lined up, uncomplaining. The long wait was an act of affirmation in the country. Like Mrs. Winstone, visitors saw themselves as bearing witness to something profound and mystical. The nation had survived for one hundred years; who were they to complain about a three-hour wait?

Every community desperately wanted the train to stop there and was aggrieved when the tight schedule made additional or undesignated stops impossible. The people of Terrace, a B.C. logging town, actually plotted to halt the train by stalling a logging truck on the tracks, after which they proposed to entertain the crew with a barbecue and square dancing. The Mounties got wind of the scheme, and the train roared through town, unimpeded, two hours ahead of schedule.

looked out at a Great War no-man's-land from inside a trench, with machine-gun fire bursting all about and the occasional star shell lighting up the sky. When they walked through a beaded curtain, there was a 1920s dress, shimmying to the Charleston, while a Mack Sennett film flickered above an ancient player piano and a nearby stock ticker recapitulated the Crash of '29.

They found buttons to press. One caused an ice cap to descend over a map of Canada; another showed a jigsaw puzzle of the country's provinces and territories coming together between 1849 and 1949. They walked on the steel deck of a World War Two fighting ship, put their hands on the huge wheel of a Red River cart, sat in an eighteenth-century French-Canadian chair, played with Joseph Howe's flat-bed

Why Can't We Talk to Each Other?

By the time of Canada's centennial, English Canadians could no longer ignore the fact that many French Canadians in Quebec saw little reason to celebrate. As late as 1960, most big businesses in Quebec were owned by anglophones (English speakers), and English was the language of many offices and stores, even though it was the mother tongue of only 18 per cent of Quebec's population. However, the 1960s, the years of the so-called Quiet Revolution, brought new confidence to Quebec, and new demands from the Québécois. Jean Lesage became premier in 1962 by using the campaign slogan "Maîtres chez nous" (masters in our own house). One of Canada's first responses to Quebec's concerns was the Official Languages Act of 1969, which said that both French and English were to be used in Parliament, federal courts, and government of Canada offices. Federal employees had to be able to speak both official languages, and all products had to have labels in English and French. Between the 1960s and the end of the century, some Quebec leaders tried to hammer out a better deal for Quebec within Confederation. Other Quebec leaders felt that separating Quebec from Canada was the only solution. Many times over those years, while Quebec struggled to work out its future, the rest of the country held its breath.

Mary Peate
Neighbours

Mary Peate wrote about her Montreal childhood in a book called *Girl in a Red River Coat,* from which this story is taken. The book describes Montreal in the 1930s as a city where the French and the English seemed to live in two different worlds. In the neighbourhood of Notre Dame de Grace, where Peate lived, she seldom heard French spoken, even though French speakers greatly outnumbered the English in the rest of the city. "Neighbours" tells what happens when a French-speaking family moves in next door. Mary and her new friend, Louise, try to bridge the gap between two languages and cultures. Unfortunately, Mary's mother is unwilling to make the same effort.

THE NEXT DAY WAS ONE OF THOSE DAYS when the snow is of the exact right consistency for making snowballs and snow forts. So I put on my Red River coat and two pair of mitts, and went out to make a snow fort on our front lawn. After a while, Louise, the little French girl next door, came out and started to half-heartedly shovel her front walk, pausing every now and then in her labours to watch as I started to build the walls of the fort. Noticing her apparent interest, I gestured to her to come over, so she did, and started to help me pack the snow. This was something we could do together without having to talk, and we worked for most of the afternoon until we had built an impressive fortress of snow, behind which we could hide after lobbing the snowballs we were piling up as ammunition against any enemy that might happen along.

Crouched behind the snow wall, rounding and making firmer the snowballs in our cache, we didn't see the enemy when he came along. It was Walter, the boy who had been hit by a car. The first we saw of him was when he leapt on the wall of our fort, crumbling it and covering us with snow. Louise and I jumped up yelling and he said, "Well, well, if it isn't the philosopher," and kicked down what remained of the wall. Then, to add injury to insult, he put snow in the hood of my coat and pulled it over my head, causing the snow to trickle down my neck. He was as one possessed as he danced on our pile of snowballs, squashing them and chanting at Louise, "French pea soup. French pea soup."

I picked up one of the snowballs that had eluded his feet, and, as he danced off down the street, I jumped up on the remains of the fort, made a flying leap and tackled him. I landed on his back, knocking him down. Then I pounded him on the head as hard as I could, and rubbed his face in snow, taking advantage of the fact that when I knocked him down I'd knocked the breath out of him. When he began to show signs of getting his wind back, I jumped up and ran back to Louise. He made as if to follow me, then apparently thought better of it and continued down the street.

Louise said something derogatory about him in French, and I muttered darkly about him in English, and then she motioned for me to go home with her.

Mrs. Lalonde, Louise's mother, was a plump, jolly-looking woman, and, when she opened the door and saw our wet, snowy condition, she drew us inside and led the way out to the kitchen.

It was the first time I'd been in the flat since Mrs. Donovan lived there, and, though there was a tantalizing smell coming from the oven, it seemed as if I could still smell Mrs. Donovan's cats.

Louise's mother took our mitts and toques from us and spread them out on the radiator to dry, and, clucking sympathetically as Louise told her what had happened, she sat us down at the kitchen table, which was covered with seven or eight pies that smelled heavenly.

"*Tourtière*," she said to me, as she cut into one of the pies and gave us each a piece.

It was delicious. It was the first time I'd eaten *tourtière*, although I knew about them. I knew that French Canadians traditionally ate these meat pies on Christmas Eve after Mass, and on New Year's Eve, when they gathered together for a family party called *le réveillon*. Mrs. Lalonde must have been preparing for such a party now. As I ate, I kept saying, "Is it ever *bonne! Très bonne!*" and Mrs. Lalonde and Louise smiled.

When I'd finished, I took my toque and mitts off the radiator, said "*Merci*," and left by the kitchen door, which was just across the driveway from ours. When I went in I told my mother about how good the *tourtière* had been.

"I've always wanted to know how to make a real French-Canadian *tourtière*," she said.

"Why don't you ask Mrs. Lalonde for the recipe?" I asked.

"Does she speak English at all?" my mother asked. "We always wave hello to each other whenever we're out on our back porches at the same time, but we've never actually spoken."

Thinking back, I realized Mrs. Lalonde hadn't spoken a word of English the whole time I'd been there, but I hadn't noticed it at the time. All the sympathetic

sounds she made as she took our wet things, the clucking she did as she listened to the story of nasty Walter, the beaming she did as I gobbled up her pie; all these things had been neither French nor English, but just the sounds mothers make in any language.

"No, she doesn't speak English," I had to reply.

"Well, I couldn't very well get the recipe then," my mother said.

I had the feeling that if my mother had gone with me across the way and sampled some of Mrs. Lalonde's *tourtière* and said, "Mmmm," and had pointed to Mrs. Lalonde and then at the pie, and made pie-making motions, Mrs. Lalonde would have caught on to the fact that my mother wanted to know how to make one. Then they would have laughed and kept misunderstanding each other and had lots of fun, and my mother would have wound up knowing how to make *tourtière*. But I didn't try to put these thoughts into words, and, as it turned out, my mother, what with being busy with my aunt and all, never did get a chance to visit with Mrs. Lalonde. The Lalondes moved away the following May.

Ian Tyson and Peter Gzowski
Song for Canada

"Song for Canada," written in 1965, was a well-intentioned but naive appeal to French Canadians to remember their shared history with English Canadians. Its words reflect the bewilderment of many anglophones, who were just waking up to Quebec's discontent. In those years, a very small revolutionary group, the Front de libération du Québec (FLQ), was getting a great deal of media attention. They advocated violence to achieve independence for Quebec. In 1963, they began to place bombs in Montreal, and they eventually killed several people. But their most shocking acts—the 1970 kidnap of the British trade commissioner, James Cross, and the murder of Pierre Laporte, Quebec's minister of labour—were yet to be committed when this song was written. These events prompted Prime Minister Pierre Trudeau's government to impose the War Measures Act. Army tanks rolled through the streets of several cities and hundreds of people were arrested. Almost all of them were later released without being charged with anything. This was one of the most controversial actions of government in Canadian history—but it also marked the end of the FLQ's terrorist activities.

1.
HOW COME WE CAN'T TALK TO EACH OTHER ANY MORE?
Why can't you see I'm changing too?
We've got by far too long to end it feeling wrong
And I still share too much with you.

Chorus:
Just one great river always flowing to the sea,
One single river rolling in eternity;
Two nations in the land that lies along each shore,
But just one river rolling free.

2.
How come you shut me up
As if I wasn't there?
What's this new bitterness you've found?
However wronged you were,
However strong it hurt,
It wasn't me that hurled you down.

Chorus

3.
Why can't you understand?
I'm glad you're standing proud;
I know you made it on your own,
But in this pride you earned,
I thought you might have learned
That you don't have to stand alone.

Last chorus:
Lonely northern rivers
Come together till you see
One single river rolling in eternity;
Two nations in the land
That lies along each shore
But just one river, you and me.

Gilles Vigneault
Mon Pays

Gilles Vigneault is a much-loved Quebec poet and songwriter. He wrote "Mon Pays" in 1964, when he was working on a film being shot in -35°C weather. Its haunting refrain—"My country is not a country, it is winter"—popped into his mind, and the rest of the song soon followed. "Mon Pays" quickly became Quebec's unofficial anthem. Vigneault has long been associated with the Quebec independence movement. The Parti Québécois, whose long-term goal is Quebec's separation from the rest of Canada, first stood for election in Quebec in 1970. From 1976 until 1985, under the leadership of Premier René Lévesque, the party formed the government of Quebec. The PQ won power again in 1994 under Jacques Parizeau. In a 1995 referendum, the people of Quebec voted against beginning the separation process—but by only a tiny margin.

1.

MON PAYS, CE N'EST PAS UN PAYS, C'EST L'HIVER;

Mon jardin, ce n'est pas un jardin, c'est la plaine;

Mon chemin, ce n'est pas un chemin, c'est la neige;

Mon pays, ce n'est pas un pays, c'est l'hiver.

Dans la blanche cérémonie / Où la neige au vent se marie,

Dans ce pays de poudrerie / Mon père a fait bâtir maison

Et je m'en vais être fidèle / A sa manière, à son modèle.

La chambre d'amis sera telle / Qu'on viendra des autres saisons

Pour se bâtir à côté d'elle.

2.

Mon pays, ce n'est pas un pays, c'est l'hiver;

Mon refrain, ce n'est pas un refrain, c'est rafale;

Ma maison, ce n'est pas ma maison, c'est froidure;

Mon pays, ce n'est pas un pays, c'est l'hiver.

De mon grand pays solitaire / Je crie avant que de me taire

A tous les hommes de la terre / "Ma maison, c'est votre maison."

Entre mes quatre murs de glace / Je mets mon temps et mon espace

A préparer le feu, la place / Pour les humains de l'horizon,

Et les humains sont de ma race.

3.

Mon pays, ce n'est pas un pays, c'est l'hiver;

Mon jardin, ce n'est pas un jardin, c'est la plaine;

Mon chemin, ce n'est pas un chemin, c'est la neige;

Mon pays, ce n'est pas un pays, c'est l'hiver.

Coda

Mon pays, ce n'est pas un pays, c'est l'envers

D'un pays qui n'était ni pays ni patrie.

Ma chanson, ce n'est pas ma chanson, c'est ma vie;

C'est pour toi que je veux posséder mes hivers.

FIRST VERSE IN ENGLISH
Land of mine, not a land but a long wintertime
Garden plot, not a garden but a snowy white plain
Highway long, not a road but a white frosty song
Land of mine, not a land but a cold wintertime

PART SEVEN

Fun and Games

Illustrated by

Kim Fernandes

Tim Shortt

Animals Wild and Mild

 No matter where you live in Canada, you are never far from the wild. Even in the middle of Canada's largest cities, you may meet a raccoon or a skunk if you go for a stroll after dark. It's not surprising that so many Canadians have written stories, based on their own experiences, in which people help out a needy wild creature, usually an orphaned baby animal. Two of these stories—which feature a young porcupine and two beaver kittens—are collected here. But it's also not surprising that Canadians have written so vividly about the unpleasant side of getting close to nature. As we all know, something small, fast, and humming may be after our blood.

Grey Owl
Big Small and Little Small

Big Small and Little Small are two beaver kittens rescued by an Ojibwa hunter after they are attacked by an otter. He takes the kittens home to his daughter, Sajo, and her brother, Shapian, who take care of them until they are old enough to be released into the wild again. Grey Owl, the author of this story, was an Englishman, but he lived as a Native person in Canada. Although he had once been a trapper, he was persuaded by his Mohawk wife to become a protector of wildlife. *The Adventures of Sajo and Her Beaver People*, from which this excerpt is taken, was written for their daughter, Dawn, in 1935. It is based on Grey Owl's own experience raising orphaned beavers.

THE KITTENS QUICKLY TOOK A LIKING TO their new way of living, and although no human beings could ever quite take the place of their own parents, everything possible was done to make them feel at ease.

Shapian partitioned off the under part of his bunk with sheets of birch bark, leaving one end open; and this was their house, in which they at once made themselves very much at home. Gitchie Meegwon cut a hole in the floor and fitted down into it a wash-tub, for a pond—not much of a one perhaps, but it was as large as the plunge-hole had been, and they spent nearly half their time in it, and would lie on top of the water eating their twigs and leaves. Whenever they left the tub, they always squatted their plump lit-

tle personalities upright beside it, and scrubbed their coats, first squeezing the hair in bunches with their little fists to get the water out. That done, the whole coat was carefully combed with a double claw that all beavers are provided with, one on each hind foot, for this purpose. All this took quite a while, and they were so businesslike and serious about it that Sajo would become as interested as they were, and would sometimes help them, rubbing their fur this way and that with the tips of her fingers, and then they would scrub away so much the harder.

It was their fashion, when drying themselves off this way, to raise one arm high above their heads, as far as it would go, and rub that side with the other hand,

and being upright as they were, it looked as if they were about to dance the Highland Fling. They often sat up in this manner while eating the bark off small sticks, and as one or other of them held a stick crossways in his hands, rolling it round and round whilst the busy teeth whittled off the bark, he looked for all the world like some little old man playing on a flute. Sometimes they varied the show, and when the sticks were very slim they ate the whole business, putting one end in their mouths and pushing it on in with their hands, while the sharp front teeth, working very fast, chopped it into tiny pieces. The rattle of their cutting machinery sounded much the same as would a couple of sewing machines running a little wild, and as they held up their heads and shoved the sticks, to all appearances, slowly down their throats, they looked a good deal like a pair of sword swallowers who found a meal of swords very much to their taste.

They had to have milk for the first two weeks or so, and Sajo borrowed a bottle and a baby's nipple from a neighbour in the village, and fed them with it turn about. But while one would be getting his meal (both hands squeezed tight around the neck of the bottle!), the other would scramble around and make a loud outcry and a hubbub, and try to get hold of the bottle, and there would be a squabbling and a great confusion and the can of milk was sometimes upset and spilled all over; so that at last there had to be another bottle and nipple found, and Shapian fed one kitten while Sajo fed the other. Later on they were fed bannock and milk, which made things a little easier, as each had his own small dish which the children held for him. The beavers would pick up the mixture with one hand, shoving it into their mouths at a great rate; and I am afraid their table manners were not very good, as there was a good deal of rather

loud smacking of lips, and hard breathing to be heard and they often talked with their mouths full.

At first they had no names, and the children just called, "*Undaas, undaas, Amik, Amik,*" which means "Come here, come here, Beaver, Beaver." But a little later on Sajo remembered the day that the two wooden dolls had seemed to be looking on when the kittens first had come, and how these new arrivals had so quickly taken their place. Well, she thought, they may as well take their names too, and called the beavers Chilawee and Chikanee, which means Big Small and Little Small. It was not long before they got to know these names, and would always come out from the house under Shapian's bunk when called on; but the names sounded so much alike, that when one was called they both would come, and as they themselves were as much alike as two peas, the difference in size being not very great, it was often pretty hard to tell which was which. To make matters worse, they did not grow evenly; that is, one would grow a little faster than the other for a while, and then he would slacken down and the other would catch up, and get ahead of him. First one was bigger than the other, then the other was bigger than the one! And it would be discovered that Little Small had been Big Small for quite some time, whilst Big Small had been going around disguised as Little Small. No sooner would that be fixed up than they would change sizes again, and when they evened up, in the middle stages as it were, they could not by any means be told apart.

It was all very confusing, and Sajo had just about decided to give them one name between them and call them just "The Smalls," when Chilawee settled matters after a manner all his own. He had a habit of falling asleep in the warm cave under the stove, between the stones, and one day there was a great smell of burning hair, and no one could imagine where it came from. The stove was opened and examined, and swept off, and the stove-pipes were tapped and rapped, but the smell of burning hair was getting stronger all the time; until some one thought of looking *under* the stove, to discover Chilawee sleeping there unconcernedly while the hair on his back scorched to a crisp, and he was routed out of there with a large patch of his coat badly singed. This made a very good brand, something like those that cattle are marked with on a ranch, and it stayed there all summer, making it very easy to tell who was who; and by calling one of them (the burnt one) *Chilawee*, and the other Chik*anee*, so as to be a little different, they got to know each his name, and everything was straightened out at last.

They followed the children around continuously, trotting patiently along behind them; and their legs were so very short and they ran so low to the floor on them that their feet could hardly be seen, so that they looked like two little clockwork animals out of a toy-shop, that went on wheels and had been wound up and never *would* stop. Anything they found on the floor, such as moccasins, kindling wood, and so forth, they dragged from place to place, and later, when they got bigger and stronger, they even stole sticks of firewood from the wood-box and took them away to their private chamber, where they sliced them up into shavings with their keen-edged teeth and made their beds with them; and nice, clean-looking beds they were too. Any small articles of clothing that might happen to fall to the floor, if not picked up at once, quickly disappeared into the beaver house. The broom would

be pulled down and hauled around, and this broom and the firewood seemed to be their favourite playthings; greatly, I suspect, on account of the noise they could make with them, which they seemed very much to enjoy.

But their greatest amusement was wrestling. Standing up on their hind legs they would put their short arms around each other as far as they would go, and with their heads on each other's shoulders, they would try to put each other down. Now this was hard to do, as the wide tails and the big, webbed hind feet made a very solid support, and they would strain, and push, and grunt, and blow until one of them, feeling himself slipping, would begin to back up in order to keep his balance, with the other coming along pushing all he could. Sometimes the loser would recover sufficiently to begin pushing the other way and then the walk would commence to go in the opposite direction; and so, back and forth, round and round, for minutes at a time, they would carry on this strange game of theirs, which looked as much like two people waltzing as it did anything else. All the while it was going on there would be, between the grunts and gasps, loud squeals and cries from whoever was getting pushed, and much stamping of feet and flopping of tails, trying to hold their owners up, until one of them, on the backward match, would allow his tail to double under him, and fall on his back, when they would immediately quit and scamper around like two madcaps. It was all done in the greatest good humour, and the two children never grew tired of watching them.

Lenore Keeshig-Tobias
The Porcupine

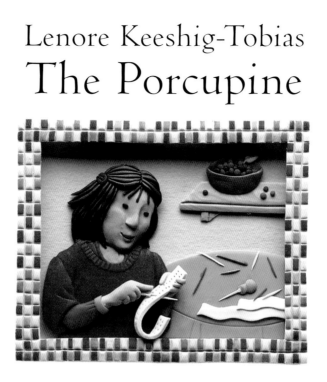

Lenore Keeshig-Tobias is an Ojibwa who grew up on the Bruce Peninsula of Ontario. She was the oldest of ten children, and telling stories was always an important part of her family life. As an adult she has continued the tradition, participating in many storytelling events for children and adults. "The Porcupine" is a true story about her childhood, and particularly about the experiences of her younger sister, Towdy, who "had a special way with animals." Because the author used her family members' real names in the story, she asked their permission before presenting "The Porcupine" to an audience.

DAD WORKED IN THE BIG CITIES—Toronto, Niagara Falls, Buffalo, and Detroit. High steel, industrial painting, and window washing—*Indian* men have always been famous for their equilibrium in high places—something to do with the middle-ear position. Anyway, my dad was away a lot. So, Mom had to look after us kids herself and supplement Dad's earnings with her craft work.

She worked with porcupine quills and birch bark, making headbands, something simple, easy to make, and something tourists could pick up for a dollar or two.

Mom would sort her quills into fat ones and thin ones, and long ones and short ones. She'd dye them using crepe paper and vinegar, or a commercial product. Sometimes she would use a natural dye—berries or bark or something like that. Carefully she'd sketch designs onto strips of birch bark, and then with an awl or darning needle she would begin to embroider, punching a hole, pushing the sharp end of a softened quill into the hole and tightening it by pulling the quill partway through with tweezers. The sharp end she'd snip off and flatten.

The embroidery done, she would then sew a strip of felt to the birch bark, join the ends and—there was a headband. The headbands she then took to the reserve general store to buy milk and bread and other supplies.

We older kids, of course, learned quill embroidery. And soon we were making the headbands, thus giving Mom time to spend creating the pictures—blue jays, chickadees, deer, other wildlife and wildflowers. We were in awe of her artistry, and so very proud when a reporter came by to do a story about her.

One spring Mom's supply of quills ran low and so she asked my brother Tony to go out and find a porcupine. "Down the road about a mile or so, near that big elm tree. I saw a porcupine there the other day. Must have been hit by a car. Bring it to me," she told him.

Tony went off and he walked and walked, past the elm tree and farther down the road. But he didn't see any porcupine. Tony knew how Mom needed the quills and so he decided to hunt for a porcupine. He would also prove that he too was a hunter, a good hunter. He found a good-sized rock at the side of the road and headed into the bush.

It wasn't long before he spotted a great big porcupine. Taking careful aim, he hurled the rock. It struck with a dull thud and the porcupine lay down and died. Tony pulled a length of rope from his pocket, thinking how proud Mom would be that he had fetched a porcupine for her, a big one too. But my brother's heart stopped as he reached down to tie the forepaws of the animal. There beside the dead porcupine was a little pink porcupine baby.

He wasn't sure what to do, so he tied up the dead animal as fast as he could and dragged it home. With a lump in his throat he told Mom about the porcupine kitten.

Towdy was listening. A year younger than Tony, and four years younger than me, Towdy always had a special way with animals. She could stand outside with a handful of crumbs and all kinds of birds would gather round. Some would light on her head or shoulders, others right in her hand. When she heard about the porcupine, she questioned Tony carefully, and then headed off through the bush, around the trees and over the boulders. There, curled up on the spot where its mother had died, she found the little pink baby. She scooped it up carefully, cupped it in her hands, and instinctively held it close to her heart so the baby could hear the rhythm of her heartbeat and feel the motion of her breathing. She then hurried home.

Tony was quickly sent off to the general store, with an armload of headbands. He returned with a can of baby formula and a box of pablum. That's what Towdy fed her critter. In fact, she was getting up for night-time feedings every two or three hours.

That year taught us wonderful things about porcupines. For one, porcupines purr like cats. Porki was as cuddly as a kitten and just as playful too. Towdy would hold her left hand down to Porki. Porki would crawl into the palm of her hand. Towdy would then hold him up into the air. Porki would creep along her arm, sit on her left shoulder and whisper sweet porcupine nothings into her ear. He would then nuzzle the back of her neck, perch himself on her right shoulder, and whisper more sweet nothings. Towdy would then extend her right arm, the porcupine would waddle out to her fingertips

and she would lower him to the floor.

Porki played with each one of us, but slept with Towdy. He would curl up beside her pillow and sometimes on cold nights he would wiggle his way down under the blankets. And yes, sometimes Towdy did wake up to pull a quill or two from her side. This is how we learned that porcupines don't shoot quills. We all knew that, but didn't necessarily believe it.

Whenever strangers tried to pick up Porki or when people Porki didn't like tried to pick him up or whenever he was frightened by a loud or unfamiliar noise or something unfamiliar, Porki turned himself into a prickly little ball. Anyone who tried to handle this little fuzz ball ended up with a handful of prickles; everyone except Towdy, of course.

The days and weeks went by and soon Porki was going out to the garden, out to nibble yellow beans and tomatoes and lettuce. The days and weeks went by and Porki was venturing farther and farther into the garden. We knew it had to be. Mom said so. Porcupines needed that space, and we really couldn't expect Porki to live with us forever, although we all wished it could be. The days and weeks went by and Porki was venturing beyond the garden, coming home late at night or the next day, and sometimes not for a couple of days.

One day Porki didn't come home. That was a sad time—for Towdy and the rest of us. Mom said Porki had heard "the call of the wild." Other times she said it was "a lady porcupine" he'd heard. And another time she told us that Porki wanted a family of his own. And we couldn't deny him that.

Months passed, and one day my brothers were heading off to the general store again. Way up in front them, they could see a small animal lumber onto the road. As they got closer they could see it was a porcupine doing its flatfooted waddle across the dirt road. "Hey, *Porki!*" they called just for fun. The porcupine stopped, turned slowly around and waddled towards them. "Hey, Porki," they shouted again and knew it *was* our pet. Porki waddled closer, grunting his porcupine greetings *kugg kugg. Kugg kugg kugg.* The boys and the porcupine talked for a while. When it was time to go, Porki turned slowly away and waddled across the road. They say he turned back for one more look before disappearing into the tall grass and the bush.

We had many pets during those years— flying squirrels, red squirrels, ducks, rabbits, raccoons, bees, and butterflies. But Porki was always the special one.

Those were good times back then when we were children. The years went by and Mom and Dad were able to build a new house, just across the yard on the other side of the white oak tree. My sisters and brothers and I went off to high school, college, and university. Tony now works for the government. I'm a storyteller and writer. Towdy is a day-care worker, has four children of her own, and still takes in and looks after injured or orphaned animals.

One summer evening, not too long ago, Towdy and Mom were having a nice quiet visit, just the two of them. They were talking, listening to the crickets, talking, listening to the tree frogs. They were talking, watching the shooting stars overhead and waiting for grandmother moon to rise over the limestone bluff. After a bit they became aware of a noise, a scratching noise somewhere over by the old house. They found a flashlight and quietly made their way across the lawn, past the oak tree and through the tall grass. The noise stopped briefly and then continued. Towdy and Mom crept round to the front porch of the old house. They shone the light into the corners of the porch. Nothing. They shone the light along the door frame. Nothing. Then they shone the light along the bottom of the door. And there it was—one great big *old* porcupine scratching to get in. It stiffened and blinked at the brightness of the light. "Hello, Porki," they said. And the big old porcupine relaxed, then lumbered round to look at them. There they sat for a good two hours or so, Towdy, Mom, and the porcupine. Once again Towdy and Mom listened to the sweet porcupine nothings *kugg kugg. Kugg kugg kugg.*

Porki had come back to an empty house. How many times, we wondered, how many times had he come back and scratched at the door? That old porcupine never came back again, even though Mom and Towdy waited and watched. The house is gone now, but we know that Porki had not forgotten us after all those years, and he had come back to say goodbye one last time.

Myra Stilborn
A Mosquito in the Cabin

Canada is home to about seventy-four different kinds of mosquitoes. Only the females
feed on blood, which they need for egg production. The female's long proboscis (mouthpart) pierces
the victim's skin. While she draws blood out, she injects a substance that keeps it flowing. This is what produces
the itchy, red bump on your skin. Mosquitoes are a summer nuisance in many parts of Canada, but they are particularly maddening in northern woodlands, where clouds of the insects may make it impossible for people to
be outside without protective gear. But as Myra Stilborn's humorous poem reminds us, just one
mosquito, if it's inside with you in the dark, can be pretty annoying too.

ALTHOUGH YOU BASH HER,
  swat her, smash her,
and go to bed victorious,
    happy and glorious
     she will come winging,
     zooming and zinging,
    wickedly singing
       over your bed.
You slap the air
      but she's in your hair
      cackling with laughter.
You smack your head,
     but she isn't dead—
     she's on the rafter.
She's out for blood—
     yours, my friend,
and she will get it, in the end.
She brings it first to boiling point,
       then lets it steam.
With a fee, fi, fo and contented fum
    she sips it
     while you dream.

Just for Laughs

It has often been suggested that Canadians are funny because they're willing to laugh at themselves. The Canadian attitude seems to be that it's often wiser and healthier not to take yourself too seriously. All the pieces in this section poke fun at some aspect of Canadian life—from people trying to survive in the extreme conditions of the North to people wanting to add some excitement to their quiet lives in a small Ontario town—however, none of them does it in a mean-spirited way.

Traditional
When the Ice Worms Nest Again

"When the Ice Worms Nest Again" was first sung by fishermen, trappers, and prospectors of Canada's North in the early 1900s. There are many different stories about how the song originated. However, Edith Fowke, who devoted her life to collecting Canadian folklore and folk songs, believed that Robert Service (the author of "The Cremation of Sam McGee" on p. 98) may have written the words to the song. Service may also have invented ice worms, to play a trick on a newcomer to Dawson City who was annoying the locals by calling himself a sourdough (an experienced prospector). They challenged him to prove himself by drinking the true beverage of the North: an ice-worm cocktail. The bartender brought out a jar of worms and dropped them, one by one, into drinks. Everyone guzzled them right down except for the sickened newcomer. Of course, they all knew something he did not: the "worms" were really pieces of spaghetti, with two red ink spots for eyes.

1.

THERE'S A TRUSTY HUSKY MAIDEN IN THE ARCTIC
And she waits for me but it is not in vain
For some day I'll put my mukluks on and ask her
If she'll wed me when the ice worms nest again
In the land of pale blue snow where it's ninety-nine below
And the polar bears are roaming o'er the plain
In the shadow of the Pole I will clasp her to my soul
We'll be married when the ice worms nest again.

2.

For our wedding feast we'll have seal oil and blubber
In our kayak we will roam the bounding main
All the walruses will look at us and rubber
We'll be married when the ice worms nest again
When some night at half-past two I return to my igloo
After sitting with a friend who was in pain.
She'll be waiting for me there with the hambone of a bear
And she'll beat me till the ice worms nest again.

Stephen Leacock
The Sinking of the Mariposa Belle

In *Sunshine Sketches of a Little Town*, Stephen Leacock made gentle fun of the people of Mariposa, a fictional town based on Orillia, Ontario. *Sunshine Sketches* was first published in 1912, just after the *Titanic* sank, and you can find many references to that event in Leacock's story, including mention of Harland and Wolff of Belfast, who built the *Titanic*, and the famous lifeboat order "Women and children first!" But as you'll see, things work out quite differently for the *Mariposa Belle*—after all, it's only a little excursion steamer on Lake Wissanotti, where the water is no more than two metres (six feet) deep!

I SUPPOSE YOU HAVE OFTEN NOTICED the contrast there is between an excursion on its way out in the morning and what it looks like on the way home.

In the morning everybody is so restless and animated and moves to and fro all over the boat and asks questions. But coming home, as the afternoon gets later and the sun sinks beyond the hills, all the people seem to get so still and quiet and drowsy.

So it was with the people on the *Mariposa Belle*. They sat there on the benches and the deck chairs in little clusters, and listened to the regular beat of the propeller and almost dozed off asleep as they sat. Then when the sun set and the dusk drew on, it grew almost dark on the deck and so still that you could hardly tell there was anyone on board.

And if you had looked at the steamer from the shore or from one of the islands, you'd have seen the row of lights from the cabin windows shining on the water and the red glare of the burning hemlock from the funnel, and you'd have heard the soft thud of the propeller miles away over the lake.

Now and then, too, you could have heard them singing on the steamer,—the voices of the girls and the men blended into unison by the distance, rising and falling in long-drawn melody: "*O—Can-a-da—O—Can-a-da.*"

You may talk as you will about the intoning choirs of your European cathedrals, but the sound of "O Can-a-da," borne across the waters of a silent lake at evening is good enough for those of us who know Mariposa.

I think that it was just as they were singing like this: "O—Can-a-da," that word went round that the boat was sinking.

If you have ever been in any sudden emergency on the water, you will understand the strange psychology of it,—the way in which what is happening seems to become known all in a moment without a word being said. The news is transmitted from one to the other by some mysterious process.

At any rate, on the *Mariposa Belle* first one and then the other heard that the steamer was sinking. As far as I could ever learn the first of it was that George Duff, the bank manager, came very quietly to Dr. Gallagher and asked him if he thought that the boat was sinking. The doctor said no, that he had thought so earlier in the day but that he didn't now think that she was.

After that Duff, according to his own account, had said to Macartney, the lawyer, that the boat was sinking, and Macartney said that he doubted it very much.

Then somebody came to Judge Pepperleigh and woke him up and said that there was six inches of water in the steamer and that she was sinking. And Pepperleigh said it was perfect scandal and passed the news on to his wife and she said that they had no business to allow it

and that if the steamer sank that was the last excursion she'd go on.

So the news went all round the boat and everywhere the people gathered in groups and talked about it in the angry and excited way that people have when a steamer is sinking on one of the lakes like Lake Wissanotti.

Dean Drone, of course, and some others were quieter about it, and said that one must make allowances and that naturally there were two sides to everything. But most of them wouldn't listen to reason at all. I think, perhaps, that some of them were frightened. You see, the last time but one that the steamer had sunk, there had been a man drowned and it made them nervous.

What? Hadn't I explained about the depth of Lake Wissanotti? I had taken it for granted that you knew; and in any case parts of it are deep enough, though I don't suppose in this stretch of it from the big reed beds up to within a mile of the town wharf, you could find six feet of water in it if you tried. Oh, pshaw! I was not talking about a steamer sinking in the ocean and carrying down its screaming crowds of people into the hideous depths of green water. Oh, dear me no! That kind of thing never happens on Lake Wissanotti.

But what does happen is that the *Mariposa Belle* sinks every now and then, and sticks there on the bottom till they get things straightened up.

On the lakes round Mariposa, if a person arrives late anywhere and explains that the steamer sank, everybody understands the situation.

You see when Harland and Wolff built the Mariposa Belle, they left some cracks in between the timbers that you fill up with cotton waste every Sunday. If this is not attended to, the boat sinks. In fact, it is part of the law of the province that all the steamers like the *Mariposa Belle* must be properly corked,—I think that is the word,—every season. There are inspectors who visit all the hotels in the province to see that it is done.

So you can imagine now that I've explained it a little straighter, the indignation of the people when they knew that the boat had come uncorked and that they might be stuck out there on a shoal or a mud-bank half the night.

I don't say either that there wasn't any danger; anyway, it doesn't feel very safe when you realize that the boat is settling down with every hundred yards that she goes, and you look over the side and see only the black water in the gathering night.

Safe! I'm not sure now that I come to think of it that it isn't worse than sinking in the Atlantic. After all, in the Atlantic there is wireless telegraphy, and a lot of trained sailors and stewards. But out on Lake Wissanotti,—far out, so that you can only just see the lights of the town away off to the south,—when the propeller comes to a stop,—and you can hear the hiss of steam as they start to rake out the engine fires to prevent an explosion,—and when you turn from the red glare that comes from the furnace doors as they open them, to the black dark that is gathering over the lake,—and there's a night wind beginning to run among the rushes,—and you see the men going forward to the roof of the pilot house to send up the rockets to rouse the town,—safe? Safe yourself, if you like; as for me, let me once get back into Mariposa again, under the night shadow of the maple trees, and this shall be the last, last time I'll go on Lake Wissanotti.

Safe! Oh yes! Isn't it strange how safe other people's adventures seem after they happen? But you'd have been scared, too, if you'd been there just before the steamer sank, and seen them bringing up all the women on to the top deck.

I don't see how some of the people took it so calmly; how Mr. Smith, for instance, could have gone on smoking and telling how he'd had a steamer "sink on him" on Lake Nipissing and a still bigger one, a side-wheeler, sink on him in Lake Abbitibbi.

Then, quite suddenly, with a quiver, down she went. You could feel the boat sink, sink,—down, down,—would it never get to the bottom? The water came flush up to the lower deck, and then,—thank heaven,—the sinking stopped and there was the *Mariposa Belle* safe and tight on a reed bank.

Really, it made one positively laugh! It seemed so queer and, anyway, if a man has a sort of natural courage, danger makes him laugh. Danger! pshaw! fiddlesticks! everybody scouted the idea. Why, it is just

the little things like this that give zest to a day on the water.

Within half a minute they were all running round looking for sandwiches and cracking jokes and talking of making coffee over the remains of the engine fires.

I don't need to tell at length how it all happened after that.

I suppose the people on the *Mariposa Belle* would have had to settle down there all night or till help came from the town, but some of the men who had gone forward and were peering out into the dark said that it couldn't be more than a mile across the water to Miller's Point. You

could almost see it over there to the left,—some of them, I think, said "off on the port bow," because you know when you get mixed up in these marine disasters, you soon catch the atmosphere of the thing.

So pretty soon they had the davits swung out over the side and were lowering the old lifeboat from the top deck into the water.

There were men leaning out over the rail of the *Mariposa Belle* with lanterns that threw the light as they let her down, and the glare fell on the water and the reeds. But when they got the boat lowered, it looked such a frail, clumsy thing as one saw it from the rail above, that the cry was raised: "Women and children first!" For what was the sense, if it should turn out that the boat wouldn't even hold women and children, of trying to jam a lot of heavy men into it?

So they put in mostly women and children and the boat pushed out into the darkness so freighted down it would hardly float.

In the bow of it was the Presbyterian student who was relieving the minister, and he called out that they were in the hands of Providence. But he was crouched and ready to spring out of them at the first moment.

So the boat went and was lost in the darkness except for the lantern in the bow that you could see bobbing on the water. Then presently it came back and they sent another load, till pretty soon the decks began to thin out and everybody got impatient to be gone.

It was about the time that the third boat-load put off that Mr. Smith took a bet with Mullins for twenty-five dollars, that he'd be home in Mariposa before the people in the boats had walked round the shore.

No one knew just what he meant, but pretty soon they saw Mr. Smith disappear down below into the lowest part of the steamer with a mallet in one hand and a big bundle of marline in the other.

They might have wondered more about it, but it was just at this time that they heard the shouts from the rescue boat—the big Mackinaw lifeboat—that had put out from the town with fourteen men at the sweeps when they saw the first rockets go up.

I suppose there is always something inspiring about a rescue at sea, or on the water.

After all, the bravery of the lifeboat man is the true bravery,—expended to save life, not to destroy it.

Certainly they told for months after of how the rescue boat came out to the *Mariposa Belle*.

I suppose that when they put her in the water the lifeboat touched it for the first time since the old Macdonald Government placed her on Lake Wissanotti.

Anyway, the water poured in at every seam. But not for a moment,—even with two miles of water between them and the steamer,—did the rowers pause for that.

By the time they were half-way there the water was almost up to the thwarts, but they drove her on. Panting and exhausted (for mind you, if you haven't been in a fool boat like that for years, rowing takes it out of you), the rowers stuck to their task. They threw the ballast over and chucked into the water the heavy cork jackets and lifebelts that encumbered their movements. There was no thought of turning back. They were nearer to the steamer than the shore.

"Hang to it, boys," called the crowd from the steamer's deck, and hang they did.

They were almost exhausted when they got them; men leaning from the steamer threw them ropes and one by one every man was hauled aboard just as the lifeboat sank under their feet.

Saved! by Heaven, saved, by one of the smartest pieces of rescue work ever seen on the lake.

There's no use describing it; you need to see rescue work of this kind by lifeboats to understand it.

Nor were the lifeboat crew the only ones that distinguished themselves.

Boat after boat and canoe after canoe had put out from Mariposa to the help of the steamer. They got them all.

Pupkin, the other bank teller, with a face like a horse, who hadn't gone on the excursion,—as soon as he knew that the boat was signalling for help and that Miss Lawson was sending up rockets,—rushed for a row boat, grabbed an oar (two would have hampered him), and paddled madly out into the lake. He struck right out into the dark with the crazy skiff almost sinking beneath his feet. But they got him. They rescued him. They watched him, almost dead with exhaustion, make his way to the steamer, where he was hauled up with ropes. Saved! Saved!!

They might have gone on that way half the night, picking up the rescuers, only, at the very moment when the tenth load of people left for the shore,—just as suddenly and saucily as you please, up came the *Mariposa Belle* from the mud bottom and floated.

FLOATED?

Why, of course she did. If you take a hundred and fifty people off a steamer that has sunk, and if you get a man as shrewd as Mr. Smith to plug the timber seams with mallet and marline, and if you turn ten bandsmen of the Mariposa band on to your hand pump on the bow of the lower decks—float? why, what else can she do?

Then, if you stuff in hemlock into the embers of the fire that you were raking out, till it hums and crackles under the boiler, it won't be long before you hear the propeller thud—thudding at the stern again, and before the long roar of the steam whistle echoes over to the town.

And so the *Mariposa Belle*, with all steam up again and with the long train of sparks careering from the funnel, is heading for the town.

James De Mille
Sweet Maiden of Passamaquoddy

Writing roughly one hundred years apart, James De Mille and Dennis Lee had the same idea—that Canadian place names have an amusing rhythm if you string them together in the right way. (For a more serious approach, see Meguido Zola's "Canadian Indian Place Names," p. 267.) James De Mille, a nineteenth-century writer from New Brunswick, also makes fun of the flowery romantic poems of his day by imagining a shy courtship on the banks of a river called Skoodawabskooksis, a name that takes a little practice to roll off your tongue.

Sweet maiden of Passamaquoddy,
Shall we seek for communion of souls
Where the deep Mississippi meanders,
Or the distant Saskatchewan rolls?
Ah no! in New Brunswick we'll find it—
A sweetly sequestered nook—
Where the sweet gliding Skoodawabskooksis
Unites with the Skoodawabskook…

Let others sing loudly of Saco,
Of Passadumkeag or Miscouche,
Of the Kennebecasis or Quaco,
Of Miramichi or Buctouche;
Or boast of the Tobique or Mispec,
The Mushquash or dark Memramcook;
There's none like the Skoodawabskooksis
Excepting the Skoodawabskook.

Dennis Lee
Kahshe or Chicoutimi

If I lived in Temagami,
Temiskaming, Kenagami,
Or Lynx, or Michipicoten Sound,
I wouldn't stir the whole year round

Unless I went to spend the day
At Bawk, or Nottawasaga Bay,
Or Missinabi, Moosonee,
Or Kahshe or Chicoutimi.

Good Sports

Taking part in sports activities, or simply rooting for favourite players and teams, has long been a way for Canadians to enjoy themselves. Baggataway (which the French called the *jeu de la crosse*) was an exciting, sometimes violent, ball game invented by Canada's Native peoples, and ice hockey and baseball have been played in Canada since the mid-nineteenth century. Some sports help us to make the best of the long, cold Canadian winter, while others allow us to enjoy the brilliant summer sunshine. The excitement of playing in a game, or cheering for the home team, has the power to bring people together. Sometimes—during the Olympics, for example—it can even bring the entire nation closer together.

Roch Carrier
The Hockey Sweater

Hockey has been an important part of Canada's history for almost as long as the nation
has existed. From its early roots in eastern Canada, the game had spread all the way to British Columbia
by the 1890s. The creation of the Stanley Cup in 1893 made hockey even more popular. By the 1900s, almost
every city and town had its own team, but from 1939 to 1969 the Montreal Canadiens and Toronto Maple Leafs
were the only Canadian squads in the National Hockey League. People all across the country followed the two
teams, and their rivalry came to mean more than just hockey. The Maple Leafs were the team of English
Canada, while the Canadiens represented French Canada. No player ever captured the hearts of Quebeckers
more than Maurice "the Rocket" Richard, the first player to score fifty goals in a season and five hundred
in his career. Roch Carrier's *Hockey Sweater* is a humorous look at growing up in small-town Quebec
during Richard's heyday. The English translation is by Sheila Fischman.

THE WINTERS OF MY CHILDHOOD were long, long seasons. We lived in three places—the school, the church and the skating-rink—but our real life was on the skating-rink. Real battles were won on the skating-rink. Real strength appeared on the skating-rink. The real leaders showed themselves on the skating-rink.

School was a sort of punishment. Parents always want to punish their children and school is their most natural way of punishing us. However, school was also a quiet place where we could prepare for the next hockey game, lay out our next strategies.

As for church, we found there the tranquillity of God: there we forgot school and dreamed about the next hockey game. Through our daydreams it might happen that we would recite a prayer: we would ask God to help us play as well as Maurice Richard.

I remember very well the winter of 1946. We all wore the same uniform as Maurice Richard, the red, white and blue

uniform of the Montreal Canadiens, the best hockey team in the world. We all combed our hair like Maurice Richard, and to keep it in place we used a kind of glue—a great deal of glue. We laced our skates like Maurice Richard, we taped our sticks like Maurice Richard. We cut his pictures out of all the newspapers. Truly, we knew everything there was to know about him.

On the ice, when the referee blew his whistle the two teams would rush at the puck; we were five Maurice Richards against five other Maurice Richards, throwing themselves on the puck. We

were ten players all wearing the uniform of the Montreal Canadiens, all with the same burning enthusiasm. We all wore the famous number 9 on our backs.

How could we forget that!

One day, my Montreal Canadiens sweater was too small for me; and it was ripped in several places. My mother said: "If you wear that old sweater, people are going to think we are poor!"

Then she did what she did whenever we needed new clothes. She started to look through the catalogue that the Eaton company in Montreal sent us in the mail every year. My mother was proud. She

never wanted to buy our clothes at the general store. The only clothes that were good enough for us were the latest styles from Eaton's catalogue. My mother did not like the order forms included in the catalogue. They were written in English and she did not understand a single word of it. To order my hockey sweater, she did what she always did. She took out her writing pad and wrote in her fine school-teacher's hand: "Dear Monsieur Eaton, Would you be so kind as to send me a Canadiens' hockey sweater for my son, Roch, who is ten years old and a little bit tall for his age? Docteur Robitaille thinks

he is a little too thin. I am sending you three dollars. Please send me the change if there is any. I hope your packing will be better than it was last time."

Monsieur Eaton answered my mother's letter promptly. Two weeks later we received the sweater.

That day I had one of the greatest disappointments of my life! Instead of the red, white and blue Montreal Canadiens sweater, Monsieur Eaton had sent the blue and white sweater of the Toronto Maple Leafs. I had always worn the red, white and blue sweater of the Montreal Canadiens. All my friends wore the red, white and blue sweater. Never had anyone in my village worn the Toronto sweater. Besides, the Toronto team was always being beaten by the Canadiens.

With tears in my eyes, I found the strength to say: "I'll never wear that uniform."

"My boy," said my mother, "first you're going to try it on! If you make up your mind about something before you try it, you won't go very far in this life."

My mother had pulled the blue and white Toronto Maple Leafs sweater over my head and put my arms into the sleeves. She pulled the sweater down and carefully smoothed the maple leaf right in the middle of my chest.

I was crying: "I can't wear that."

"Why not? This sweater is a perfect fit."

"Maurice Richard would never wear it."

"You're not Maurice Richard! Besides, it's not what you put on your back that matters, it's what you put inside your head."

"You'll never make me put in my head to wear a Toronto Maple Leafs sweater."

My mother sighed in despair and explained to me: "If you don't keep this sweater which fits you perfectly I'll have to write to Monsieur Eaton and explain that you don't want to wear the Toronto sweater. Monsieur Eaton understands French perfectly, but he's English and he's going to be insulted because he likes the Maple Leafs. If he's insulted, do you think he'll be in a hurry to answer us? Spring will come before you play a single game, just because you don't want to wear that nice blue sweater."

So, I had to wear the Toronto Maple Leafs sweater.

When I arrived at the skating rink in my blue sweater, all the Maurice Richards in red, white and blue came, one by one, and looked at me. The referee blew his whistle and I went to take my usual position. The coach came over and told me I would be on the second line. A few minutes later the second line was called; I jumped onto the ice. The Maple Leafs sweater weighed on my shoulders like a mountain. The captain came and told me to wait; he'd need me later, on defence.

By the third period I still had not played.

Then one of the defencemen was hit on the nose with a stick and it started to bleed. I jumped onto the ice. My moment had come!

The referee blew his whistle and gave me a penalty. He said there were already five players on the ice. That was too much! It was too unfair! "This is persecution!" I shouted. "It's just because of my blue sweater!"

I crashed my stick against the ice so hard that it broke.

I bent down to pick up the pieces. When I got up, the young curate, on skates, was standing in front of me.

"My child," he said, "just because you're wearing a new Toronto Maple Leafs sweater, it doesn't mean you're going to make the laws around here. A good boy never loses his temper. Take off your skates and go to the church and ask God to forgive you."

Wearing my Maple Leafs sweater I went to the church, where I prayed to God.

I asked God to send me right away, a hundred million moths that would eat up my Toronto Maple Leafs sweater.

Lois Simmie
Face-Off

Hockey is a tough game. Cuts, bruises, and missing teeth have
long been the marks of an NHL star. Nowadays, better helmets and face masks mean
that young hockey players don't have to suffer the same kinds of
injuries as the child in Lois Simmie's poem.

I GOT A FAT LIP LAST SATURDAY NIGHT
When the goal post said hi to my head;
Then a stick got stuck in the blade of my skate
And I turned the blueline red

I flattened my nose up against the boards;
I'm thinking it must be a sign
Not to forget my helmet again,
Or the *face off* is going to be mine!

Raymond Souster
Wild Pitch

When the Blue Jays won the World Series in 1992, it was the first time that the baseball championship had been held by a team outside the United States. Toronto had been in the American League only since 1977, and the Montreal Expos had joined the National League in 1969. But baseball in Canada is much older than that. In fact, the first known game in the country took place way back in 1838—one year before the sport was supposedly "invented" in Cooperstown, New York—and the first Canadian baseball league was formed in 1876, the same year the National League was started. Some teams were even paying star players to join their teams, a practice many fans thought wasn't right. More than 120 years later, players' huge salaries still concern us. But the game has not become so serious that we can't sometimes laugh at it, as in the poem "Wild Pitch."

Again for Cid

IN THAT BLUE JAYS/
Red Sox game
one beautiful
one hysterical moment
to stop all cameras—

batter set in the box,
big bat swinging,
sweat of concentration
beading his face;

the catcher crouched,
signal just given
and the big glove ready,
body taut spring
ready to uncoil anywhere;

umpire bent low,
set squarely behind him,
chest mask moved up
underneath his chin,
his attention focused
on that white projectile

soon to hurtle in;

then all three frozen
in one glorious second
when the ball's released
from the pitcher's fingers;

comes bulleting in
to sail high high
higher
over batter
catcher
umpire
six feet above their heads;

with no motion made
so great their disbelief,

all eyes
refusing to look up
to catch,
winging high and wide and far

the screwball
that came unscrewed.

Anne Hart
The Friday Everything Changed

This story is set in Nova Scotia in the 1940s. In those days, most people believed that certain games and activities were only for boys or only for girls. The longer story from which this excerpt is taken describes the one-room schoolhouse the children attended. The school has a new teacher, Miss Wilson, from another, larger community called River Hibbert. Children of all ages are taught together, in a classroom heated by a coal stove in the centre of the room. A bucket full of drinking water sits on a shelf in the corner. It has always been the boys' job to leave class and go to the pump, about a quarter of a mile away, to fetch the drinking water. But one day, a girl named Alma gathers the nerve to ask Miss Wilson if girls can get the water next time. Instead of reacting with shock, Miss Wilson says she'll think about it and let them know on Friday. The boys, faced with losing their special privilege, decide to retaliate...

THE FIRST THING CLEARLY EVIDENT BY recess on Monday morning was that the boys had decided not to let us girls field at softball any more.

Softball at our school used to go like this: every Monday morning at recess two of the bigger boys—that year it was usually Ernie Chapman and Junior LeBlanc—used to pick their teams for the week. Whichever one came out on top in laddering their hands up the softball bat got to pick first and the loser second and so it went—back and forth—until all the boys who were considered good enough to be on a team had been picked. Then Ernie and Junior laddered the bat again to see which side would get up first and the losing side took to the field to be joined by the little boys who hadn't been picked and us older girls who were allowed to act as sort of permanent supplementary fielders. And for the rest of the week the teams remained locked, at every recess and lunchtime, in one long softball game which had, as we discovered to our surprise several years later when the television came through, unusually complicated rules.

The way we played, for example, every single boy had to get out before the other team could come in. And any boy hitting a home run not only had the right to bat straight away again but also to bring back into the game any boy who had got out. Which led to kids who couldn't remember their six times table properly being able to announce—say, by noon on Thursday—"The score's now forty-six to thirty-nine, because, in the last inning starting Tuesday lunchtime, Junior's team was all out except for Irving Snell who hit three homers in a row off Lorne Ripley and brought in Ira and Jim and Elton who brought in the rest except for Austin who got out for the second time on Wednesday with a fall ball one of the girls caught behind third base...."

Some days it got so exciting that at noon we couldn't wait to eat our lunches but would rush straight into the schoolyard, gobbling our sandwiches as we ran, towards that aching moment when the ball, snaking across the yellow grass or arching towards us from the marsh sky, might meet our open eager hands.

So Monday morning recess, when Ernie Chapman whirled the bat around his head, slammed it down as hard as he could on home base and announced, "The first girl that goes out to field, we break her neck," was a hard blow. We clustered forlornly around the girls' entry door knowing there was nothing we could really do. "Oh Alma," mourned Minnie Halliday, biting the end of her long, brown braids, "why couldn't you just have kept your mouth shut?" It was a bad

moment. If we'd tried to go out to field they'd have picked us off one by one. We couldn't even play softball on our own. None of us owned a bat and ball.

If it hadn't been for Doris Pomeroy we might have broken ranks there and then but Doris, who was in Grade Nine and had had a home permanent and sometimes wore nail polish and had even, it was rumoured, gone swimming in the Quarry all alone with Elton Lawrence, flicked a rock against the schoolhouse wall in the silence following Minnie's remark and steadied us all by saying: "Don't be foolish, Minnie. All we have to do is wait. They need us to field and, besides, they kind of like to have us out there looking at them when they get up to bat."

But it was a long, hard week. Besides not letting us field, the boys picked on us whenever they got the chance. I guess they figured if they made things bad enough for us, sooner or later we'd go to Miss Wilson and ask her to forget the whole thing. But all their picking on and bullying did was to keep us together. Whenever one of us was tripped going down the aisle or got an ink ball in her hair or got trapped in the outhouse by a bunch of boys it was as if it was happening to all of us. And looking back on that week—when there were so many bad feelings and so many new feelings in the air— it was kind of nice, too, because for the first time we girls found ourselves telling each other our troubles and even our thoughts without worrying about being laughed at. And that was something new at our school.

As for Alma, who kept getting notes thrown on her desk promising her

everything from a bloody nose to having her pants pulled down, we stuck to her like burrs. But maybe Alma's hardest moment had nothing to do with bullying at all. It was when her cousin Arnold came over to see her Wednesday after school and asked her to drop the whole idea of girls going for the water.

"If they find out about it, Alma," said Arnold, "they'll probably take away the water bucket."

"Who's they?" asked Alma. She and Arnold played a lot together when they were little kids and she was used to listening to his opinions.

"Well, the Health Inspector," said Arnold, "and guys like that."

"They'll never take away that water bucket," said Alma, though she wasn't all that sure. "They don't care who carries the water as long as it gets carried."

"Alma," said Arnold, "the other guys would kill me if they ever found out I told you this but sometimes carrying the water isn't that much fun. On cold days it's real hard work. You're better off in the warm school."

Alma knew what it cost Arnold to tell her this but she stood firm. "I'm sorry, Arnold," she said, "but I'm used to cold weather. In winter I walk to school the same as you." So Arnold went away.

If Miss Wilson, as the week wore on, noticed anything unusual going on in her school she gave no sign of it. She passed out the usual punishments for ink balls, she intercepted threatening notes and tore them up unread. She looked at Alma's white face and all she asked about was the principal rivers of Europe. Nor were we surprised. Nothing in our experience had led us to believe that the grown-ups had the slightest inkling—or interest—in what really went on with kids.

Only Doris Pomeroy thought differently. "Miss Wilson looks real mad," said Doris as we trailed in thankfully from Friday morning recess.

"Mad?"

"Yeah. Like when she comes out to ring the bell and we're hanging around the entry door like scared chickens. She rings that old handbell as if she wished all those yelling boys' heads were under it. Of course, they do things differently in River Hibbert. I know for a fact that girls there get to play on softball teams just like the boys."

"On teams? Just like the boys?" But it was too much for us to take in at that moment, so preoccupied were we with that afternoon's decision on the water. All that long, hard week it was as if Friday afternoon and Junior Red Cross would never come again. Now that it was almost upon us, most of us forgot, in our excitement—at least for the time being—Doris's heady remarks about softball.

So at lunchtime, just as the boys were winding up their week's game ("And real great, eh? Without the girls?" Ernie Chapman was gloating loudly from the pitcher's mound), when Miss Wilson, without her bell, leaped through our clustered huddles at the entry door and headed straight towards the softball field. She took us all completely by surprise. Crunch, crunch, crunch, went Miss Wilson's bright red loafers against the cinders and the next thing we knew she'd grabbed the bat from Irving Snell and, squinting against the sun, was twirling and lining it before our astonished eyes.

"Come on! Come on!" cried Miss Wilson impatiently to Ernie, who stood transfixed before her on the pitcher's mound. "Come on! Come on!" she cried again and she banged the bat against the ground. "Come on! Come on!" cried Doris Pomeroy and we all rushed after her across the cinders.

The first ball Ernie threw was pretty wobbly and Miss Wilson hit it at an angle so that it fell sideways, a fall ball, towards George Fowler's outstretched hands. "Ah-h-h-h-h-h," we moaned from the sidelines and some of us closed our eyes so we wouldn't have to look. But George jumped too eagerly for such an easy ball and it fell right through his fingers and rolled harmlessly along the ground.

Ernie took a lot more time over his second pitch. He was getting over the first shock of finding Miss Wilson opposite him at bat and by this time he was receiving shouts of encouragement from all over the field.

"Get her! Get her!" the boys yelled recklessly at Ernie and they all fanned out behind the bases.

Ernie took aim slowly. None of us had ever seen the pirouettings of professional pitchers but there was a certain awesome ceremony, nevertheless, as Ernie spat savagely on the ball, glared hard at Miss Wilson, slowly swung back his big right arm and, poised for one long moment, his whole body outstretched, threw the ball as hard as he could towards home base where Miss Wilson waited, her sturdy feet braced against the cinders, her body rocking with the bat.

For a fleeting moment we had a glimpse of what life might be like in River Hibbert and then Miss Wilson hit the ball.

"Ah-h-h-h-h-h," we cried as it rose high in the air, borne by the marsh wind, and flew like a bird against the sun, across the road and out of sight, into the Ox Pasture on the other side.

"Ah-h-h-h-h-h…" We all stared at Miss Wilson. "School's in," she announced over her shoulder, walking away.

Hitting the ball into the Ox Pasture happened maybe once a year.

That afternoon, towards the end of Red Cross, there was a big hush all over the room.

"Next week," said Miss Wilson, closing the school register, tidying her books, "next week Alma Niles and Joyce Shipley will go for the water."

She swept her hand over the top of her desk and tiny dust motes danced in the slanting sun.

PART EIGHT

From Far and Wide

Illustrated by

Harvey Chan

From Bonavista to Vancouver Island

Canada is an immense country, stretching some five thousand kilometres (three thousand miles) from Newfoundland to British Columbia. The southernmost point in Canada reaches as far south as Northern California in the United States, while the territory of Nunavut stretches into the Arctic Ocean. Only one country, Russia, is larger. Canada has the longest coastline in the world, one more than ten times as long as Australia's, as well as the largest freshwater lake system—the Great Lakes. Each piece in this section celebrates Canada's landscapes, from E. J. Pratt's description of the turbulent waters of Cape Race, Newfoundland, to Chief Dan George's appreciation of British Columbia's natural beauty. "Something to sing about," as Oscar Brand says, "this land of ours."

E. J. Pratt
The Way of Cape Race

Cape Race is at the southeastern tip of Newfoundland. Its name sounds as if it might have something to do with the waves crashing on its shores, or perhaps the ships that navigate its treacherous waters. Indeed, Newfoundland-born E. J. Pratt, one of Canada's most renowned poets, describes Cape Race as a dangerous place in the time of the Vikings and, despite foghorns and bells, still a dangerous place a thousand years later. But the cape's original name, given to it by Portuguese mariners, was Cabo Raso. "Raso" means "shaven," and is probably a reference to its flat-topped, treeless slate cliffs, which reach 30 to 45 metres (100 to 150 feet) above the ocean.

LION-HUNGER, TIGER-LEAP!
The waves are bred no other way;
It was their way when the Norseman came,
It was the same in Cabot's day:
A thousand years will come again,
When a thousand years have passed away—
Galleon, frigate, liner, plane,
The muster of the slain.

They have placed the light, fog-horn and bell
Along the shore: the wardens keep
Their posts—they do not quell
The roar; they shorten not the leap.
The waves still ring the knell
Of ships that pass at night,
Of dreadnought and of cockle-shell:
They do not heed the light,
The fog-horn and the bell—
Lion-hunger, tiger-leap!

Chief Dan George
And My Heart Soars

Dan George was chief of the Squamish band, on Canada's West Coast, from 1951 to 1963. When he was more than sixty years old, he became a well-known actor in CBC dramas and Hollywood movies, and also published two collections of his writings: *My Heart Soars* (1974), from which this piece is taken, and *My Spirit Soars* (1982). He wrote, "I am a chief, but my power to make war is gone, and the only weapon I have is speech. It is only with my tongue I can fight my people's war." There is no anger in this poem, however, only joy at Canada's natural beauty.

THE BEAUTY OF THE TREES,
the softness of the air,
the fragrance of the grass,
   speaks to me.

The summit of the mountain,
the thunder of the sky,
the rhythm of the sea,
   speaks to me.

The faintness of the stars,
the freshness of the morning,
the dew drop on the flower,
   speaks to me.

The strength of fire,
the taste of salmon,
the trail of the sun,
And the life that never goes away,
   They speak to me.

And my heart soars.

Meguido Zola
Canadian Indian Place Names

From the West Coast (Bella Bella) to the East Coast (Shubenacadie and Malagash in
Nova Scotia) and back again (Yahk and Quaw), Meguido Zola has set down some of the names that
Native peoples gave to Canada. Zola's poem is also a record of the sounds of many different Native languages.
Some of them, including Cree, Ojibwa, and Athapaskan, are still spoken by thousands of people, but
others have vanished or are spoken by only a handful of elderly people.

Bella Bella, Bella Coola,
Athabaska, Iroquois;
Mesilinka, Osilinka,
Mississauga, Missisquois.
Chippewa, Chippawa,
Nottawasaga;
Malagash, Matchedash,
Shubenacadie;
Couchiching, Nipissing,
Scubenacadie.
Shickshock
Yahk
Quaw!

Oscar Brand
Something to Sing About

Oscar Brand is a Canadian-born folksinger and songwriter. This rousing song about Canada's natural beauty was written in 1963 for a television special. It later became the theme song for the Canadian pavilion at Expo 67. As more than one fan of the song has pointed out, walking "on the Grand Banks of Newfoundland" is actually impossible, since this area is underwater!

I have walked 'cross the sand on the Grand Banks of New-found-land,
Lazed on the ridge of the Mi - ra - mi - chi. Seen the
waves tear and roar at the stone coast of Lab - ra - dor,
Watched them roll back to the great north - ern sea ___ From the
Van - cou - ver Is - land to the Al - ber - ta High-land, 'Cross the
prai - rie, the Lakes to On - ta - ri - o's ___ towers. From the
sound of Mount Roy - al's chimes out to the Mar - i - times,
Some - thing to sing a - bout, this land of ours. ___

1.
I HAVE WALKED 'CROSS THE SAND ON THE GRAND BANKS OF NEWFOUNDLAND,
Lazed on the ridge of the Miramichi.
Seen the waves tear and roar at the stone coast of Labrador,
Watched them roll back to the great northern sea.

Chorus:
From the Vancouver Island to the Alberta Highland,
'Cross the prairie, the Lakes to Ontario's towers.
From the sound of Mount Royal's chimes out to the Maritimes,
Something to sing about, this land of ours.

2.
I have welcomed the dawn from the fields of Saskatchewan,
Followed the sun to the Vancouver shore.
Watched it climb shiny new up the snow peaks of Cariboo,
Up to the clouds where the wild Rockies soar.

Chorus

3.
I have heard the wild wind sing the places that I have been,
Bay Bulls and Red Deer and Strait of Belle Isle.
Names like Grand'Mère and Silverthrone, Moose Jaw and Marrowbone,
Trails of the pioneer, named with a smile.

Chorus

4.
I have wandered my way to the wild wood of Hudson Bay,
Treated my toes to Quebec's morning dew.
Where the sweet summer breeze kissed the leaves of the maple trees,
Sharing this song that I'm singing to you.

Chorus

5.
Yes, there's something to sing about, tune up a string about,
Call out in chorus or quietly hum
Of a land that's still young with a ballad that's still unsung
Telling the promise of great things to come.

Chorus

A New Start

 Canada has been a multicultural country from the time Native peoples first arrived here with their many different languages and ways of life. Today, about ten million Canadians trace their ancestry to the British Isles; more than six million trace their ancestry to France. But Canada is also home to one million people of German descent, more than 700,000 of Italian descent, 500,000 of Ukrainian descent, and almost 350,000 whose families originally came from China. Nearly every country in the world has now contributed people to Canada, with Hong Kong, India, and the Philippines providing the greatest numbers in the 1990s. All the pieces in this section are about immigrants and how they feel about their new lives in Canada.

John Robert Colombo
My Genealogy

Since Canada is a country populated by immigrants from all over the world, it's not surprising that
people from different cultural backgrounds meet and marry. This is what happened in John Robert Colombo's
family, giving him a rich and varied inheritance. Perhaps, Colombo concludes in this poem, his confused feeling that
the blood is "flowing through his veins at different speeds" is a way of knowing that he's a Canadian.

1.
MY GREAT-GREAT-GRANDFATHER
played in the streets
of Milano, I am told.
I take it on faith.

2.
His son, the artisan,
immigrated to Baden, Ontario,
as a decorator or builder.
I believe this, but never met him.

3.
My grandfather was born
in Baden, and he married
a German girl there.
I remember him well—
he spoke English
with a German accent.

4.
My grandparents lived
in Berlin, Ontario,
when it changed its name
to honour Lord Kitchener.
They made an unusual couple—
he was more than six feet tall,
she barely five—but together
they produced fourteen children.

5.
One of these fourteen Colombos
was my father. He spoke English
with a Pennsylvania-Dutch accent.

6.
He married a Kitchener girl,
and I was born in that city—
with its light industry
and its farmers' market—
in that city, an only child.

7.
I remember quite distinctly
my mother's parents, my grandparents. My grandfather spoke
with a thick Greek accent,
and my larger grandmother,
a nasal Quebec French. Yes,
they made a colourful couple.

8.
They first met in Montreal,
lived in Toronto for a while,
finally settled in Kitchener.
They had five children,
and their arguments had to be
heard to be believed.

9.
Blood flows through my veins
at different speeds:
Italian, German.
Greek, French-Canadian.
Sometimes it mixes.

10.
At times I feel close
to the Aegean.
the Côte d'Azure,
the Lombard Plain,
and the Black Forest.

11.
I seldom feel close
to the Rocky Mountains,
the Prairies,
the Great Lakes,
or the cold St. Lawrence.
What am I doing in Toronto?

12.
If this means being Canadian,
I am a Canadian.

Ian Wallace and Angela Wood
The Sandwich

How do you find a place in your new homeland while still respecting your family's cultural traditions? Generations of immigrant children have faced this challenge. *The Sandwich* is about a boy named Vincenzo who comes from an Italian-Canadian family. Vincenzo's mother has died, and his *nonna* (grandmother) has come over from Italy to look after him while his father is at work. When Nonna has to go into the hospital, Vincenzo begins to take his lunch to school instead of eating at home. In his lunch is a sandwich with traditional Italian ingredients: provolone cheese and mortadella…

"VINCENZO!" SHOUTED MATT. "COME'N eat with us!"

"Okay," he replied, running towards his friend.

Matt threw an arm around Vincenzo's shoulder and like a two-headed monster they strutted down the hall. Hans, Cindy, Rita, and Paul were waiting at the table by the window. Vincenzo dropped his lunch on the table and sat on the end of the bench beside Rita.

"Vincenzo," she asked, "how's your nonna today?"

"She's still sick. Papa took her to the hospital yesterday. That's why I am eating here instead of at home."

"She'll get better," assured Rita. "Don't worry. At least you get to eat lunch with us!"

Vincenzo turned and glanced around the table at the lunches which were now coming out of their bags.

"They're all the same except mine," he whispered to himself.

"Peanut butter and jam is my favourite sandwich," stated Paul.

"Mine too," said Rita, holding hers in front of her face. "I won't eat any other sandwich and that makes my mother so mad. She says that someday I am going to turn into a peanut! That would be neat, eh?"

"Yeah. Rita the Peanut," giggled Cindy. Everyone nodded, laughing.

"*Peeeeww*," shouted Matt, "What's that stink? I've never smelled anything like it at our table before."

"*Dead socks*," screeched Rita, grabbing her nose. Heads turned, sniffing back and forth, up and down.

"Vincenzo," sniffed Matt. "It's Vincenzo's sandwich!"

His friends covered their noses and began to laugh.

"Vincenzo eats stinky meat!" laughed Matt.

"Vincenzo eats stinky meat!" sang Rita, Hans, Paul, and Cindy.

"Vincenzo eats stinky meat!" rang throughout the cafeteria.

Vincenzo didn't sing or laugh. He dropped his head onto his chest and wiped away the stinging in his eyes. The sandwich was staring him in the face. With one quick movement, he grabbed it and shoved it into the bag.

"The garbage," he thought, "that's where it belongs and then I can run out of the cafeteria!"

But he didn't run outside. His friends, finishing their lunch, went into the schoolyard to play tag. They'd asked him to come along, but he didn't want to go. Instead, he sat alone for the remainder of the lunch hour. He returned to the classroom and quickly shoved the lunch into his desk.

"No one will see or smell it there," he thought.

The afternoon passed even more slowly than the morning.

When Vincenzo returned home that day his father noticed that he was still carrying his lunch.

"Vincenzo," asked his father, "what did you eat for lunch?"

"Nothing."

"Nothing! You took a good lunch to school and ate nothing? What's the matter, are you sick?"

"No, Papa, I'm not sick. I didn't feel like eating, that's all."

"The day that you don't eat your lunch, Vincenzo, there *is* something wrong. Please, tell me what it is!"

Vincenzo shifted his weight from one foot to the other and back again. His left hand moved across his face and stopped behind his ear where it began to scratch.

"My friends...umm...they...uh... laughed at my sandwich and shouted, 'Vincenzo eats stinky meat!'"

"Ohhh," sighed his father. "So that's it. Come here." Vincenzo climbed into his father's lap as he had done many times before and waited for him to speak.

"Why do you think they laughed at you?"

"Because my sandwich stinks, that's why! But, it is a good sandwich, isn't it?"

"Do you like mortadella and provolone, Vincenzo?"

"Yes, Papa, I do."

"Then it is a good sandwich. Your friends laughed because it was different. It smelled strange, looked different, and it was new to them."

Late that night, he dreamed. He was seated at a table twelve feet high in the

middle of a large room while bears danced around the walls. There, set in front of him, was the biggest and most beautiful jar of peanut butter and jam that he had ever seen. With a large gold knife, he dug into the glass jar and spread a huge brown and red glob across a slice of bread. He smiled down with delight at his family who looked very sad and kept eating and eating and eating.

"Vincenzo, why are you taking so long?"

"I'll be there in a minute, Matt. You go ahead."

"Hurry up, then. We have to eat fast so we can play outside longer," shouted Matt, racing off down the hall.

When Vincenzo reached the cafeteria table, his friends were seated as they had been the day before.

"Vincenzo," asked Matt, "what did you bring for lunch today? Something stinkless I hope."

Everyone laughed, except Vincenzo.

"No," he replied firmly, "I have stinky meat and cheese."

"Oh no. Vincenzo eats stinky meat again," groaned Rita, grabbing her nose, "and I have to sit beside him!"

Matt laughed, and Rita laughed, as did Hans, Cindy, and Paul. But louder than them all laughed Vincenzo.

"I eat stinky meat!" he shouted at the top of his lungs.

Startled, his friends looked towards him.

"I dare you to eat some

peanut butter and jam!" blurted Cindy.

"I don't want your peanut butter and jam. I have my own sandwich that my papa and I made."

"I dare you!" threatened Matt. "I dare you!"

Vincenzo glanced around the table and met five pairs of eyes staring into his. He felt sweaty all over and wondered if it showed on his face.

"No," he thought, "I won't take a dare," and took a big bite into his sandwich and another bite and another.

His friends sat and watched in amazement. Vincenzo was eating a stinky meat sandwich and seemed to like it!

Everyone began to eat except Matt, who stared intently at the other half of Vincenzo's sandwich. Slowly, his arm crept across the table and, picking the sandwich up with one hand, lifted it to his mouth. There it sat for a few moments. He closed his eyes tightly and took a bite.

Vincenzo, seeing what had happened, smiled to himself.

"Papa was right," he thought.

Arm over arm and hand over hand the stinky meat sandwich moved around the table. It reached its way to Rita who took a bite, chewed, and stopped.

"It's not bad. It's not bad!" she whispered to Paul and handed the one small bite left to Vincenzo. He popped it into his mouth and reached into his lunch bag for the anisette cookies and orange juice.

Uma Parameswaran
Show and Tell

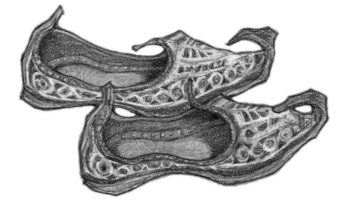

This is a story about how some imaginative immigrant parents from India help their children
with their "show and tell" projects. When Sita needs to make a presentation at school, her mother teaches
her some *mudras* (hand positions) from the classical dance of India. The many different postures and intricate hand
positions date back thousands of years, and each one has a meaning. Many Indian dances are based on stories about
Hindu gods and goddesses, such as Sita, for whom the little girl in this story is named. When Sita's brother,
Dilip, also has to perform for his class, his father comes up with some exciting theatre: he shows Dilip
how to perform a story about Rama, the hero of one of the most famous Hindu epics, the *Ramayana*.

DILIP, IN HIS PYJAMAS, RAN TO THE
kitchen for one last check that his new
toy airplane was in perfect condition for
his Show and Tell class next morning.
The carpeted floor of the bedroom and
hallways was not suited to the wonders his
plane could do. The linoleum floor of the
kitchen was just right. The plane ran
smoothly and had a soft whistle just like
real planes.

"Dilip, off to bed!" His mother's voice
came from the living room. Dilip
switched off the battery and carefully carried the airplane back to his bedroom. He
placed it on his desk, next to his pencil
case.

Sita, his twin sister, was rummaging in
her toybox. She was close to tears. Their

mother came in. "Into your beds," she
said, giving Dilip a fond slap on his rear.

"Sita didn't brush her teeth properly,"
Dilip said gleefully, getting back into his
bed. "What story are you going to read
tonight? I want Rocky and Sherman."

"I don't have anything for Show and
Tell," Sita burst out crying. Their parents'
friends, who had given Dilip the airplane,
had given Sita a dress, and one cannot
very well take a dress for Show and Tell.

Their mother knelt down and hugged
her. "Sweetheart, why do you always need
things for Show and Tell? Why don't
you…"

"Because everyone else brings toys.
Everyone," Sita interrupted.

Her mother patted her and continued,

"Why don't you do something nice and different?"

"Like what?"

"Like..." Their mother had to think fast. "Like a little story." She thought some more. "A little dance-story of your name! You know it already, but I'll tell it to you in a new way."

She wiped her daughter's tears and seated her on her bed. She was not only a doctor; she had been a dancer in her teens, and so could enrich a story with the language of hand gestures. As she told the story, her hands and fingers moved in the language of dance and the children could see the sun and the moon, and the bees sipping honey from flowers, and water running downstream, and all the scenes that she spoke about in the story of Sita, the princess after whom her own daughter had been named.

"That's a nice story," Sita said, when the story was over, "but how can I remember all that at Show and Tell? And learn all those dance things?"

"Before breakfast tomorrow, I'll teach you some of the *mudras*, that's what the hand movements are called," her mother said. "Get into bed, and I'll tell you the story again."

And this was the story that she told them for the second time:

Once upon a time there lived a princess called Sita. She was the daughter of King Janaka. She was a gentle and beautiful girl who loved to do gentle, beautiful things. She loved to walk in the palace gardens, where there were sweet-smelling rosebuds, fragrant white jasmine that she could string into garlands, and many other flowers around which bees hovered, sipping

sweet nectar. Sita was truly a child of Mother Earth and loved everything around her—the bright sun and the lovely moon, the river cascading down the hill, the nimble-footed doe that frolicked in the parks, the gentle-eyed cows that grazed in the meadows, and the birds that nested in the trees.

When Sita grew to be a woman, she married the strongest, bravest, gentlest, most noble prince in the whole world and they lived happily ever after.

Many days later, their mother found Dilip sitting at the kitchen table, moodily stirring his bowl of rice crispies. They had already lost all their crackle.

"What is it, Dilip?" his father asked. "Anything I can do to help?"

"How does one become a writer?" the boy asked. "I have to tell a story."

"You don't have to be a writer to tell a story. There are lots of stories you can read."

"But I don't know how to read!"

His father felt like laughing but he knew that would upset the boy.

Dilip slowly ate his soggy cereal. "Why can't they just ask me to turn a cartwheel? Or to stand on my head? Why do I have to tell a story? I could even walk on my hands with some practice. But to tell a story..." he complained. "And only girls dance anyway."

His parents knew just what the problem was. Dilip didn't want to compete against Sita. Sita's story of her name had been praised by the teacher. The teacher had even called their mother and asked her to teach the kids more *mudras*, that is, how to show through hand movements such things as sun and moon and birds and

flowers. Everyone had made a big to-do about Sita, and Dilip was feeling left out.

"Well," his father said, "boys too *can* dance, but you don't *have* to dance in order to act out a story. Let us try."

He drummed his fingers on the table and thought for a minute. He then pulled out a paper from the telephone pad on the wall behind him and drew a bow:

"This is Siva's great bow," he said, "and the story is about how Rama broke it. You know Rama already, from Grandma's stories, but I'll tell you this story in a new way."

He looked at his wife, who was cleaning the breakfast table. He said, "I'll need a sword and mace and such." She took out a ladle and a roll of aluminum foil.

Their father stood at the centre of the kitchen, cleared his throat and acted out the story.

"Long ago in the land of Ayodhya, there was a prince called Rama. He was of the royal house of Dilip."

"Dilip?" Dilip shouted.

"Yes, Dilip of the Solar Dynasty of Kings who lived centuries ago in India. Rama was Dilip's great-great-grandson. Of course, Rama was brave and strong. Rama and his younger brother spent a year in the forests of their father's kingdom, helping hermits by chasing away the wicked people who kept disturbing the hermits' peaceful life in the forest. The boys fought with swords (Dilip's father wrapped a ladle in aluminum foil and fenced with it) and with mace (he lifted Dilip's baseball bat and swung it over his head) and with bow and arrow (he drew a make-believe arrow from a make-believe quiver on his back and shot it *wheeesh*)."

By now Dilip was imitating his father

and there was a lot of action and sound in the kitchen.

"After a few months, all the evil people had been killed or chased away and the hermits were happy and the forests were peaceful again. Then the two princes, with their teacher, came to the Kingdom of Mithila. Now, the King had a beautiful teenaged daughter…"

"And Rama married her and lived happily ever after," Sita piped in.

Her father said, "Yes, I guess you could end the story there."

"What about the bow?" Dilip asked. "Didn't he have to kill more people, *bang, bang, swish, swish?*" Dilip was moving around the room with war cries and his imaginary bow.

His father continued, "Yes, of course, the bow. The king of Mithila had a bow that had been given to him by Lord Siva. The bow was so heavy that two men were needed to move it from one spot to another.

"The king decided that his daughter deserved the strongest archer in the world and so he announced (here the father put the ladle to his lips and blew like a trumpet) that his daughter would wed the prince who could string the great bow of Siva.

"Many princes came to try but all of them only made fools of themselves. One lost his balance as he bent down and so fell on his nose. One fell backwards and hurt you know where. One raised one end of the bow but had to drop it because he was out of breath and he limped away with a stubbed toe."

Dilip had caught on and now he hopped around the kitchen, holding his toe.

"One twirled his bushy moustache with great confidence but when he tried to lift the bow, he almost choked because he exerted himself too much. No one, just no one, could lift the bow more than a few centimetres off the ground.…And then came…" Their father paused dramatically.

"Dilip," Dilip shouted.

"Rama, you stupid!" said Sita.

Their father drew himself up, very straight and tall. "Yes, Rama came to the Assembly Hall of Mithila. He planted his feet firmly on the ground, took one deep breath and bent down. He lifted the great bow as easily as you lift your baseball bat and he strung it. Then he placed an arrow in the bow and pulled it against the string. Suddenly *twang*, the bow broke (he gave a saucepan lid to Dilip who took the hint and clanged it with a spoon) and the whole palace resonated with its sound."

"And Rama married the princess and lived happily ever after," Sita shouted.

"Do you know the name of the princess?" their father whispered. "Sita."

"Sita, Sita!" The girl danced happily.

"Aw," Dilip said, turning away as though he was five years and not just five minutes older than his sister. "I think I'll end the story with the *twang*."

The parents smiled at each other as the children went to their rooms to get ready for school. Their mother said, laughing, "In India we told them fairy tales from Grimm and Andersen. Now we have to tell them stories from our own epics."

"In India, grandmother and school books would have told them," their father said. "Now we have to double as grandmothers and books!"

Nancy Prasad
You Have Two Voices

Immigration is especially challenging for those who do not speak the language of their new homeland. Nancy Prasad's poem is a sympathetic response to someone struggling to learn English. She recognizes that the same person who speaks English in a halting voice has a first language in which his words can "flow like rivers." Prasad suggests that just as the immigrant has two voices, she has two ears to listen. Even if she doesn't understand the words, she can take pleasure in the joy of people speaking their mother tongue.

YOU HAVE TWO VOICES WHEN YOU SPEAK
in English or your mother tongue.
When you speak the way your people spoke
the words don't hesitate but flow
like rivers, like rapids, like oceans of sound,
and your hands move like birds through the air.

But then you take a stranger's voice
when you speak in your new tongue.
Each word is a stone dropped in a pool.
I watch the ripples and wait for more.
You search in vain for other stones to throw.
They are heavy. Your hands hang down.

You have two voices when you speak;
I have two ears for hearing.
Speak to me again in your mother tongue.
What does it matter how little I understand
when the words pour out like music
and your face glows like a flame.

A Suitcase Full of Stories

Because Canada is rich in immigrants from so many lands, it is also rich in their stories, songs, and celebrations. In this section you will find just a few of these treasures, brought to Canada and lovingly preserved and shared here.

Harry Gutkin
How to Make a Two-Room Hovel Roomier

Many Jewish Canadians are descended from Jews who lived in Eastern Europe. Before the Second World War, Poland had a Jewish population of more than three million—10 per cent of the country's people. Some lived in cities and some lived in traditional villages known as *shtetls*. They spoke a language, Yiddish, that was related to German. Sadly, this way of life came to end when most of the Jews of Europe were murdered in the Holocaust. However, the Yiddish language and its songs and stories have not been lost. Some of the best-known stories are about Chelm. The actual Chelm is a town in Poland, some sixty-five kilometres (forty miles) east of Lublin. But in Jewish folklore, Chelm is a town inhabited entirely by fools—endearing, well-meaning fools. This Chelm story has been retold by Harry Gutkin, a Jewish historian from Winnipeg.

WHEN IT COMES TO BEING POOR IN Chelm, how much unhappier can you get than Chatzkel, his wife, Surkeh, their nine children and Surkeh's parents, all living together in a two-room hovel? They literally bumped into each other coming and going. One evening Chatzkel kissed his mother-in-law in the dark, mistaking her for his own wife.

This was enough for Chatzkel, who rushed over for an audience with the good Rabbi Eliezer. "Holy Rabbi," he blurted out, "our nerves are on edge. We quarrel all the time; we have no privacy. We can't go on living cooped up one on top of the other. The way we live in cramped quarters, hell would be heaven by comparison."

The good rabbi considered the matter most gravely. He stroked his beard, scratched his head, coughed three times, and asked sagely:

"Tell me, Chatzkel, what animals do you own?"

"I have a cow, a goat, a flock of chickens. Without them we would have no milk for our children, or meat for the Sabbath."

"Good!" exclaimed the good rabbi. "Go home and take the cow into your living room."

Chatzkel was bewildered by the rabbi's advice, but he went home and took the cow into the living room. It didn't take more than a day before Chatzkel burst into the rabbi's study, screaming, "Things are worse than ever! The cow keeps us awake with its mooing, and there is cow dung all over the floor."

Rabbi Eliezer calmly went through his wisdom routine: stroke beard, scratch head, cough three times. Then he said, "Go home, Chatzkel, and take the goat and chickens into your kitchen and living room!"

An exasperated, overburdened, bewildered Chatzkel went home and did as the rabbi dictated, much to the mounting unhappiness of his wife, his children, and his in-laws. It didn't take more than a day for Chatzkel to return to his rabbi. "The animals have turned our home into a stable, the goat has destroyed what little fur-niture we have and the cow dung stench has made living impossible. Chicken feathers and refuse are everywhere—save us, Rabbi, save us!"

The rabbi went through his wisdom routine and said, "Chatzkel, go home and take out the chickens and return them to the chicken coop!"

Chatzkel raced home and did as the rabbi instructed him, much to the relief of all the occupants. He returned to the rabbi, reporting, "I removed all the chickens and it's a bit easier with them out of the house, but the goat continues to rampage up and down, pulverizing what he has already destroyed!"

"Chatzkel," replied the rabbi calmly, "go home and take the goat out of the house. God will help you!"

Chatzkel raced home and dragged the goat out of the house as his family cheered him on, then he returned once again to the rabbi. "Thank God, it's easier with the chickens and the goat out of the house, but the cow dung is piling up and the mooing is getting louder."

"Chatzkel," replied the rabbi calmly, "go home and take the cow out to the back-yard. God will help you!"

Chatzkel raced home and took the cow out to pasture. He and his family then cleaned up the cow dung and scrubbed the floors and walls, and all breathed a sigh of great relief.

A happier Chatzkel returned to report to the good Rabbi Eliezer. "Rabbi," exclaimed the poor man, "in your great wisdom, you've sweetened our miserable lives. We have so much room in the house now. It's so quiet and sweet-smelling. Thank God, life is full of promise!"

Rita Cox
How the Agouti Lost Its Tail

Rita Cox is a storyteller who grew up on the island of Trinidad, in the Caribbean. There were once many French planters living in Trinidad, and a French dialect is still spoken there today. Cox likes to tell this story, which is well known in Trinidad, to groups of Canadian children. An agouti is a tailless rodent that lives in Central and South America and the Caribbean. For flavouring, Cox has used a couple of French words from Trinidad in her story: *Compère* means "godfather" and *Macumère* means "godmother."

THERE WAS A TIME WHEN ALL THE animals were good friends.

Compère Dog and *Compère* Agouti lived near to each other. Dog was a handsome fellow, and so was Agouti, with his long beautiful bushy tail. They planted a vegetable garden together, sharing the crops. They hunted together and shared the meat. They were very good neighbours.

One day as Agouti was passing near a clearing in the forest, he came upon a crowd of animals talking and laughing. There was great excitement in the air. Agouti was curious. He stopped to greet his friends and heard *Compère* Goat addressing the crowd. "What's going on

here?" he asked *Macumère* Cow. "What's all the excitement about?"

"*Compère* Goat is having a picnic next Sunday. We'll be going by boat to Gasparee Island and we're making plans for it," she replied. "I must hurry home and tell *Compère* Dog about this," said Agouti.

"Oh, no!" replied Cow. "You can't come. Only animals with horns are invited." Agouti's face fell. "But we have no horns— and we are your friends. How could he do that to us?"

"Sorry, you just can't come," said Cow, moving away haughtily.

Agouti went home, sad and worried. He told Dog about the picnic to which only animals with horns were invited, and they both sat there, feeling very unhappy about being left out. Picnics were such fun and they did enjoy sailing. They talked about it for a long time, but nothing would console them. "Well," sighed Agouti at last, "I suppose we'll have to stay home by ourselves." Dog said nothing, just nodded his head.

Suddenly Agouti had an idea. "Why don't we get some wood and make two pairs of horns, one for you and one for me? We'll fasten them on with glue so they'd stay fixed; then we could go to the picnic." "What a wonderful idea!" Dog said. "Let's go now and find some wood."

It took a long time for them to find pieces of wood that would work, but at last they did. Then they shaped and smoothed and polished them until they were just right.

Sunday came. They got up early, packed their picnic baskets with all kinds of good things to eat and drink—roasted breadfruit, peas and rice, curried chicken, sorrel, beer, coconut bread. Then they put on their horns and helped each other to fasten them into place.

First Agouti fastened Dog's horns carefully and neatly so that no glue showed and they were just right. Just as he finished they heard the voices of the animals coming from the boats. They were getting ready to cast off. "Hurry, Dog, hurry and get my horns on now, before they leave us behind!" cried Agouti. But Dog didn't even hear. He picked up his basket and ran away as fast as he could, not even looking back to see if Agouti was following.

Poor Agouti was left behind. Try as he

could he couldn't fasten his own horns—he needed assistance, and Dog had gone and left him behind. At first he was sad, and then he got angry. Quickly he ran to a hill overlooking the harbour and he could see the boat full of animals just sailing by. Standing proudly on the deck with the other animals was Dog. Agouti ran up to the top of the hill and shouted as loud as he could:

Examine the horns.
Examine the horns.
Captain Goat, hear me.
One of the animals has no horns.

Dog heard this and tried to distract the captain. He opened his basket. "Have some sorrel, Captain. It will keep you cool in this bright sun…"

Agouti ran higher up the hill and shouted even louder:

Examine the horns.
Examine the horns.
There's a traitor on board
Who has no horns.

"Captain, do you hear that racket the wind is making?" said Dog. "Here, have some coconut bread." But Agouti shouted again, loud and clear:

Examine the horns.
Examine the horns.
There's a traitor on board
Who has no horns.

This time Captain Goat heard. He stopped the boat and made all the animals stand in line. He tested all their horns—*Compère* Ram's, *Compère* Bull's, *Macumère* Cow's, but before he could reach Dog, Dog had jumped overboard and was swimming for shore. He was furious as he made for the hilltop from where Agouti had called out.

Agouti saw him coming. He ran as fast as he could to reach his hole, but he wasn't fast enough. As he dived into the hole, Dog made a great leap, got hold of Agouti's tail, and bit it off.

That is how the Agouti lost his tail, and from that day to this Agouti and Dog have been enemies. Dog pursues Agouti whenever he catches sight of him. He's still angry because Agouti had made him the laughingstock of the forest. The animals poked so much fun at him that he had to move away and live with man.

Traditional
Tet Troom Too

Many Asian Canadians celebrate a moon festival in mid-autumn, when the full moon is particularly bright. The Vietnamese moon festival is called Trung Thu (in this song, Troom Too). In Vietnam, children parade in the streets, wearing masks and carrying lanterns. Families enjoy special sweet pastries called mooncakes. In Canada, Vietnamese communities also celebrate with parades and lanterns. The song "Tet Troom Too" tells of a beautiful girl, Hang, and a kind old man, Tahn Goyee, who live in the moon. With their lanterns and their song, children beckon to Tahn Goyee, trying to persuade him to let down a ladder from the moon so Hang can come down and play with them. The English translation of this song is by Mary Martin Trotter.

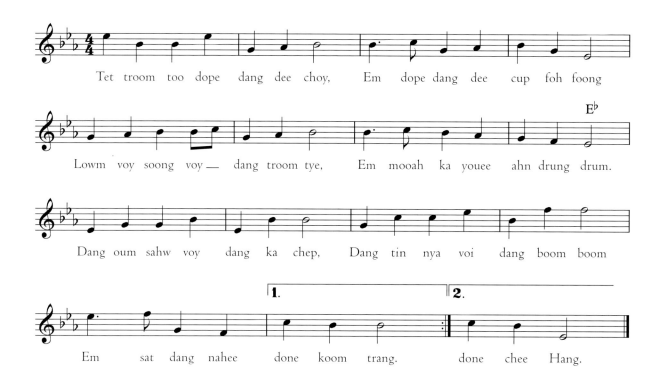

Tet troom too dope dang dee choy, Em dope dang dee cup foh foong

Lowm voy soong voy — dang troom tye, Em mooah ka youee ahn drung drum.

Dang oum sahw voy dang ka chep, Dang tin nya voi dang boom boom

1. Em sat dang nahee done koom trang.

2. done chee Hang.

1.
TET TROOM TOO DOPE DANG DEE CHOY,
Em dope dang dee cup foh foong
Lowm voy soong voy dang troom tye,
Em mooah ka youee ahn drung drum.
Dang oum sahw voy dang ka chep,
Dang tin nya voi dang boom boom
Em sat dang nahee done koom trang.

2.
Tet troom too dope dang dee choy,
Em dope dang dee cup foh foong
Lowm voy soong voy dang troom tye,
Em mooah ka youee ahn drung drum.
Tome yin yin kak tome yin yin,
Tome yin yin kak tome yin yin
Em sat dang nahee done chee Hang.

1.
Full moon as you rise tonight,
I will light my candle bright.
From my lantern it will glow,
Marching through the streets below.
"*Tome yin yin kak,*" sound the drum!
"*Tome yin yin kak,*" children come!
Show the moon maid up above.
"*Tome yin yin kak,*" sound the drum!
"*Tome yin yin kak,*" children come!
To the moon maid show your love.

2.
To the moon we want to go,
Swinging lanterns all aglow.
Lanterns of all shapes we bring.
As we go, we dance and sing.
"*Tome yin yin kak,*" sound the drum!
"*Tome yin yin kak,*" children come!
Oh the joy my lantern gives!
"*Tome yin yin kak,*" sound the drum!
"*Tome yin yin kak,*" children come!
Come to where the moon maid lives!

Written and Illustrated by
Duke Redbird
I Am a Canadian

"I Am a Canadian" was originally printed in a limited edition of two thousand copies. It was presented to Queen Elizabeth II in Ottawa on October 17, 1977, in honour of the twenty-fifth year of her reign. It's surprising, more than twenty years later, how little "I Am a Canadian" has dated. Redbird's portrait of Canada includes darkness and loss: last week's unpaid rent, the mother who lost a son. But "I Am a Canadian" is, more than anything, a celebration: of Canada's sheer size and its many kinds of natural beauty; of its famous citizens; and above all, of ordinary people taking pride in their work and enjoying life.

I'M A LOBSTER FISHERMAN IN
NEWFOUNDLAND
I'm a clambake in P.E.I.
I'm a picnic, I'm a banquet
I'm mother's homemade pie
I'm a few drafts in a Legion hall in
Fredericton
I'm a kite-flyer in a field in Moncton
I'm a nap on the porch after a hard day's work
is done.
I'm a snowball fight in Truro, Nova Scotia
I'm small kids playing jacks and skipping rope
I'm a mother who lost a son in the last great war
And I'm a bride with a brand new ring
And a chest of hope
I'm an Easterner
I'm a Westerner
I'm from the North
And I'm from the South
I've swum in two big oceans
And I've loved them both
I'm a clown in Quebec during carnival
I'm a mass in the Cathedral of St. Paul
I'm a hockey game in the Forum
I'm Rocket Richard and Jean Béliveau
I'm a coach for little league Expos

I'm a baby-sitter for sleep-defying rascals
I'm a canoe trip down the Ottawa
I'm a holiday on the Trent
I'm a mortgage, I'm a loan
I'm last week's unpaid rent
I'm Yorkville after dark
I'm a walk in the park
I'm Winnipeg gold-eye
I'm a hand-made trout fly
I'm a wheat-field and a sunset
Under a prairie sky
I'm Sir John A. Macdonald
I'm Alexander Graham Bell
I'm a pow-wow dancer
And I'm Louis Riel
I'm the Calgary Stampede
I'm a feathered Sarcee
I'm Edmonton at night
I'm a bar-room fight
I'm a rigger, I'm a cat
I'm a ten-gallon hat
And an unnamed mountain in
the interior of B.C.
I'm a maple tree and a totem pole
I'm sunshine showers
And fresh-cut flowers
I'm a ferry boat ride to the Island
I'm the Yukon
I'm the Northwest Territories
I'm the Arctic Ocean and the
Beaufort Sea
I'm the prairies, I'm the Great
Lakes,
I'm the Rockies, I'm the Laurentians,
I am French
I am English
And I am Métis
But more than this
Above all this
I am a Canadian and proud to be free.

About the Authors

MARGARET ATWOOD, born in Ottawa in 1939, is one of Canada's most honoured novelists and poets. She was educated at the University of Toronto and Radcliffe College in Massachusetts. Atwood first won the Governor General's Award in 1966, for a collection of her poetry called *The Circle Game*. *The Journals of Susanna Moodie* (1970), from which the poem in this anthology is taken, was her fourth poetry book. Atwood won the Governor General's Award again in 1986, this time for fiction, and the Giller Prize in 1996. Atwood has also written several books for children, including *Princess Prunella and the Purple Peanut* (1995). She has been the chair of the Writers' Union of Canada and president of PEN Canada, a group concerned with human rights. She was made a Member of the Order of Canada in 1974 and a Companion in 1988.

ARCHIBALD STANSFELD BELANEY (Grey Owl) was born in England in 1888 and immigrated to Canada when he was seventeen. He travelled to Northern Ontario, where he became a trapper and told everyone he was a Native person. After his Mohawk wife persuaded him to give up killing animals, Grey Owl became a world-famous writer and environmentalist. His books include *Pilgrims of the Wild* (1935) and a children's book, *The Adventures of Sajo and Her Beaver People* (1935). It was only after he died in 1938 that the public learned he was really an Englishman.

PIERRE BERTON was born in Dawson City, Yukon, in 1920. He began his career as a journalist, and in 1956 published *The Mysterious North*, which won the Governor General's Award for Non-fiction. Berton went on to write many best-selling popular histories, including *The National Dream* (1970) and *Vimy* (1986). Meanwhile, he had become one of the country's best-known television personalities through his appearances on the long-running television program "Front Page Challenge." In recent years he has also been working on a series of novels for children called Adventures in Canadian History. Pierre Berton won two more Governor General's Awards for Non-fiction in 1958 and 1971, as well as the Stephen Leacock Medal for Humour in 1959. In 1986, he was made a Companion of the Order of Canada.

OSCAR BRAND is a folksinger and songwriter who was born in 1920 in Winnipeg, Manitoba, although he has spent much of his life in the United States. Over the course of his sixty-year career, he has released ninety-three albums of songs. He hosted a radio program called "Folk Song Festival" from New York City for more than fifty years, beginning in 1945. From 1966 to 1968, Brand hosted a CBC Television program, called "Let's Sing Out," that featured the top folksingers of the day. The show's theme song was "Something to Sing About," written by Brand, which is included in this anthology.

JEAN DE BRÉBEUF (1593–1649) was born in France and became a Jesuit priest. In 1629, he sailed to New France to become a missionary to the Huron people. Brébeuf learned their language and became one of the first to write it down, translating many books into Huron, but he is best remembered as the probable author of "Jesous Ahatonhia" (The Huron Carol). In 1649, Brébeuf was captured and killed by the Iroquois, who were at war with the Huron.

JOSEPH BRUCHAC, an Abenaki storyteller and writer, was born in 1942 in Saratoga Springs, New York. After graduating from Cornell University, he obtained his Ph.D. at the Union Graduate School in 1975. For the past twenty-five years, Bruchac has been a major voice in Native storytelling and writing. He is the author of more than sixty books for both adults and children. Bruchac's children's books include *The Boy Who Lived with the Bears* (1995). With Michael Caduto, he has compiled several books of Native legends and beliefs, including *Keepers of the Earth* (1989), from which "Manabozho and the Maple Trees" is taken, and *Keepers of the Animals* (1991).

ROCH CARRIER was born in the little village of Ste-Justine-de-Dorchester, Quebec, in 1937. His first published works, in the 1950s, were collections of poems. His novel *La Guerre, Yes Sir!* (1968), the first in a trilogy, won him acclaim in both French and English Canada. Carrier continues to be one of the best-known Québécois writers, and his work is widely available in English translation. He has also written plays, a film script, and several children's books, including one of Canada's most beloved children's stories, *The Hockey Sweater* (1979), which is in this anthology. Carrier was made an Officer of the Order of Canada in 1992, and was director of the Canada Council from 1994 to 1997.

BARBARA CASS-BEGGS (1904–1990), music teacher and folk-music scholar, was born in Nottingham, England. Immigrating to Canada after the Second World War, she became a music teacher, first in Toronto and later in Saskatchewan, Ottawa, and British Columbia. Her special interest was music for young children, and she was the founder of the Canadian Listen, Like, Learn program for babies and pre-schoolers. In 1982 she won the Children's Service Award from the Association of Early Childhood Educators of Ontario. She published many collections of folksongs, including *Canadian Folksongs for the Young* (1975). That collection includes "Song of Louis Riel" (included in this anthology), which Cass-Beggs translated into English.

JOAN CLARK was born in Liverpool, Nova Scotia, in 1934. She now lives in Newfoundland, the setting for her young people's novel *The Dream Carvers* (1995), from which the excerpt in this anthology was taken. Clark graduated from Acadia University and then taught school. Her short stories were published in numerous magazines before being collected into her first book. Her first novel for adults, *The Victory of Geraldine Gull*, was shortlisted for the Governor General's Award, while *The Dream Carvers* won both the Geoffrey Bilson Award for Historical Fiction and the Mr. Christie's Book Award. In 1999, Joan Clark won the Vicky Metcalf Award for a Body of Work.

JOHN ROBERT COLOMBO, born in Kitchener, Ontario, in 1936 and educated at the University of Toronto, is probably best known for compiling *Colombo's Canadian Quotations*, first published in 1974, as well as many other reference books about Canada. He has edited more than 120 books, contributed pieces to CBC Radio and Television, and reviewed films. Colombo is also a poet who has published numerous collections of poetry, including *The Sad Truths*, from which "My Genealogy" is taken.

THOMAS CHARLES CONNORS was born in Saint John, New Brunswick, in 1936 and grew up in great poverty in Prince Edward Island. He began writing songs when he was eleven years old. As an adult, he has written hundreds more, often about the lives of ordinary Canadians. He first began to perform in 1964 in Timmins, Ontario, and was soon known as Stompin' Tom for his habit of keeping time by stamping his cowboy boot on the stage. Among his best-known songs are "Bud the Spud," which he turned into a children's book in 1994, and "The Hockey Song." Connors was made an Officer of the Order of Canada in 1996.

RITA COX, born in Trinidad, is a storyteller who has brought the magic of literature to thousands of young people. For many years, she was head librarian of Toronto's Parkdale Public Library, where she developed Literacy and Learning programs that became models for other libraries to follow. She also assembled a Black Heritage and West Indian Collection that is considered the finest in Canada. In 1997, Rita Cox was made a Member of the Order of Canada.

DONALD CREIGHTON (1902–1979) was born in Toronto and attended the University of Toronto and Oxford University in England. He was a member of the history department at the University of Toronto from 1927 into the 1970s. Creighton wrote several important and widely read books about Canadian history. He won the Governor General's Award for Non-fiction in 1952 for *John A. Macdonald: The Young Politician*, from which the excerpt in this anthology is taken. He won again in 1955 for the second volume of this biography. In 1967, he was made a Companion of the Order of Canada.

MARY HELEN CREIGHTON (1899–1989) was born in Dartmouth, Nova Scotia. During her long career, she gained an international reputation as a pioneer-ing collector of folksongs and folklore in the Maritimes. She recorded more than four thousand folksongs and folktales, in English, French, Gaelic, Mi'kmaq, and German, for the Library of Congress in Washington and the National Archives in Ottawa. She gave lectures throughout North America and received five honorary doctorates. In 1976, she was made a Member of the Order of Canada. Her books include *Bluenose Ghosts* (1957) and a children's book called *With a Heigh-Heigh-Ho* (1986).

JAMES DE MILLE (1833–1880) was born in Saint John, New Brunswick, and spent most of his adult life teaching history and literature at Dalhousie University in Halifax. He was at one time one of the most popular novelists in North America. He also wrote two series of books for boys. Today most of his writings are forgotten, although his fantasy novel *A Strange Manuscript Found in a Copper Cylinder* (1888), published after his death, is still read and appreciated. He is represented in this anthology by his humorous poem "Sweet Maiden of Passamaquoddy."

MARY ALICE DOWNIE was born in Illinois to Canadian parents in 1934. She is a graduate of the University of Toronto and now lives in Kingston, Ontario. Her first children's book was *The Wind Has Wings*, a collection of Canadian poetry, and she also published several other children's anthologies. Downie has co-written a number of historical novels for young people, including *Honour Bound* (1991) and *A Proper Acadian* (1980), from which the excerpt in this anthology is taken.

WILLIAM "WILLIE" DUNN is a folk musician and filmmaker whose Native name is Roha'tiio, meaning "his voice is beautiful." Of Mi'kmaq-Scottish descent, he was born in Montreal in 1941. Dunn has recorded six albums of his music, and has written and performed music for films and radio programs. He has also made several films for the National Film Board, including *The Ballad of Crowfoot* (whose theme song is included in this anthology).

DAN FERGUSON was a Saskatchewan farmer with twelve children when the drought years of the 1930s struck. When he heard his youngest son, Jim, boast about the clothes he would buy when he earned money by trapping gophers, Ferguson wrote the song "Flunky Jim," which is included in this anthology. Many years later, his grandson sang the song for Barbara Cass-Beggs, who added it to her folksong collection.

BEATRICE FINES was born in Fort Frances, Ontario, in 1917 and later moved to Manitoba, where her family farmed. On a nearby farm lived a Ukrainian family, and their pioneering experiences inspired "No Flour in the Barrel," which is included in this anthology. Fines worked for many years as a staff writer for the Winnipeg General Hospital, while also writing short stories and articles for many periodicals and anthologies. Her writing awards include the Lady Eaton Award from the Manitoba branch of the

Canadian Authors' Association. She has also taught creative writing at several universities and participated in Manitoba's Artists in the Schools program.

EDITH FOWKE (1913–1996), one of Canada's foremost folklorists, was born in Lumsden, Saskatchewan. After receiving an M.A. from the University of Saskatchewan, she moved to Ontario, where she began to make field trips to collect folksongs and folklore. Through radio broadcasts and university lectures, recordings she supervised, and books she published, she greatly increased our knowledge of traditional music and culture. *Sally Go 'Round the Sun*, her collection of children's songs, rhymes, and games, won the Canadian Library Association's Children's Book of the Year Award in 1970. In 1978, Edith Fowke was appointed a Member of the Order of Canada.

FRANCES FRASER (1920–1989) was born in Bossano, Alberta, and raised on a farm that bordered the Blackfoot (Siksika) Reserve. She spent a great deal of time among the Siksika as she was growing up, and as an adult began, with their permission, to write their traditional stories for the *Calgary Herald* and other newspapers. The author W. O. Mitchell encouraged her to submit her stories to the *Globe and Mail* in Toronto, where they came to the attention of book publishers. In 1959, her first book, *The Bear Who Stole the Chinook and Other Stories*, was published and was an instant success. In 1968, her second collection of stories, *The Wind along the River*, appeared.

BILL FREEMAN, born in 1938 in London, Ontario, has had several occupations, including teaching and social work. He has written many novels with historical settings for young people, including *Shantymen of Cache Lake* (1975), which is excerpted in this anthology and was his first book. Its six sequels, including *Prairie Fire* (1998) trace the further adventures of Meg and John Bains. In 1984, Bill Freeman won the Vicky Metcalf Award for a Body of Work.

RHINEHART FRIESEN is the grandson of Mennonites who were among the first group of settlers in Manitoba. Born in 1914, he graduated from the faculty of medicine at the University of Manitoba in 1944. For almost forty years, he practised as an obstetrician, earning an international reputation. After his retirement from medicine, he turned his attention to writing. He is the author of a children's book, *Almost an Elephant* (1987), and *Mennonite Odyssey* (1988), a collection of historical short stories based on his grandparents' experiences.

ROBERT E. GARD (1910–1992) was born in Iola, Kansas. He was a professor of history at the University of Wisconsin, the author of more than forty books, and an important figure in the cultural life of the state. He was director of the Wisconsin Idea Theater, and also founded the Wisconsin Regional Writers' Association. In the 1940s, he travelled north to Alberta, where he organized the Alberta Folklore and Local History Project. Out of the materials he collected came a book called *Johnny Chinook: Tall Tales and True from the Canadian West* (1945). "Johnny Chinook" is one of the stories from that book.

CHIEF DAN GEORGE (1899–1981) was born on the Burrard Indian Reserve in British Columbia and was chief of the Squamish band from 1951 to 1963. When he was sixty years old, after decades of work as a logger and longshoreman, he became an actor. He first appeared on stage and television in Canada, and later in Hollywood movies. He was also the author of *My Heart Soars* (1974) and *My Spirit Soars* (1982). In 1971, he was appointed an Officer of the Order of Canada.

ANTOINE GÉRIN-LAJOIE (1824–1882) was born in Yamachiche in Lower Canada (later Quebec). He was only fourteen years old when the Rebellion of Lower Canada broke out, and a few years later, while a student at Nicolet College, he wrote a poem about an exiled rebel called "Un Canadien errant," to be sung to an old French folk tune. Gérin-Lajoie went on to a distinguished career as a lawyer and an author, and he was very involved in the cultural life of Quebec. He was a founding member and first president of the Institut Canadien, a group of intellectuals who advocated freedom of thought and political reform in Quebec.

BOBBY GIMBY (1918–1998) was born in the small community of Cabri, Saskatchewan. He was a trumpeter and a bandleader, as well as a composer of popular songs. In 1961, while on tour to the Far East, he wrote a song called "Malaysia Forever," which became the unofficial Malaysian national anthem. In 1967, he had another hit, the song "CA-NA-DA." Gimby toured the country as the Pied Piper of Canada, performing his song with groups of children. In the same year, he was appointed an Officer of the Order of Canada.

MONA GOULD (1908–1999), born Mona McTavish in Prince Albert, Saskatchewan, began writing poetry in the 1930s. During her long career, she worked as a journalist and advertising copywriter, and was also the host of several radio programs. She continued to write poetry even after losing her eyesight in the last years of her life. It is for one of her poems that Mona Gould is best remembered: "This Was My Brother," written for her brother, a lieutenant-colonel killed during the Second World War, at Dieppe in 1942.

BARBARA GREENWOOD was born in Toronto in 1940 and educated at the University of Toronto. Before turning to writing historical fiction for children, she taught elementary school. She now teaches creative writing for grades 6 through 12 and has taught numerous adult writing courses. She was president of the Canadian Society of Children's Authors, Illustrators and Performers (CANSCAIP) from 1983 to 1985. Her books include *The Last Safe House: A Story of the Underground Railroad* (1998) and *A Pioneer Story: The Daily Life of a Canadian Family in 1840* (1995), which won several awards, including the Mr. Christie's Book Award and the Ruth Schwartz Award.

GREY OWL (*see* Archibald Stansfeld Belaney)

HARRY GUTKIN was born in 1915 in Winnipeg, where he still lives today, and educated there and in Chicago. He is past-president of the Jewish Historical Society of Western Canada. His books for adults include *Journey into Our Heritage: The Story of the Jewish People in the Canadian West* (1980) and, with his wife, Mildred Gutkin, *Profiles in Dissent: The Shaping of Radical Thought in the Canadian West* (1997). Both these books received awards from the Manitoba Historical Society. His textbook *The Jewish Canadians* has been used in many junior high schools across Canada. The story in this anthology is from a collection that he is currently compiling.

PETER GZOWSKI was born in Toronto in 1934 and grew up in Galt, Ontario. He edited the student newspaper while he was at the University of Toronto, then began a long career in journalism. Gzowski became a household name as host of the CBC Radio programs "This Country in the Morning" and "Morningside." He has also hosted several television programs, and is widely admired for his warmth, humour, and curiosity as a host and an interviewer. In 1995 he won a Governor General's Award for the Performing Arts, and in 1998 was made a Companion of the Order of Canada.

ANNE HART was born in Winnipeg and grew up in rural Nova Scotia. She has lived in Newfoundland for more than thirty years, many of them as head of the Centre for Newfoundland Studies at Memorial University Library. Her short stories and poems have appeared in a number of Canadian periodicals and anthologies, and have been adapted for CBC Radio. "The Friday Everything Changed" appeared in *Chatelaine* magazine in 1976.

SAMUEL HEARNE (1745–1792) was born in England and joined the British navy at the age of eleven. In 1766, he joined the Hudson's Bay Company, which sent him to search for a water route from Prince of Wales's Fort, on Hudson Bay, to the Pacific Ocean. In 1770, led by a skilful Chipewyan guide named Matonabbee, Hearne followed the Coppermine River to the Arctic Ocean. Hearne's account of his epic journey, *A Journey from Prince of Wales's Fort in Hudson's Bay to the Northern Ocean*, was published three years after his death.

ALOOTOOK IPELLIE was born in 1951 on the north shore of Frobisher Bay in the Northwest Territories (an area that is now in Nunavut), where his family still followed a traditional, semi-nomadic life. He was educated in Iqaluit, Yellowknife, and Ottawa, where he now lives. He has worked for the CBC as an announcer/producer, and as a freelance writer and editor for many publications, including *Nunavut* and *Nunatsiaq News*. In 1993–94, his artwork was included in a National Library exhibition entitled *North: Landscape of the Imagination. Arctic Dreams and Nightmares*, which he wrote and illustrated, was published in 1993.

PAULINE JOHNSON (1861–1913) was born on the Six Nations Reserve in Canada West (later Ontario). She was the daughter of a Mohawk chief and a non-Native mother and later adopted the Native name Tekahionwake. Johnson began to write poetry as a child. After her father died in 1884, the family was short of money, so Johnson started to write poems for magazines to pay the bills, and to give public recitals of her work. By 1892, she was performing for audiences in Canada, the United States, and England, often wearing a colourful buckskin costume she had created. Many of her poems were collected in *Flint and Feather* (1912). Pauline Johnson retired from touring in 1909 and settled in Vancouver, where she died.

LENORE KEESHIG-TOBIAS is an Ojibwa (Anishinabe) writer and traditional storyteller. She was born in 1949 on the Neyaashiinigmiing (Cape Croker) Reserve in Ontario, where she now lives, and she holds a B.F.A. degree from York University. She has given public readings across North America and in Scandinavia, and is involved in groups promoting racial minority writers and Aboriginal rights. Keeshig-Tobias has written several children's books, including *Emma and the Trees* (1996). Her book *Bird Talk* (1992), illustrated by her daughter Polly, won the Living Dream Award, given in memory of Dr. Martin Luther King to a book that "provides positive cultural images and dispels prejudice."

KIAKSHUK (1886–1966) was a distinguished Inuk artist and storyteller. His prints were exhibited widely in Canada and the United States, and are in the collections of the Canadian Museum of Civilization in Hull, Quebec, and the Art Gallery of Ontario in Toronto. One of his prints, called *Summer Tent*, was reproduced on a Canadian postage stamp. Kiakshuk appeared as the storyteller in the National Film Board of Canada's film *The Living Stone*. His poem "The Giant Bear" was first printed in an anthology of Inuit writings called *Paper Stays Put* (1981).

CALIXA LAVALLÉE (1842–1891), composer and musician, was born in Verchères, Canada East (later Quebec). He studied music first in Montreal and later in Paris. As a professional musician, Lavallée gave concerts in the United States and Europe, playing the piano, violin, and cornet. For a few years, he established a music studio in Montreal, and was twice president of the Académie de musique du Québec. By 1880, he had been dubbed "Canada's national musician," so it was natural for the lieutenant-governor of Quebec to ask him to compose a piece for Quebec's Congrès national des Canadiens-Français. Today it is the melody of Canada's national anthem.

STEPHEN LEACOCK (1869–1944) immigrated to Canada from England with his family when he was still a child. He became a professor of economics and political science at McGill University in Montreal, and won the 1937 Governor General's Award for Non-fiction for *My Discovery of the West*. Today he is best remembered for his collections of comic stories, such as *Literary Lapses* (1910) and *Sunshine Sketches of a Little Town* (1912), from which the excerpt in this anthology is taken. The Leacock Medal, given annually to the best book of humour by a Canadian, was named in his honour.

DENNIS LEE, born in 1939 in Toronto, is a poet, novelist, and editor. Although he first gained recognition as a writer for adults, he became famous for his entertaining books of poetry for children, including *Alligator Pie* (1974) and *Garbage Delight* (1977). Among his many literary honours are the Governor General's Award for Poetry in 1972 and, for his children's writing, the 1992 Mr. Christie's Book Award for *The Ice Cream Store* and the 1986 Vicky Metcalf Award for a Body of Work. In 1994, he was made a Member of the Order of Canada.

GORDON LIGHTFOOT is a singer and songwriter who was born in Orillia, Ontario, in 1939. His best-known songs include "Early Morning Rain," "If You Could Read My Mind," "The Wreck of the Edmund Fitzgerald," and "Canadian Railroad Trilogy," which appears in this anthology. He has recorded more than fifteen albums, which have sold, in total, more than ten million copies. Lightfoot's recordings have won sixteen Juno Awards, and he was inducted into the Juno Hall of Fame in 1986. He was made an Officer of the Order of Canada in 1971, and in 1995 won the Governor General's Performing Arts Award.

DELL J. MCCORMICK was the American author of *Paul Bunyan Swings His Ax*, the source for "Paul Bunyan Digs the St. Lawrence River." This book, first published in 1936, is still in print and has sold more than one million copies. McCormick followed up with a second Paul Bunyan collection called *Tall Timber Tales* (1939). "Paul Bunyan Digs the St. Lawrence" was also published in a reader called *Beckoning Trails*, which was used in Ontario schools in the 1940s.

JOHN MCCRAE (1872–1918) was born in Guelph, Ontario, and received a medical degree from the University of Toronto. During the First World War, he served in the medical corps until his death from pneumonia. His poem "In Flanders Fields" was published in the British magazine *Punch* in 1915, and it quickly became one of the best-known poems of the war. His only collection of poems, *Flanders Fields and Other Poems*, was published in 1919, after his death.

EDGAR MCINNIS (1899–1973) was born in Charlottetown, Prince Edward Island. In the First World War, he served with the Canadian artillery. Out of these experiences came *Poems Written at the Front* (1918), which includes "Our Dugout." After the war, he was a Rhodes Scholar at Oxford University in England. In his long, distinguished career as a historian, he taught at the University of Toronto and York University, wrote numerous books, including a six-volume history of the Second World War, was a delegate to the United Nations, and became president of the Canadian Institute of International Affairs. In 1966, he received the Tyrrell Medal of the Royal Society, its highest award for history.

WILLIAM LYON MACKENZIE (1795–1861) was a journalist and politician who became the leader of the Rebellion of Upper Canada in 1837. He was born near Dundee, Scotland, and immigrated to Canada in 1820. Mackenzie was first elected to the Legislative Assembly of Upper Canada in 1828, but he was expelled for publishing attacks on the Tory government in his newspaper, the *Colonial Advocate*. In 1834, he was elected the first mayor of York (Toronto), and he held a seat in the legislature from 1834 to 1836. After his Reform Party was defeated in an election, Mackenzie advocated open rebellion, but his march on Toronto was quickly put down. He fled to the United States, returning to Canada in 1849, after he received a government pardon. He resumed his outspoken career, serving as member of the Legislative Assembly for Haldimand until 1857.

JOHN GILLESPIE MAGEE, JR. (1922–1941), was born in China, the son of missionary parents. His father was American and his mother was British. In 1939, he earned a scholarship to Yale University in the United States, but he instead enlisted in the Royal Canadian Air Force to fight in the Second World War. Magee trained in Canada and then was sent to Britain to join a Spitfire (fighter plane) squadron. While on a training mission, he was killed in a plane crash in December 1941. He was only nineteen. In the months before his death, he had been including poems in his letters home to his parents. One of them was "High Flight," which is reprinted in this anthology. The Royal Canadian Air Force distributed plaques with the words to this poem to their airfields and training stations. It is probably the most famous aviation poem ever written.

AINSLIE MANSON was born in Montreal in 1938 and now lives in Vancouver. In between, she lived, worked, and studied in London and the United States. Her first book for children was published in 1982. In recent years, she has specialized in books with historical settings: biographies of Alexander Mackenzie and Simon Fraser for older readers, and picture books based on incidents in Canadian history, including *A Dog Came Too* (1992), which is excerpted in this anthology, and *Baboo* (1998), about John A. Macdonald's physically challenged daughter. Manson was a founding member of the Canadian Society of Children's Authors, Illustrators and Performers (CANSCAIP).

SUZANNE MARTEL was born in 1924 in Quebec City. She writes in French, but many of her children's books have been translated into English. Martel has won numerous awards for her children's books, including the 1994 Governor General's Award for *Une belle journée pour mourir* (A beautiful day to die), the Vicky Metcalf Award for a Body of Work in 1976, and the 1981 Ruth Schwartz Award for *The King's Daughter*, from which the excerpt in this anthology is taken. She currently lives in Montreal.

EVA MARTIN was born in Woodstock, Ontario, and graduated from the University of Toronto with a degree in library science. Since her childhood, she has loved fairy tales, and through her work as a children's librarian she became very knowledgeable about this form of traditional story. In 1984, she collaborated with the artist Laszlo Gal on a collection called *Canadian Fairy Tales*, from which "Ti-Jean Brings Home the Moon" is taken.

L. M. (LUCY MAUD) MONTGOMERY (1874–1942) was born in Clifton (now New London), Prince Edward Island, and raised by her grandparents in Cavendish. She studied at Prince of Wales College in Charlottetown and later at Dalhousie University in Halifax. Her first novel, *Anne of Green Gables*, was published in 1908 and became an instant best-seller. It was followed by eight more books about Anne over the years, as well as three popular books in the Emily series, including *Emily of New Moon*. During her lifetime, Montgomery published twenty-two works of fiction, more than four hundred poems, and more than five hundred short stories. In 1911, Montgomery married a minister and moved to Ontario, where she lived until her death. Today Anne of Green Gables is known all over the world, and the books about her have been made into several movies, a musical stage play, and a television series. L. M. Montgomery was awarded the Order of the British Empire in 1935.

SUSANNA MOODIE (1803–1885) immigrated from England to Upper Canada (later Ontario) with her husband, John Dunbar Moodie, in 1832. For a few years, they pioneered in the backwoods north of present-day Peterborough. After the Moodies and their children moved to the town of Belleville, Susanna Moodie wrote about her experiences in *Roughing It in the Bush* (1852). Although she produced many other books, including children's novels and even some poetry collections, only *Roughing It* is still well known today.

KIM MORRISSEY was born in 1955. She was a founding member of the Saskatchewan Playwrights' Centre and is the author of many acclaimed plays. Her black comedy about Sigmund Freud, *Dora*, has been produced in Canada, the United States, Britain, and Germany. This anthology includes an excerpt from *Batoche*, her collection of poems about Louis Riel and other leaders of the Northwest Rebellion. *Batoche* won poetry prizes from the Saskatchewan Writers' Guild and the CBC Radio Literary Competition. Another of her poetry collections was adapted as an opera and performed by the Winnipeg Symphony in 1993.

FARLEY MOWAT was born in Belleville, Ontario, in 1921, and later, as related in *The Dog Who Wouldn't Be* (1957), moved with his family to Saskatchewan. As a child he was an avid naturalist, and many of his more than twenty-five books for both children and adults reflect his love of animals and his environmental concerns. They include, for children, *Owls in the Family* (1961) and, for adults, *A Whale for the Killing* (1972) and *Never Cry Wolf* (1963), which was later made into a film. He has won most of the literary awards Canada has to offer, including a Governor General's Award for *Lost in the Barrens* (1956) and the 1970 Vicky Metcalf Award for a Body of Work. He was made an Officer of the Order of Canada in 1981.

ALEXANDER MUIR (1830–1906) was born in Scotland and immigrated to Canada as a child with his parents. After obtaining a B.A. from Queen's University, he became a schoolteacher and later a principal at various schools in what is now the Greater Toronto Area. Muir was also a poet and amateur musician. In 1867, he wrote both the words and the music for "The Maple Leaf Forever." Although for many years this was English Canada's unofficial anthem, Muir never received, or sought, a penny in payment for his song.

RICHARD NARDIN was born in New York City in 1952, and has loved the simplicity and grace of folk music from the time he was a child. In 1976, he moved to the Upstate New York community of Saratoga Springs, where he composed numerous songs about the history and legends of the region, including "The Piper's Refrain." Nardin is now a computer software professional living in North Carolina.

bp (BARRY PHILLIP) NICHOL (1944–1988) was born in Vancouver. In his relatively short life, Nichol published many books of acclaimed poetry, including four volumes that won the Governor General's Award in 1970. He performed sound poetry in solo concerts and with a group called the Four Horsemen. In the 1980s, he created musical plays and also wrote for the children's television program "Fraggle Rock."

UMA PARAMESWARAN was born in Madras, India, and educated in India and the United States, eventually obtaining a Ph.D. from Michigan State University. In 1966, she moved to Winnipeg, Manitoba, where she still lives. She is a professor of English at the University of Winnipeg, and has published critical studies, poems, and short stories, including "Show and Tell," the story reprinted in this anthology. She is now at work on several longer works of fiction. Parameswaran has been heavily involved in the Writers' Union of Canada, the Manitoba Writers' Guild, and several other cultural organizations.

MARY PEATE was born in Toronto and grew up in Montreal in the 1930s and 1940s. She had a twenty-five-year career in Canadian radio and television, both as a writer and broadcaster. Peate has written two books of reminiscences: *Girl in a Red River Coat* (1970) and *Girl in a Sloppy Joe Sweater* (1980). In 1980, she moved to California, where she has written for various newspapers and magazines.

NANCY PRASAD was born in Toronto and graduated from Queen's University. She is a freelance writer with a particular interest in poetry and fantasy, but she has also written a number of non-fiction books for children, including *What It Means to Be Honest* (1987). Her stories and poems have appeared in literary magazines and school textbooks, as well as in *The Dancing Sun* (1981), a multicultural anthology in which her poem "You Have Two Voices" first appeared.

E. J. (EDWIN JOHN) PRATT (1882–1964) was born in Western Bay, Newfoundland. After studying at St. John's Methodist College, he obtained a Ph.D. from the University of Toronto. He then joined the department of English at UofT's Victoria College and was a much-loved professor there for more than thirty years. Pratt was also one of Canada's most renowned poets. His first two books of narrative verse (poems that tell a story) were about the sea, and one of his short poems about the sea—"The Way of Cape Race"—is included in this anthology. He won the Governor General's Award for Poetry for "Brébeuf and his Brethren" (1940) and again for "Towards the Last Spike" (1952).

GEORGE RAWLYK (1935–1995) was born in Thorold, Ontario. He won a Rhodes Scholarship to study at Oxford University in England, and then returned to Canada to become a professor of history. He taught at Queen's University for almost thirty years. Rawlyk was a leading scholar of Christian history and also had an interest in the history of the Maritimes, writing many books on these subjects. With Mary Alice Downie, he co-wrote the children's novel *A Proper Acadian*, which is excerpted in this anthology.

JAMES REANEY was born in 1926 in South Easthope, a rural community near Stratford, Ontario. He combined an academic career, teaching English at the University of Western Ontario, with work as a playwright, poet, and novelist. His poetry collections for adults have won three Governor General's Awards, in 1949, 1958, and 1962, and his plays have been staged across Canada. Among his plays for children are *Listen to the Wind* (1980) and *Ignoramus*; his novels for children are *The Boy with an R in His Hand* (1965) and *Take the Big Picture* (1986). In 1976, he was appointed an Officer of the Order of Canada.

DUKE REDBIRD, an artist, poet, and performer, was born in 1939 on the Saugeen Reserve, on the Bruce Peninsula, near Owen Sound, Ontario. During the 1970s, he performed his poetry throughout Canada and the United States. In 1977, a multi-media revue based on his writings was performed for Queen Elizabeth in Ottawa during her Silver Jubilee celebrations. In 1978, Redbird obtained an M.A. from York University. He published *We Are Métis* in 1980, and his poems were included in the anthology *Canada: Pictures of a Great Land* (1976). Redbird is former president of the Ontario Métis and Non-Status Indian Association and a former vice-president of the Native Council of Canada. In 1998, he became the arts and entertainment reporter for CityPulse News in Toronto.

QUENTIN REYNOLDS (1902–1965) was an American author, screenwriter, journalist, and—during the Second World War—war correspondent. He wrote many non-fiction books for both adults and children, usually with military subjects. During the 1950s, he appeared on a CBS television show called "It's News to Me," hosted by Walter Cronkite. Reynolds's short story "A Secret for Two" was published in a reader called *Beckoning Trails,* which was used in Ontario schools in the 1940s.

LOUIS RIEL (1844–1885) was a Métis leader born in the Red River Settlement in what is now Manitoba. In 1869, he became head of the provisional government that was negotiating with the Canadian government to make Manitoba a province. But when he authorized the execution of Thomas Scott, who had opposed Métis leadership in Red River, English Canadians in the East were appalled. Eventually, Riel fled into exile in the United States. In 1884, the Métis of what would become Saskatchewan asked Riel to return and present their grievances to the Canadian government. When their petitions were not heard, the Métis and other Native groups rose in a short-lived rebellion. Riel was taken prisoner by Canadian forces and put on trial for treason. The jury found him guilty but recommended mercy. However, Riel was hanged in November 1885.

STAN ROGERS (1949–1983) was born in Hamilton, Ontario, and died in a fire on an airplane in 1983, when he was only thirty-three. During his short career, he had already established himself as a singer-songwriter, and had six albums to his credit. (Three more were released after his death.) Many of his songs were about events in Canadian history, including "Northwest Passage" (from the album of the same name) and "MacDonnell on the Heights" (from the album *From Fresh Water*), whose words are included in this anthology.

A. B. (ADOLPHE-BASILE) ROUTHIER (1839–1920) was born in St-Placide in Lower Canada (later Quebec). He became a lawyer and, in 1873, a judge.

But he was even better known in his own day as a poet, and was a founding member of the Royal Society of Canada. In 1880, the lieutenant-governor of Quebec asked him to write words to a melody by Calixa Lavallée for a large public celebration, the Congrès national des Canadiens-Français. Routhier's French words for "O Canada" are still sung today.

A. R. (ARTHUR) SCAMMELL (1913–1995) was born in the Change Islands, Notre Dame Bay, Newfoundland. He wrote his most famous song, "The Squid-jiggin' Ground," when he was just fifteen years old. Scammell originally taught school in Newfoundland, then followed that with many years of teaching in Montreal. In 1970, he retired to St. John's. In 1987, Scammell was made a Member of the Order of Canada, an honour he earned for keeping Newfoundland's history alive through his songs, verses, and stories.

ELMA SCHEMENAUER, born near Elbow, Saskatchewan, was educated at Briarcrest Bible College and the Universities of Saskatchewan and Toronto. She has written more than fifty books, many of them for young people, including the Yesterstories series, from which "Hunting for Unicorns" and "The Lady and the Cowcatcher" are taken. Her children's novel *Jacob Jacobs Gets Up Early* draws on her Prairie Mennonite background.

ROBERT W. SERVICE (1874–1958) was born in England and immigrated to Canada in 1894. He settled in British Columbia and went to work for the Canadian Bank of Commerce. The bank later sent him to Whitehorse and Dawson City, which led him to write his collection of poems about the north and the Klondike gold rush, *Songs of a Sourdough* (1907). The collection was an immediate success, and Service became known as the Poet of the Yukon. He followed it with several other collections of poetry, as well as novels. During the First World War, Service was an ambulance driver, which he described in his collection of poems *Songs of a Red Cross Man* (1916). After the war, he lived in France, where he died in 1958.

MARK SHEKTER was born in Hamilton, Ontario, in 1946. He is a writer and composer with more than one thousand hours of television productions to his credit. His shows, including "Laugh-In" and, more recently, "The Elephant Show," have garnered Emmys and other international awards. Shekter has been the director of development for the Canwest Global Network and has lectured on media topics at universities. With Charles Weir, he co-authored the 1980 musical *Toronto Toronto*, from which "The New Land" is taken.

SHINGUACOUSE (1773–1854), also known as Little Pine, was born in what is now Ontario. He fought against the Americans during the War of 1812, and later became a leader of the Ojibwa people. In 1832, he was successful at persuading the lieutenant-governor to establish a Native settlement near Sault Ste. Marie. However, he was later ignored when he tried to obtain benefits for the Ojibwa from mining operations on their land. In 1850, he was involved in the negotiations for the Robinson Treaty, but once again was disappointed in his efforts to gain more Native control over their own lands.

LOIS SIMMIE was born in 1932. She has supported herself as a writer for many years, winning a literary award from the Saskatchewan Writers Guild in 1983. Her adult fiction includes the novel *They Shouldn't Make You Promise That* (1987). Her children's books include *An Armadillo Is Not a Pillow* (1986), *Who Greased the Shoelaces?* (1989), and *Betty Lee Bonner Lives Here* (1993). Lois Simmie lives in Saskatoon.

JOAN SKOGAN was born in Comox, British Columbia, in 1945. She has lived and worked most of her life along Canada's West Coast, and has even had stints on commercial fishing boats. As a journalist, she has written for CBC Radio, *Saturday Night* magazine, and many other publications. Her books for adults include *Voyages at Sea with Strangers* (1992) and *Moving Water* (1998). Her children's books include *The Princess and the Sea Bear and Other Tsimshian Stories* (from which "Scannah and the Beautiful Woman" is taken) and *The Good Companion* (1998).

WILLIAM W. SMITH, a businessman in Swift Current, Saskatchewan, wrote the humorous words of the song "Saskatchewan," which is reprinted in this anthology. It was sung to a hymn tune called "Beulah Land," and appeared in many versions on the American plains, usually with lyrics bemoaning the dust and starving animals brought by years of drought. But Smith's version ends more hopefully than most of the American songs, with a sense of looking forward to better times.

RAYMOND SOUSTER was born in Toronto in 1921 and, except for wartime service in the Royal Canadian Air Force, has lived there his whole life, working for the Canadian Imperial Bank of Commerce. His first poem was published in the *Toronto Daily Star* when he was twelve years old. His first collection of poetry was published in 1946, and he won the Governor General's Award for Poetry in 1964. Throughout his career, he has encouraged younger poets, publishing their work in numerous poetry magazines and anthologies he has edited. In 1995, Souster was made an Officer of the Order of Canada.

KEN STANGE, poet, artist, and teacher, was born in Chicago in 1946, and has lived in Canada for many years. He has produced several books of his poetry, including *Advice to Travellers* (1994). Stange's art has been published in a book called *A Smoother Pebble, A Prettier Shell* (1996). He also maintains a Web

site of his artwork and publishes a Netzine. He is now a teacher at Nipissing University in Ontario, where he specializes in studying the links between science and literature.

MYRA STILBORN, born in 1916, grew up on a farm in Indian Head, Saskatchewan. She attended a one-room rural school, where she also later taught. Her poetry, including "A Mosquito in the Cabin," as well as her prose, has been published in periodicals and anthologies in Canada, the United States, England, and Australia. Her haiku—a Japanese poetry form—have been published in Japan and four of her sonnets have been read on CBC Radio. Stilborn now lives in Saskatoon, where she is working on a project to encourage seniors to write their memoirs.

SHIZUYE TAKASHIMA was born in 1928 in Vancouver. When she was fourteen, she and her family were uprooted from their home and sent by the Canadian government to a Japanese internment camp called New Denver. The experience became the subject of *A Child in Prison Camp* (1971), which she illustrated with her own watercolours. The book won the Amelia Frances Howard-Gibbon Illustrator's Award, the Canada Council Award (predecessor of the Governor General's Award for Children's Literature), and a literary award in Japan. A dramatized version of the book was later staged in that country. In 1988, she illustrated the children's book *Kenji and the Cricket* by Adele Wiseman.

C. J. (CARRIE) TAYLOR was born in Montreal in 1952 and raised in the Eastern Townships. She is the daughter of a Mohawk father of the Deer Clan, whose heritage has provided the subject matter for her work. Her mother, of British-German descent, encouraged her artistic talent. Taylor is a self-taught artist who began to paint at the age of sixteen. Her first children's book was *How Two-Feather was Saved from Loneliness* (1990), a traditional Abenaki tale originally illustrated by her own paintings. She has followed this with numerous other books retelling the legends of many different Native groups, including *The Messenger of Spring* (1997).

DAVID TIPE grew up in the area of Toronto known as Cabbagetown in the early 1900s, when it was home to low-income families, many of them Irish Canadians. Years later, he contributed two stories about his childhood to a book called *CORE: Stories and Poems Celebrating the Lives of Ordinary People Who Call Toronto Their Home*. One of these stories was "Picking Coke," which is included in this anthology.

CATHARINE PARR TRAILL (1802–1899), the older sister of Susanna Moodie, was born in Kent, England, and immigrated to Canada in 1832. Before leaving England, she had already published several books for children, and she continued her writing in Canada. Her most famous books for adults are *The Backwoods of Canada* (1836) and *The Canadian Settler's Guide* (1854), which described the life immigrants would face in Upper Canada and supplied many ideas for making the best of it. Her novel for children, *The Canadian Crusoes* (1852), also worked a great deal of practical pioneering information into an adventure story about three children who must survive on their own in the wilderness.

IAN TYSON was born in Victoria, British Columbia, in 1939. His plan to become a rodeo cowboy ended with an accident when he was nineteen. He first took up the guitar while recovering, and by the 1960s had become famous as a partner in the folksinging duo Ian and Sylvia, with Sylvia Tyson. In the 1970s, Tyson became an Alberta cattle rancher and also established a solo singing and songwriting career with such albums as *Cowboyography*, for which he won a Juno award in 1987. He was inducted into the Juno Hall of Fame in 1992.

GILLES VIGNEAULT is a poet and songwriter who has always been deeply committed to French Canada. He was born in Natashquan, Quebec, in 1928. He obtained an arts degree from Laval University in 1953, and taught for a number of years while also performing his songs and working in the theatre. He won the Governor General's Award for French-language poetry in 1966 for *Quand les bateaux s'en va*. That same year, his song "Mon Pays," reprinted in this anthology, won the International Song Festival, which is held in Europe. "Mon Pays," although it does not mention Quebec by name, became the unofficial anthem for many Québécois. In recent years, Vigneault has also concerned himself with environmental issues. Among his many awards, he has received three honorary doctorates and has been named a Chevalier of the Order of Quebec.

IAN WALLACE was born in Niagara Falls, Ontario, in 1950 and moved to Toronto, where he now lives, to study at the Ontario College of Art. He has spent more than twenty years writing and illustrating children's books. With Angela Wood, he co-wrote *The Sandwich*, which is included in the collection, in 1975. Travelling across Canada from one end to the other, Wallace has given readings to more than two hundred thousand young people and adults. He won the Mr. Christie Book Award for his *Name of the Tree* illustrations in 1990, and the IODE Book Award and the Amelia Francis Howard-Gibbon Illustrator's Award for *Chin Chiang and the Dragon's Dance* (1985).

CHARLES WEIR was born in Toronto in 1934. After teaching high school, he became a television writer, and worked for ten years for the long-running CBC panel show "Front Page Challenge." He also created television specials for André Gagnon and Ginette Reno, among others, and his Toller Cranston special "Dream Weaver" won an international award in 1980. With Mark Shekter, he wrote the musical productions *All for One* and *Toronto Toronto*, from which the piece for this anthology, "The New Land," was taken. *All for One* was performed at the National Arts Centre in Ottawa and later televised.

ROBERT STANLEY WEIR (1856–1926) was born in Hamilton, in Canada West (later Ontario), and studied law in Montreal.

He excelled in his profession, eventually becoming a judge at the Exchequer Court of Canada. Weir also represented the riding of Argenteuil in the Quebec Legislative Assembly from 1903 to 1910. He wrote both legal works and poetry, and was elected a fellow of the Royal Society of Canada. Today, he is best remembered as the author of the English words for "O Canada," which he wrote in 1908 in honour of the three-hundredth anniversary of the founding of Quebec City.

STELLA WHELAN (1910–1998) was born in St. John's, Newfoundland, and graduated from Memorial College in 1930. She was secretary to the convention that decided Newfoundland would join Confederation, although she herself was against it. After Newfoundland became part of Canada, she continued to work for various provincial government departments. Throughout her life she wrote poetry, including the piece "Mary March," about the last Beothuks, and she won several prizes in provincial literary competitions.

ANGELA (ANNIE) WOOD was born in Northern Greece, of Macedonian ethnicity, and came to Canada as a baby. As one of the founding members and past publisher of Kids Can Press, she contributed to the development of the Canadian children's publishing industry. Her book *The Sandwich* (1975), co-written with Ian Wallace, has sold tens of thousands of copies. It has been translated into Braille, turned into a performance by the National Tap Dance Company, and will soon be an animated film from the National Film Board of Canada. Recently, Wood has organized a Macedonian textile exhibit, *From Baba's Hope Chest*, for the Royal Ontario Museum, and has founded Inventive Women Inc. to develop multimedia projects showcasing female inventors.

PAUL YEE was born in Spalding, Saskatchewan, in 1956, grew up in Vancouver, and now lives in Toronto. He studied history at the University of British Columbia and did volunteer work in Vancouver's Chinatown. He has written several children's books about Chinese Canadians, including *Tales from Gold Mountain* (1989), from which the story "Spirits of the Railway" is taken. Yee has won numerous awards for his work, including the Governor General's Award for *Ghost Train* (1996) and the Ruth Schwartz Award for *Roses Sing on New Snow* (1992).

MEGUIDO ZOLA was born in 1939 in Cairo, Egypt. His first name means "storyteller" in Hebrew. Today he lives in Vancouver and is a member of the faculty of education at Simon Fraser University. He has written children's books about Karen Kain, Terry Fox, and Wayne Gretzky, as well as a collection of folktales called *Noodle, Nitwit, Numskull*, published in 1990.

About the Illustrators

 HARVEY CHAN was born in Hong Kong and came to Canada in 1976. In 1982, he graduated from the Ontario College of Art. His paintings, often on his favourite subject, modern dance, have been exhibited in galleries in Toronto and New York. But it is as a children's book illustrator that Chan has been particularly honoured. *Roses Sing on New Snow* by Paul Yee won the Ruth Schwartz Award in 1992, as did Yee's *Ghost Train* in 1996. Chan's illustrations for *Ghost Train* also won the Amelia Frances Howard-Gibbon Award and the Elizabeth Mrazik-Cleaver Award. For this anthology, Harvey Chan illustrated "From Bonavista to Vancouver Island," "A New Start," and "A Suitcase Full of Stories."

 ALAN DANIEL was born in Ottawa. He now lives in Kitchener, where he works as an artist and illustrator, often in collaboration with his artist wife, Lea. Together they created the art for, among other books, *Bunnicula Escapes* by James Howe (1994), *Sody Salleratus* by Aubrey Davis (1996), and *The Dream Collector* by Troon Harrison (1999). They have also written and illustrated eight short historical fiction novels for the Voyages in Time series. In 1993, Alan Daniel won the IODE Book Award for his detailed historical paintings for *The Story of Canada*. For this book, Daniel illustrated "Explorers and Adventurers," "New France," and "The Great Northwest."

 KIM FERNANDES creates her three-dimensional illustrations with a modelling compound called FIMO. She is the illustrator of Clement C. Moore's classic Christmas story *A Visit from St. Nicholas* (1998) and *One Gray Mouse* by Katherine Button (1995). She is also the author and illustrator of *Zebo and the Dirty Planet* (1991). Her mother, Eugenie Fernandes, who is also a well-known children's author and illustrator, worked with Kim on the design of some of the illustrations for *The Spirit of Canada*. Kim Fernandes illustrated "Animals Mild and Wild" and "Just for Laughs."

LAURA FERNANDEZ and RICK JACOBSON are a husband-and-wife team who trained at the Alberta College of Art. They now live in Toronto with their three children. They have illustrated several book jackets and a number of children's

 picture books, including *Tchaikovsky Discovers America* by Esther Kalman (1994) and *Jeremiah Learns to Read* by Jo Ellen Bogart, which won the 1997 Ruth Schwartz Award. For this book, Fernandez and Jacobson illustrated "O Canada!," "A Vanished Way of Life," and "The Wars."

 ZHONG-YANG HUANG was born in Guangzhou, China, and now lives in Regina, Saskatchewan. Since immigrating to Canada, he has built an impressive career as an artist, and his work can now be found in private and corporate collections around the world. He teamed up with the author David Bouchard to produce two Chinese folktales: *The Great Race* (1997) and *The Dragon New Year* (1998). *The Dragon New Year* was nominated for the Governor General's Award for Children's Illustration. For *The Spirit of Canada*, Zhong-Yang Huang illustrated "Tall Tales" and "Ghosts and Spirits."

 DON KILBY is an award-winning illustrator based in Toronto. He has extensive experience in the advertising and publishing industries in both Canada and the United States, and he also teaches courses in drawing and illustration at George Brown College in Toronto. Kilby has illustrated several children's books, including *Forts of Canada* by Ann-Maureen Owens and Jane Yealland (1996), *Hold On, McGinty* by Nancy Hartry (1997), and *The Prairie Fire* by Marilynn Reynolds (1999). For this book, Kilby illustrated "Settlers," "Loggers," "The True North," and "Voices of Sadness."

 GEORGE LITTLECHILD was born in Edmonton, Alberta, in 1958. He is the son of a Plains Cree mother and a Scottish-French-Maliseet father. In 1988, he graduated from the Nova Scotia College of Art and Design with a Bachelor of Fine Arts degree. Since then, his paintings have been exhibited in Canada, the United States, Japan, Germany, and Australia. His work is also included in the collections of the Canadian Museum of Civilization, the Edmonton Art Gallery, and many others. He has illustrated

many children's books, including *What's the Most Beautiful Thing about Horses?* by Richard Van Camp (1998). Littlechild is also the author/illustrator of several books for children, including the award-winning publication *This Land Is My Land* (1993). For this book, he illustrated the opening section, "When the World Was New."

LUC MELANSON is a well-known commercial artist and illustrator who lives in Montreal. He has provided editorial illustrations for *Saturday Night* magazine, *Les Éditions du Seuil* in France, and *L'Actualité* in Montreal. He has also illustrated two French-language children's books, and his first English-language children's book, *Little Kim's Doll* by Kim Yaroschevskaya, was published in 1999. For *The Spirit of Canada*, he illustrated three sections: "The Dirty Thirties," "Canada at 100," and "Why Can't We Talk to Each Other?"

PAUL MOMBOURQUETTE was born in Moose Jaw, Saskatchewan, in 1962. He grew up on air force bases across Canada. He is a graduate of the computer graphics and computer animation programs at Sheridan College in Oakville, Ontario. Among the books he has illustrated are *Emma and the Silk Train* by Julie Lawson (1997) and *Fog Cat* by Marilyn Helmer (1998), which won the IODE Book Award and the Mr. Christie's Book Award. For this book, he illustrated "Railway Builders" and "Seafarers."

MIKE ROOTH was born in 1975 in Brampton, Ontario, and is a recent graduate of the interpretive illustration program at Oakville's Sheridan College. Along with preparing the icons that illustrate each subsection opener in *The Spirit of Canada*, Rooth apprenticed with Laura Fernandez and Rick Jacobson on their illustrations for "A Vanished Way of Life" and "The Wars."

TIM SHORTT was born and lives in Sarnia, Ontario. He is a graduate of the University of Windsor and an avid baseball fan who is widely admired for his comical sports illustrations. In 1996, he wrote and illustrated his first book for children, *The Babe Ruth Ballet School.* For *The Spirit of Canada*, he illustrated "Good Sports."

BILL SLAVIN was born in 1959 in Belleville, Ontario, and attended Sheridan College in Oakville, where he studied cartooning and graphic story illustration. Today he lives in the small village of Millbrook, Ontario. The many children's books he has illustrated include *The Cat Came Back* (1992), *Rosie Backstage* by Amanda Lewis and Tim Wynne-Jones (1994), and *One Is Canada* by Maxine Trottier (1999). Slavin is also the writer/illustrator of *Stone Lion* (1996). For *The Spirit of Canada*, he illustrated "Turbulent Times," "Rebels," and "Freedom-Seekers."

JANET WILSON was born in the Toronto area in 1952. After her children had started school, she pursued her lifelong interest in art, graduating from the Ontario College of Art in 1985. She has become a prolific and sought-after illustrator of children's books, and has more than thirty books to her credit. Her illustrations for *Selina and the Bear Paw Quilt* by Barbara Smucker won the 1995 Elizabeth Mrazik-Cleaver Canadian Picture Book Award. That same year, she won both the IODE Book Award and the Children's Roundtable Information Book Award for *In Flanders Fields* by Linda Granfield. For *The Spirit of Canada*, Janet Wilson illustrated "Confederation" and "Pioneering in the West."

EDITOR'S ACKNOWLEDGEMENTS

Many people have participated in the creation of *The Spirit of Canada*. Above all, I must thank my publisher, Malcolm Lester, for his enthusiastic and unswerving support from the first moment we discussed the book.

As the anthology took shape, I received much-appreciated help at the Canadian Children's Book Centre in Toronto, the University of Toronto's libraries, the Toronto Reference Library, the North York Central Library's Canadiana Collection, and especially the library at the Ontario Institute for Studies in Education, which has non-circulating collections of Canadian children's literature and music books, among other gems. Thanks to Kathie Imrie, I was also able to spend long hours in OISE's Textbook Archives.

While tracking down rights-holders and securing permissions, Elizabeth d'Anjou showed her flair for detective work, as well as for sweet-talking in both official languages. Many other people whom I met only on the telephone and the Internet helped me to identify elusive authors and obtain permissions. I want to thank particularly Francine St-Denis of Les Nouvelles Éditions de l'Arc, Montreal; Carleen Rummery of the Manitoba Writers' Guild; Martha DiSalle of Kids Can Press, Toronto;

and Christiane Talbot of the National Film Board Reference Library, Ottawa. The authors themselves were a delight. I was able to tell many of them how much I admired their work, and I must single out a quartet of Prairie octogenarians for their courtesy and *joie de vivre*: Beatrice Fines, Harry Gutkin, Rhinehart Friesen, and Myra Stilborn.

For making *The Spirit of Canada* look so beautiful, I am grateful to all the talented artists who illustrated the book, in a stunning array of media and styles, as well as to the creative director, Scott Richardson, and to Jean Lightfoot Peters, who assembled the pages and contributed to the design. Alison Reid's careful proofreading saved us from several embarrassing errors, and Jamie Hopkings not only did a fine job of typesetting the music, but also tracked down more complete versions of several folk songs.

Janice Weaver, as project manager, handled a broad range of tasks with dedication, professional skill, and élan. Janice was my trusted sounding board for questions of style, content, and aesthetics; she knew when to be a tough critic and when to be my cheerleading squad.

My daughter, Amanda, inspired me with her bright mind and her interest in the project, and my husband, Eric, a writer and editor himself, gave good advice and clever suggestions when asked—the perfect mate! Together they came up with the title for the book, and they embody it, too.

ACKNOWLEDGEMENTS

PART ONE: WHEN THE WORLD WAS NEW

"How Two-Feather Was Saved from Loneliness" by C. J. Taylor. From *How Two-Feather Was Saved from Loneliness*, © 1990 by C. J. Taylor, published by Tundra Books. "Manabozho and the Maple Trees" by Joseph Bruchac. Reprinted from *Keepers of the Earth: Native American Stories and Environmental Activities for Children* by Michael J. Caduto and Joseph Bruchac. © 1988, 1989, 1997. Fulcrum Publishing, Inc., Golden, CO. All rights reserved. "How the Thunder Made Horses" by Frances Fraser. From *The Bear Who Stole the Chinook: Tales from the Blackfoot* by Frances Fraser, published in 1990 by Douglas & McIntyre. Reprinted by permission of Douglas & McIntyre. "Scannah and the Beautiful Woman" by Joan Skogan. From *The Princess and the Sea-Bear and Other Tsimshian Stories*, copyright © 1990 by Joan Skogan. Used by permission of Polestar Book Publishers, Victoria, B.C.

PART TWO: THE NEW FOUND LAND

Explorers and Adventurers

"Thrand and Abidith" by Joan Clark. From *The Dream Carvers* by Joan Clark. Copyright © 1995 by Joan Clark. Reprinted by permission of Penguin Books Canada Limited. "Hunting for Unicorns" by Elma Schemenauer. From *Yesterstories A: Fish and Ships*, copyright © 1981 by Elma Schemenauer. Used by permission of the author. "The Village That Stretched from Sea to Sea" by Barbara Hehner. Copyright © 1999 by Barbara Hehner. Used by permission of the author. "Chickabash and the Strangers" from *Chickabash*. Told by Geordie Georgekish, William Kapsu, and John Mukash. Translated from Cree to English by Susan Iserhoff. Story adaptation by Jane Pachano. Copyright © Jane Pachano. Published by the James Bay Cree Cultural Education Centre.

New France

"The Huron Carol" by Jean de Brébeuf. English text by J. E. Middleton. © The Frederick Harris Music Co., Limited, Mississauga, Ontario, Canada. All rights reserved. "The King's Daughter" by Suzanne Martel. From *The King's Daughter*, copyright © 1980 by Suzanne Martel, translation copyright © 1980 by David Homel. A Groundwood Book/Douglas & McIntyre. "Mon Canot." From *Folklore of Canada* by Edith Fowke. Used by permission, McClelland & Stewart, Inc. *The Canadian Publishers*.

The Great Northwest

"The Long Journey of 'Our Dog'" by Ainslie Manson. From *A Dog Came, Too*, copyright © 1992 by Ainslie Manson. A Groundwood Book/Douglas & McIntyre. "Northwest Passage" by Stan Rogers. From the album *Northwest Passage*. Copyright © 1980 by Fogarty's Cove Music. Used by permission of Fogarty's Cove Music and D. Ariel Rogers.

PART THREE: CREATING A COUNTRY

Turbulent Times

"Leaving Acadia" by Mary Alice Downie and George Rawlyk. Selection from *A Proper Acadian* by Mary Alice Downie and George Rawlyk used by permission of Kids Can Press Ltd., Toronto. Copyright © 1980 by Mary Alice Downie and George Rawlyk. "The Piper's Refrain," words and music by Richard Nardin. Copyright © 1983 by Richard Nardin. Used by permission of the author. "MacDonnell on the Heights" by Stan Rogers. From the album *From Freshwater*. Copyright © 1984 by Fogarty's Cove Music. Used by permission of Fogarty's Cove Music and D. Ariel Rogers.

Rebels

"The Boy with an R in His Hand" by James Reaney. From *The Boy with an R in His Hand*, copyright © 1965 by James Reaney. Used by permission of the author.

Freedom-Seekers

"A Visit from the Slave Catcher" by Barbara Greenwood. From "A Parcel for Joanna," copyright © 1985 by Barbara Greenwood. Used by permission of the author.

Settlers

"The Two Fires" by Margaret Atwood. From *The Journals of Susanna Moodie* by Margaret Atwood. Copyright © Oxford University Press Canada 1970. Reprinted by permission of Oxford University Press Canada.

Loggers

"Big Joe Mufferaw" By Tom C. Connors. Copyright © 1970 by Crown Vetch Music. Used by permission. All rights reserved. "The Log Jam" by Bill Freeman. From *Shantymen of Cache Lake*, copyright © 1973 by Bill Freeman. Used by permission of James Lorimer & Company Limited.

The True North

"The Cremation of Sam McGee," copyright © 1907 by Robert W. Service. Used by permission of M. Wm. Krasilovsky, Agent, New York. "I Shall Wait and Wait" by Alootook Ipellie. From *Musicanada 2*, Phyllis Shafer and Yvette Stack, eds. (Holt Rinehart and Winston, 1991).

Voices of Sadness

"The Ballad of Mary March" by Stella Whelan. From *Passages: Literature of Newfoundland and Labrador*, edited by Eric Norman, June Warr, and Ray Goulding. St. John's, Newfoundland: Breakwater Books, 1983. Copyright © by Stella Whelan. Reprinted with permission of Breakwater Books, Ltd. "Ballad of Crowfoot" by Willie Dunn, copyright © 1971. Used by permission of the author.

PART FOUR: THE NEW NATION

Confederation

"The First of July, 1867" by Donald Creighton. From *John A. Macdonald: The Young Politician* by Donald Creighton. Copyright © 1952, republished 1998. Used by permission of the Estate of Donald Creighton. "Address to the Jury" by Kim Morrissey. From *Batoche* (1989), published by Coteau Books. Used by permission of the publisher. "Song of Louis Riel" from

Subject Index

Project manager: Janice Weaver
Creative director: Scott Richardson
Layout and electronic assembly: Jean Lightfoot Peters
Music typesetter: James Hopkings
Proofreader: Alison Reid
Rights and permissions: Elizabeth d'Anjou
Historical consultant: McGill Institute for the Study of Canada
Colour separations: Colour Technologies
Printing and binding: Friesens
Text set in Centaur
Text printed on 70 lb. Luna Matte